Taking C[...]

Susan Lewis is the bestselling author of twenty-two novels. She is also the author of *Just One More Day*, a moving memoir of her childhood in Bristol. She lives in France. Her website address is www.susanlewis.com

Acclaim for Susan Lewis

'One of the best around' *Independent on Sunday*

'Spellbinding! . . . you just keep turning the pages, with the atmosphere growing more and more intense as the story leads to its dramatic climax' *Daily Mail*

'Mystery and romance *par excellence*' *Sun*

'Deliciously dramatic and positively oozing with tension, this is another wonderfully absorbing novel from the *Sunday Times* bestseller Susan Lewis . . . Expertly written to brew an atmosphere of foreboding, this story is an irresistible blend of intrigue and passion, and the consequences of secrets and betrayal' *Woman*

'A multi-faceted tear jerker' *heat*

Susan LEWIS

Taking Chances

arrow books

Published by Arrow Books 2009

2 4 6 8 10 9 7 5 3

First published in Great Britain in 1999 by
William Heinemann
Random House, 20 Vauxhall Bridge Road,
London SW1V 2SA

www.rbooks.co.uk

Addresses for companies within The Random House Group Limited can be
found at: www.randomhouse.co.uk/offices.htm

The Random House Group Limited Reg. No. 954009

A CIP catalogue record for this book
is available from the British Library

ISBN 9780099534341

The Random House Group Limited supports The Forest
Stewardship Council (FSC), the leading international forest
certification organisation. All our titles that are printed on
Greenpeace approved FSC certified paper carry the FSC logo.
Our paper procurement policy can be found at:
www.rbooks.co.uk/environment

Typeset by SX Composing DTP, Rayleigh, Essex
Printed and bound in Great Britain by
CPI Bookmarque Ltd, Croydon, CR0 4TD

To Lesley

Acknowledgements

My love and thanks go to Rose Garcia for her research, translation and support during our extraordinary adventure in Colombia. A time certainly never to be forgotten. Nor will Timothy Ross who so generously shared his great knowledge of Colombia, who introduced us to some exceptionally special young people, and who so painstakingly checked the manuscript – any inaccuracies that remain are solely mine. Thank you to Kelly Rodriguez, Birgitte Bonning and Martha Cardenas de Cifuentes. A very big thank you to Francisco Santos for sharing the experience of his own kidnap at the hands of the drug lords; to Maria Christina Morales, for retelling the story of her father's kidnap at the hands of the guerillas; and to Miguel Caballero, for demonstrating the fashion and foibles of bullet proof jackets.

Love and affection to Leidy Johana Valle, Diana Perez and all the lovely children at the Fondacion Renancer, in Bogotá and Cartagena.

I also extend my deepest thanks to Dr Barry Heller of St Mary's Medical Center in Long Beach for providing so much valuable medical detail for the relevant parts of the story. Also to Joan Leeds, not only for taking me around Cedars Sinai, but for being such a good friend.

I am extremely grateful to Clive Fleury for helping me with the 'takeover' and to all my family and friends who have supplied so much character detail, humour and support.

Prologue

Nothing had happened, yet the threat, the absolute danger, was a presence even before the car was forced off the road. It rushed in with the wind, a terrifying premonition, an advance notice of something too horrible to imagine.

The omen paused, then with sublime synchronicity it began locking into reality. The car was rammed off the road. The driver was swearing, struggling with the wheel. With a jarring crash another car hit from behind, projecting theirs into a ditch. Within seconds a swarm of slight young men, toting mini-Uzis and M16s, were surrounding the car. Her driver was grabbed from his seat, thrown to the ground and shot through the head. The window beside her was smashed, the door torn open and someone yelled at her to get out.

Her limbs were like sand. Shock was hammering through her body. The terror was so great she couldn't move. But she had to, or they would kill her.

'Muevete!' one of them snapped. Move yourself!

In the glaring light of day she stepped out of the car. The countryside around was tranquil and swathed in mountainous beauty. Traffic sped past – no-one was insane enough to get involved.

She was taken to the car in front and pushed into the back seat. She was handed a pair of Porsche wraparounds. They were painted over with nail polish. She

1

put them on and only then became aware of the dampness between her legs. At some point in the last few minutes terror had loosened her bladder.

The car started up. She could smell the grease on the guns, the sweat on her captors' bodies. Bile rose to her throat. She choked it back. She thought of Tom and tried not to think of Tom. He'd sent her here, to Cartagena in the north of the country, thinking she'd be safer. They were due to leave in a couple of days.

She was a journalist, American. Her agenda was complete, the tragedy of street children and child prostitution in Bogotá, Colombia, was reported. She'd named names: the pimps, procurers, paedophiles and European package-tour agents. Italians, Swedes, French, Spanish, they came here to violate the tender young bodies of children so small it was a miracle they survived. Drugs helped, muted the pain and dulled the senses. Glue, basuco, sometimes smack. But that wasn't why she was being taken. No-one here cared about those kids.

Tom. How soon would he know they had taken her?

Some hostages were held for months, even years. Most were killed. She was going to die. She would never see Tom again. Her throat tightened with panic. Dank, polluted air shuddered in and out of her body. Someone spoke. She didn't understand the dialect. Were they talking to her?

Finally the car stopped. She was dragged out. The glasses remained on as she was led forward. Birds were singing, a dog was barking. The scent of flowers assailed her. A sudden image of her dead driver caused her to shake harder than ever. She vomited. It came from her in a bitter, fast stream.

'*Hijueputa!*' one of them muttered. Son of a bitch.

They stood aside and waited as she wiped a hand over her mouth. She took off the glasses. No-one seemed to care. Her captors wore masks – only their eyes were visible.

2

She was in a dense, tropical garden. They were approaching a house whose former glory was now faded and scarred by neglect.

She was taken up the stairs and pushed into a darkened room. A light was turned on, casting a dull glow over the worn floorboards and old-fashioned bed. Dark, chunky furniture was pushed against the walls, the windows were boarded up, planks nailed across them. She was drowning in fear. It was filling her up like a shadow. Chains were put about her ankles and she was pushed onto the bed. Her lovely face was stained with tears, smeared with dust. The whites of her eyes glowed in the waning light.

She was left alone.

She tried to remember the procedure now. They would contact Tom, maybe with a phone call, more likely with a hand-delivered note. They would tell him which radio to get and the frequency he should tune to. How long would that take? Hours? Days? But there was no time. This wasn't a guerrilla operation, so there would be no notes, no radios, no bargaining. Just demands, instant results, or death. Tom would have to back off now. The investigation that he had been working on for six months and more must be terminated, annihilated, expunged from existence. The evidence he had gathered that would blow apart the Tolima Drug Cartel, as well as half the Government, would be written in her blood if it ever went to print.

Hours later the door opened. The man who came in was shoddily handsome, tall and thin with mocking brown eyes and a beak of a nose. A neat moustache crooked over his narrow lips, an expensive suit masked his meagreness of muscle. She'd seen him only once before, but knew instantly who he was. He was the man who used social cleansing as a means to disappear children from the streets and subject them to the perversions of loathsomely sick men. Her reports on his

3

iniquity had been so explicit, and so shocking to the world, that he had been forced into hiding ever since.

He spoke quietly through a smile, the resonance of a Medellín accent curling through his pleasure as he told her what she already knew – who had ordered him to take her, and why. This was about her now, as well as Tom.

There were two others with him, standing in shadow. He came forward and she knew there was nothing Tom could do to save her from this. As each of them took their turn she tried to put her mind in another place: an attempt to rescue it from the driving pain, the blood and tears, the savagery and utter degradation. Everything they did they captured on film, which she knew they would send to Tom. She would rather die than have Tom see this; the world was no longer a place for her once this was over.

For the next two days she saw no-one except a boy who brought her food and water, and stood over her while her body did the things it must. The pain was intolerable. She was broken, bruised, torn and not always conscious. With her mind and soul she talked to Tom and felt him reaching her through the intangible, yet vital bond they shared. She listened for God, but never heard Him. She spoke to death and to life, and felt both embrace her as she tried to climb from the earthly weight of fear.

On the third day he came back with the other two. They unchained her and forced her to kneel. Then he put a gun to her head. She closed her eyes, so afraid she could feel the urine running down her legs. A terrible rushing sound drowned her ears. No-one moved. There was only stillness: a dreadful, cruel stillness.

The hammer clicked. Her lips pulled back over her teeth; her heart was in a stampede. Someone moved. The gun left her. She sank forward, whimpering and sobbing. It was over. She wasn't going to die now. Air

4

seeped back into her lungs. Her chest was too tight. She choked. Gasped with relief. She wanted life. Not death. No matter what they did to her, she wanted life. She could survive this. Oh, thank God, thank God. She was still alive.

Then the gun was at her head again, and this time they killed her.

Chapter 1

'As a success she's awesome, as a woman she seems to be a work in progress.'

Sandy Paull tossed the magazine aside and tried not to be irritated. *Work in progress!* It made her sound like one of God's little unfinished jobs. Something he might get round to one Sunday afternoon when he was through perfecting the misery in Africa and temporarily bored with heaping happiness and riches on everyone but her.

Well, OK, riches she had, to a degree, but happiness . . .

Snatching up the magazine she stuffed it in the bin and rotated her chair to face the computer screen. She was, in fact, perfectly happy and had good reason to be. At twenty-six she was co-owner of the McCann Paull Theatrical Agency, and Chief Executive Officer of World Wide Entertainment. Actually, it was just the London division of World Wide, but it was a pretty crucial part of the international operation, and though she had a team of trusty advisers and experienced industry consultants backing her, she was the one in charge. And that wasn't bad for a kid from the sticks whose sisters worked at the bus depot, brothers were either on the dole or in the process of getting sacked, whose father had just written to her from clink after a six-year silence, and whose mother worked the checkout at Safeways in between bingo sessions and treatment for her varicose veins.

She was in touch with them as rarely as possible, but sent money every time they asked, which was often, and had even had her mother to stay a couple of months ago which was a disaster. Sandy was a different person now: she mixed with classier people, had opinions that were listened to and a life that was about as far removed from Fairweather Street as her mother's manners were from good. Not that Gladys, with her powdered cheeks and cheap shampoo and set, was deliberately offensive, she just had to tell it as it was, and if that meant upsetting someone then she was sorry, but that was the way she was and she wasn't changing for no-one. In truth she had been so way out of her depth during the visit that Sandy, once she'd got over the shame, had ended up feeling sorry for her mother, who was just a simple soul really and certainly no match for all the snobs who were turning up their noses, or laughing at her behind her back. Gladys might not be as well-dressed, or educated, or well-connected as any of them, or the kind of mother who appreciated Quaglino's or the latest West End show, but she was still a person and there was truly nothing to admire in the way the upper classes looked down on those who weren't so well off – much like the little she-devil from the over-priced glossy who'd come here to interview Sandy a couple of months ago.

Just what was it with these journalists and their amateur character analyses? What gave them the right to decide if a person was complete or not? *Work in progress!* Anyone would think she was propped up here in her office like a blob of marble awaiting the finishing hand of today's answer to Michelangelo, whoever that might be. And how would she know when she barely had time to read all the scripts piling up in her office, or to get to the screenings and shows her clients were in, let alone worry about traipsing round art galleries trying to figure out which way was up.

As she waited to connect to her e-mail she took a

mouthful of the café latte she'd brought in with her, quickly checked her watch and jotted down a couple of reminders to herself. It was just after seven in the morning. As usual she was the first in the office, but this early couple of hours, before everyone else arrived, were often two of the most valuable in the day. It was a time when she cut the jumble from her mind, pasted it to the computer and attempted to make some sense of actors' demands, writers' unreliabilities, directors' contracts, the other agents' needs for decisions or backup, and the company's ongoing performance.

Of course there were a zillion other things to deal with as well, and there was no question that, as a boss, Sandy Paull was as hands-on as an eager lover. And she knew all about *them*. At least she used to, but there wasn't much time for them these days. Or maybe there wasn't the need, as just about every lover she'd had since she'd abandoned her mother's crappy little terraced house in the Midlands to come and make it big in London, had been paired up with her through an escort service. That was in the days when she'd had no other way of paying the rent, or even eating. And the truth was she hadn't always slept with her 'dates', unlike Nesta, her best friend and flatmate, who was still an escort and proud of it.

In fact, Sandy wasn't particularly ashamed of this episode in her past, especially when it was through the escort business that she had met Maurice Trehearne, the property tycoon, and her own personal mentor. The magazine article hadn't mentioned him, because no-one knew about him. It had mentioned the fact she was unattached though, phrasing it in a way that had made her feel like the star prize in one of life's smaller lotteries, which was just typical of a skin and bone Sloane whose idea of style owed everything to Laura Ashley, with knickers and tights from Next. At least she'd managed to get Sandy's couturiers right, Ralph Lauren for weekends – though that could change now that Lauren had done a

8

deal with Tesco! – Chanel, Dior or occasionally Max Mara for the office; Donna Karan or Dolce and Gabanna for evenings; undies specially imported from France.

In her description of Sandy's looks the journalist had been almost magnanimous, calling her an 'exceptionally attractive blonde (not natural), with surprisingly long legs for a woman of only five feet four, handspan hips and a bust (natural) that's as arresting, and perhaps as predatory, as her piercingly turquoise eyes'. Bitch! Still, what could be expected from a woman who had no more to put in a bra than a limp pair of nipples and a few stray hairs.

Going back to Maurice, without him there was just no way Sandy would be where she was today, for it was his skill and fortune that had put her in a position to ruin Michael McCann, the boss who had flirted with her, screwed her, then cruelly fired her when she had become an embarrassment. In fact it was only a little less than six months ago that she'd come so close to destroying him that the fall-out had already begun. But then, at the very last minute, Michael had performed a miraculous feat of recovery that had not only regained him control of the agency, but of World Wide Entertainment and American Talent International, one of Hollywood's biggest agencies. Exactly how he had managed to pull it off was still a mystery to Sandy, and one she remained determined to uncover, even though in her heart she was glad Michael was back at the top, for, if she had a weak spot anywhere, it was very definitely where he was concerned.

He was living in Los Angeles now, with Ellen Shelby, an American who was gorgeous, talented and the newly appointed Head of Development for World Wide Entertainment. Michael was CEO. Ellen oozed the kind of sophistication that Sandy would kill for, and made love every night with the man Sandy would die for. Hating Ellen wasn't just something Sandy did, it was something she thrived on. But quietly, subtly so: watching, storing and waiting for the day to dawn when she could not only push Ellen aside, but actively crush her. And that day was going to come, for the seeds were already sown.

Noticing a light flashing on her console Sandy picked up the call, while continuing to read her e-mail.

'Sandy? Is that you?'

'Nesta?' Sandy responded in amazement. 'Where are you? I thought you were in Hong Kong.'

'I was. I got in an hour ago and was just on my way back to the flat when I realized I'd . . .'

' . . . forgotten to take your keys,' Sandy finished.

'Are you going to be there for a while?' Nesta said. 'I could get the taxi to stop by to pick up yours.'

'Bring me another latte and a Danish,' Sandy replied, and rang off.

She wasn't normally so brusque with Nesta; in fact she'd really missed her this past week, and was looking forward to seeing her, it was just that damned article! Just who the hell did that weedy little hack who made a good case for female Viagra think she was, criticizing her for still sharing a flat with her best friend? So what if she was rich enough to buy a house in Belgravia, or a luxury apartment right here on the river? If she chose to stay in the two-bedroomed flat she and Nesta had had virtually since they'd met, that was her business. And besides, it wasn't just any old flat. It was in a listed building just off Sloane Square, and was big enough to swallow up her mother's council house a couple of times over.

She turned back to the computer, busied herself with a few instant replies, downloaded the rest of her mail and took a couple of videos from her briefcase ready to hand back to her assistant. They'd been sent in by a young director, fresh from film school, who'd been referred to her by an existing client. As she mainly represented directors – though she had a few actors and a couple of writers on her list too – she had taken the videos home the night before. She'd watched both short films right the way through, and in her opinion nothing in them had shown the kind of flair that would persuade her to take this newcomer on.

She never allowed herself to become personally involved with all the rejections she sent out, if she did she'd never keep McCann Paull at the top. The article had accused her of being ruthless, but since when did that budding little profiler with her queer, fuzzy hair and red-hot freckles have to deal with a persistent bombardment from the nation's young wannabes or sad has-beens who believed Sandy Paull was the entertainment industry's answer to the Second Coming? Anyway, since the accusation had been coupled with a more or less flattering description of the way she looked, she was prepared to accept the remark with less indignation than the others. In fact, she had to admit she was pretty ruthless, but she'd also been the power behind a dozen or more dazzling success stories these past couple of years, not just her own. She definitely had a knack when it came to spotting talent, not only in actors but in writers and directors too. Even Michael, with his killer reputation, hadn't launched as many careers as she had in such a short space of time, nor at such a young age, and, being Michael, he was the first to admit it.

Waiting for the computer to search out some contract details she needed, she took a moment to turn in her chair and look out of the window. It was a beautiful morning, rich with sunlight, sharp with cold. The sky was brazenly blue and the buildings across the river looked somehow less depressed, more alive than usual. The river itself was a wide band of sludge-coloured liquid with a couple of old barge wrecks thrown up on its banks, stripped bare and left to rot like plundered chests. Sandy loved this view, night or day, rain or shine. It was her view.

Once it had been Michael's, before he'd gone to LA. This office had been his too, and still could be for she'd changed nothing, not even the framed photographs on the walls that showed a heartstoppingly handsome Michael with any number of famous faces. Of course Sandy was in some of them too, it would be too weird to have only pictures of Michael on her wall, she just wished there was one of the two of them together. The large mahogany desk was in the exact same position Michael had chosen, in front of the window, facing towards the inner office of the agency where bookers, secretaries, agents' assistants, contracts managers and accounts clerks all had their desks. The agents in the offices that ringed the inner well were all agents Michael had employed. The computer terminal she used was the one Michael had used; the books on the shelves were the same, though added to now; even Jodi, Michael's personal assistant, was still in the next room. Jodi was the agency manager now, and shared her office with Stacy, Sandy's personal assistant, one of the very few changes that had been made to McCann Walsh when it had become McCann Paull. Dan Walsh, Michael's brother-in-law, and the agency's chief accountant, was still a shareholder, but he had had no problem with having his name removed from the title when Sandy and Michael had merged their agencies.

There had been another change. A very major one in fact, and that was the acquisition of the offices on the floor below which housed the business managers, finance experts and freelance personnel of World Wide Entertainment. But other than that almost everything was the way Michael had built it and left it. In fact it was all so very reminiscent of the days he had worked there that there were even times she was sure she caught the scent of him drifting in the air like the passing of a ghost. And then the memories would come flooding in. She didn't often think back though, they weren't happy days, nor did they get better with the convenient gloss of time.

Abruptly she turned back to her desk. Nesta would be here any minute. She'd deal with her then call Michael in LA. She was certain he had something big cooking for World Wide, and though she knew better than to push Michael until he was ready to tell, she was on the phone to him regularly knowing that he would include her in his plans any time. The fact that Ellen was doubtless already involved incensed her to the point of fury, but she'd have no problem walking right over Ellen when the time came, and if there was any glory being handed out she'd take whatever steps were necessary to make sure she was the one who shone in Michael's eyes, never Ellen.

Getting up from her chair, she kicked the bin and its magazine out of sight. There was no doubt the article was right when it said that success helped to smooth the rough edges of life: what it had failed to point out, however, was that it did nothing to lower the heat, or temper the madness of obsession.

'Remind me, what time do you have to be at the airport?' Ellen said.

'Four o'clock,' Matty answered. 'Can you manage it?'

'I think so. How long are you going to be in Florida?'

'A month. Then we're in Denver for a couple of weeks. I guess it's a silly question to ask if you'll be able to make it out to the set?'

Ellen laughed, then quickly flung out an arm to prevent her cousin stepping off the sidewalk into the path of a speeding car. She was about to take the lead in a major new mini-series, so having her in one piece would be helpful.

They were currently power-walking through the early morning streets of Beverly Hills, something they tried to do at least three times a week. Lately, if they managed one they were lucky. Still, for the time being at least, they were both in pretty good shape. Ellen's sensuously curvy figure was enhanced by her soft mane of chestnut waves and haunting hazel eyes. By contrast Matty was much slimmer, with narrow, boyish hips, small breasts, endlessly long legs, and sleek, dark brown hair that framed her lovely face in short feathery spikes.

'I had a call from your mother last night,' Ellen said.

'Mmm, me too,' Matty responded.

Ellen smiled. 'It's hard to imagine Aunt Julie being nervous about anything, but she sure sounded that way.'

'Well, it's been thirty years since she married my dad and caused a rift between him and your dad. Who'd have thought having a sister-in-law who was once a showgirl in Paris could upset Uncle Frank so much?'

'Oh come on,' Ellen laughed. 'You know my dad. He's as stubborn as he's puritanical, and he's got more pride than a congress full of hypocrites. Still, it's good that they're all meeting up at last. Mom is really looking forward to it. They don't have too many visitors to the farm these days, so it'll be good for her to have some company.'

'Yeah. And it's about time Dad and Uncle Frank got together again. Your mom says they were pretty close when they were young. I guess finding out that he couldn't live your life for you, made him realize that he couldn't live my dad's life for him either.'

'It's all based in love,' Ellen said. 'He just wants to protect those he cares about. And finally coming to terms with the fact that I now live in LA and won't be returning to Nebraska to marry a neighbour and take over the farm, doesn't mean that he's stopped worrying. About either of us.'

'Tell me about it,' Matty groaned. 'He's set me a dozen passages of the bible to read while I'm away, did I tell you that?'

14

Ellen laughed. Then changing the subject as they crossed the road she said, 'Did I mention we're moving the World Wide offices over to the ATI building on Wilshire today? Michael's going to be working from home while I run around like a lunatic making sure it all happens.'

Matty cast her a look.

'Actually, he's pretty stressed out with everything right now,' Ellen explained. 'Raising development funds isn't proving as easy as he'd hoped. And he hasn't had a call from Tom Chambers in over a week.'

'But Tom's in Colombia, right?'

'Uh-huh.'

'Tracking down his girlfriend's killers?'

'That's right.'

'The man's got to be insane. I mean, I think it's a great idea for a movie, but Colombia! Drug cartels! I guess he knows what he's doing.'

'I guess we have to hope so.'

'Does anyone know about the movie yet? I mean apart from us.'

'Just a select few. I'm not sure how hopeful Tom was about finding the killers, and if he doesn't . . . Well, I guess we deal with that if it happens. For now, setting it all in motion is taking up most of Michael's time, while I get to play mom, mistress, movie mogul and misunderstood producer.'

Matty laughed. 'Why misunderstood?'

'It goes with the territory.'

'I thought you were Head of Development?'

'I'm that too. Jeez, do you think we could slow up a bit, I'm busting my buns here.'

'That's the point,' Matty reminded her, slowing her pace.

They rounded another corner and began heading along a beautiful, maple-lined street full of multi-million dollar homes. The sun was already hot, and the perfume of exquisitely flowering gardens was filling the air.

'So tell me,' Matty said, watching a stretch limousine drive by, 'how does life feel when it gets to be perfect?'

Ellen laughed. 'Scary as hell,' she confessed.

Matty's eyebrows went up. 'So you're prepared to admit it's perfect?' she challenged.

'It's good, but believe me, it's a long way from perfect.'

'Well, I've got to tell you, it looks pretty much that way from where I'm standing. Michael's crazy about you . . . '

' . . . and I'm crazy about him. But I don't think we should ever take anything for granted.'

'You're right, we shouldn't, but you've got to agree, you've got a lot more than most.'

Ellen shot her a look. 'Maybe I have,' she said sharply, 'but if you think I'm going to apologize for it just because you didn't meet anyone since you and Gene split up, forget it.'

They marched on in silence for a while, both wondering where the tension had suddenly sprung from, until finally they glanced at each other and started to laugh.

'If you had any idea what a knife-edge I was on half the time,' Ellen said. 'You know what Michael's like. He can be pretty volatile at times – and Robbie's much the same,' she added, referring to Michael's five-year-old son.

'But you're all totally besotted with each other, so if you ask me the knife-edge is of your own making. Did you talk to Michael yet about me playing the part of Rachel Carmedi?'

Ellen grimaced. 'I mentioned it,' she admitted.

'And he hated the idea.'

'No. He just said that when the time comes we should be going for big star names.'

'Isn't the time already here? I mean, if you get some

development money you'll be wanting to attach a star right away, won't you?'

'Yeah. But I think the plan is to create a much bigger part for whoever's playing Tom Chambers than for his girlfriend.'

'I thought the story was about her. After all, she was the one who was kidnapped and murdered.'

'But men are bigger box office,' Ellen reminded her, 'and this is going to be World Wide's first major feature, so Michael wants to play it as safe as he can. Which sounds like a pretty dumb thing to say when Tom Chambers is down there somewhere in Colombia very likely about to get his head blown off.'

A few minutes later they jogged up to Matty's luxurious, Spanish-style apartment complex, where Ellen went to collect her car keys from the security guard she'd left them with.

'OK, I'll be by around three thirty to pick you up,' she promised, giving Matty a hug. 'It's going to be a crazy day, so wish me luck.'

'You don't need any more,' Matty told her grudgingly.

Ellen cast a meaningful look over her shoulder, then, reversing her car out of its spot, she headed off towards the Hollywood Hills.

Much later that day, after dropping Matty at the airport, Ellen made a quick stop at the grocery store, then deciding not to go back to the chaos in the office, she called Michael to let him know she was on her way home.

With its Mulholland Drive address, elegant Spanish-style architecture, stunning views of the San Fernando valley and glorious mountains beyond, the house she and Michael shared in the Hollywood Hills was without question one of LA's more desirable residences. And since it could boast a spectacular swimmer's pool with spa, Japanese gazebo, five bedrooms, four bathrooms, gourmet kitchen, separate guest or maid's apartment and marble floors throughout, it was currently worth somewhere in the region of two million dollars. That was a good half a million more than Michael had paid for it just over six months ago – a staggering increase in value by anyone's standards, but that was the way real estate was going right now.

After dumping the groceries in the kitchen, she turned up the air-conditioning and went to find Michael. He was in the study, his head buried in the results of a recent survey they'd commissioned.

'This is amazing,' he said, sliding a hand absently along her thigh as she stooped to kiss him on the head. 'Do you realize that three out of five people surveyed actually remember who Rachel Carmedi is, and one point five out of the remaining two caught on as soon as the Colombian kidnap and murder was mentioned?' He looked up. 'Can you believe that? Something that happened over three years ago, and more than three-quarters of the nation didn't even need prompting into remembering who she was.'

Cupping his face in her hands, Ellen kissed him lingeringly on the mouth. She knew she was biased, but with his wonderful thick black hair, dark blue eyes and exquisitely defined features, he really was devastatingly attractive. And since they'd only been living together for just over six months, the incredible passion and excitement of their relationship had yet to shift down a few gears, which was fine by them both.

'If you'd been here at the time you'd have seen for yourself that it was pretty big news,' she told him, walking over to her desk to check on her messages. 'And what I want to know is how you get one point five of a person?'

Michael's eyes still showed the effects of her kiss as he laughed. 'This was well worth the money,' he said, indicating the survey. 'Whose idea was it?'

Ellen leaned forward to switch on her computer. 'Mine,' she airily responded.

Michael eyed her sceptically, and waited until she started to grin.

'OK, it was Rufus's,' she confessed, referring to one of their lawyers. 'So, aren't you going to ask me how the move's coming along?'

'How's the move coming along?'

'Not bad. We just need to know which office you want.'

'Oh, I guess the one next to yours,' he answered, distractedly.

'Not Ted's?'

He looked at her, and waggled his eyebrows. 'No, not Ted's,' he said.

Laughing, Ellen clicked on to her e-mail.

Ted Forgon was the majority shareholder of World Wide Entertainment, which would have made him president of the new company, had Michael not very neatly seized the position for himself by using the exact same tactics Forgon had so ruthlessly subjected his many rivals to over the years.

Blackmail. It was an ugly word, and an even uglier business. But threatening to reveal Forgon's affair with an underage girl was the only way Michael had been able to regain control of his London agency, and the burgeoning new production company, World Wide, when Sandy Paull had gone behind his back and done a deal with Forgon that had come very close to wiping Michael off the face of the entertainment world.

Michael was fully aware that Forgon was now biding his time, waiting for the statute of limitations to expire on his crime, in order to avoid prosecution. Were Michael able to raise the capital, he'd already have taken advantage of Forgon's weakened position to buy the man out of World Wide completely. But since he'd already put up just about everything he owned as security against his colossal loans – his share of McCann Paull, the London agency; his penthouse apartment in Battersea, and a small, private villa in the Caribbean – he simply didn't have the means, or the collateral, right now to force Forgon out.

Turning to his computer he called up the latest investment reports from World Wide's offices in New York, London and Sydney. He had yet to inform the company's other shareholders of his intention to sink over 80 per cent of their resources into developing Tom Chambers's script – that was a piece of news he felt it would be more prudent to deliver when he had managed to gain a similar stake from some major Hollywood investors.

When finally he looked up again Ellen was watching him, so she saw his eyes go to the phone that was sitting apart from the others on his desk. It was the private line he'd had installed just over a week ago, for the sole use of Tom Chambers. There was an individual answering machine attached to the phone too, but lately neither the line nor the machine was getting anywhere near as much use as Michael would have liked.

Forcing a smile, Michael said, 'The hell-raiser should be home any minute.'

Ellen shook her head. 'He called at lunch-time to ask if he could go to Jeremy's right after school. He'll be back around seven.'

Michael looked at his watch, then reached for another of his phones as it started to ring.

'Michael McCann,' he said into the receiver. 'Oh, hi Sandy,' he answered, glancing at his watch, then at Ellen. 'It's got to be midnight over there, are you still at the office?'

Not much wanting to listen while he spoke to Sandy Paull, Ellen put in a call to Maggie, the personal assistant she and Michael shared.

A few minutes later Michael ended his call and got up from his desk.

'Everything OK?' Ellen asked.

He nodded, then opening the double doors that closed them off from the rest of the house, he walked across the huge, white-carpeted sitting-room where sumptuous pale linen-covered sofas, glass- and marquetry- topped coffee-tables and an eclectic assortment of pottery, paintings and sculptures faced on to the sunny patio and pool.

Knowing where he was heading Ellen put down the phone and got up to follow him. By the time she joined him at the wet bar, which was in a cosy sunken niche between the kitchen and the den, he'd poured himself a very large neat Scotch and was sitting on a bar stool gazing at the mirrored shelves of bottles.

'It's been four days now,' he said as Ellen helped herself to a drink too. 'Something's got to be wrong.'

Though Ellen had yet to meet Tom Chambers personally, she knew that a unique kind of friendship had developed between the two men during the time they had been together in Rio, trying to rescue Michael's son Robbie, and younger brother Cavan, from a ruthless gang of kidnappers. Since that time, Michael had made several trips to Washington where Chambers generally based himself whenever he was in the States, and now both men were totally committed to making the three-year-old murder of Chambers's girlfriend, and the failure ever to bring anyone to justice, the subject of World Wide's first major movie.

'I shouldn't have agreed to him going back there,' Michael said.

'It was his decision,' Ellen responded.

'Then I should have tried to stop him. But what do I do instead? I tell him if he can get the names of those who did it, there'll be no way they can escape justice once Hollywood immortalizes them on film.'

'You told him that to stop him from killing them,' Ellen reminded him firmly. 'You knew, when he told

21

you he was going back, that there was a chance he was going after revenge, so you offered him another means of achieving it. Now for God's sake stop blaming yourself here. You did what you thought was best, and if anything's happened to him, we'd be sure to know.'

He sighed and pressed his fingers to his eyes. 'You're right,' he said. 'I guess it just seems crazy, us going to all this trouble, when we don't even know if he's going to come back in one piece.' His laugh was grim. 'Of course, if he doesn't, it'll make the movie an even hotter property than it already is, two American journalists going down at the hands of a Colombian drug cartel, and lovers at that.'

'You see, there's a bright side to everything,' Ellen responded, and he couldn't help but laugh at the blackness of her humour.

Turning to look at her he felt his tension starting slowly to ebb. She was a truly beautiful woman, in every imaginable way, and sometimes he wondered if he'd really known what love was before he met her. He guessed he had, for Robbie's mother, Michelle, had damned near broken his heart when she'd left, but that seemed such a long time ago now, and as much as he had loved Michelle, he just couldn't remember feeling the way he did now.

'What are you thinking?' Ellen asked.

Though his eyes started to dance he didn't answer right away. Instead he tried to imagine what the past six months must have been like for her, being thrown in the deep end of a relationship, motherhood and fresh career. If they'd been living together before he'd got custody of Robbie the relationship and motherhood package might have been easier for her to deal with; or if he'd got the company going sooner she'd at least have had some time to adjust from being an agent to a producer. As it was, it had all happened at once, and though she was never backward in asserting herself or her opinions, she had never once complained about the way he had so completely and cavalierly turned her entire life upside down. Nor, despite the heavy load of their upcoming commitments, was she averse to the idea of providing a brother or sister for Robbie.

'Will you marry me?' he said.

Ellen laughed. 'Is there something about that particular question that you like?' she teased. 'I mean this has got to be the sixteenth time you've asked me, not that I'm counting, you understand.'

'We keep talking about it, I just think we should do it,' he said, lifting a hand to touch her hair. 'And what I like about the question is the way you answer.'

She frowned, trying to recall the way she'd answered in the past. Then her eyes started to shine. 'You don't have to bribe me into satisfying your insatiable sexual needs,' she told him.

'You think I don't know that,' he countered. 'You're a pushover. I just think we should get married. Soon.'

She smiled and watched him as he began to look her slowly up and down, his eyes travelling her body with all the power of an intimate caress.

'Sooner still I think you should fix me another drink,' he said, resting his gaze on her mouth in a way that caused a delicious bite of lust to clench between her legs.

'I'll go get some ice,' she said, and sliding down off the bar stool she sauntered into the kitchen.

Minutes later she was back, carrying a small silver bucket of ice and wearing nothing but a pair of white hipster jeans and a single pearl drop necklace. She fixed him another drink, pushed it across the bar, then wandered round to stand next to him, her back to the bar, her elbows resting on it in order to better show him her gloriously full breasts.

As they spoke their dialogue made them sound like strangers – he the travelling salesman, she the obliging bar girl. She touched herself regularly and provocatively, smoothing her breasts, and flicking her hair. Then she invited him to touch her too, and almost lost her breath as his hands took the heaviness of her breasts and began to squeeze and rotate. Then he was kissing them, sucking on her nipples and unzipping his fly.

Finally he pulled her mouth to his and pushed his tongue deep inside. As they kissed he opened her jeans and eased them down over her hips, moaning softly as her hand tightened on his penis. Then sliding off the stool he stood in front of her and pushed himself into the join of her legs. Her knees were held together by her panties, and the way he was rubbing himself against her made her ache for the feel of him inside her. He pushed himself back and forth, faster and faster, until her breath was ragged and she could feel the encroaching power of orgasm pressing against every place he was touching. Then suddenly he lifted her up on a stool, pulled off her panties and opened her legs wide.

Even as he entered her he could feel the pulsing pressure of her climax claiming him, pulling him in deeper and deeper. He jerked himself into her brutally hard and fast, giving her the full length of him, catching her cries in his mouth as her orgasm pounded. Then he was coming too, the seed tearing from his body in a long, sweeping rush of exquisite release. He held her to him, buried in her as deep as he could go. She clung to him, her arms around his neck, her legs gripping his waist. He searched for her mouth again and kissed her harshly, then tenderly, sucking her lips between his, covering her mouth with his own.

'This just gets better and better,' he said when finally his breathing was steady.

'I know,' she whispered.

She looked into his eyes and they both started to smile. Then from the study came the sound of a telephone ringing.

As she pulled on her jeans Ellen could hear him

shouting in an effort to make himself heard. Obviously the elusive Tom Chambers had finally made contact.

Returning to the kitchen for the bra and T-shirt she had discarded, she was about to start making plans for dinner, when she became aware of a strange uneasiness descending over her spirits. Stopping in front of the refrigerator she stood staring at Robbie's magnetized works of art, trying to figure out where the feeling was coming from. This wasn't the first time she'd had it, but though it had been happening for a while now, she still couldn't quite work out why.

'He's arrived in Cartagena,' Michael said, strolling into the kitchen and looking around for something to eat. 'Apparently someone there saw the kidnapping. Someone who was driving by.'

'But still no word on the names of the kidnappers?' Ellen said, taking the salad tray from the fridge.

He shook his head. 'Though there's not much doubt the drug lord, Hernán Galeano, was behind it,' he said, biting into an apple.

'Did he say why he hasn't been in touch for the past few days?' she asked.

Michael shook his head. 'You know, I've been thinking,' he said, after he'd finished chewing. 'If Virago Knox do come up with the two million we're after for development, we could put this house up as collateral for the remaining two and go right ahead and get ourselves a star. I mean, as I see it, it's the only way we're going to raise the rest of the money this side of the millennium, and if we're really serious about this, we're going to have to accept that we need to take a few risks.'

'But the house?' Ellen protested.

There was the sudden crash of a door, followed by running footsteps and 'Daddy! Ellen! Daddy!'

Michael's eyes started to twinkle. 'Sounds like the hell-raiser's back early,' he said, as the kitchen door flew open and Robbie burst in. 'Five minutes earlier . . . ' he grinned, as Robbie came breathlessly towards them, his loyal puppy, Spot, bouncing eagerly at his heels.

'Daddy, Ellen, Jeremy says I can go watch the Raiders with him and his dad. They're outside in the car. Can I go? Thanks, you're cool. See you later.'

'Not so fast,' Ellen cried, grabbing his arm and swinging him back. 'Did you eat yet?'

'Not hungry.'

'Have you got any money?'

'Jeremy's dad'll pay. He's loaded.'

'Is this my son?' Michael demanded.

Robbie looked up at his father, his thick, untidy dark hair badly in need of a wash, his bright blue eyes glowing with impatience. 'I've got to go, Dad, this is a real important game.'

'Really,' Michael corrected.

'Yeah, really,' Robbie responded.

Michael rolled his eyes. 'Then I guess I'd better go and talk to Jeremy's dad.'

'Michael,' Ellen called after them as they headed off, Spot tacking on behind them, clearly thinking he was going too. 'Why don't you go with them?'

'Oh yeah!' Robbie cried, punching his fist in the air. 'Please Dad, please, please, please.'

Michael looked at Robbie, then at Ellen. Tonight would be the first they'd had free for over a month, and the plan had been to spend it together, at home.

'Go on,' Ellen prompted.

'Sure you don't mind?' he said.

'Why would I?' she laughed.

He came back, deposited Spot in her arms, then kissed her lingeringly on the mouth while Robbie made like he was throwing up in the background.

They'd only been gone a matter of minutes when Michael's private line started to ring again. As Ellen was trying to catch Spot, who was attempting to head off down the road after his master, the answerphone had already picked up by the time she got to the study.

'Michael, I forgot to ask just now,' Chambers was saying, 'did you speak to Michelle? I really think we could be on for this, that is, if I manage to hang on to my mortal coil. Say hi to Robbie. Be in touch in a couple of days. Over and out.'

The line went dead and Ellen stood staring at the machine, trying not to feel offended, and failing. OK, she and Chambers had never met, while he and Michelle, Robbie's mother, were practically old friends, but she didn't much like the way he had just made her feel as though she wasn't a part of Michael's life. After all, he must know that she was every bit as involved in the movie as Michael was, so at the very least he could have had the good manners to remember she was there.

Rewinding the tape she listened to the message again and wondered what Chambers, Michael and Michelle might be on for. Whatever it was, it didn't seem to include her, and though she disliked herself for such pettiness, she was sorely tempted to erase the message altogether. She didn't, but she knew she'd regret it bitterly if Michael had some crazy notion of going down there to join Chambers in Colombia, because it was precisely the kind of thing Michelle, the highly acclaimed British actress turned devoted humanitarian, could be relied upon to suggest. But no, Michael wouldn't, couldn't, leave LA right now. There was too much going down with World Wide and besides, he just didn't have the kind of training Chambers did in handling such hostile and dangerous conditions as those offered by Colombia and its infamous cartels.

Chapter 2

Getting up from the spare, rough-hewn table he was working at, Tom Chambers took a beer from an icebox in the corner of the shady room and went to look out the window. The narrow street was quiet, just a couple of kids kicking around a punctured ball, scuffing the gutters and scattering clumps of filth-sodden trash. The cacophony of boombox music and honking, angry traffic from nearby streets resounded through the tightly packed maze of the ghetto, where the walls were smeared with graffiti, windows and doors were constantly barred and violence stalked every sidewalk.

Being here could easily turn out to be the dumbest thing he had ever done. Except that accolade had already been awarded to the decision he had made three years ago – the decision that was going to punish him for the rest of his life.

It had brought him to where he was now – a city that had to be one of the most exquisite he had seen, on a mission that was infinitely more suicidal than any he had taken. But despite all his discussions with Michael, when Michael had tried to talk him out of coming, he'd had no choice in the matter, for his conscience was burning with enough guilt and remorse to launch him into a karmic cycle of everlasting chaos. Were he a Catholic he would probably go to confession. A few hundred years of Hail Marys, a hair-shirt and a couple of

28

lifetimes of abstinence on all counts might do the trick. But he wasn't a Catholic, nor did he have much faith in any religion giving him any kind of peace for what he had done. That was mainly because he believed it had to come from within him, which was why he was here, in a country that instilled fear in most right-thinking citizens of the world, in a town where Rachel, the woman he'd loved, had lost her life as a direct result of his stupidity and arrogance.

Her kidnap, three years ago, had been a warning from the Tolima Drug Cartel for him to back off his investigation *now*. Of course the warning had told him just how nervous they were, and they'd had good reason to be, for by then he'd connected up with a whole bunch of their enemies who were to be found not only in rival cartels and regular law enforcement, but within many of the left-wing terrorist groups that virtually controlled the country's interior.

Exactly who the Galeanos – the family who ran the Tolima Cartel – had paid to kill Rachel he still didn't know. Hernán Galeano, the head of the cartel, was now in prison, but it wasn't the kind of work a man like Galeano carried out personally, so what Chambers wanted to know was, who had been responsible.

Looking beyond the rooftops opposite, he allowed his eyes to move out to the distant grey walls of the Castillo de San Felipe. The fort was only for tourists now – and the troubled ghosts of a bygone era. It was from atop the sloping walls of that fort that the Spanish had finally beaten back the English; more recently it was from one of the *casas mata* inside that a security guard had come running to announce the discovery of a woman's dead body.

Rachel's dead body.

A horrible heat burned in his chest as he dragged his mind through the memory of the day they had found her. He knew already what they had done to her, they'd sent pictures that had spared no detail, nor shame. All that had been missing were the faces of her abductors. Not *her* face though, and the terrible degradation, the helplessness and pain, had buried itself so deep inside him that it had become his now to endure in a way she, mercifully, no longer did. But God, how he missed her. How he still longed for her, and how bitterly he wished he could turn back the clock.

When they'd met she'd been the editor of a human rights publication based in New Orleans. Weeks later she had unshackled herself from the frustrations of a desk and brought herself and her journalistic skills into the field.

Was he to blame for that? Had he talked her into giving up the security of her position for the madness of passion and front-line assault? Or was it more arrogance on his part to assume that he could wield such influence over a woman who was as headstrong and wayward as she was sensuous and caring? From the moment they'd met, at a Washington party, it had been clear to them both that all roads in their lives had led to this point, and that all roads from there would be travelled together. He'd made love to her that night and had known such hunger, sensation, tenderness and bewilderment that she had laughed at his surprise and confusion, as though understanding something he didn't. She was a mystery, a force so vibrant, wild and untamable – such a contradiction to the dignified and sober image of a do-gooder that even now it could make him smile.

Despite the shadows of the room, the humidity crept silently, intrepidly in, coating his body in sweat as the memories swathed his soul in pain. He put the beer to his lips and drank deeply. Coming back here, raking up the past and searing open his wounds was crazy, but he'd always known that one day he would.

Cartagena, the city they'd never got to meet up in, nor ever would. He'd spoken to her, less than an hour before they'd taken her. He'd been in Cali then, she had been here, almost a stone's throw away, in the splendid Santa Clara hotel. She might have been safe if she'd stayed there, not ventured out, and waited for him to come. But after six gruelling weeks in Bogotá, who could blame her for wanting to get out into the country for a while, to breathe a less polluted air and feast her eyes on the soothing infinity of nature. And she wasn't so far from town when they'd taken her, close enough for there to have been a hundred witnesses or more, but only one had come forward, and now he was nowhere to be found.

He walked back to the makeshift desk where a laptop computer, 9mm automatic, and stacks of papers cluttered the pitted surface. He was attempting to put together her story, trying as best he could to encapsulate the essence of her, while indulging in a self-absorbed purging of grief, and punishing himself with the imagining of her final terrible hours. While his own mission in Colombia had been to expose the Galeanos and the government officials they controlled, Rachel's had been to bring world attention to what was happening to the children, those who were referred to as *desechables* – disposable people – or as human waste, or filth. Though she'd gotten some good coverage, her kidnap and death had received so much more, for it had made headlines all over the world. But so too had the story she had syndicated a week before her death, the story that Chambers was staring down at now.

The first time he'd seen it was when Rachel had shown him herself. He had just arrived at the Casa Medina hotel in Bogotá, having flown in from the northern town of Montería where he'd spent the previous few days. She was waiting for him and the minute he walked into their room she had thrust the typewritten pages into his hand, insisting he read them right away. It was one of the things he'd loved most about her, the passion she'd felt for her work. This particular story concerned an invitation that had been posted all over the Bogotá district of Los Mártires announcing the introduction of a new 'social cleansing' campaign. It read:

FUNERALS
The industrialists, businessmen, civic
groups and community at large in the
Los Mártires area
INVITE ALL
to the funerals for the delinquents who work
in this part of the capital, which will begin
as of today and continue until they are
exterminated.

As his eyes scanned the words now he could still hear her anger and frustration as she demanded to know how anyone could get away with this, and why no-one cared.

'What the hell's wrong with the world that a story like this doesn't even make a front page?' she yelled, her brown eyes glittering with rage, her lovely face wrought with confusion. 'Don't they matter? Because they're not American or Jewish, or French or British, don't they count? We're as guilty as those goddamned bastards who're sticking the posters all over the streets, don't you see that? Merv Hemlisch should be held to account for this, and all those other godless editors who don't know a moral from a fucking menu. And you, Tom Chambers, could give me some support here. God knows I need it.'

'Hey, you've got it,' he assured her. 'And you've got to learn to give them a chance to go to print. I heard you've got a front page lead-in in the *New York Times* tomorrow. Did you know that?'

That silenced what she'd been about to say next, and she looked at him in amazement, before her eyes started to shine. 'Are you kidding me?' she asked suspiciously.

'Call them up. Ed's on the desk tonight. I spoke to him in the taxi on the way over here.'

'You talked him into it,' she accused.

'No, you did! The story did. It's big news, honey. I'll lay money right now you get above-the-fold coverage in London, Paris, Toronto, you name it.'

She looked at him, her eyes glowing, then put on a smile that showed him how much she wanted to believe that, though wasn't quite sure she could. 'We had the fire department in there tearing those posters down,' she told him. 'Boy, someone was running scared once we got ahold of it. Take a shot at who organized putting them up? Yeah, you guessed it, Salvador Molina. That slimeball should be taken out and butchered.'

She turned away, and going to stand at the window behind her he slipped his arms around her, hugging her to him. He knew how personally she took the tragedies she reported, and how impotent she sometimes felt in trying to expose the iniquity and corruption of lowlife like Molina – and God knew there were plenty of them.

After a while he felt some of the tension sliding from her and as she lifted her head they looked at each other's reflection in the darkened glass. Her smooth dusky skin, just like her passion, denoted the mix of her native-American and Creole roots. Her thick, ebony hair, cropped short for convenience rather than style, made her eyes seem larger and somehow more vulnerable, despite their fire. Her cheekbones, so high and proud, the regal flare of her nostrils, the perfect fullness of her mouth, and exquisite sensuousness of her body, all contrived to capture his heart in a way he no more understood than he could deny.

Lifting a hand she touched his handsomely rugged face, the face that had seen more tragedy than most, had watched more suffering and fought more injustice. She loved him beyond her own life, and knew he was as committed to exposing the torment of this nation's weak and poor as she was. He was the only one on whom she could vent her fury and frustration and know he understood. He was always there in her moments of hopelessness and exhaustion, with strength to spare and a wicked humour to make her laugh.

'I spoke to Francisco on the way in too,' he said. 'He was trying to get ahold of you. He's prepared to give the posters an inside page in *El Tiempo* tomorrow. It can be your byline, your story, if you want it.'

Her dark eyes narrowed. 'Why wouldn't I want it?' she said.

He waited.

'Oh God!' she groaned, as understanding dawned. 'You mean it might just serve to extend the invitation?'

He nodded.

She shook her head in despair. 'This country isn't Christian, it's barbaric.'

'Which is why I want you out of here by the end of the week,' he said.

She turned to face him. 'That must mean things are hotting up for you,' she said.

'Someone made contact from the Cali Cartel a couple of days ago,' he told her. 'They're going to connect me up with one of their lieutenants, a defector from the Tolima ranks. I'm flying to Cali in the morning. I want you to meet me in Cartagena next Thursday. If this guy's got some real goods to unload there's a chance we might have to ship out right away. If not, I thought we could spend some time together, just you and me.'

Her head went to one side, the appeal of the suggestion lighting her eyes. 'And do what?' she teased.

He moved his hands to her shirt buttons and started to undo them. 'Pretty much this sort of thing,' he responded.

She waited for him to finish, and as her shirt fell to the floor she slipped her arms around his neck. 'I had a dream about you last night,' she told him.

His eyebrows went up. 'Is that so?' he responded. 'Are you going to tell me about it?'

Her eyes were clouding as his mouth came very close to hers. 'It was real kinky,' she warned him.

'I'm liking the sound of it already,' he murmured. 'So what did we do?'

Standing on tiptoe she whispered in his ear.

His eyes widened for a moment, then pulling her more tightly against him, he said, 'I reckon it's time we made that dream come true.'

The images of their last night together were too painful for him to deal with now. It wasn't just the eroticism, it was the crazy laughter, the madness and abandonment, as well as the incredible intimacy and tenderness. Worst of all, though, was the knowledge that he was to blame for the fact that it would never happen again, for it was while he was in Cali, hammering the final few nails in Hernán Galeano's coffin, that Galeano had ordered the hit.

The message had taken no time to get through: the *gringo* is to give up his investigation of certain Colombian businessmen and politicians and get out of the country now or the *gringa* will die. And that was when Chambers had made the biggest mistake of his life.

Looking back, in the weeks, months, years that followed, he had never been able to make himself understand why he hadn't just done what they'd said and got out right away. There was no acceptable explanation for what had made him stay to get his story over before heading out, he could always have done it later – after Rachel's release. But it hadn't happened that way. Instead, Pacho, the friend whose cousin's apartment he was using now, had worked alongside him, translating and editing and filing the story through to *El Tiempo* and *El Espectador* in Bogotá, so by the time Chambers had reached the airport and reconnected with

35

the Galeano contact, the damage was already done – and two days later Rachel's body was discovered in the Fort San Felipe.

So why in God's name hadn't he done as he was told, when he of all people knew what little regard the *narcotraficantes* had for human life? His only answer was one of such blinding arrogance and stupidity that he'd never been able to admit it to another living soul. He had assumed, because she was American, and a woman, that they wouldn't dare to harm her. What a fool! What a goddamned, fucking madman. Surely to God he deserved to be in the kind of torment he'd been in ever since, he deserved it never to end.

'Hey, man, it is time to close up the shop and come have some fun!'

Chambers frowned. He'd been so deep in thought, so lost in her memory, he'd barely been aware of the phone ringing, or even of answering.

'Pacho,' he said to his friend.

'Come, join me at the café. I order you *empanadas*. I think you are hungry now.'

Chambers's stomach growled, a handsome and pressing response to the accuracy of Pacho's guess. 'Give me an hour,' he said and clicked off the phone.

The bar was in the exclusive section of the old town, not far, but in this heat he was in sore need of a shower. And there was no way he was leaving this room without first packing up his work – the reams of notes and sketchy outline of a screenplay that he had fed into his computer. He would leave it for safe keeping with Lioba, the motherly old soul who lived across the hall. The floppy disk backups he took with him wherever he went.

Just how much danger he was in was hard to gauge. Cartagena wasn't, by Colombian standards, a violent city, but should what was now left of the Tolima Cartel get wind of the fact he had re-entered the country, he'd rate his chances of getting out again a whole lot higher if it were as a corpse than as a passenger on an American Airlines 757. Thanks to his investigation three years ago, no less than twelve key members of the cartel, as well as half a dozen elected politicians, had experienced an ignominious end to their liberty, and in a couple of cases to their earthly existence. Because of that they felt Chambers owed them, and he was pretty damned sure that Rachel's death hadn't even come close to settling the sum.

'There is news, my friend,' Pacho said, as Chambers joined him at a table in front of a noisy bar. A jukebox inside throbbed with the heavy, fast rhythm of salsa, and a half-drunk couple in bright shorts and straw sombreros swung and gyrated around their rowdy friends.

Chambers watched them and waited for Pacho to continue.

'They receive a call at the Santa Clara today. Someone is looking for you,' Pacho told him.

Chambers felt his pulses start to speed. 'Any idea who the someone is?' he asked, picking up his beer as it was put down on the table. With the exception of Michael McCann he had told no-one he was coming here, and McCann knew very well he couldn't be reached at the Santa Clara.

'Not yet. But the fact that someone is asking means that someone either knows or suspects you are here.'

Chambers drank deeply and trailed his eyes across the elaborate, flower-covered balconies that fronted the whitewashed buildings on the other side of the plaza. Above them the red-tiled roofs baked in the afternoon sun; the only movement across the endless blue sky was that of an occasional bird or faraway plane. No sign of anyone watching him from there.

His eyes moved to the dappled shade of the trees that draped their luscious foliage over the square. Horses clattered by, and he could see any number of thin, half-naked men slouching on the grass, staring out of their thoughts and seeing nothing of the beauty that surrounded them. All strangers, all potential assassins.

As he waited Pacho chuckled. His round, warm face was pitted with pinprick scars, his chocolate-brown eyes, as merry as the impish tilt of his moustache, were watching Chambers closely.

'How much longer you plan to stay?' Pacho asked.

'Another week, maybe two.'

'How the work coming along?'

'It's coming. The witness, the one who came forward, did you track him down yet?'

'*Sí, sí.* I find man who live in Manga. He knows the man who see what happened. He is willing to talk. He knows what his friend see. He tell us.'

Chambers arched an eyebrow. 'So he knows I'm in town,' he pointed out.

'But I pay him to keep mouth shut,' Pacho protested.

'Maybe Hernán Galeano paid him more.'

'No, no, Galeano in prison. Thanks to you that scum is arrested and locked away, along with all the other hoozos from Tolima Cartel.'

'Come on, Pacho, you're not that naïve. Galeano might be behind bars, but he's still running what's left of the show and we both know that there's a bounty on my head that's making me more popular around here than Simon Bolívar. Galeano's been waiting for me to come back, and my guess is your guy from Manga has already sent him word.'

There was no contradiction in Pacho's expression. Evidently, having had it pointed out, he now suspected the same.

Chambers drank more beer, then sat quietly staring across the busy plaza at the Palacio de la Inquisicion, with its spectacular baroque stone entrance topped by the very regal Spanish coat of arms. The devil only knew what manner of suffering had been endured in the salons of torture behind those walls, but what was concerning Chambers now was the possibility that someone had got to Pacho with much the same methods – that maybe someone was paying him enough, or threatening him enough, to lead a Galeano hit man right to Chambers's door.

His death, if it came, wouldn't be swift, of that he could be certain. He had few friends in high places now, his investigation had put most of them behind bars. And of those who were left – well, three years had gone by, there was no knowing now who owned whom, or who was fighting on which side. Besides, no-one was ever going to thank him for the pressure that had been brought to bear upon the Colombian government to hand over Rachel's killers. Of course, they never had, and that he, an American journalist, had been responsible for so many investigations, trials and imprisonments, was as big an insult to the cartels as it was to the corrupt politicians and lawless bands of insurgents. He guessed the only incorruptible he'd ever met in this hopeless, war-torn land was one of the police chiefs, General Garcia Gómez, who was currently on vacation in Spain and not expected back for at least another month.

But Chambers was here now, and, even if it cost him his life, he was going to find out who had really killed Rachel. Though there was no question that Hernán Galeano had ordered the hit, the ones Chambers wanted were the bastards who had held her prisoner, raped her, then put a gun to her head and killed her. The score was going to be settled, and his vengeance was going to reach a scale that those miserable sons of bitches could never imagine.

'I think,' Pacho said, 'that you must leave the apartment. Maybe it no longer safe.'

Chambers looked at him and said nothing.

'I know you suspect me, my friend,' Pacho said, 'and it is right that you do. You must suspect everyone. Hernán Galeano want you very bad, and he pay lot of money for someone to find you. We no speak to friend of witness. We forget him now. There are others. I find them and make them talk. I bring them to you, before they have chance to get word to Galeano's people. After you speak with them you disappear. You understand? We find places for you, lots of them. You must stay on the move.'

Once again Chambers's harsh grey eyes searched the milling crowds in the plaza. Were they being watched now? Out here in the open like this he was a sitting target for even the most inept of assassins, and cartel *sicarios* were anything but that. Which meant that if they did have eyes on him, then his suspicions were correct: for the moment they wanted him alive – probably for much the same reasons that he wanted them alive too.

Pacho got to his feet and dropped a few coins on the table. 'I will come for you in the morning, just after dawn,' he said. 'Be ready to leave.'

Chambers watched him walk off down the street, then finishing his beer he got up from the table and began the twenty-minute stroll back to the apartment. Though he had the sense of being followed, and checked several times, he spotted no-one, nor did he put too much store by the feeling. It was one he'd had ever since arriving, and he knew it probably had its roots in paranoia rather than truth.

After collecting his papers and computer from Lioba, he crossed the hall to his own apartment and locked the door firmly behind him. He wouldn't go out again tonight.

The following morning, as the golden orb of the sun began to rise from the far horizon, Pacho came quietly up the worn concrete stairs outside Chambers's apartment. There was no-one else around, the only sounds coming from the early stirrings of life in the streets, and the wail of a baby somewhere else in the block. He stopped outside the apartment door, looked back down the hall, then raised a hand to knock. His fist connecting with the wood pushed the door open. Immediately Pacho stepped back, reaching for his gun as he pressed up against the wall. He waited, listening, hardly breathing.

He moved forward, pushed the door wider and called Chambers's name.

His mouth was turning dry, his heart beat a thick, loud tattoo in his brain. Bracing himself, he pulled out his gun and stepped quickly into the room, thumbing down the safety ready to fire.

The place was empty. He looked over at the bathroom. The door was open, the mirror reflecting a bare, white-tiled wall. The bed had been slept in. A pan of cold coffee rested on the stove. There was no sign of a struggle, nor of a hasty retreat. But everything had gone, Chambers, his computer, his papers, his clothes.

Spotting something on the floor by the bed, Pacho went to pick it up. It was a letter, addressed to Chambers at his Washington apartment, many pages long and neatly folded inside a torn blue envelope. He pulled it out and started to read. It didn't take him long to work out who it was from, even without looking for the name at the end. Prior to returning to Colombia, Chambers had been in Brazil working with a British woman by the name of Michelle Rowe. Pacho knew about her, Chambers had told him himself. There had been no romance between the two – their only objective had been to expose the activities of a certain Brazilian whom Chambers, and many others, had suspected of employing his own death squad, as well as running a private prison for the incarceration and torture of street children.

Pacho knew that there was a whole lot more to the story with Michelle Rowe, and judging by this letter there was still more to come. But that wasn't interesting him now. All he wanted to know was where the hell Chambers had gone.

Hearing footsteps in the hall outside, he quickly stuffed the letter inside his jacket and turned to face the door. As he expected, the footsteps stopped and two men peered cautiously into the room.

'*Ya se fué,*' Pacho said sharply. He's already gone.

'Where?' the shorter of them asked.

'I don't know,' Pacho answered. 'Maybe to hell.'

Chapter 3

Michael was sitting in a lone swivel chair facing a panel of five grey-suited businessmen. They were studying the thick files of information he had messengered over to them the day before, detailing his own personal and career backgrounds and the companies he was currently involved with.

It had been a while now since anyone had spoken, but he could see that several of them had reached the Profit Picture page for the movie, and, though the figures were certainly ambitious, he didn't consider them beyond the realms of achievement. Indeed, should the returns only amount to half of what he had forecast, Virago Knox would still stand to make something in the region of twelve million dollars, for a mere two-million-dollar investment.

Interminable minutes ticked by, until finally Truman Snowe, the company chairman, took in a silent verdict from the rest of the board before returning his sharp eyes to Michael.

Then, in true American style, with no preamble at all, Snowe said, 'The two-million-dollar investment for development will be transferred to the World Wide account as soon as the relevant documents have been drawn up.'

Until that moment Michael hadn't realized how tense he was. After weeks of being turned down, he'd now finally achieved the funds he needed to get the movie underway. Relief brought an irrepressible grin to his face as he got to his feet and reached for Snowe's hand. 'You won't regret this,' he told him. 'In fact, it's probably one of the safest investments you've ever made.'

'The names of the killers are to remain secret until the movie's release?' Snowe said, closing up the file.

'That's right,' Michael confirmed, not letting on that they didn't even know the names yet.

'Can we ask who's in the frame for the part of Chambers?' the man next to Snowe enquired.

'Richard Conway's favourite,' Michael answered.

'And the part of Rachel?' one of the others wanted to know.

Michael threw out his hands. 'Give me a name and I'll tell you she's there,' he answered. 'It'll be easier, though, once we know for sure that Conway's on board. Your backing at this stage is really going to help us secure that.' He looked at his watch. 'Now, if you'll excuse me, gentlemen, I'm already running late. I'll be in touch at the beginning of next week to set up a time to come and sign the necessary papers.'

Ten minutes later he was in the car on the way to the bank and listening to the message on Ellen's voice mail. 'Put the champagne on ice,' he said when the recording had finished, 'we're in business. If I don't hear from you in the next hour, I'll put a call in to Conway's people to set up a meeting. Oh, and by the way, we need to talk some more about hiring an investment manager. Did you mention it to Rufus yet? Call me when you get this message, I guess you're still tied up with Gromer. Are you free for dinner tonight? I'll cook. Love you.'

Hoping the good news would go some way to easing the tension that seemed to have arisen between them lately, he rang off, and making a left onto the freeway he started heading down town.

Not even the fact that Chambers had failed to call

again could take the edge off his exhilaration right now. In fact he was feeling so charged up and good about everything that he was actually allowing himself the fantasy of an Oscar speech, and whom he was going to thank. If things carried on the way they were going then the list would certainly be long, and could even include Ted Forgon, since, to Michael's amazement, the old boy had recently contacted Ellen from the bar at the Hillcrest and pledged a million dollars of his personal money if they managed to sign Richard Conway. Quite some vote of confidence considering its source, and in truth it had done more to buoy Michael than he was prepared to admit.

'Maggie,' he said into the phone.

'Ah, my lord and master,' his Scottish assistant responded. 'Where are you? And how did it go with Virago Knox?'

'We got it,' Michael told her, and grinned as she squealed with excitement, then relayed the news to the rest of the office. More cheers went up and, laughing, he waited for everyone to call out their congratulations before speaking to Maggie again.

'It's time,' he told her, 'to e-mail the rest of the gang in London, Sydney and New York, and let them know that I'm proposing to allocate eighty per cent of World Wide's capital to Tom Chambers's movie. The fact that we're going to be calling on them to come up with a further fifteen-plus million in the next couple of months we'll save for a later date.'

Sandy Paull was looking down at an e-mail printout and the set of spreadsheets that had come with it, as she left her office, threaded a path through the usual mayhem going on in the agency's main office, and pushed open Zelda Frey's door.

'I knew he was aiming for something big,' she said, looking at the extremely large and colourfully dressed agent, who was one of Michael's closest friends and confidantes. 'Did you get the same e-mail? Or don't tell me, you already knew.'

'About the Tom Chambers and Rachel Carmedi story?' Zelda said, cutting short the number she was dialling. 'I guessed it was the direction he was heading in. No sign of a script, I suppose?'

Sandy shook her head. She was scanning the spreadsheets again. 'I need to talk to him about this,' she said. 'Eighty per cent of our capital . . .' She looked up as Zelda's phone rang, then seeing Zelda grimace to say she had to take this call, she turned back to her own office.

After checking her watch to calculate the time in LA, she picked up the phone and dialled the ATI number. If this 'Untitled Feature' was going to be as big a project as the proposed budget was suggesting then she wanted to know more, and she wanted to know it now.

As she waited for someone to answer the phone she quickly checked her calendar to make sure World Wide LA's move to the ATI building had already taken place. Yes, it had happened a week ago, which meant that Michael and Ellen were no longer working from home. Sandy didn't allow herself to dwell on how snug and secure it all seemed over there for those two, it was best, she found, to blot that from her mind – at least for the time being.

'Michael McCann, please,' she said when someone finally picked up. There was an abrupt click, the strains of Satie or Chopin, then a voice said, 'Michael McCann's office.'

'Is he there?' Sandy asked.

'Who's speaking, please?'

'Sandy Paull.'

'Sandy Ball?'

'*Paull*. With a 'p' Peter,' she said, irritated that whoever this idiot was she appeared never to have heard of her.

'Can I tell him what it's about?' the girl said.

'Just tell him I'm on the line,' Sandy responded shortly.

'I'm afraid he's not here at the moment. Can I have him return?'

'Is he at home?' Sandy asked.

'Actually, he's at a meeting over on . . .'

'Is Ellen there?' Sandy snapped.

'Can I tell her what it's about?' the girl enquired, like a robot.

'Is she there?' Sandy repeated.

'I'll check. Can I tell her what your call is in connection with?'

'What's your name?' Sandy demanded.

'Olivia.'

'Then listen to me, Olivia. My name might mean nothing to you right now, but if you're at all interested in hanging on to your job, I'd put me through to Ellen and then go and do some homework on exactly who your bosses are.'

'Uh, excuse me?' the girl said.

It was hard not to scream as, too late, Sandy remembered it was never wise to speak in long sentences when dealing with American secretaries. She had no idea whether it was her accent they had a problem with, or if they were all just plain stupid. What she did know, however, was that when finally Ellen's voice came on the other end of the line, for once in her life she was almost glad to hear it.

'Sandy? What can I do for you?' Ellen said coolly.

'I'm fine, thank you. How are you?' Sandy replied.

'Michael should be back in an hour if you want to speak to him,' Ellen told her.

'I'm glad you're well too,' Sandy responded. 'I'm calling about the "Untitled Feature" that's just appeared on the spreadsheets. All it says is that it's a Tom Chambers' script. Do you have a copy? I'd like to read it.'

'You and me both,' Ellen retorted.

Sandy hesitated, noting the edge in Ellen's voice. 'You mean all this money's been set aside without anyone seeing the script?' she said.

'In Hollywood that's not so unusual,' Ellen informed her.

'Well, if such a large proportion of World Wide's current resources is being directed into one project,' Sandy said, 'then I think the rest of us should have been consulted.'

'I'm sure you're right,' Ellen said.

Sandy was intrigued by this answer, as it seemed to be confirming what she'd suspected a moment ago, that Ellen was pissed off about something and it sounded very much like it could be this movie. 'As the Head of Development, perhaps you could tell me when a script's likely to be available,' she said, enjoying the dig.

'As far as I'm aware no funds are being reassigned from any of your UK projects,' Ellen responded, neatly avoiding the question, 'so I don't understand your concern.'

'Not concern, interest,' Sandy corrected. 'If it's going to be World Wide's first major feature, I'd like to know more about it. I'm sure that goes for Chris Ruskin in New York and Mark Bergin in Sydney too.'

'I haven't heard from either of them on the matter,' Ellen told her, 'but you can be sure that as soon as there are any positive moves towards raising more finance for the project, or if a script should be approved, everyone will be notified.'

'More finance?' Sandy said. 'Exactly how big is this budget likely to get?'

'It's impossible to say right now,' Ellen answered, clearly annoyed by Sandy's persistence.

'What about stars? He must have someone in mind.'

'Richard Conway is looking pretty certain for the Tom Chambers role,' Ellen answered.

Sandy was extremely impressed. 'Well, when it comes

time for the rest of the casting I hope you're not going to forget McCann Paull's clients here in London,' she said. 'After all, we're supposed to be an international company and if you're intending to sink 80 per cent of our resources into a project that doesn't have a script . . .'

'Your clients won't be forgotten,' Ellen cut in. 'Now, if you'll excuse me, I'm already late for a meeting.'

As the line went dead Sandy muttered 'bitch' under her breath and hung up too. She almost always enjoyed talking to Ellen, mainly because she knew how little Ellen trusted her and how powerless Ellen was to do anything about it.

'Jodi,' she said, walking into the office next door, 'are either of World Wide's project researchers in today?'

Jodi, who was Michael's assistant when he was in London and general office manager when he wasn't, looked at the schedule board behind her. 'No,' she answered, as Sandy's assistant, Stacy, came into the office, loaded down with scripts. 'They're due in tomorrow – Stace they're going to fall!'

'It's OK, I've got them,' Sandy said, catching half a dozen scripts as they toppled towards her. 'Why don't you get the chaps in the post room to do this? What are they, anyway?'

'Rejects from the readers,' Stacy answered, her flushed face showing only relief as she deposited the rest of the pile on her desk. 'I brought them up in case you wanted to do a spot check,' she added, flopping down in her chair. With her short, plump body and shiny brown hair she looked the picture of schoolgirl health, despite being a mere eight days from her thirtieth birthday.

'Call downstairs to World Wide and find out if either of the researchers have put in an unexpected appearance,' Sandy told her. 'If not, find one of them and get him on the phone.' She was about to leave, then suddenly turned back. 'I'm going to talk to Zelda, but I'll take the call in my office.'

Some ten minutes later she was back at her desk talking to Jeremy Whittaker, one of the World Wide researchers, on the phone. 'I want you to find out everything you can about an American woman by the name of Rachel Carmedi,' Sandy said. 'She was shot and killed in Colombia three years ago. There was apparently quite a lot in the press about her at the time, so it shouldn't be too difficult to get some background.'

'I vaguely remember the story,' he said. 'Was she from New Orleans?'

'I think so. Get back to me as soon as you can. Actually e-mail me whatever you come up with.'

As she rang off Craig Everett, the senior literary agent, put his handsome blond head round her door. 'Fancy a screening tonight?' he invited. 'It's at BAFTA. None of our clients, so it could be a bit of a relaxer. Zelda's up for it. I'm about to ask the others. *OK, I'll be right there,*' he called back over his shoulder as someone yelled for him.

Sandy looked at her watch. 'What time does it start?' she asked.

'Drinks at seven. Movie at eight.'

'Sounds tempting,' she responded, 'but I've got a meeting at six over at the Beeb. I suppose I could make the movie.'

'Try,' Craig said. 'You don't get out enough. What it did to Jack it can do to Sandy.'

Sandy frowned and watched him go. Then, realizing he was referring to all work and no play, she started to smile. She really was fond of Craig, felt much more relaxed with him than any of the other agents, even though, amazingly, none of them ever appeared to have a problem with her. Hopefully none of them guessed how daunted she sometimes was by the fact she was their boss, but it wasn't an insecurity she gave much rein to, mainly because there wasn't the time – as Craig had just pointed out.

How many women's hopes had he crushed over the

years by being gay, she wondered. And when was the last time the two of them had sat down and had a good old gossip over dinner, putting the world, the industry and their complicated love lives to rights? Actually, his was much more complicated than hers, as the great love of his life was not only married with three kids, but just happened to be a highly respected cabinet minister too. For her part, since there wasn't any love life to speak of, there weren't any complications either.

Smiling ruefully to herself she thought of Ellen Shelby and her ill-disguised fears that Sandy was going to do something to disrupt the picture-book perfection she, Michael and Robbie were enjoying over there in Hollywood. It was whenever she thought of that cosiness that Sandy was thankful for how busy she was, because knowing that Michael was making love to another woman, when no-one was making love to her, was even worse than the forced abstinence itself. She fantasized regularly about Michael, reliving the night he had made love to her all over his apartment, taking her in every position and making her come like she never had before or since. She wasn't sure what hurt the most now, the fact that they had never done it again, or that he had then turned round and fired her.

'Hello, Michael?' she said into the phone much later that night.

'Sandy?' he responded. 'How are you? Burning the midnight oil again?'

She smiled and looked at the e-mail on the screen in front of her. 'I wanted to talk to you about the Untitled Feature,' she said. 'If it's what I think it is, you've got me really excited.'

Michael laughed, and she felt the pleasure steal through her. 'Then I hope it's what you think it is,' he answered.

'The story of Rachel Carmedi?' she asked. 'And her kidnap and shooting by a Colombian drug cartel? I think it's brilliant. It's got everything. Drugs, sex, love, terrorism, street children and truth. Ellen tells me there's no script yet.'

'Tom Chambers is writing it. He's in Colombia right now, but I'm hoping he'll be back in the next couple of weeks. We should have the first draft shortly after.'

'Can I see it, when it comes? I'd really like to get behind this. If you're looking for more finance, then I'd be happy to do what I can over here. We've built up some good contacts in the past six months.'

'Sandy, you don't know how wonderful it is to hear you say that,' he told her, 'because I certainly will be asking you to call on your contacts. I've got to warn you though, the kind of investments we'll be looking for aren't going to be in the tens of thousands. They're more likely to be in the hundreds of thousands, if not millions.'

'Wow!' Sandy responded. 'You really are thinking big. But having Richard Conway attached should certainly help smooth the way. In fact, I can hardly wait to see my backers' faces when I start dropping Conway's name.'

Michael laughed. 'You know, it's really good to hear your enthusiasm,' he said. 'Ellen seems to have developed a bit of a down on it lately. I mean, she knows it's a great story, but she's started thinking we're in danger of upsetting the Colombian cartels, and considering their propensity for kidnap and murder . . . Well, to quote her, Robbie went through enough in Rio, we shouldn't be putting him in the firing-line again.'

'She's got a good point,' Sandy responded. 'It takes real courage to make this sort of film . . .' She let those words hang for a moment, then said, 'Who are you thinking of for the female lead?'

'It's still under discussion,' Michael answered.

'Directing?'

'Hopefully Vic Warren. He's got a conflict at the moment, but he's working on it.'

'And producing? Apart from you, obviously.'

'Ellen and I are the executives. She'll concentrate more on the creative side, while I take on the finance. The actual hands-on producers have yet to be hired, Ellen's currently working on that. We reckon the team will number around eight, including associates, by the time we're ready to roll. Tom's down as a producer too . . .'

'I'd like to be included, if I come up with some of the funding,' Sandy interrupted.

'I don't see any problem with that,' he replied. 'Hey listen, my other line's ringing. It's one of the ones I had set up for Chambers. I'll catch you later, OK?'

Sandy rang off and after hitting a button on her computer to print out some documents she needed she began packing up to go home. Inside she was glowing, the way she often did after speaking to Michael, though tonight she was feeling a particular elation at how readily he had accepted the idea of her being included as a producer. She tried to imagine how Ellen would react when she was informed, and spent some time enjoying the various effects it would probably have.

Chapter 4

For the past five days Chambers had had one hell of a time trying to figure out where he should be from one minute to the next. Nowhere, it seemed, was safe, yet anywhere was a haven. Since abandoning Cartagena, over a week ago, he had slept in ditches, ridden on mules, eaten from banana leaves and bathed in slimy lakes. Each day brought a totally new and unexpected experience, from having his face shaved by a cutthroat's apprentice, to secretly watching the harvest of a coca crop, heavily guarded by one of the nation's most notorious paramilitary groups – men who were known to clear villages by decapitating peasants and using their heads as footballs, a sure-fire way of getting the rest to flee.

Deciding whom to trust was like a game of Russian roulette with only one empty barrel. When Orlando Morales, his former contact from the Cali Cartel, had visited him in the dead of night in Cartagena, the man had been easy to believe. After all, Morales had proved himself in the past, so why not trust him again? And Pacho Martínez, the notorious Mr Fixit and friend to the cutting edge of Colombian society, was no more invincible than any other man with a passion for survival. Chambers knew that Pacho wouldn't willingly sell him down the river, but he knew too that if it came to his skin or Pacho's, then the Colombian's masseuse was in a pretty safe job.

So he'd opted to go with Morales, whose past allegiance to the Tolima Cartel was a big chapter in the little man's history. That Morales was still alive could only be down to the protection he received from the Cali Cartel, and, if the past five days were anything to go by, there were more than a few debts owed to the FARC – one of the country's leading guerrilla groups, and arguably the most dangerous – for more often than not it was they who had escorted them over some of the most dangerous and bitterly contested terrain of the Colombian interior.

Chambers still didn't know how Morales had come to find out he was in Colombia, but the fact that he'd shown up just hours after a call was made to the Santa Clara hotel looking for Chambers, had been enough to confirm that word of his arrival was out. Morales hadn't made the call to the hotel, but, as he'd pointed out later, he hadn't had much trouble locating Chambers once he'd known he was in Cartagena. And if Morales could find him that fast, so could others. Which was why Chambers had driven out of the city with Morales and two others in the early hours of Friday morning, and travelled with them over the next five days to this remote border village that time had clean forgot.

It was certainly the most peaceful place Chambers had visited in this war-torn land, with barely a car to be seen on the narrow dirt roads that were edged with decrepit old houses and ran with mud for the best part of the year. The rain came every day, sweeping in a fine, gauze-like mist down over the gloriously rich green mountains of the Magdalena valley, washing the huge, succulent leaves of the banana trees and glimmering on the red-tiled roofs of the village. Dry or wet, the humidity was stifling, and the sun so bright on the whitewashed walls it stung the eyes and drowned the streets in dazzling light.

Chambers and Morales had taken over a small two-storey house at the far end of the main street. No-one paid them much attention, and they rarely went out. Throughout the day locals trotted by on their trusty steeds, while others postured and swaggered about street corners in their wide-brimmed hats and thick checked ponchos. Every one of them smoked tobacco, or chewed coca leaves, indulging in rowdy games with unfathomable rules, while the women inspected hanging slabs of meat for supper and kids scuffed around in the dirt.

It had been a quiet and easy couple of days after the ordeal of the journey, and should remain that way until Morales's cohorts returned with word from *El Patron* that it was safe to move on, or necessary to stay put a while longer. *El Patron* – the boss – was a man without a name, though Chambers knew he was very probably paramilitary, for that was how members of such groups referred to their ranking officer.

Thanks to Morales he now knew the name of one of Rachel's killers. Gustavo Zapata. It had come as no surprise to learn that the kid, for he was barely in his twenties, was a near relative of Hernán Galeano's: this would account for the older man's refusal to hand anyone over at the time the pressure was on. Morales had obtained Zapata's identity from one of his 'sleepers' inside the Tolima Cartel, but so far the other two names were proving hard to come by. But there were ways of finding out, and Chambers wanted to be around when the Zapata kid squealed.

Morales was putting up no objection to that; he understood the need to look a killer in the eye and let him know how much worse it was going to be for him. What he didn't understand was Chambers's professed reluctance to execute the scumsuckers who had carried out the job on his girlfriend. But Morales was losing no sleep over it. It was Chambers's call, he was only there to continue the payback for what the Galeanos had done to his son after the boy had been seduced by Galeano's bitch of a cockteasing wife.

It was evening now, a time when the veil of rain was absorbed by the humid air and the strange stone statues on the hillsides, carved by the hands of long-dead craftsmen, basked in the fiery glow of sunset. Chambers was standing before one now, gazing at the curiously monstrous face and stout cribbed body. He wondered about its origins, its creator, its link to the long-lost civilization that had once inhabited these hills. He felt a sense of timelessness stirring inside him, connecting him to the past, or maybe the future. Rachel was never far from his mind. He wondered if she was with him now, looking at this ancient symbol of indecipherable meaning. Her presence felt so real, he was sure if he turned he would find her there. Would she speak to him? Would she tell him to give up on this earthly torment and come join her in a place where vengeance had no meaning or purpose? Or would she guide him to those who had wrenched her from the bonds of their love and consigned them to this hell of divided worlds?

Turning, he looked down over the hillside to where the village lay cradled in the bowl of the valley. It was several moments before he noticed the girl climbing the path towards him. Her thick dark hair hung loosely around her shoulders, her strong, athletic legs moved gracefully over the grassy ascent. She waved, and though she was still too distant for him to see her face, he could feel himself warming to the childlike brightness of her eyes and guileless beauty of her smile. Her name was Carlota: she was a whore's daughter who had ridden with them from the nearby town of Popayán to this village where her grandmother lived. She looked fourteen, though insisted she was twenty.

'I was looking for you,' she said as she joined him. She was breathless from her walk; her clear olive skin was sheened in sweat. 'They are saying in the bar that you are wanted in your country for more than a hundred crimes.'

Chambers crooked an eyebrow. '*Are* there that many?' he said.

'Oh yes,' she assured him. 'And I think you have committed them all. Morales, he says you did, and that no-one should mess with you, because you are a very wicked and dangerous man.'

Chambers pushed his hands in his pockets and started back down the hill. He liked the girl, enjoyed her prattle, and knew he should dissuade her from seeking him out.

'Where is your wife?' she asked, falling in beside him.

He threw her a sidelong glance, and carried on walking.

She skipped up over a rock, then came down to block his way. 'I want to be your wife,' she told him, her slanted green eyes shining with mischief. 'I am a virgin. I could be your wife.'

Picking her up, he set her aside to clear his path, then laughed as she threw herself to the ground and tried to pull him down with her. 'Morales says I must seduce you,' she smiled up at him. 'He says you are in need of a woman.'

'And you are a girl,' he said, pulling her back to her feet. 'A child.'

'A woman!' she cried. 'I am a woman. I can give you love, and I can make you special rate.'

They walked on in silence, until finally she said, 'The men who were with you and Morales before we leave Popayán, they arrive just now.'

Chambers felt a rapid beat in his heart. 'Did Morales send you to find me?' he said.

'He told me to find you, and love you, then bring you back to the house.'

Despite the sudden edge to his nerves there was a glint of humour in Chambers's eyes. 'Here,' he said, dragging a twenty-dollar bill from his pocket, 'tell him you succeeded.'

She snatched the money, buried it inside her dress, and said, 'It is too soon. He will know that there was no love, because we come back too soon.'

Ordinarily Chambers wouldn't have cared what Morales thought, but the man had been on his case for days about a woman, and this could be an easy way of getting him off. Let him think that he had taken the girl, maybe then his celibacy would cease to be an issue. 'Come here,' he said to Carlota, and taking her hand he pulled her behind a boulder and pushed her down on the grass. 'I want you to lie there and be quiet,' he told her, sitting down facing her and resting his back against the rock. 'I need to think, and I need you to tell Morales we made love.'

'Then let's make love,' she said. 'It will be easier that way.'

There was great irony in Chambers's eyes as he surveyed her. Lying there like that, so fresh and inviting, she looked as desirable as any woman he'd known, and God knew he needed the release. But no matter how many times she had given herself before, sex with a minor was no more his scene than sex with a horse.

It wasn't that he'd been celibate since Rachel died, far from it, it was just that being back in this country was reconnecting him to her in a way that made him want to exclude other women. Were he being honest, he'd have to admit, on an emotional level, it was pretty much that way wherever he was. It certainly wasn't that he set out to hurt a woman, but after he'd slept with her he just didn't want the additional involvement.

He thought about Michelle Rowe, the British actress who'd worked with him on bringing down the Brazilian businessman Pedro Pastillano. In the time they were together he had probably felt closer to her than he had to anyone since Rachel's death, but, as beautiful as

Michelle was, there had never been a question of anything more than friendship between them. He wondered where her most recent letter was. It seemed he'd mislaid it somewhere between Cartagena and here. It wasn't important, he could always get her address from Michael – as he recalled, she was currently working in the Afghan refugee camps on the borders of Pakistan. He liked the suggestion she'd come up with in her letter, and wondered if she'd put it to Michael yet. Chances were Michael wouldn't go for it, not now he had another woman in his life. On the other hand Chambers could make it a condition of his contract, when it finally got drawn up.

Héctor Escobar and Dario Galvis were drinking beer with Morales when Chambers returned to the house. Carlota left him at the door and gave a star performance of having just been laid. Morales looked pleased and handed Chambers a congratulatory beer.

'We have news,' he told Chambers, settling back in his chair. 'Good news.' He signalled Héctor to continue.

'We've got another name,' Héctor said, his permanent scowl allowing only a trace of satisfaction.

Chambers looked at him, his iron-grey eyes as sharp as flint. 'How?' he said.

Héctor shrugged. 'Never dump on a woman and never trust one either.'

Morales said, 'Galeano's wife, the bitch my son was killed for, is getting even with the husband who just dumped her from a prison cell.'

'He found himself a nice young boy to take her place,' Dario sniggered.

Morales looked at him, then turned back to Chambers.

'How do you know she's telling the truth?' Chambers said. 'Who spoke to her?'

'*El Patron* spoke to her,' Héctor answered. 'One of the names she gave him is Julio Zapata. Gustavo Zapata's older brother. They are the sons of Galeano's sister.' He

60

paused, then looked Chambers right in the eye. 'The third name is Salvador Molina,' he said.

Chambers's insides turned to ice.

Morales and the others waited. In the end Morales spoke again. 'It is the same Salvador Molina as Rachel named in her reports, the one who fucks with kids.'

Inside Chambers was shaking. Of course, he'd always suspected Molina, but there had never been any proof. There was probably none now, but he didn't need it. All he needed was a moment to make himself accept finally that no matter what he had done back then, Molina would have killed her anyway. It still didn't let him off the hook, but it sure as hell sorted out any lingering problem he might have had about taking another man's life.

'How do you know?' he said.

'*El Patron*'s men did the kidnap,' Morales answered. 'After that, they handed over to Molina and the Zapatas.'

It figured. 'So what now?' he said.

'Now, you decide,' Morales answered. 'You want these scumsuckers dead, you give the word. You want to do it yourself, we will arrange it. Or maybe, now you have the names, you want to leave and go back to your own country.'

Chambers looked at the three men and saw their contempt for the third choice, and for any man who would take it. He thought of Rachel and what it must have been like for her in those final moments when the gun was pressed to her head. He felt her terror, her desperation, her hopelessness . . .

There had never been any choice.

'You know, you didn't have to come,' Michael said. 'We'd have understood if you had other things to do.'

'What makes you think I had other things to do?' Ellen countered as they watched Robbie and his two friends leaping in and out of the water jets at Universal Studios' Citywalk.

'We've always got other things to do,' Michael replied, glancing over his shoulder as someone in the crowd nudged past him.

Ellen sighed, then suddenly she was dodging behind Michael and shrieking as Robbie made a dive towards her in his soaking wet clothes. 'Robbie! No!' she cried. 'Robbie! *Michael stop him!*'

But it was too late as, much to the enjoyment of the crowd, Robbie embraced her vigorously, drenching the light cotton pants and pale silk shirt she was wearing.

'Right, you've asked for it now,' she declared, and scooping him up she gave him a whopping great kiss right in front of his friends.

'No! No! Oh, yuk! Ugh! Dad, stop her!' Robbie yelled, struggling to get free as his friends clapped and jeered and Michael looked on with great amusement.

Laughing, Ellen started to put him down, then suddenly threw him at Michael. Instinctively Michael caught him, clutching the sopping little body to his own and soaking himself.

'Oh no, I don't want you kissing me too,' Robbie cried in disgust, and quick as a flash he wriggled out of Michael's arms and escaped back to his friends.

Michael looked at Ellen and they laughed. That Robbie had taken so well to life in LA was a constant source of surprise and relief to them both, though they were always on the lookout for any repercussions to the trauma he had suffered while in Brazil. He had been four years old when he was kidnapped, an ordeal that was sure to bear some kind of adverse consequences the psychologists had told them. But so far there had been none, and more than six months had passed since Michael and Tom Chambers had rescued him. It was also six months since his mother had relinquished custody and allowed him to come and live with his father, which, considering how well he was adapting, went to show how remarkably resilient children could sometimes be.

Watching them together now, it was hard to credit that Michael's first meeting with his son had taken place on that terrifying night of rescue, for their closeness seemed to derive from a relationship that had started with birth. But that hadn't been the case, for when Michelle had ended her relationship with Michael and taken off for Sarajevo, she had taken their unborn child with her. And in an effort to punish her Michael had refused ever to have anything to do with the child. Of course, it hadn't worked that way, for the only one who had really suffered as a result of his pride and stubbornness was Michael. Now he was making up for lost time, and Ellen had to hand it to Robbie's mother, the woman was far braver and more generous than she could ever be, for handing her son to his father and a strange woman wasn't something Ellen could ever imagine herself doing. In truth, Ellen knew it hadn't been easy for Michelle, because she was often there when Michael spoke to her on the phone and tried to comfort and reassure her that Robbie was happy and settling in well at school and at home. Ellen wondered if it hurt Michelle to know that. It had to, even though she'd never want him to be lonely or miserable, she wouldn't be human if she didn't crave the comfort of knowing he missed her. Which of course he did, but he loved Michael so much and was so proud to be living with the daddy his mother had told him so much about, that like any other five year old he was often too busy to dwell long on anything, even missing his mother.

Ellen smiled as she watched him and felt her heart fill with love and gratitude for the ease with which he had accepted her into his life. It could have been hell, but because he was such an exceptional little boy, so full of mischief and humour, as well as kindness and love, he had gone a long way towards making these past six months the most special she had ever known. In fact there were times when she fervently wished that his father was even half as easy to deal with.

'I wish I knew why you were mad at me,' Michael said softly as he slipped an arm around her.

'Who said I was mad at you?' she responded.

'Well, the cold shoulder you keep treating me to lately's a bit of a give-away,' he said, his eyes twinkling with humour even though she knew he meant it.

She looked off along one of the walkways to where a vast, lifesize model of King Kong loomed out over the teeming masses below.

'I don't get it,' he told her. 'You set a date for the wedding, then you can barely bring yourself to speak to me. So what did I do?'

Lifting her eyes to his, she smiled and shook her head. 'Now's not the time,' she said. 'We've got Jurassic Park and Back to the Future to get through yet, never mind ET and the Hard Rock café.'

'You really didn't want to come, did you?' he challenged quietly.

'Sure I did. I've just got a lot on my mind, that's all.'

For a moment it seemed he was going to let it go, then, turning her to him, he said, 'It's to do with the movie, isn't it?'

Her eyes fell away as she wondered if it would be a lie to say that it was.

'A couple of weeks ago you were right behind it,' he said, 'so what's happened to change your mind?'

She looked up into his face and, seeing his confusion and concern, she felt such love swell in her heart that all she wanted was to hold him and forget about what was eating her. But sadly it wasn't going to go away that easily. 'Nothing's happened,' she said, 'except that not knowing what we're up against in a bunch of Colombian drug lords doesn't exactly make for a restful night's sleep.' She shrugged. 'Maybe, once the script is in and we've got some idea what we're really dealing with, I won't feel quite so concerned.'

He was still looking at her, as though waiting for her to say more. 'Are you sure that's all?' he prompted, when she only looked back at him.

She smiled and marvelled at how well he knew her. 'Why do you say that?' she countered.

'I just sense it,' he said. 'So am I right?'

'OK, yes, I am holding something back,' she admitted, 'but only because we've been so frantic these past couple of weeks that there hasn't been a chance for us to talk about anything except work or school. I thought we could today,' she said, looking at Robbie, 'but this comes first.'

Michael looked at Robbie too, and when she saw the frown on his face Ellen turned him quickly back to her. 'It's got nothing to do with him,' she said, 'I swear it.' And, seeing the anguish retreat from his eyes, she stood on tiptoe and kissed him. 'I love you both,' she whispered.

He grinned. 'So you're not going to back out?'

'Of the wedding?' she laughed in surprise. 'Is that what you were thinking?'

He shrugged. 'It crossed my mind.'

Still laughing, she rested her head on his shoulder. 'In a little over three months from now,' she said, 'despite the utter chaos our lives are going to be in because of this film, I'm going to become your wife, and nothing or no-one is going to stop me.'

'Well, there's a relief,' he sighed, 'because I've already booked the honeymoon and there's no way I can get my deposit back now. Ouch!' he grunted as she nudged him.

'And what,' she said, 'makes you think we're going to have time for a honeymoon?'

'We'll make time,' he assured her, then pulled a face as

her cellphone started to ring. 'It's Sunday,' he protested.

'Look on it as a honeymoon rehearsal,' she advised, digging around in her bag. 'It could be Jackie Bott. I told her to call me as soon as she had an answer. Hello, Ellen Shelby,' she said, into the receiver. 'Oh hi, Jackie! How's it looking?' Her eyes were on Michael's as she listened to the reply, and, as she started to grin, so did he. 'That's fantastic,' she laughed, giving him the thumbs up. 'I'll get a contract sent round to you first thing tomorrow. No rush, have your lawyers look it over and get back to me if there's a problem. Michael and I are meeting with Reece and Otto on Tuesday at four, can you make it? Terrific. We'll see you then. No, still no script I'm afraid, but I've done a breakdown of the story and the kind of locations, facilities, crewing, casting etc. it's going to need, so I'll get Maggie to fax it over in the morning.'

As she rang off Michael cupped her face in his hands and kissed her hard. 'I take it,' he said, 'you just added the famous Jackie Bott to the producers' team.'

'It sure looks that way,' Ellen beamed, and, kissing him on the mouth, she went to round up Robbie and his friends to move them on towards the Jurassic Park ride.

It was way past eight o'clock when they finally dropped off Robbie's friends and headed towards home. Robbie, surrounded by souvenirs of the day, was struggling to stay awake in the back, while Ellen went between dictating notes for Maggie into a recorder, and talking over the week's madcap agenda with Michael.

It really was going crazy now, as a couple of World Wide's smaller projects were gaining some interest from the networks, and ATI was getting ready to go official with the new packaging format Ellen and Michael were introducing. Most of the other big agencies in town operated like that – putting together directors, producers, actors and writers – and though a number of ATI agents had long been working that way as part of their personal deal, it was only since Michael had involved himself in the company that ATI was starting to be recognized as a heavyweight contender on that front.

As they pulled up outside the house Lucina, their new live-in housekeeper, opened the door for Spot to come hurtling down the steps to greet his master.

'Hey Spot,' Robbie cried, scooping him up and letting the dog lick him all over the face. 'We brought you some hamburger. Can I give it to him, Ellen?'

'Sure,' she answered, 'let's just take everything inside. Everything OK, Lucina?'

'Oh yes,' Lucina beamed, her round olive-skinned face gazing upon Robbie and Spot with unabashed devotion.

'Any calls?' Michael asked, taking damp towels, a Hercules mask and a helium balloon from the back of the Land Cruiser.

'Lots,' Lucina answered. 'The machine take them. My English no good yet. You ready for bath, Robbie?'

Robbie's eyes grew wide as he looked up at Ellen. 'It's OK,' she whispered, trying not to laugh, 'Daddy'll come in with you.'

'Hey, you, me and Lucina in the bath, sounds like fun,' Michael joked.

'I can bath myself,' Robbie said grumpily as he buried his face in Spot. Then suddenly he brightened again. 'Can Spot come in too?' he said eagerly.

'I don't think so,' Ellen answered, taking one of the bags Michael was passing her. 'Are your clothes still damp. Give them to Lucina, she'll put them in the drier.'

By the time the front door had closed behind them Michael was already in the study, playing back their messages. There was nothing on the machine that took calls from Chambers, but he was getting used to the erratic nature of contact from Colombia now, so he wasn't unduly concerned. The other tape took some minutes to rewind, and by the time the first couple of messages had played Ellen had left Robbie in the bathtub and come in to join him. It was just as Michelle's voice began that she happened to walk in the door.

'Hi darling, it's Mummy,' Michelle began. 'Sorry I missed you. Hope you're having a good time, whatever you're doing. How's Spot? Is he being a good boy? Your letter was wonderful, and the photographs. I've put them up next to my bed. I've got a surprise for you, sweetheart. I'm coming over to Los Angeles in a couple of weeks. Isn't that great? I hope it's going to be OK with Daddy. Ask him to call me, will you? 'Bye darling. I love you.'

Michael stopped the tape and looked over at Ellen.

'I'll get Robbie,' she said.

'Wait.'

She turned back.

'Is it OK with you?' he said.

'Even if it weren't, you don't think I'd stop him seeing his mother, do you?' she snapped.

He stared at her, waiting for her to say more.

'What?' she cried, throwing up her hands.

'If she's coming she'll have to stay here,' he said.

Ellen's eyes flashed. 'Well, won't that be cosy?' she responded tartly.

Michael's face darkened. 'I don't think I like the way this is going,' he said.

'Oh, is that so? Then try seeing it from where I'm standing, you'll like it a whole lot less. "I hope it's OK with Daddy," like *I* don't live here. Like I'm not the one who takes her son to school every day, who helps him with his reading, or takes him horseback riding, or to the dentist, or nurses him when he's sick, and dries his tears when he's missing her . . .'

'You sound like you resent doing it,' Michael cut in.

'How dare you say that?' she seethed, almost failing in the effort to keep her voice down. 'You know how much I care for that boy, so don't you ever accuse me of that. What I resent is her calling up and saying she's coming, like I don't exist. And then *you* saying she's going to be staying here, like I don't get a say in it.'

'So what are you suggesting, that she goes to a hotel?'

'I wasn't aware I suggested anything.'

He was silent for a moment, clearly trying to deal with his anger. In the end, he said, 'You know, I didn't realize you had such a big problem with Michelle.'

'Me? You think I'm the one with the problem?' she responded caustically. 'I think it's you.'

He stared at her in genuine amazement. 'I need a basis for that,' he said tightly.

'Maybe it's not a problem,' she said. 'Maybe it's something you just don't want to share with me.'

'What the hell are you talking about?' he demanded.

Instead of answering she stared at him, furiously, until finally she averted her eyes, not sure she wanted to get into this while their tempers were so frayed.

'Come to the point,' he said shortly.

'Why don't you?' she shot back. 'You're the one who's got something to hide, or secrets to keep, or whatever the hell you're doing. So *you* come to the point. Just what is it that you, Michelle and Tom Chambers have got cooking together? I heard the message Chambers left, and I've been waiting, Michael, more than two weeks for you to tell me what the hell it's all about.'

'What message? I don't know what you're talking about.'

' "Did you speak to Michelle?" ' she repeated, her voice shaking with anger as she quoted Tom Chambers. ' "I really think we could be on for this." On for what, Michael? You've got something planned, the three of you? Are you intending to go down there, is that what it's about? You're just going to take off and go play heroes again . . .'

'Hold it! Hold it!' he shouted across her. 'First, I'm not going anywhere, OK? And if this is the reason you've been so fucking difficult with me lately, then it's time you grew up and learned to say what's on your mind instead of bottling it up . . .'

'Well, I think I just did,' she raged. 'So, what's the answer?'

'The answer is, I don't know what the message meant any more than you do. Whatever he's discussed with Michelle, neither of them have told me. Is that OK? Does that answer your question?' His fist suddenly hit the desk in frustration. 'Jesus Christ, what is this, that you think I'd hold back on you over something? Why would I? What the hell do you think I've got to hide? And I don't see you getting this way about any other project, so while we're at it, maybe you'd like to tell me just what you've really got against Tom Chambers and Rachel's story?'

'Oh, so it's got a title already?' she said. 'Thanks for keeping me informed.'

Michael rolled his eyes. 'That wasn't a title,' he said. 'But maybe it could be. Have you got a better idea? If you have, then let's hear it. You're as much a part of this damned movie as anyone else around here. And as far as I can see, you're the only one who's got a problem with it. So let's get it all out in the open, shall we?'

Ellen glared at him.

He glared back, waiting.

In the end she was the first to look away. 'I don't have a problem with the movie,' she said, knowing how ludicrous she would sound if she told him how shut out Chambers had made her feel when he'd left that message – and how Michelle had just managed to do the exact same thing. The insecurity was hers, so she had to be the one to deal with it. 'I just think we should . . . Oh, great timing!' she snapped, as the private line on Michael's desk suddenly burst into life.

Michael snatched it up. 'Tom?' he said, looking at Ellen. 'Everything OK?'

Chambers's voice was fractured by static on the line.

'I've got the names,' he shouted. 'I put them on the e-mail.'

'You've got them?' Michael cried incredulously as he reached over to turn on his computer. 'Are you sure about them? I mean, that's fantastic. Brilliant. But we can't afford for there to be any doubt . . .'

'There's no doubt,' Chambers assured him.

'Then congratulations, if that's the right word. This is going to make all the difference. So tell me you'll be on the next plane.'

'There are a couple more things I need to clear up before I leave,' Chambers responded. 'I'll call you again in a couple of days,' and the line went dead.

'He's got the names,' Michael said as he rang off. Then, looking up, he saw that Ellen had gone. He stood staring at the empty doorway. He guessed she had gone to supervise Robbie out of the bath and into bed, but despite loving her for how much she did for Robbie, he knew that on this occasion she had used it as an excuse to disappear while Chambers was on the line. It seemed this movie was becoming a really big deal with her, and for the moment he could only thank God that she didn't yet know he had agreed to make Sandy Paull one of the producers. That was a battle he really wasn't looking forward to, but it seemed they had a few more to get through before that one eventually reared its head.

Crossing the lounge, he stopped a moment to flick on the outside lights, illuminating the pool and garden, then continued on to the wing that contained Robbie's bedroom and bathroom, the playroom, a guest-room and the stairs to Lucina's basement apartment. He found Ellen sitting on his son's bed, rubbing Robbie down with a towel as he playfully attacked her with Buzz Lightyear. She glanced up as Michael came in, then reached for Robbie's pyjamas.

'Daddy,' Robbie said, as Ellen pulled him onto her lap, 'do you think Spot could have a pony?'

71

Michael's eyebrows went up.

'I mean, one day,' Robbie added hurriedly.

'What's Spot going to do with a pony?' Michael enquired.

'Well, he could ride him,' Robbie answered.

'While you run along next to them?' Michael suggested.

Robbie looked up at him and grinned. 'Will you come riding with me this week?' he said. 'They're letting me go on Frisky, because I was good last time, and if you're good you get to go on Frisky, don't you, Ellen? Will you come, Dad, and watch me?'

'I'll certainly try,' Michael promised.

'Ellen's coming, aren't you, Ellen?' he said, and putting his arms round her neck and his head on her shoulder he promptly fell asleep.

Smiling and kissing him, Ellen laid him down and covered him with a sheet. 'And you stay there,' she said to Spot, who was sitting up in his basket eager for attention. 'No jumping on the bed, do you hear me?'

Spot wagged his tail and started to pant.

Michael came forward and leaning over his son dropped a kiss on his forehead, while roughing Spot's shaggy little coat. 'You didn't tell him?' he said softly to Ellen.

'About Michelle? No. I thought you should.' She carried on picking up Robbie's clothes, folding them and putting them away, or tossing them aside for the laundry.

'Can I fix you a drink?' Michael offered.

'No. I'm kind of tired. I'm going to take a bath, then go to bed.'

'Is there room in there somewhere for me?' he asked. 'Like the bath?'

Ellen looked at him, but there was no smile in her eyes.

Swallowing his irritation Michael turned and left the

room. He was waiting for her when she finally came into the lounge. 'We're going to have to decide something about Michelle,' he reminded her.

'I thought it was already decided,' she responded.

'She stays here?'

'That's what you said.'

'Ellen, for Christ's sake, she's his mother. How can I tell her she can't stay here when we've got more than enough space, and when she's going to want to be with him as much as she can?'

'It's OK,' she said. 'I'll go stay with Matty while she's here.'

'The hell you will!' he barked. 'This is your home . . .'

'No, it's yours. You're the one who bought it, then mortgaged it, you make all the decisions concerning it. I just happen to live here . . .'

'Will you stop this,' he snapped. 'This is *our* home and if you feel that strongly about Michelle staying here, then I'll book her into a goddamned hotel and be done with it.'

Though Ellen would have liked nothing better than to leave it at that, she knew she couldn't. 'You just don't get it, do you?' she cried. 'I've got no rights here, Michael. I don't have any say in what goes on. He's her son and I don't want to be here when she walks through that door and makes me feel as though I'm some kind of understudy, living with *her* son and his father while she's off saving the world.'

Michael dropped his head and pushed a hand through his hair. 'I'm sorry,' he said, 'I guess I didn't see it that way.' He looked up at her face and saw the anguish in her eyes. 'You do have rights,' he told her, 'and you do have a say. She's a reasonable woman, I'm sure she'll understand.'

Ellen closed her eyes and sucked in her lips to stop herself exploding again, or maybe it was to hold back the tears. 'I guess I'm not being reasonable,' she said finally.

'She's his mother and I've got to accept that.'

'He loves you,' Michael said softly. 'We both do.'

Ellen swallowed, then took a breath.

'And think how it's going to make her feel if she knows she's driven you out,' he added.

Ellen's eyes flashed with fury. 'Do you seriously think I give a damn about the way she feels, when she doesn't even have the courtesy to remember I live here when she leaves a message on the machine? Do you think she's given a single thought to how difficult it might be for me, having her around? Has she hell? She just assumes she can come swanning in here and we're all going to welcome her with open arms like it's all we've ever been waiting for to make up our little family. That's presuming, of course, she's remembered I exist. I mean, do you ever talk about me to her, Michael? Does my name ever get mentioned? And what about Tom Chambers? Surely he knows I live here? Or maybe he doesn't. Maybe you forgot to tell him too. You keep saying I'm one of the executives on this movie, but that's not really true, is it? It's all yours, Michael. You're taking all the decisions and I don't remember you consulting me on a single damn thing since the day you flew over to Washington and worked it all out with Chambers. You've never brought the movie up for discussion with any of us. You just decided it was going to be made and expected us all to go along with it. Well, that's OK. Since you're pulling the strings at World Wide you can do that. But stop making out like I've got some equal share in all this, when it's total bullshit and you know it.'

Michael's eyes were glittering hard with anger. 'So what do you want, that I cancel it just to make you feel like you've got some power? Or would you prefer that I handed Chambers over to you every time he calls?'

'I don't think what I want features here any more,' she responded. 'So you just do what you have to do,' and moving past him she went through the door that led to the master bedroom suite.

It was an hour later, after a long, and partially relaxing jacuzzi bath while Michael showered in the cubicle next to her, that Ellen finally donned a cover-all nightie and walked through their dressing-room into the spacious bedroom that looked out on one side to a fabulous view of the glittering valley lights below, and in front to the beautifully lit pool terrace.

She already knew she would find Michael there as she could hear the TV, but she was surprised to discover the bed littered with scripts and videotapes. Normally they never brought their work into the bedroom, so she was unsure what kind of gesture this was. But being in no mood to start fighting all over again, she merely pulled back the fresh cotton cover her side and slipped into bed.

Michael turned to look at her, then searched for the remote and shut off the TV. 'Whatever I have to do to make you believe that you're more important to me than anything or anyone, I'll do it,' he told her.

Ellen looked up at him and felt what remained of her anger starting to dissolve.

'Just please don't ever wear a nightie like that into my bed again,' he implored. 'The punishment is too severe for the crime.'

Unable to stop herself, Ellen laughed. 'Your bed?' she said.

Michael pulled a face. 'Oh God, *our* bed,' he corrected.

'So what's all this?' she said, indicating the scripts and videotapes.

He glanced at her sheepishly, and she wondered if he knew how like Robbie he was when he put on that look. 'I need to do some work, and this is where you are,' he said.

She laughed again, then sitting up she drew the nightie over her head and tossed it to the floor.

Leaning over her he began kissing her neck and

breasts, while sliding a hand beneath the covers. She lay back, feeling the desire slake through her as he began teasing her in a way he knew she could never resist. Because of tension and tiredness this was the first time they'd made love in almost a week, and though they both knew that the issues between them weren't entirely resolved, they welcomed the closeness – or they would have, had Robbie's voice not come across the intercom at that moment calling for Michael.

He was gone much longer than he expected, and by the time he returned Ellen was already asleep. He looked down at her and silently prayed that she hadn't heard the talk he'd just had with his son. But he was pretty certain he'd managed to turn off the intercom in time, and besides, there was no way she'd be asleep right now if she had overheard what'd been said.

Chapter 5

It had taken a while to set up the safe passage, so by the time word finally came for them to move out, Chambers felt a rough edge of frustration to his relief. Carlota was becoming too regular a visitor now, and presenting such a temptation that he was almost ready to damn his own morality for forbidding it.

'We leave at sundown for Popayán,' Morales said, spreading a map over the cluttered table. 'From there we will head for Neiva.'

Chambers looked at him sharply. Neiva was a hot, Huila lowland town of small significance. It would take them several hours to get there from Popayán, provided they didn't run into any marauding gangs of *bandoleros* and cutthroat guerrillas on the way. He could wish it was going to happen faster than this.

'What's at Neiva?' he asked.

'*El Patron* is sending someone there to meet us,' Morales answered. He looked long and hard into Chambers's eyes. '*El Patron*'s men have taken Salvador Molina,' he said, switching from Spanish to English. '*El Patron* wishes for you to know that it is all right to kill him.'

Chambers's steely grey eyes remained on Morales. He was developing his own theories on what was happening here and he didn't much like them – especially not when it seemed as if he was about to be set up to take the rap for a killing that he was not alone in wanting. No-one, but no-one was to be trusted, it seemed. Not even Morales.

Still silent, he walked up the narrow stone staircase to the small room he had shared with no-one and began to pack up his belongings. Were it not for how badly he wanted Molina he'd be figuring out how to give Morales the slip the minute they hit Popayán. As it was, he was prepared to believe they had Molina, and there wasn't any doubt in Chambers's mind that Molina was the one who had pulled the trigger on Rachel. Question was, who else had he pulled the trigger on for *El Patron*, or was it the Cali Cartel, to want him dead and a fall guy for the killing?

With his bag packed he walked over to the window to close it and noticed Carlota sitting on a wall opposite, waiting for him to come out for his walk. He looked at his watch, then up over the hills to see how far the sun was from setting. No time for a final visit to the strange and silent statues of the valley, but he wouldn't leave without saying goodbye to the girl.

'You are late today,' she chided, as he crossed the street towards her. 'Did you forget me?'

Chambers smiled to himself. He hadn't realized that she saw their afternoon strolls as pre-arranged trysts. 'How could I forget you?' he teased.

Her dark eyes shone with pleasure as she got up from the wall and stepped in close to him. 'You like my hair this way?' she said coyly, tilting her head to one side so he could better see how she had folded it around a carved bone slide.

'It's lovely,' he answered, unable to stop himself noticing the exquisite length of her neck, nor the softly inviting flesh of her shoulders. 'I've come to say goodbye,' he told her.

Her head snapped up and he felt a genuine sorrow in his heart as he saw the confusion in her eyes. 'But why? Where do you go?' she asked.

He smiled and touched her face with his fingers. 'You knew I wasn't going to stay,' he said gently.

Her eyes were desperately searching his and for one minute he thought she was going to cry. Instead she looked off down the street to where her neighbours and friends were going about their business. 'Will you kiss me once?' she asked, turning back. 'Will you make them think that you care for me?'

'I do care for you,' he smiled.

'You don't make love to me. That means you don't care for me,' she replied sulkily.

He looked into her eyes and wondered if one day she would understand that it was because he cared for her that he wouldn't make love to her.

'Will you remember me?' she said.

'Of course I'll remember you.'

She gazed up into his face and he looked at the seductive moistness of her mouth and noticed the gentle rise and fall of her girlish breasts. For a moment he felt engulfed by her femininity, and wished desperately that life could be so easy that all he had to do was stay right here with her.

'Will you send me letters?' she said shyly. 'Flowers?'

He nodded, and felt his throat tighten as he remembered how much Rachel had loved to be sent flowers.

'And come again one day to see me?' she said.

'I can't promise that,' he answered and watched her eyes fill with anger.

Then, very tentatively, she came up on tiptoe and with her eyes closed she parted her lips for his kiss. He looked at her a moment, then, gathering her gently in his arms, he put his mouth to hers. It was as beautiful, naïve and alluring as he'd expected and no hardship at all to hold her for a long, long time, as though they were lovers who dreaded to let go.

'Do you promise about the flowers?' she said, when

finally he lifted his head and looked into her eyes.

'I promise,' he said.

It was the early hours of the morning by the time Galvis steered the jeep into a brightly lit suburban street in one of the better parts of Popayán.

It wasn't until they were inside the impressive colonial mansion that Chambers realized they were entering a hotel. It seemed they were expected, as an elegant middle-aged woman was waiting to hand them their keys. A smartly uniformed porter led them upstairs to their rooms. There were two, with an adjoining door. Morales and Chambers took the first, Galvis and Escobar the other.

'We rest here only until morning,' Morales said, dropping his backpack on one of the beds. 'We take the chopper just after sunrise.'

Chambers nodded, then turned as Escobar came in through the adjoining door.

'It's for you,' he said, handing Morales a note.

Morales read it quickly then tore it into pieces. 'The chopper will come at midday,' he informed him. 'Now we should sleep.'

Escobar left, and as Morales began to haul off his boots Chambers disappeared into the bathroom. When he returned the room was in darkness, and he could hear Morales snoring softly. He made his way to the second bed, and lay down in the slender, silvery rays thrown in by a street light. The journey had been rough; he was bruised and exhausted, so it wasn't long before he too was sleeping.

An hour later he woke with a start, certain he had heard a noise. He lay very still, straining his ears. On the opposite bed he could hear Morales breathing. There were no other sounds. After a while his heart rate lessened, and soon after he was heading back for his dreams.

80

He woke several more times, always with a jolt and a quick rush of adrenalin. It proved how ragged his nerves were, as there was never anything more sinister in the room than the empty shadows in the corners, and the rhythmic wheezes from Morales's open mouth.

When finally the sun came up he knew he would sleep no more. He went to the window and stood watching the streets come to life. He was trying to get a sense of Rachel, wanting to feel her presence the way he had so many times these past few weeks. To his dismay it seemed she had gone, leaving a void in his heart and the vague impression of a face that might or might not have been hers. He found himself thinking of Carlota, and the craziness that had come over him one day when he had thought she was Rachel, returned in a forbidden body to torment him for the way he had betrayed her.

Morales stirred and turned over. Chambers glanced at him, then feeling the need to get out he grabbed the leather bag that contained his computer and notebooks and went silently from the room.

The streets were warm and finding a stall just opening up he ordered himself a *fritanga* of two sausages and a small black coffee. He carried it to a nearby park and sat down on a bench to eat and watch the early-morning world pass by. He was becoming increasingly uneasy about the upcoming trip to Neiva and was certain he knew why.

Checking his watch for the time in LA, he decided to give it another hour before calling Michael to fill him in on his plans. Then picking up his bag he continued to walk through the park, barely seeing the schoolchildren, businessmen and street workers as they passed. Those he never failed to notice, though, were the *gamines*, the homeless children Rachel had cared so much about. A lot of them would be runners for the *jibaros*, the small-scale dope-dealers who were the lowest of the low when it came to the peddling of drugs. And the kids, who were randomly and viciously beaten up by cops, crooks and even each other, hung about in gangs that only fools or addicts ever willingly approached.

It was some time later, as he stepped from the shady interior of the magnificent Iglesia de Santo Domingo, that he noticed an old woman selling flowers on the plaza outside. Without giving it much thought he went over and bought some for Carlota, then realized he now had to find and pay someone to take them to her.

The entire process took an hour or more, as a crowd of taxi-drivers, motor cyclists, *baquianos*, and even a Telecom engineer gathered round, each swearing the other was a thief in a bid to win the healthy fee for carrying flowers to the village.

It was a farce. God only knew how the word spread, but as the throng grew thicker and the good-natured banter began to give way to menace, Chambers finally parted with his money and flowers to a handsome young motor cyclist who might just appeal to Carlota. He still had no real confidence they would ever get there, but he had to take a chance on someone and after watching the boy roar off down the street on his Honda, he summoned one of the taxi-drivers to take him back to the hotel. It was past eleven by now and Morales was probably working up a sweat wondering where in the hell he was and if they were going to make the chopper at midday.

When he got to the hotel the lobby was quiet, just a couple of guests poring over a map of the city and an overweight maid polishing the *tunjo* figurines on the mantelshelf. He realized suddenly that he had forgotten to call Michael, and made a mental note to do it the first opportunity he got.

Now that the time of departure was approaching he could feel his tension returning. Already he could see Molina's shock as he, Chambers, walked into whatever place they were holding him, and the hatred he felt as he imagined himself face to face with Rachel's killer was only made bearable by planning how greatly he was going to make that son of a bitch suffer.

As he walked up the stairs he was going over it in his mind. The Zapata brothers he had decided to leave to Morales. It was Molina he wanted, Molina who was going to know every moment of pain, every heartbeat of fear, and unanswered plea for mercy.

At a turn in the stairs he stood aside for a woman and her young son to pass. The boy looked up at him and he thought fleetingly of Robbie, Michael and Michelle's son, the child he'd never imagined Michelle would give up. He wondered, once they arrested him for Molina's murder, if there would be a way he could still get his notes to Michael. Or maybe it wasn't an arrest that was planned, maybe they would shoot him down too and make out of it what they would.

The floorboards creaked beneath his feet as he walked along the hallway towards the room he had left a few short hours ago. It suddenly felt like a lifetime. He wished the next few hours were already over, that Molina's mutilated and lifeless body was already slumped at his feet.

The old grandfather clock opposite his door chimed the quarter-hour. He could see a maid, vacuuming in a room further on. There was a 'Do Not Disturb' sign hanging on his door. The street door opened downstairs, briefly letting in the noise from outside. Music was playing, somewhere in the depths of the house. The smell of polish mingled with the freshly-cut flowers in a vase beside him. Suddenly all his senses felt heightened. His head was pounding as though the ordeal to come were already upon him. The bag on his shoulder was strangely heavy. The stubble on his chin felt like nails. He looked around. Then he pushed open the door and went inside.

The curtains were still pulled, though pools of

brilliant sunlight spilled into the room. Everything was as he'd left it: the bathroom door half open, a glass of water on the night stand, Morales's boots on the floor. He looked at the bed. Morales was still there.

The sudden shaking was so fierce it paralysed him. Terror grabbed him, crushed his bladder and closed his chest. A machete. It could only have been a machete that had split Morales's head in two.

With a strange, jerky movement he turned round. The door between the two rooms was ajar. He stared at it, then went to it, hardly even thinking about whom or what he might find. The curtains were drawn, but this time he could smell the blood even before he saw it. Escobar and Galvis were on their beds. There was so much blood it was dripping into two small pools on the floor.

The beat of his heart was the only sound he could hear. His whole body was stiff. He had to get out of there as fast as was humanly possible.

Turning back he grabbed his holdall and took one last look at Morales. The blood hadn't yet congealed, the body would still be warm. It had happened less than an hour ago, as he stood on the plaza arguing and bantering with half of Popayán's drivers over who was to take flowers to a dark-haired girl with the eyes of a child and the heart of a woman. There was no doubt in his mind that were it not for those flowers he would be lying there on the only empty bed, soaked in his own blood, all but minus his head.

Twenty minutes later he was at Machangara airport waiting to board the next flight out. He had gone deeper into the throes of shock, and the shaking was so bad people were staring. He stayed with the crowds, hoping to blend in and avoid the eyes of any possible pursuers. It was anyone's guess now whether he would make it out of this city, but, even if he did, there was still every chance he was never going to make it out of the country.

*

It was late the following morning when Michael came out of his office to the reception area of the executive suite he shared with Ellen. Maggie, their joint personal assistant, and her two-man backup team, Bob and Olivia, were all at their desks, either fielding phone calls, dealing with mail or, in Maggie's case, fighting to achieve workable structures to Michael and Ellen's impossible schedules.

Most of the reception was cluttered up with a dozen or more half-opened boxes, unpacked patio furniture and cellophane-wrapped plants, all waiting to take up residence on the large, empty veranda outside. But on the whole they were now sufficiently installed in their new location to have started hanging paintings on the walls, and assigning a telephone each to the growing number of the movie's production personnel who were currently housed in three recently-combined conference rooms just across the hall. As soon as things really got going Michael would relocate them to wherever he could get the best deal on a soundstage and accompanying offices.

'Is Ellen still down in the screening room?' Michael asked, stopping at the cooler to help himself to water.

'No, she's gone over to Raleigh to meet with Jill Stoner,' Maggie answered, 'she should be back around one.' Her permanently flushed cheeks and tousled dark curls made her look as romantic as the novels she feasted on, and her gentle Scots brogue was always a welcome reminder to Michael of his good friend and senior agent in London, Zelda Frey.

'Here, did you see this?' Maggie said, searching the scattered paperwork on her desk. 'It's from Richard Conway's managers. Ah, here it is.' Her dark eyes were alive with mischief. 'Brace yourself, hen,' she advised, 'the man wants everything from a chef for his dog to a coach for his voice. He's got a team of fourteen assistants, all of whom need to be on the payroll; and added to that he's got his own hairdresser, make-up artists, dentist, that's right, dentist; manicurist, dialogue coach, personal trainer and therapist. He needs four winnebagos to house this royal entourage, and a fleet of limousines to ferry them back and forth from the set.'

Michael was laughing. 'Give me that,' he said, snatching it from her.

'He thinks I'm joking,' Maggie informed the other assistants. 'Watch his face when he finds out I'm not.'

And sure enough the humour made a fast demise as Michael's eyes scanned the unbelievable list of star demands. 'Put a call in to his manager,' he said. 'Has Ellen seen this?'

Maggie nodded as she swallowed a mouthful of coffee. 'She thought it was hysterical, like the rest of us, and can't wait to see what your incredible powers of negotiation do to the list. Our money's on it getting longer.'

Despite himself Michael laughed.

'Call for you,' Olivia told him. 'It's Jonathan Bridge at Fox Searchlight.'

'I'll take it,' Michael said, reaching for the receiver. 'Jonathan? What news?'

'Three million, six per cent and you keep total control,' the voice at the other end told him.

'Four and a half and the deal's done,' Michael responded.

'I'll get back to you. Is there a script yet?'

'Any day now.'

'I'm sticking my neck out for you here,' Bridge reminded him. 'It would help to have a script.'

'You're not kidding,' Michael muttered as he hung up. He was only too aware of how many favours he was being done, and just hoped to God that Tom Chambers was going to come through with this script. If Chambers failed them, he and Ellen would be in bigger trouble than either of them wanted to think about.

As if on cue the private line in his office started to ring. 'Tom?' he said, snatching it up.

'Thank God you're there,' Chambers responded.

'Where are you?' Michael demanded. 'What happened? You sound stressed.'

'You could say that,' Chambers remarked drily. 'I'm in Bogotá. The guys I was with got involved with a machete in Popayán, just hours before we were due to connect up with Molina.'

'Jesus Christ, are you OK?'

'Yeah, I'm fine. I'm pretty sure I was supposed to go the same way, but I was out buying flowers.'

Michael frowned. 'Flowers?'

'Another time. The important thing is I managed to get out. I'm with someone I can trust now, at least for one night. But just in case anything goes wrong I'm going to e-mail you the bare bones of a script and all my notes.'

'Tom, it's more important that you get yourself out of there. Is there anything I can do this end?'

'If there is, I'll let you know. Check the e-mail and with any luck, the next time you hear from me I'll be in Miami en route to LA.'

Much later in the day Michael walked into Ellen's office and found her sitting in a corner of a tan leather sofa, her long bare legs curled under her. She was reading the partially-written script and notes they had downloaded and printed from Tom Chambers's e-mail a couple of hours ago.

'So what do you think?' Michael said, closing the door behind him.

Ellen looked up. 'The first word that comes to mind is relief,' she responded. 'I mean, at least we've actually got something now, so we don't have to keep lying and stalling. But yeah, it's good. Needs a lot of work, but on the whole it's better than I expected. What about you, what did you think?'

'I agree it needs work,' he answered, coming to sit on the coffee-table in front of her.

She stretched out her legs, putting her feet in his lap, and moaned luxuriously as he began massaging her calves. 'Did I tell you, I got your son the whole way to school this morning,' she said, 'then he reminded me he had gym first thing and I had to go all the way back again for his kit. Boy, was he mad at me, like it was my fault. I could have crowned him, especially as it made me forty minutes late for Jill Stoner. Mmm, don't stop that,' she murmured, letting her eyes close as he began squeezing her toes. 'Have you got any idea how much this turns me on?'

'Well, seeing as you've fallen asleep on me three nights in a row,' he reminded her, 'I could be up for taking my chances while I've got them.'

Ellen's eyes started to dance. 'Don't tempt me,' she said, and inhaled deeply as he pressed his thumbs into the soles of her feet.

Grinning, he relaxed his grip. 'So will you take it on?' he said, nodding towards the script. 'Help him get it into shape?'

Ellen eyed him for a moment, then smiled. 'Is this the carrot?' she said. 'Get her involved in the script, it might soften her up a bit. Make her feel more needed.'

'Oh, come on,' he said. 'You're so far into this now you surely can't be in any doubt about that. No, what I'm saying is, we both know you've got a gift for making scripts work, and I happen to think you could really make something of this.'

'While you do what, exactly?'

'Fight with Richard Conway's managers to see if he'll agree to Spot's chef taking on the catering for the Conway cur, and for my manicurist to fix up the acrylics.'

Ellen was laughing. 'Since when did Spot get himself a chef?' she enquired.

'You're looking at him,' he replied. 'And as you know, I come cheap.'

Still laughing, Ellen returned to the notes in front of her. 'You know, if I didn't have a wedding to sidetrack me I'd be pouring all my excitement into this,' she said. 'I really think it's going to work, especially now I've seen what Tom's already done. And we're pulling a terrific team together, in case you hadn't noticed. Some of the best.'

'Thanks to you.'

'And you. After all, you're the one who's raising the money to pay them.'

'For now. We've still got a way to go, and if we don't come up with more investment by the end of the month, the payroll's in jeopardy.'

She sighed and chewed thoughtfully on her lip. He wasn't telling her anything she didn't already know. 'Do you reckon we're going to be able to afford another big name to play Rachel?' she asked.

He took a breath to answer, then suddenly changed course. 'Don't let's get into the casting now,' he said, knowing she was about to start making a case for her cousin Matty. 'Let's just sort the script out, 'cos without it we're dead. Will you take it on? I mean, we could get another writer in, but I don't think Tom'll go for that and . . .'

'It's OK, I'll do it,' she said. 'Though God only knows where I'm going to find the time. Which reminds me, we're supposed to go see Robbie's teacher this evening for his progress report. Can you make it?'

He shook his head. 'I'm meeting with the Touchstone people at six,' he said. 'And there's a chance Tom might fly in later. I got a call from him saying he was on a flight out of Bogotá. From what he told me on the phone it seems things got pretty hairy down there.' He was about to enlarge further when he remembered how nervous she already was about the Colombian cartels, so keeping it brief he said, 'Maggie's working on getting him a connection in Miami.'

'Will he be staying with us?' Ellen said. 'Silly question. I'd better call Lucina, tell her to get one of the guest-rooms ready. We could put him in the suite upstairs.' She looked at her watch. 'I've got a five o'clock with Rosa and Gerry,' she said, referring to a couple of the ATI agents, 'can you call Lucina? Or no, I'll do it. I'll have to give her a list for the market. Did you leave her some money for taxis? Oh God, she's got her driving lesson today, she won't be back until six. I'll get Maggie to call her. God, I wish the woman could cook.'

'Why don't we order in tonight?' he suggested.

'Good idea. Chinese?'

'Thai?'

'That's settled then, Chinese it is?'

Michael glanced over his shoulder, as though searching out the extra voice that had voted against him. 'I was wondering,' he said, getting to his feet.

Ellen looked up from the script. 'Wondering what?' she prompted.

'If we came to a decision about Michelle?' he asked tentatively. 'I'm going to have to call her back . . .'

Ellen smiled and got to her feet. 'I've had a good idea about that,' she informed him. 'Why don't you ask her if she can put off her visit until the wedding, then she can stay with Robbie while we're on honeymoon.'

Michael grinned, and tilted her face up to his. 'You're a genius,' he stated.

'You didn't ask your mother to take that on yet, did you?' she said cautiously.

'No, not yet,' he assured her. 'But there's every chance she'll stay on anyway. How many guests are we up to now?'

'I'm keeping it to a hundred,' she answered. 'I just wish I knew where everyone was going to stay. Can we do a deal with a hotel, do you think? I'll get Maggie on to it. But my parents and your mother will definitely stay at the house. Matty can put up her own parents,' she continued, walking over to her desk. 'Thank God my dad's worked things out with Aunt Julie and Uncle Melvin. Did you hear, Eugene pulled off a great deal with Sony. He's using their studios to shoot the pilot of that sitcom we can never remember the name of.'

'Which means we should find another title,' he said. 'Are you producing?'

'No, I've handed over to Kelly. Are you getting involved in the script auction at five thirty, or am I?'

'Which script? And are we buying or selling?'

She cocked an eyebrow. 'Remind me, what do you do all day over there in that office of yours?'

'You mean when I'm not fantasizing about my high-powered mistress?' he responded, backing her up against the desk.

She could feel his erection pressing against her, and wished desperately that they could just lock the door and have a few precious minutes to themselves. But even as she thought it Maggie's voice came over the intercom.

'Rosa's just arrived,' she said. 'Gerry's on his way. You missed lunch, so do you want me to send out for some food?'

'We'll finish this later,' Michael said, kissing her softly on the mouth.

'Do you think you can wait that long?' she teased.

His eyes narrowed as he looked at her. 'Can you?' he countered.

Smiling, she leaned over for the intercom. 'Ask Rosa if she wants something,' she instructed Maggie, 'and I'll have the same.' She let go of the button just in time, for Michael's hand was slipping under her skirt and as he pushed it between her legs she groaned out loud.

'Gerry's here now,' Maggie's voice informed them. 'Shall I ask them to wait, or shall I send them in?'

Ellen reached for the button again, inhaling deeply as Michael's fingers moved inside her panties and started to stroke her.

'Give us a moment,' she managed to respond, then let go fast as Michael pushed his fingers deep inside her. 'Oh God, Michael, this is cruel,' she murmured, as he lifted her skirt to her waist and pulled down her panties. 'Someone might come in.'

'They won't hang about,' he assured her, making her laugh. 'And I thought we were supposed to be trying for a baby.'

'We are,' she confirmed.

'Then this is the way to do it,' he said, and unzipping his fly, he took out his penis and pushed it right up inside her.

'Oh yes,' she whimpered. 'Yes, yes,' and as her legs circled his waist, his mouth came crushing down on hers and his hips began to jerk against her.

Within minutes they were both struggling to silence their orgasms, and almost as soon as it was over they were laughing.

'Sssh,' she whispered, stepping back into her panties. 'I thought we made a pact, no sex in the office. Remember?'

'I never was any good at playing to the rules,' he responded. He lifted her face up to his. 'Love you,' he whispered.

'Love you too,' she smiled. Then she started to laugh again. 'Do you think they're going to know?' she asked.

His eyes twinkled. 'Who cares?' he responded, and kissing her briefly on the lips he turned back towards the door.

As she watched him go she was surprised to find herself thinking about Sandy Paull. It was this very kind of relationship Sandy had always wanted with Michael, to be his partner in every way, though why on earth that should have come into her mind now, she didn't have a clue.

'Oh by the way,' he said, turning back as he opened the door. 'Thanks.'

Ellen's eyes widened.

He grinned. 'About Michelle,' he said. 'I'll call her tonight.'

After greeting Rosa and Gerry he returned to his own office and the mountain of work that was piling up on his desk. Though his mind was fully on what he was doing, it was only a few minutes before he was stopped by his conscience and his thoughts returned to Ellen – or, more precisely, to the conversation he'd had with Robbie a couple of nights ago.

It was the first time Robbie had mentioned anything about wanting his mummy and daddy to get back together, and though common sense told Michael that this problem was long overdue, he couldn't help but be uneasy when it had happened to coincide with Ellen's own insecurity over Michelle. Were it not for that, he might have discussed it with Ellen so that the three of them could try to work through it together, but with the way things stood he really wasn't sure how to play it.

Nor was he feeling very comfortable with the way he had as good as lied to Ellen when he'd claimed not to know what Chambers and Michelle were cooking up. Not that either of them had actually told him what they had in mind, but he had a pretty good idea. And, if he was right, he didn't even want to think about how Ellen was going to take that.

'Do you know what's most interesting about this script?' Sandy said, looking up as Nesta came into the sitting-room of the flat they shared in Chelsea.

'What's that?' Nesta yawned, sinking down on the adjacent sofa and kicking off her high heels. 'I thought you'd have been in bed by now.'

'The message from Michael that came over the e-mail with it,' Sandy replied. 'Did you have a good time? Where did you go?'

'It was OK. Ronnie Scott's. What message?'

'He's asked me not to discuss the script with Ellen for the time being,' Sandy answered.

Nesta yawned again. 'Do you think I'm getting too old for all this?' she said, looking down at her expensive purple and black dress that was cut so low in the front that her breasts were barely covered.

'Probably,' Sandy answered. 'You're back early, so I take it it was just a date, no extras?'

'No extras,' Nesta confirmed, her small, kittenish face looking pale and tired. 'So what's it like, the script? Any good?'

'Not bad, what there is of it. Apparently Ellen's going to work on it with the writer, you know, Tom Chambers, to get it in shape. Apparently that's her forte, whereas the role I've been allocated is coming up with some of the finance. I've made a start, but I could do with some help.'

Nesta chuckled. She was a good person to ask, for there were any number of men she could call on who might be interested in coughing up the odd ten grand or more. In fact, it wouldn't be the first time Sandy had found backers through Nesta's private network, though so far she had only been seeking to raise finance for World Wide UK projects. This was going to be a much bigger deal, meaning that the brokerage fee Nesta would receive would provide a serious boost to her early-retirement fund. 'I'll get back to you on it,' she said. 'Any news on Maurice, by the way?'

Sandy shook her head sadly. Right up until three weeks ago, when he'd had a stroke from which he wasn't expected to recover, Maurice Trehearne, the well-known property tycoon and Sandy's mentor, had continued to pay someone to advise her and take care of her interests. It wasn't that she really needed his support any more, it was simply that the old man had wanted a professional excuse to stay in her life, and being as indebted to him as she was, as well as caring for him deeply, Sandy was happy to do whatever he wanted.

'His daughter was at the hospital earlier,' she said. 'Looked right through me.'

Nesta's eyebrows rose with interest. 'Makes you wonder what's in the will,' she commented. 'Could be you'll end up backing this movie yourself.'

Sandy threw her a look.

'Just a thought,' Nesta said. 'So what about Michael asking you not to discuss the script with Ellen? What do you reckon that's all about?'

Sandy shrugged. 'Probably that he hasn't told her yet that he's making me a producer,' she answered. 'That is, provided I come up with some finance, of course. Anyway, it doesn't exactly speak of total harmony between them, does it? And long life to all the discords in their cosy little opera, is what I say. Except, to continue with the musical theme, there don't appear to be enough bad notes for them to call off the wedding.' Her eyes were dancing as she added, 'Stay sitting for this one – I've been invited.'

Nesta's large hazel eyes grew bigger than ever. 'You're kidding! They've invited *you*!'

'You don't have to say it like that,' Sandy objected. 'And if you think about it, they don't really have a lot of choice. I mean, they can hardly invite every other agent at McCann Paull and not me, can they?'

'So, are you going?'

Sandy yawned and stretched. 'To LA, of course,' she said. 'But not to the wedding. How can I, when there's not going to be one?'

Nesta looked at her and shook her head in dismay. 'I've never known a woman hold on to a lost cause for so long,' she said bluntly.

Sandy was unruffled.

'You really think you can break them up?' Nesta said.

Sandy pulled a face as she thought, then, looking Nesta straight in the eye, she smiled and nodded.

Chapter 6

'OK, everyone,' Ellen said, calling the meeting to attention. 'Grab your coffee and take your places. I think we're all here now. Tom Chambers won't be joining us, I'm afraid. He flew in late last night, so he's catching up on some sleep. And for those of you who haven't yet met Michael, this is he. Be nice to him because he's paying the bills.'

Everyone laughed and, as they settled down at their desks, they turned their chairs to face Ellen and Michael who were sitting on the edge of a very long table at the front of the office. Ellen was about to speak again when Maggie put her head round the door and waved at her.

'I've got someone from *Marie Claire* on the line,' she said, 'wanting to know if you'll talk to them about being a working stepmother. Or maybe that should be wicked,' she added, frowning curiously at her notebook.

Michael laughed and Ellen nudged him. 'If there's time in the schedule,' Ellen answered. 'When do they need it by?'

'I'll ask. They want to bring their own photographer as well, and I think they want to do it at the house. I'll check all that, but in principle, are you up for it?'

'Yes,' Michael answered. 'We need all the publicity we can get.'

'OK, let's get started here,' Ellen said, as Maggie disappeared. 'Cissy Carr and her assistant, Kyle, just joined us today. I'm sure you've all met already, but just in case, Cissy's in charge of casting. And Joe Kenyon, who's sitting at the back over there, is our art director, who Vic Warren appointed a couple of weeks ago. Obviously, you all know that Vic's going to be directing the movie, but as he's still tied up on another project, which he's currently shooting over in France, he won't be joining us for a while yet.'

She glanced down at her notes and was about to continue when a voice just in front of her said, 'Uh, before we really get started, there's something I'd like to say.'

Ellen looked up and gave a smile of encouragement to Billy Christopher, the tall red-headed guy from Texas, whose explosion of freckles was as sunny as his nature.

'Um, I'd just like to say on behalf of us all here,' he began, getting to his feet, and glancing round at the dozen or so of his colleagues, 'that we're all real proud to be getting involved in this movie, and that it's a big honour to us all to be working with you, Ellen, and you, Michael. And thank you, both of you, for giving me my stripes as a fully-fledged production manager. I promise I won't let you down – and thank you for all the courage you're showing in giving a lot of other people in this room their breaks too, I know they won't let you down either.'

'Hear, hear!' Cissy called out. 'We're right with you, Ellen and Michael.'

As everyone broke into applause, Ellen turned to Michael and tried not to laugh, for she knew how uncomfortable he was with this kind of Californian emotion.

'Thank you for that,' Ellen said, once the applause had died down. 'Speaking for both Michael and myself, we know what a great team we have here, and I think we're all in agreement, considering the story and what you've seen of the script, that we'd have to work pretty hard to fail at this one.'

Everyone laughed and murmured agreement, then Ellen turned to Michael for him to take over.

'OK,' he said, 'I'm going to start the ball rolling by talking to you a bit about the financing of the picture, and then we'll get on to your individual budgets. You all know what a risky business it is, raising the investment, and keeping the whole thing rolling, and it's my intention to keep you informed every step of the way, even if we're in danger of running out of funds – which frankly we're pretty damned close to now. Yeah, believe it or not we're already heading fast towards the wall, but I've had word from one of my partners in the UK that something could be coming through over there any time, so no need to start sweating just yet.'

Half an hour later, having confirmed that Richard Conway was now signed, which should help the financing no end, and having assured them that the many possible legal problems they could run into, given the subject of the movie, were being investigated, Michael took the topped-up coffee Ellen passed him and was about to carry on when she leaned over to whisper in his ear.

'I'd better go get Robbie now,' she said. 'Don't forget to tell them about the cocktail party next Friday when they can get to meet Tom Chambers and Richard Conway.'

'OK,' Michael nodded. 'Will you be back in time for lunch?'

'I should be. Where will I find you?'

'Probably at the Four Seasons. I'll give Tom a call in an hour, see if he's feeling human yet.'

It was almost three in the afternoon by the time Ellen finally abandoned her car to the valet at the Four Seasons hotel and ran inside the plush marble lobby to take the elevator to the fourteenth floor. She was over an hour and a half late, having got to Robbie's school to find out he didn't feel sick any more and wanted to go join his friends at T-ball practice. Of course the bus was long gone, so Ellen had to drive him over to Culver City herself, then go back to the school to pick up the briefcase she'd managed to leave there.

She was on her way back to the office when she'd got a call from the wedding organizer with a thousand questions that needed answers right away, so she'd detoured over to Crescent Heights to go calm him down. Just roll on when Matty got back from Denver where she was just finishing up filming a mini-series for Lifetime, with any luck she'd take over some of the wedding plans and provide Ellen with the odd five-minute respite from total madness.

By the time the elevator doors opened to let her out she had managed to tidy her hair and touch up her make-up, though why she was doing it for Tom Chambers, who had insisted on staying in a hotel rather than with them, she had no idea. Then she remembered that it was for Michael, who was already there. He would know if she hadn't bothered to make an effort and she didn't want to let him down when she knew how much it meant to him that she and Chambers got along. And she was certain they would, provided he didn't ostracize her with his thoughtlessness again.

It seemed she was going to have to turn it all on for Michelle much sooner than she'd expected as well, for, as it happened, though Michelle would be delighted to come to the wedding, she had to make a trip to LA next week anyway to co-host some kind of fund-raiser for a children's charity. She'd be staying for ten days and the only positive aspect Ellen could find to that was that maybe she could take over some of the ferrying around of her son. Except even thinking about that scared Ellen half to death, for she loved Robbie so much that despite the chaos he was causing in her life, she just couldn't imagine it without him now. She was over-reacting of course. Michelle was only coming for a visit, not to take Robbie away, at least she hoped to God that wasn't going to happen. Maybe if she could get pregnant herself . . . But it was ludicrous to think that a child of their own could ever replace Robbie, and besides, just where was she going to find the time to have a baby, when lately they barely had time even to make love?

She was about to knock on the hotel room door when her cellphone sprang into life. Fumbling in her bag, she found it, clicked it on and knocked the door.

'Ellen Shelby,' she said into the phone

'Hi, Ellen, it's Gretta Monk, I got your message.'

'Oh Gretta!' Ellen cried. 'Thanks for calling me back. I was wondering, are you going to pick up Matthew from T-ball later? You are? Great! Could you pick up Robbie too and drop him by the house?'

'Oh gee, Ellen, I'm sorry. My folks are flying in from Boston at five so we're going right on to the airport to collect them, then we're going to my sister's in Rhodondo Beach for dinner. Any other time, honey.'

'Sure, OK,' Ellen responded, her heart sinking as Gretta rang off and Michael opened the door.

'Hi sweetheart,' he said. 'Come on in. Are you OK?'

'Oh yeah, yeah,' she answered, forcing a smile. 'Sorry I'm late. You got my messages?'

'Sure. Do you want some coffee? You look like you could do with some.'

'I could,' she replied, looking around the large, beautifully furnished suite with its tall, sunlit windows, subtle grey and rose pink drapes and upholstery, and impressive assortment of technology.

'Tom's in the other room, on the phone,' Michael told her, crossing to a table that was cluttered with the remains of the lunch she should have joined them for. 'Sit yourself down. Was Robbie OK?'

'I think so,' she answered, grimacing at her reflection in a full-length mirror – it seemed her quick-fix job in the elevator wasn't as effective as she'd thought. But then there was precious little she could do about the heat, which was the main cause of the creases in her limp-looking tangerine silk top and brown linen skirt. 'God I look a mess,' she groaned, trying to straighten herself out. 'Anyway, how's it going? Obviously he got out of Colombia OK. Have there been any repercussions?'

'A few,' Michael responded, discarding the coffee on the table and going to the phone to order fresh. 'They're trying to load him with three murders in Popayán, but they don't stand much chance of getting away with that. Yeah, room service, could you bring some fresh coffee to room 1426?' He turned to Ellen. 'Have you eaten?'

'No, and I'm starving,' she answered. 'Order me a chicken sandwich, or no, some bruschetta and goat's cheese.'

Michael placed the order then rang off. 'Ah, here he is,' he said, as the bedroom door opened and Tom Chambers came into the sitting-room.

Ellen looked up and to her surprise felt the welcome fade on her lips as she met the intense grey eyes of a tall, casually dressed man with dark, silver-streaked hair, a strong, rugged face, and an extremely impressive physique. It had never even occurred to her that he might be attractive, and certainly not as attractive as this. Quickly, she reasserted her smile and got to her feet. 'Tom,' she said, holding out her hand as he came towards her. 'It's really good to meet you at last. I've certainly heard enough about you.'

Chambers laughed and Ellen's eyes widened at the surprising transformation it made to his otherwise dark and austere features. 'Well, I've got to tell you, it's good to meet you too,' he responded, shaking her hand. 'And one thing's for sure, you're a hell of a lot prettier than him.' He grimaced. 'I guess I could be shot for making remarks like that in this town, so I take it back, and replant it as a mere thought.'

Ellen's eyes were dancing, she was enjoying the flirtation and the fact that Michael was starting to scowl was making her enjoy it all the more. 'It was a relief to find out you'd got here safely,' she told him. 'Michael tells me you're being accused of murder,' she added, startling herself with the casualness of her tone.

Chambers's eyes were alive with humour. 'Well, it won't be *that* that causes me to lose any sleep tonight,' he assured her, and she felt herself flush at the subtle implication that she just might.

'I ordered more coffee,' Michael said as someone knocked on the door and Ellen's cellphone started to ring.

As she dealt with the call, and the three others she had to make as a result of it, Michael poured them all coffee and steered her to the table to sit down with her food. Then he and Chambers returned to the sofas and the coffee-table between them that was littered with Chambers's maps, reference books, newspaper cuttings, photographs, notebooks, a laptop computer and portable printer.

'It's kind of hard to figure out how we're going to end the script when I didn't actually get near any of the killers,' Chambers was saying as Ellen, licking her fingers, went to kneel on the floor next to Michael. 'I mean, we can go either way, stick to how it is, me getting out before I got my head split in two, which, the way I see it, kind of dead-ends the drama, or fictionalize. Then we can go whichever way we want, and I could get the satisfaction of seeing the bastards shot down on film, even if it's not going to happen in reality.'

'I think we should go for both,' Ellen said, putting down her napkin and helping herself to Michael's coffee. 'Gruesome as they are, the machete murders are too powerful to lose, and knowing it's an end that you're going to meet if you stay, it makes sense for you to get out of the country fast – the way you did. So in my

103

opinion, that's the way it should go – exactly as it happened. And from there we fictionalize. Script it in a way that could feasibly be true. My suggestion is that we explore what might happen should Galeano's people come looking for you here.'

Michael and Chambers looked at her. 'In LA?' Michael said.

She nodded. 'If we bring it into the States,' she explained, 'it could have a much greater impact on an American audience than if we kept it in Colombia. And I'm just praying to God that I'm not making some kind of prediction here,' she added with a smile that in no way belied her seriousness.

Michael looked at Chambers. 'Is that likely to happen?' he asked.

Chambers shook his head. 'Not unless Galeano's nephews, the Zapata brothers, start making some serious progress in pulling the Tolima Cartel back together,' he answered. 'And that's not looking likely.'

'Do any of them know you're planning to make a movie?' Ellen asked.

Again Chambers shook his head. 'No-one in the Tolima Cartel,' he answered. 'And that's the only one that matters.'

'These nephews are the ones who were involved in Rachel's kidnap and murder?' Michael said.

Ellen looked at Chambers to see how he responded to the mention of his dead girlfriend's name, but there was no expression in his eyes as he answered Michael's question.

'The very same,' he said. 'So we bring the chase to LA,' he went on, returning them to the script. 'What then?'

'We don't need to decide on that right now,' Ellen answered. 'There's going to be a lot of time for discussion, and what we really need is to get the opening straightened out. It's got to start with a good, strong background on Rachel. I take it this is her?' she said, picking up a glossy ten-by-eight photograph of a strikingly beautiful dark-haired woman. 'She's lovely.'

Chambers's eyes remained on Ellen.

'How old was she?' Ellen asked.

'When she was killed? Twenty-nine.'

'And when you met her?'

'Twenty-seven.'

Ellen nodded and looked at the photograph again.

'Do you have copies of the journal she worked on in New Orleans?' Michael asked.

'Sure, they're right here,' Chambers answered, sorting through the scattered piles on the table. 'And photographs of the office. I thought they'd help if you were going to build the set here in LA.'

'They will,' Michael answered, taking the journal and photographs and flicking quickly through them.

Chambers got up to go for more coffee.

'Now's not the time,' Ellen said, 'but at some point I'd like to sit down with you and have you tell me everything you can about Rachel. You know, what kind of personality she had; the things she liked, or didn't like to do; stuff she felt passionate about; the people in her life who really mattered; the kind of clothes she wore; her views on politics, religion, human rights obviously; things that made her laugh or cry or get mad. You get the idea. Is that going to be OK for you?'

'Sure,' he answered.

As he poured the coffee and Michael picked up a call on his cellphone, Ellen looked at Rachel's photograph again. Though she wouldn't say so to Chambers, the image of Rachel's face was affecting her deeply, for the energy and warmth that seemed to flow from her smile, the *joie de vivre* that lit up her exotic eyes and seemed to add such abandon to her laughter, made it almost impossible to believe that she was no longer alive. It was no wonder Chambers had loved her so much, Ellen thought, it would be hard for any man not to love a woman like this.

Ellen looked up at him and wondered if now was a good time to broach the subject of Matty. Though Matty wasn't quite as striking as Rachel, she was certainly lovely, and so right for the part of Rachel that Ellen just knew, once he saw her, that Chambers would agree.

'Have you given any thought to where you're going to shoot the main stuff?' Chambers asked, picking up his coffee.

'We've discussed it briefly,' Ellen answered. 'Probably Mexico or Peru. Definitely not Colombia, anyway.'

Chambers laughed and turned to Michael as he finished his call. 'Did you talk to Michelle recently?' he asked.

'Mmm, yesterday, as a matter of fact,' Michael answered, swallowing a mouthful of coffee before passing the cup back to Ellen. 'She's coming over here next week, so you'll see her.'

'Hey, that's great,' Chambers declared. He gave a quick glance at Ellen to make sure it was, and seeing nothing to deter him, he said, 'Is your brother coming with her?'

'No. He'll be here for the wedding though.'

'Wedding?' Chambers echoed. 'Are you guys getting married?'

'In a little over eight weeks,' Ellen informed him. Then, looking up at Michael, she added, 'If we can find enough time to organize it.'

Michael grinned and touched her face. 'You don't get out of it that easily,' he warned her. 'You're going to come, aren't you?' he said to Chambers.

'Sure, if I'm invited,' he responded. 'Wouldn't miss it for the world. Will this be before or after we shoot?'

Ellen burst out laughing. 'It's going to be months before we can get this into production,' she told him. 'There's a hell of a lot of prep to do and if these phones

106

would stop ringing we could probably get on with it. Ellen Shelby,' she said into her cellphone.

'Hi, Ellen, it's Gary Negroni's mother,' the voice at the other end told her.

'Oh hi, thanks for calling me back,' Ellen responded, wondering if the woman had forgotten her own name since becoming a mother. 'I was wondering, is there any chance you could pick up Robbie when you go for Gary this evening?'

'I'm sorry, dear, but Gary didn't go to T-ball this afternoon, he hurt his ankle running on Tuesday.'

Ellen's heart sank. 'Oh I see,' she said. 'Sorry to hear that. I hope he recovers soon.'

By the time Ellen rang off Michael and Tom were exchanging more ideas on location possibilities, so she quickly dialled another number and waited for Lucina to answer. But their housekeeper wasn't at home, which was no surprise really, when today was her day off.

'Damn!' she muttered, clicking off the phone and throwing it back in her purse.

Michael turned to look at her. 'Are you OK?' he said.

'Yeah.' She hesitated, then said, 'Honey, is there any chance you can go pick up Robbie from T-ball? I've got a meeting with Richard Conway at five and that's the time Robbie gets off.'

Michael was already shaking his head. 'I've got a five thirty with Tony Brown at Fox,' he said.

Ellen looked beaten.

'I'm sorry, honey,' he said. 'Is there no-one else?'

'No-one I can find,' she sighed.

'Then why don't you give me the address and I'll go get Robbie?' Chambers suggested.

Ellen's lovely brown eyes came up to his. She couldn't have given him a more adoring look had he been the Saviour Himself.

Chambers laughed. 'It'll be like old times,' he said. 'I used to go pick him up a lot when we were in Rio.'

'Are you sure you don't mind?' Ellen said.

'It'd be a pleasure, especially if it's going to take that worried frown off your face.'

Michael turned to look at her, and slipped a hand into her hair.

'It'll make his day, seeing you,' Michael smiled.

Chambers's eyebrows rose in a way that made Ellen laugh. 'So going back to Michelle,' he said. 'Did you talk to her yet about the idea she had for the movie?'

To Ellen's surprise she felt Michael tense. Then she realized, from his next words, that he was stalling. 'You know what I did talk to her about,' he said, 'was the Brazilian guy you two brought down. Did you know he got a life sentence?'

'Much less than the bastard deserves,' Chambers commented. 'Yes, I had heard.'

'What idea did Michelle have for the movie?' Ellen wanted to know.

Chambers's eyes moved between her and Michael. Michael looked away, so Chambers was forced to turn back to Ellen. 'She wants to play the part of Rachel,' he told her. He let a beat go by, then added, 'And personally I can't think of anyone I'd rather have do it.'

Every muscle in Ellen's body had turned rigid. She looked at Michael, waiting for him to object, but he said nothing. And then she realized that even if he hadn't actually known this was coming, he'd pretty much guessed it.

'Actually,' she said, 'Michael's keen to go with star names, and no-one in the States has ever really heard of Michelle.' She looked at Michael, waiting for him to agree with her.

'Well, everything's open for discussion,' he said, avoiding her eyes.

At that Ellen's anger increased to such a pitch she could feel herself starting to shake. But there was no way she was going to lose it in front of Chambers, so forcing an icy smile back to her lips she said, 'Well that's good, because I'd like Tom to meet Matty. I think, once you see her,' she said to Tom, 'you'll agree with me that she's absolutely right for the part of Rachel.'

Chambers was starting to look awkward. 'Like I said, I kind of think Michelle will work,' he replied. 'It feels right.'

'But she's blonde,' Ellen pointed out.

Chambers looked away, clearly not wanting to argue this out at a first meeting. Even so, something inside Ellen was telling her that his mind was made up about this and he wasn't going to budge. What was more, there didn't seem much doubt, considering the silence from that quarter, that Michael was going to back him. Her fury was suddenly so great that it was like everything inside her was gripped by it.

'Well,' she said, her heart pounding in her chest, 'I guess everything's still up for discussion.' She looked at her watch. 'I should be heading out of here now, if I want to make it over to Richard's.' She looked at Chambers. 'I expect Michael's already told you it'll be me who's working on the script with you,' she said, 'so we should set up a schedule of meetings. I'll have my assistant put something together and call you.'

'Do you want to give me the address where I have to go for Robbie?' Chambers reminded her. 'And directions to your place so I can drop him off later. Will someone be there?'

'Lucina, the housekeeper, will be back by then,' Ellen answered, picking up a pen from the table and writing everything he needed on a sheet of hotel notepaper.

'Where are you going to be this evening?' Michael asked.

Not wanting to look at him, Ellen went into her purse searching for her keys. 'I'm giving a talk to a screenwriters' workshop,' she answered.

'Where?' Chambers asked.

'Santa Monica.'

He glanced at Michael, then back to Ellen. 'Can I come?' he said.

They both looked at him in surprise.

He shrugged. 'This is my first attempt,' he reminded them. 'I could pick up some useful hints.'

Michael nodded. 'Sounds like a good idea,' he said, turning to Ellen.

Ellen still wouldn't look at him. 'You'd be welcome,' she told Chambers. 'I'll come by for you around twenty of eight. Meet me downstairs, we won't have a lot of time to spare.'

As she got to her feet both men rose with her. 'It's OK, I can see myself out,' she said, heading round the table so she wouldn't have to walk past Michael. 'It was good meeting you, Tom,' she said, shaking his hand. 'Thanks for offering to go and get Robbie. I'll look forward to seeing you later,' and without even a glance in Michael's direction, she left.

It was almost midnight by the time Ellen finally returned home, and though she had calmed down considerably, she was still no closer to being talked round about Michelle than when she'd walked out of the hotel. If anything, she was even more set against it. And why the hell shouldn't she be, when the idea had no merit whatsoever, and when the role they were discussing was absolutely vital to the story.

The house was in darkness as she drove in through the gates and along the short floodlit drive to the garage. She waited for the automatic door to open, then steered her Pontiac in next to Michael's Cruiser. That reminded her, she needed his car tomorrow to go pick Matty up from the airport. Ordinarily the Pontiac would have done, but Matty had called to say she'd been shopping, not only for a few items of furniture which she was bringing on the flight with her, but for a new man as well it seemed.

110

Whoever the man was, Ellen guessed she'd meet him when she went to the airport tomorrow, which was a shame, because she could really do with having Matty to herself for a while. She needed someone to talk to, someone to reassure her she wasn't going crazy, or being unreasonable, or hurtling towards the edge of failure in just about everything from motherhood to moguldom. It was almost frightening the way her life had gone so crazy lately. It was like being in a runaway car with no brakes and an accelerator jammed to the floor. She barely had time to make all her meetings now, never mind the numerous lunches, cocktails and dinners that she and Michael were constantly obliged to attend. And as for getting her hair cut, or snatching a quick workout at the gym, these luxuries were now such a thing of the past that she was starting to despair of ever doing them again. Much like her and Michael's sex life, for they were both so busy now, and so tired by the time they eventually got to bed, that apart from the few brief moments they were stealing from the madness they were becoming more like colleagues and less like lovers every day.

After checking on Robbie and Spot, she went to read through the messages Michael had left on her desk. Then, with a tight, angry face and flashing eyes she pushed open the door and walked into the bedroom. She'd already drawn breath to let rip when, seeing him lying on the bed, the air suddenly went out of her and to her unutterable frustration she started to laugh. Though he was fast asleep, he'd obviously known he'd have to do battle and had kitted himself out accordingly. Robbie's toy sword was still grasped in his hand, the shield was lying across his chest and the helmet had slipped down over one eye. He looked so ridiculous that he completely took the wind out of her sails.

Biting her lip and sticking her tongue in her cheek, she struggled hard to control her laughter as his one visible eye opened.

111

'I hate you,' she told him, stamping her foot and hitting the door-frame.

'I thought you might,' he responded, tilting his helmet back.

'For God's sake, just look at you!' she cried. 'How can we have a sensible discussion while you're . . .'

'Sensible discussion?' he interrupted. 'Is that what you're after? I must have got it wrong, because I was sure when you left the hotel today that the next time I saw you you were going to attack me. And I want you to know, I've got my army right here as backup,' and flipping aside the sheet he revealed a small battalion of plastic soldiers.

'You're not funny,' she insisted, even though she was laughing through her anger.

'No,' he said defeatedly, 'I'm just scared.'

Ellen rolled her eyes, turned away then looked at him again. 'You should be,' she informed him, 'because I'm seriously mad at you for what happened today.'

He watched her come towards him, then swiftly blocked her with his sword and shield as she went to pummel him with her fists. 'You idiot!' she choked, still trying not to laugh. 'You're not getting round me this way.'

'Unhand me, woman,' he cried, as she grabbed his sword.

'Michael stop it!'

Suddenly he cast aside his sword and shield, seized her in his arms and pulled her onto the bed.

'Ow, ow, ow!' she protested as he rolled her over on the toy soldiers.

'I gave no order to attack,' he objected, glaring at the soldiers, and with a single sweep of his hand he brushed them to the floor. Then, gathering her tightly in his arms again, he looked down into her eyes.

'I'm sorry,' he said.

She gazed up at him, then felt her eyes flutter closed as

his lips came gently down on hers. 'So how did it go with Richard Conway earlier?' he asked afterwards.

She couldn't help but smile. 'Apparently he doesn't even have a dog,' she answered. 'It was his managers, just like we thought, trying to get every last dime. He says we should go straight to him if there's any problem like that in the future. So now you can tell me why you got me to sort that ludicrous list out rather than take it on yourself.'

'Because I had a feeling he'd be more impressed by you than he would by me,' Michael answered. 'And it seems I was right.'

'I'm not sure I like that tactic very much,' she responded.

'I'm not happy about it myself, but if it works . . .'

She looked away for a moment, then returning her eyes to his said, 'And what about this situation with Michelle and Tom? What kind of tactic are you employing there?'

'No tactic,' he said. 'And I should have warned you it was coming?'

'So you did know?'

'Let's say I guessed. And I didn't say anything, because I hoped I was wrong.'

'So why didn't you back me when I said you wanted star names?'

Sighing, he let her go and rolled onto his back.

She propped herself up on an elbow and looked down at him. 'Well?' she prompted.

His eyes returned to hers. 'After you'd gone we talked about it – did he tell you that? You did see him this evening, didn't you?'

She nodded. 'Michelle's name wasn't mentioned. So what did you talk about?'

'Well, it seems he feels more comfortable with Michelle getting inside Rachel's skin than he does a total stranger.'

'But that's ridiculous!' Ellen snapped.

'Honey, neither of us has been through what he's been through, and though it might not seem logical to us, to him . . . Well, it's got to be different. It's the only thing he's going to hold out for.'

'Are you kidding me? He's going to hold us to ransom over this?'

Michael merely looked at her.

Ellen sat up and stared hard at the lit pool outside. Her anger was returning fast and she wondered if it was fear making her this mad, or jealousy. Or was it simply that Michelle couldn't be more wrong for the part? It was probably all three, but the only valid argument she could make was the third.

She turned to look down at Michael. 'Do you think she's right for the part?' she demanded.

He took a deep breath and let it out slowly. 'I've got to admit, she wouldn't have been my first choice,' he answered, 'but if it's what Tom wants . . . Listen,' he said, as she started to object. 'I know you don't want to hear this, but whatever else she is, Michelle is a damned good actress. OK, she might not look like Rachel, she might not sound like her either, but she could bring more passion and believability to that role than anyone else I know. Not only because of her talent, but because her own sympathies are so in accordance with Rachel's.'

'So what happened to the star name?' Ellen demanded tightly.

'With Conway playing Tom, we don't necessarily need a big name for Rachel,' he replied.

She looked past him to where the bedside lamp cast an orangey glow over the silver-striped walls. It was true, one star would be enough, and as that status had gone to the part of Tom Chambers, there was no reason, other than the fact that Chambers knew Michelle and felt comfortable with her, why the part of Rachel shouldn't go to Matty. 'And if I said I really didn't want Michelle to play the part?' she said. 'Would you support me?'

Michael waited for her eyes to come back to his. 'We're in Tom's hands,' he answered.

Ellen got up from the bed, walked into the bathroom and slammed the door. As she stripped off her clothes she was seething with fury and, seeing Michael's things placed neatly around his wash-basin, she swept them all into the wastebin, marched to the chute and emptied them into the trash. Then, taking her robe from where it was hanging under his, she slipped it on and turned to the mirror. As she began cleansing her face the door opened and he stood watching her in the glass.

'Tell me,' she said bitterly, 'where will she be staying when she comes here to film? With us?'

Michael looked at her, his expression starting to harden.

'Ten days!' she seethed. 'I agreed to ten days, and a further two weeks when we're on honeymoon. I'm not having her here any longer than that. Do you hear me? And if you're making the mistake of thinking that's me agreeing to her playing the part just as long as we don't have to put her up, then disabuse yourself now, because I'm not agreeing at all. Not for one minute am I agreeing.'

Michael turned and walked away. A few minutes later she followed him into the room and got into bed beside him.

'You're jealous of a woman you've never even met,' he told her harshly.

'And you're giving me good cause to be,' she responded, turning her back.

Several minutes ticked by.

'And this isn't about jealousy,' she said, 'it's about professionalism. And you're just not professional enough to stand up for something you believe in.'

'You mean that *you* believe in,' he corrected. 'And your beliefs are all to cock because you just can't see past your own obsession with . . .'

Ellen swung round. 'There's nothing obsessed about me!' she yelled.

'You can't accept that I love you and not her,' he yelled back. 'But all right, if you want it spelt out, I don't have a problem with her playing the part. Nor do I think she should stay anywhere but here when*ever* she comes to LA.'

Ellen stared at him furiously. 'I'm giving you fair warning,' she said, 'I'm going to do everything I can to persuade Tom Chambers to change his mind, but if I don't succeed and this movie goes ahead with Michelle in the lead, then I'm out of this house, because there's just no way I'm going to live under the same roof as you, Robbie and *her*.'

Chapter 7

The afternoon sun was blazing its might along the southern California coast as the PAL flight carrying Michelle finally came in to land. It had been a long and uncomfortable journey, with little room to move in a cabin that was packed to capacity, and crowded seats that did their level best to deny any attempts at exit or access. Still, it was behind her now, and the only thing that interested her, as she cleared customs and wheeled her luggage through to the arrivals hall, was that she was going to see her darling, precious little boy for the first time in more than eight months.

The crowd waiting to greet other passengers was dense and noisy as she came through, and for a while her view was blocked by the tightly packed bodies of a slow-moving family in front. Her shoulder-length blonde hair, which had been newly cut and styled just before she left, caused her to stand out in the mainly Asian crowd, just as her height enabled her to catch an occasional glimpse up ahead. In the end, she and Robbie found each other at the same moment, and as he shrieked 'Mummy!' and came bounding towards her, she abandoned her cart and ran towards him.

'Darling!' she cried, sweeping him up in her arms. 'Oh my darling. I've missed you so much. Let me see you. Oh, Robbie, you've grown so handsome and big. Can I kiss you? You're not too grown-up to be kissed?' and she laughed through her tears as he grabbed her round the neck and pressed his lips hard against hers. 'Such passion!' she spluttered. 'Oh God, I can't believe how much I've missed you. Is Daddy here?'

'He's over there. And Tom. We all came to meet you and Daddy said we can go for a McDonald's on the way home if you're not too tired. You're not too tired, are you, Mum?'

'No,' she laughed, brushing back his hair and gazing adoringly into his face, 'I'm not too tired.'

'Any of those hugs going spare?' a voice behind her enquired.

'Tom!' she cried, turning to greet him and almost tripping over the luggage cart he had rescued. 'Oh God, look at you! It's so wonderful to see you.'

'It's good to see you too,' he told her, embracing both her and Robbie, while trying to keep hold of the cart.

'Daddy! Daddy!' Robbie shouted, wriggling from Michelle's arms as Michael came towards them. 'Let me have Spot, Daddy. Spot, come here boy. Mummy, this is Spot,' he declared, scooping the shaggy little black dog up in his arms and turning to show his mother.

'Oh, he's adorable Robbie,' Michelle laughed, taking the dog and bringing his cheeky little face up to hers. 'But where are all his spots?'

'He doesn't have any,' Robbie responded indignantly. 'He doesn't have to have spots to be called Spot, does he, Dad?'

'No,' Michael confirmed.

Michelle's lovely green eyes were shining with laughter as she looked up at Michael.

'Hi,' he said, his tone and expression seeming to close them off from the mayhem for a moment. 'How are you?'

'I'm fine,' she answered, and tucking Spot under one arm, she walked into his arms.

'Mummy, you're squashing Spot!' Robbie objected.

'Yeah, don't squash the dog,' Tom joined in.

'Sorry,' Michelle laughed, handing the dog back to Robbie. 'He's gorgeous, darling,' she said, 'and I'm really looking forward to getting to know him better.'

'Oh, you will,' Michael assured her, disentangling the lead and clipping it on Spot.

'No, Daddy, he's too little to walk,' Robbie protested. 'Someone might stand on him and kill him.'

'And that would never do,' Michael said, scooping up both Robbie and Spot. 'Come on, let's get out of here, we're causing a pile-up.'

Robbie looked at Michelle. Grinning, she held out her arms for him to come.

'You can carry Spot, Dad,' Robbie said, by way of compensation, and dumping his cherished pet he all but leapt into his mother's arms.

'I guess I get the luggage,' Tom remarked, as they began heading for the door.

'You can have a Big Mac,' Robbie informed him. 'Mummy said she's not tired, so we can go for a McDonald's. Mummy, you're sleeping in the next bedroom to me and Spot and we helped make the bed for you this morning. And do you know what, I helped Ellen choose some nice soap for you and it's in the bathroom next to my soap. I don't mind if you share my bathroom.'

'You mean you've got a bathroom all to yourself?' Michelle gasped.

'Yes. And a bedroom. And a playroom. And we've got a swimming-pool too, haven't we Daddy? Daddy won't let me go in unless he's there too, or unless Ellen's there, but I can swim. I'm a good swimmer, aren't I Daddy?'

'I know you can swim, honey,' she told him. 'You were swimming in Rio. Remember?'

He frowned, then laughed. 'Oh yes,' he said. 'Can I press the button, please,' he asked as they came to the crosswalk. After pushing the button he looked at his mother, and with a sudden burst of euphoria he threw

119

his arms around her neck and squeezed her hard.

'Oh no, Daddy's on the phone again,' he complained, rolling his eyes as Michael took out his cellphone and started to dial.

Michelle and Chambers laughed as Michael tweaked Robbie's nose and waited to make the connection. 'Line's busy,' he said.

'Where's Ellen?' Michelle asked, as they began crossing over to the parking lot. 'I'm really looking forward to meeting her. But I guess she's got a lot to do . . .'

'She didn't want to come,' Robbie stated.

'Hey, that's not true,' Michael responded. 'She was afraid she might be in the way, which I told her was nonsense, but she had a meeting to go to anyway. She'll be there when we get home. Now, what news on my reprobate brother?'

'Oh, he sends everyone his love, especially you,' she added, squeezing Robbie hard.

Michael smiled, then his eyes met Michelle's in a way that left her wondering what he really thought of her relationship with his younger brother. She didn't imagine he was jealous, but was surprised to find herself wondering if she wanted him to be. 'He would have loved to come,' she said, 'but there's so much to do in those refugee camps, and as we're going to be back here for the wedding in a couple of months . . .' Michael was walking slightly ahead by now, so, not sure whether he'd heard her, she glanced up at Tom and smiled as he winked.

'Are you sure it's OK, me staying at the house?' she said, as Michael came to a stop at the car. 'I don't want to be a nuisance.'

'It's perfectly OK,' Michael assured her. 'I just need to let Ellen know that we're stopping off at McDonald's.'

A few minutes later, with the luggage stowed in the trunk, Michelle, Spot and Robbie behind and Tom next to him, Michael drove them out of the car park and tried calling the house. Ellen picked up almost right away.

'Hello darling,' he said. 'Are you OK?'

'Fine,' she answered. 'Did Michelle arrive yet?'

'Yes, she's right here. We're in the car.'

'So you should be home in what, forty minutes?'

'Actually, we're going to be a bit longer than that,' he said, glancing quickly over his shoulder as he changed lanes to join Century. 'Robbie wants to go for McDonald's, so as a treat . . .'

'Sounds like a good idea,' Ellen replied.

The flatness of her tone caused Michael's heart to sink. 'Why don't you come and join us?' he suggested.

'No. I don't much want my first meeting with Michelle to be at a McDonald's,' she answered. 'I'll see you when you get here,' and the line went dead.

Michael clicked off his end, and as he passed the phone to Chambers his and Michelle's eyes met in the rearview mirror. Though she said nothing, Michael knew she had guessed more about that call than he wanted her to.

After speaking to Michael Ellen walked back to the kitchen and began packing away the groceries she had picked up on her way home. It hadn't been easy, clearing her calendar to allow time for shopping and cooking, but, knowing how much it would mean to Michael, she had gone to great lengths to manage it. She hadn't been planning anything fancy, just a spaghetti bolognaise, because it was one of Robbie's favourites, and some fresh fruits and ice-cream for dessert, because coming from one of the more deprived areas of the world she'd thought Michelle might appreciate something wholesome and healthy. Still, it could wait, and so too could their dreaded first meeting, for there was no way in the world she was just sitting around here waiting, when she had a ton of work to get through at the office and when there was every chance she'd work herself into a royal rage if she did.

121

'It's not that I mind having my surprise totalled,' she complained to Matty half an hour later, 'though I've got to admit it did piss me off. I'd even bought French champagne which I thought was a pretty generous gesture, considering. No, what I really mind about is how hard I'm trying to be adult and in-perspective about this and how pathetically I'm failing. I mean, look at me now. What purpose is this going to serve, me coming here to you after storming out of an empty house because they're cosying up like a happy little family down at McDonald's, feeding French fries to Spot and talking over old times and kidnaps with Tom? If I was going to go anywhere, I could at least have gone to the office. God knows, there's more than enough for me to do there. In fact there's so much I'm almost glad Michelle's here so she can help out with Robbie and give me a chance to get back on top. Except what's needing the most work right now is me and Michael, and just how the hell am I supposed to get that back on track when the very reason it went off in the first place is about to take up residence under the same roof?'

'Here, drink this and calm down,' Matty commanded, handing her a generous glass of chilled white wine and steering her out onto the veranda of her luxurious Beverly Hills apartment. The night lamps were glowing in the scented semi-darkness and Matty's damp swimsuit and a couple of towels were draped over the backs of the expensive white-cane and blue-padded chairs.

'Tell me, how are things going with Tom?' Matty said, sinking into one of the sumptuous armchairs and putting her feet on the coffee-table. 'Weren't you having a session on the script with him yesterday?'

Ellen nodded as she swallowed a much-needed mouthful of wine, then, letting her head fall back, she gazed up at the luminous red sky and opaque crescent of moon. 'And again this morning,' she said, picturing him with Michael, Michelle and Robbie now and feeling a pang of jealousy about that too. 'You know, so far working with him on this script is a dream. He's so receptive and quick-thinking and . . . Oh, I don't know, I just wish all writers were like him. He's so professional and . . .' she laughed, 'I guess, funny. Honestly, you'd never know it was his personal life we were discussing, he's so objective about it, yet at the same time I can't help thinking how difficult it must be for him reliving it all like this. You know, he believes it was Rachel who saved him from being murdered just before he left Colombia? It was all to do with a young prostitute and some flowers. Sure, it sounds crazy, but to hear him tell it, well, believe me, it sounds more than plausible, it sounds perfectly credible. He obviously loved her a hell of a lot, and still feels the bond with her now, despite her death. Don't you think that's romantic?'

Matty nodded. 'Mmm,' she said, 'and enviable, even though she's dead. I mean, how many of us ever get to love like that?'

Ellen smiled ruefully. 'A month ago I'd have said I did,' she answered. 'Now, I'm not so sure.'

Matty turned to look at her. 'You don't mean that,' she said. 'You're just mad at him, right?'

Ellen inhaled deeply. 'Yeah, I'm mad at him,' she replied, 'and I don't guess I do mean it, but I sure wish I knew how to deal with what's happening now. All we've done these past two weeks is fight or avoid each other. It's terrible, but I can't make up with him and go on like everything's OK when the truth is neither of us is backing down over Michelle.'

'Are we talking about Michelle as mother, ex-girlfriend or Rachel Carmedi?' Matty asked, her fine, dark features looking softer and more appealing than ever in the gently flickering candlelight.

'I guess all three,' Ellen sighed. 'But tell me, you've seen the pictures of her, you've seen the videos . . . Forget for a moment that we want you to play the part, and just answer me this, is Michelle wrong for it or is it just that I want her to be wrong?'

Matty took some time to consider the question before saying, 'I think it's a bit of both. She's a good actress and with some work on the accent she could probably play the part well.'

'But so could you, better even than she could and you're already a lot closer to the accent than she is. God, you even look like Rachel. I've got to introduce you to Tom. It's the only way I'm going to get through to him on this.'

'Have you talked to him about it all?' Matty asked.

Ellen shook her head. 'Not really. He knows I'm not happy about Michelle playing the part, but he probably thinks it's because I don't want her around Michael and Robbie for so long. Which he's not wrong about, because believe you me, the prospect of her being here for the next ten days is bad enough, three months or more . . .' She shuddered and took another sip of wine.

'I was thinking,' Matty said, 'if I really do look like Rachel, it could be a tough call for Tom, you know, having to see someone who looks like her stepping into her shoes and bringing it all back to life.'

Ellen stared at her with wide, disbelieving eyes. 'Matty, don't do this to me,' she said. 'For God's sake I need someone to back me on this, and if I can't depend on you, then who the hell can I?'

'It was just a thought,' Matty said. 'But I think it's one you should consider.'

'What is it, do you suddenly not want the part?' Ellen demanded.

'Sure I want the part. Under any other circumstances I'd kill for it, but we've got to see things from Tom's perspective too, and after all, he's the one who owns the rights to it. It's his story every bit as much as it's Rachel's. I just think that if we're really going to sell him

124

on me, then a better way to play it would be to let him come up with the idea on his own. Not force it down his throat.'

'And how are we going to do that now that Michelle's here and ready to sign a contract the minute it's drawn up?'

'Is it drawn up?' Matty asked.

Ellen's heart tightened. 'Not that I know of,' she answered. 'But no, Michael wouldn't do that to me. Just no way would he go behind my back and sign her up without telling me first. Note I say telling, not discussing, because we're a long way past the stage of debating anything where Michelle is concerned now. He tells me and I either like it or I lump it.'

'Why don't we take this gently?' Matty suggested. 'I mean, we don't want to frighten Tom off by introducing me like I was some kind of ghost of kidnaps past, do we? So we just bring me in as your cousin, who also happens to be an actress.'

Ellen laughed. 'Michael will see straight through it,' she said. 'But what the hell? You're right. I should at least get you two to meet, and what better time than the present? What are you doing tonight? Which reminds me, what happened to the camera operator you met in Denver? I thought he was staying here?'

'He went back to Denver on Tuesday for a couple of days reshoot. It didn't include me, but it's over anyway. You know how these things always seem like a good idea on location and turn out to be about as appealing as gout when you get home.'

Ellen smiled in sympathy. 'So you're free tonight?' she said. 'Can you come up to the house with me? Be there when they all get back?' She looked at her watch. 'They'll probably beat us to it now, but who cares? Why shouldn't I have someone from my camp around, God knows he's got enough in his.'

'You're making this sound like a war,' Matty

remarked.

Ellen looked at her, slightly shaken by that, then picking up her keys she said, 'If it is, then it's of his making.'

Michael's car was outside the garage and the lights were on in the house as Ellen drove through the gates and came to a stop next to the Cruiser. 'I'm doing this all wrong,' she declared to Matty. 'I shouldn't have walked out. I should have just called you and got you to come over.'

'But you didn't,' Matty stated, 'so quit trying to deal with what's already done, and figure out how you're going to make this work to your advantage.'

Ellen glanced at her sharply. 'I've got about thirty seconds in which to do that,' she remarked, 'so unless you've got any suggestions . . .'

'As a matter of fact I do. Get rid of that anger and stop turning yourself into the victim here. No-one's trying to shut you out of this, you're doing it to yourself. So lighten up. Smile. Remember, he chose you, not her, and you can afford to be generous in your victory.'

Despite herself Ellen laughed. 'He's going to be pretty mad that I wasn't here when they got back,' she said. 'And seeing you is going to tell him exactly where I've been and why . . .'

'Ellen shut up and get out of the car,' Matty commanded.

Ellen did as she was told, and walked in silence up to the closed front door. Slipping her key in the lock she glanced at Matty, then pushed the door open and walked into the sitting-room.

'Ah, there you are,' Michael said, getting up from the sofa. 'I was starting to worry. You didn't take your phone. Oh, hi, Matty. How are you?'

Ellen searched his expression for any signs of annoyance, but there appeared only a genuine pleasure to see Matty, and why not, they'd always got along perfectly well.

'Matty! Matty!' Robbie cried, suddenly bursting in through another door and racing across the room.

'Hey big guy!' Matty laughed, swinging him up in her arms. 'How ya doing?'

'My mummy's here,' he told her excitedly. 'She came all the way from . . . from . . . an aeroplane, and she's got the room next to mine and we're going to the movies tomorrow after school and then we're going to Magic Mountain the next day . . .'

'Hang on, calm down,' Michael chided, slipping an arm around Ellen. 'Sorry about the McDonald's,' he murmured in her ear. 'There wasn't a way out of it.'

'It's OK,' she answered, and felt her heart starting to melt as his lips came gently down on hers in the first kiss they had shared in over a week.

'Mummy!' Robbie suddenly cried, and leaping from Matty's arms he raced across the room to grab Michelle's hand. 'This is my mummy,' he told Matty proudly. 'She's staying here with us for ten whole days.'

Ellen couldn't not be aware of the way Robbie was shutting her out, and saw the slight confusion on Michelle's beautiful face as she looked from the woman Robbie was taking her to, to the woman Michael's arm was around.

'Hi, I'm Matty,' Matty said, holding out her hand. 'I'm Ellen's cousin.'

'I'm pleased to meet you, Matty,' Michelle smiled, and Ellen felt her throat tighten at the genuine warmth in her sparkling green eyes. This was a woman it was going to be shaming to dislike.

'And this is Ellen,' Michael said, keeping his arm around her as Michelle turned to them.

'Ellen. I've been so looking forward to meeting you,' Michelle said, taking her into a gentle embrace. She laughed self-consciously. 'I've heard so much about you

127

I feel I already know you. Thank you for letting me stay in your home.'

'You're welcome,' Ellen smiled, trying not to bristle at the way Michelle's greeting had seemed almost to reverse their roles of guest and hostess. 'I'm sorry I wasn't here when you arrived. I had to go back to the office for something, then I went over to pick up Matty so she could join us for dinner.'

'We don't need dinner we had McDonald's,' Robbie protested.

'Hey!' Michael said sharply. 'Less of that attitude, thank you. And just because you had McDonald's doesn't mean the rest of us wouldn't prefer something else.'

Ellen smiled past the ache in her heart. 'Did you have a good journey?' she asked Michelle.

Michelle laughed. 'It was hell,' she answered, 'but worth it to see this one.'

Ellen's smile remained in place as she looked down at Robbie, then over to Tom who was standing in front of one of the sofas watching them all. As their eyes met Ellen got the uncomfortable impression that he knew exactly how difficult she was finding this.

'Hello Tom,' she said, going to greet him. 'We're all ignoring you. Do you have a drink?'

'I do. How about you? Would it be presumptuous of me to go fix you one?'

'Not at all,' she assured him. 'But say hi to Matty first, then all the introductions'll be over.'

Unable to stop herself Ellen searched his face as he shook hands with Matty, wanting to see if there was any flicker of recognition, or perhaps any other kind of interest that went beyond mere politeness. There was nothing she could detect, but from the few occasions she had met Chambers she had already learned how very skilled he was at giving nothing away unless he wanted to.

As she turned back she briefly caught Michael's eye

and knew instantly that he had recognized her purpose in introducing Matty and Tom. From the way his eyebrow went up she realized that far from being angry, he was much closer to being sad that she was still fighting the inevitable.

'What are you having, Matty?' Tom said, as they all moved towards the sofas.

'A Chardonnay for me,' she answered.

'And I guess yours is the same?' he said to Ellen.

She smiled and sat down next to Michael as Michelle and Robbie sank down beside Matty on the opposite sofa.

'You must tell us all about Pakistan and your work there,' Ellen said to Michelle.

Michelle gave a mock frown and waved a dismissive hand. 'Believe me, it's too depressing a subject for tonight,' she said. 'Tell me about my little tearaway here instead. How's he doing at school? Top of the class I hope,' she added, digging him playfully in the ribs.

'I got a commendation last week!' he boasted. 'That's my second.'

'And what about all your black marks for talking too much?' Michael enquired.

'I only got one, and that was because Andrew kept talking to *me*.'

As Tom returned with the drinks and went to sit in the large two-seater armchair between the two sofas, Ellen watched and listened to the banter and tried not to be hurt by the way both Michael and Michelle seemed to have forgotten any part she might have played in helping to settle their son into his new school and country, never mind all the running around she had done for him since. It wasn't so much thanks that she wanted, but some kind of recognition would have been nice, or perhaps just a glance from Robbie that held some of the affection she had always been treated to before. But since she'd walked in the door he hadn't looked at her once and no-one, not even Michael, seemed to have noticed.

As the laughter and teasing grew louder and more animated she watched Michelle and found herself wondering how Michael had ever been able to leave her. With her gorgeously sleek blonde hair and flawless complexion, she was one of the most beautiful women Ellen had ever met, and her laughter was so natural and warming that even Ellen found herself smiling in response.

Yet all the time she was hating her more and more for the way she was so supremely British and shared so much background with Michael. It was as though they were all part of another world and though Tom and Matty seemed to be having no problem joining in, for Ellen it was impossible even to step up to the threshold. She had no idea what Michael's feelings were for Michelle now, but it was plain to see that there was still some kind of bond between them.

In the end Ellen got to her feet. 'I guess I should go fix some dinner,' she said. 'Is anyone else interested, or is it just me and Matty?'

'What are you offering?' Michael asked, rolling on to his back and grunting as Robbie jumped on his chest.

She shrugged. 'There's plenty in the freezer, whatever you like,' she answered. 'Chicken, pasta, fish. The question really is, are you full after the McDonald's, or would you like something else?'

'I'll have whatever you're making,' he said, trying to fend off Robbie's monster.

'Me too,' Tom added.

Ellen looked at Michelle.

'Nothing for me,' Michelle laughed. 'But I'll come and give you a hand if you like.'

'No, really,' Ellen replied. 'Stay with Robbie.' She looked at her watch. It was past his bedtime and he had school in the morning, but did she dare say so and risk being overruled by one of his parents?

As though picking up on her thoughts Robbie suddenly said, 'I want Mummy to take me to school in the morning.'

Michelle grinned and leaned over to pinch his cheeks. 'I don't have a car, silly,' she reminded him.

'You can use Daddy's, can't she, Daddy?' he responded.

Michael shrugged. 'I guess so,' he answered. 'I'll go to the office with Ellen and get cabs if I need to after that. Yeah, sure, you can use mine,' he told Michelle.

The words were out before Ellen could stop them. 'Well, if you've got a car, Michelle, perhaps you wouldn't mind taking Robbie to the dentist tomorrow as well. He's got an appointment at eleven.'

'I don't want to go to the dentist!' Robbie protested. 'I hate the dentist.'

'Don't be difficult,' Michelle reprimanded. She looked up at Ellen. 'I'm afraid I promised to check in with the Christian Children people in the morning,' she said. 'I can probably drop him off at school though.'

Ellen could feel the colour rising in her cheeks as she nodded. 'OK,' she said. 'I'll be the unpopular one and do the dentist.'

Almost as soon as the kitchen door closed behind her Michael came in after her. 'Was that really necessary?' he demanded. 'She didn't know Robbie had to go to the dentist or I'm sure she'd have arranged things so she could take him.'

'Yeah, I'm sure you're right,' Ellen responded, slamming the refrigerator door as she carried the overflowing salad tray to a nearby counter. 'So what do you want me to do? Apologize?'

'It would do for a start,' he bit back. 'And then perhaps you could take a decision to make our lives tolerable for the next ten days, instead of going the route you seem to be set on right now.'

Ellen swung round with the chopping knife. 'She's

here, isn't she?' she seethed. 'You got what you wanted, so get off my case. Or maybe *you'd* like to take Robbie to the dentist tomorrow.'

'What *is* all this about the dentist?' he snapped. 'What's the big deal? You've always taken him before. Or do you have more important things to do now you're working on this script?'

'Nothing's more important than that child, but I'm the only one who seems to think so,' she spat. 'Because I'm the only one who ever makes any time to take him where he's got to be, or go see his teachers, or check out his friends. When was the last time you put yourself out to do something for your son, except take him to the airport to meet his mother?'

'If it's too much for you, Ellen, we can make other arrangements,' he said darkly.

She stared at him, her face turning ashen with shock as the meaning of his words reached her. 'Then maybe you'd like to do just that,' she said tightly, and dropping the knife she turned to walk out.

'Stop!' he said, spinning her round. 'I'm sorry, that wasn't called for. It wasn't what I meant.'

'Then what did you mean?' she challenged, her face still taut with hurt and anger.

'I don't know,' he answered. 'I guess it just came out in the heat of the moment. It's not the way I feel. It's not what I want to happen. But we've got to stop this fighting. It's been like this for weeks now, and I love you too much to want it to go on.'

She looked away, not ready to forgive him yet, but not wanting to continue the fight either. 'Robbie should be in bed,' she said.

'Do you want to take him and I'll do what needs doing here?'

She shook her head. 'He doesn't want me, he wants his mother,' she said, with an edge to her voice that she wished wasn't there.

'Oh God,' Michael groaned, pulling her into his arms. 'I see what this is all about now. He loves you too, honey. Just give him some space, OK? The excitement'll soon wear off and then things will return to normal.'

She nodded and pulled back to wipe the tears from her eyes. 'She's much more beautiful than I realized,' she said.

He smiled. 'Have you looked in the mirror lately?' he asked. Then, tilting her face up to his, he said, 'You know, this would all be so much easier on you if you could see your way to making friends with her. And believe me, you've got nothing to be afraid of, not when I love you as much as I do.'

'I just hope to God that doesn't change,' she whispered.

Chapter 8

All six of the McCann Paull agents were gathered around the conference table with World Wide UK's accountants and business managers. Sandy Paull, dressed entirely in black, was in the chair. Though most of the south wall, which ran alongside the table, was taken up by windows that offered great views of the river Thames and Battersea beyond, the rest of the walls were covered in posters, photographs, captions, schedules, and a hundred other useful or commemorative items that World Wide's transient staff had collected since the company's inception.

The meeting presently under way was one of the regular Monday sessions that brought the two companies together either to discuss projects in progress, or to put forward new ideas and scripts that showed potential for being packaged by McCanns and produced by World Wide.

'OK,' she said, as Ginger Coulton, one of the World Wide accountants, finished her report, 'to summarize: the budget reports and early returns are looking good and we're still being judged a good risk by potential investors.' She smiled. 'Seems that right now everyone wants to throw money our way, so it shouldn't be too long before we can launch our own airline.'

Everyone laughed and Sandy cocked an eyebrow, an indication the jest might not be so idle. She glanced over at Stacy, her assistant, who was taking down the minutes. 'I'm going to spell this out,' she said, 'because I don't think we've got any one document that encapsulates everything that World Wide and McCann Paull are into right now. So for those of you who know all this I'm sorry, but I think we should have something down in writing, if only for easy reference.' She put aside the finance reports and turned to a couple of pages of handwritten notes.

It took a while to go through the many projects that were in various stages of development, and to make all the changes that had occurred during the past week, but the discussion was as lively as it was worthwhile for all the discrepancies it uncovered.

'OK, just a couple of words on *Rachel's Story*,' she said, glancing at her watch and starting to wrap the meeting up. 'Things are starting to move ahead pretty fast in LA, so I'll be making the movie a priority from now on. Between ourselves, Michael informed me when we last spoke that he's going to have difficulty meeting the payroll next month, so the need to get some really big interest going is becoming vital. That's not to say he doesn't have the backers over there, because he does, it's just that the money is taking some time to drop, and naturally it's affecting the cash flow. From what we've managed to pull together so far we can transfer three million sterling by the end of next week, which is really going to help him out, but, like I said, it's important now that we get as much investment in as we can. So, if anyone's got any other possible backers they can put me on to, please let me know.' Once again she looked at her watch. 'OK, I don't have anything else here that needs immediate attention,' she said, 'and as I have a funeral to go to at one I'd like to bring us to a close. Anyone else got anything to say?'

Her eyes moved to World Wide's business managers,

who were discussing something quietly between themselves.

'Marilyn, Clive?' she prompted.

They looked up. 'We just need to check that the three million from Deightons is going to be in on time to transfer next week,' Marilyn told her.

Sandy felt her mouth turning dry. 'I didn't realize it wasn't already here,' she said, trying to keep the irritation from her voice. 'When I last spoke to Rodney Parker-King he assured me there would be no problem.'

'I don't think there is,' Marilyn assured her. 'We just need to make sure the transfer is effected right away.'

'Well, I need an answer by the end of the day,' Sandy said. 'Michael's flying in tomorrow, and I want to be able to tell him that the immediate panic is over. For those of you who didn't know, his mother's had a fall . . . It's OK, apparently nothing to get worked up about,' she added swiftly, as all the agents appeared about to ask – everyone was extremely fond of Clodagh, with her eccentric Irish charm, and the added virtue of being something of a surrogate mother to them all.

'I went to see her last night,' Zelda informed them. 'She's just a bit shaken up. Nothing broken.'

'Is she in hospital?' Janey asked.

'She's going home this afternoon,' Zelda answered. 'You know Clodagh, hates all the fuss but would be furious if it didn't happen.'

'Will you get a chance to see Michael before you go up to Scotland?' Sandy asked her.

'We'll cross paths at Heathrow for about an hour,' Zelda chuckled. 'Did he speak to you about Vic Warren?'

Sandy nodded. 'I'm waiting for Vic to call me back,' she said. 'He's still shooting in Paris, but he's hoping to get over while Michael's here.'

'How long's he staying?' Craig asked.

'Only a few days,' Sandy answered. 'He'll be at his

136

sister's so he can see plenty of Clodagh and her grandchildren. If Vic can't get over to London, then he's thinking of going to Paris for the day before flying back to LA.' She looked at her watch. 'Oh God, look at the time. I haven't even booked a cab yet. Stacy, can you . . .'

'Where's the funeral?' Craig interrupted.

'Mortlake,' Sandy answered.

'Then I'll drive you there. I'm having lunch with Guy Foster at Teddington Studios.'

Ten minutes later they were pulling out of the underground car park and heading towards the Kings Road. Sandy was talking to Stacy on her mobile phone, while Craig tuned into the radio news.

'I take it it's Maurice's funeral,' he said, when Sandy finally clicked off.

She nodded and turned to gaze at the passing shops and pubs. 'I'm going to miss him,' she said. 'More than I ever missed my own father, wherever he might be now.'

Craig glanced at her and started to slow for a red light. 'Do you ever think about looking for him?' he said.

Sandy's laugh was more of a scoff. 'What, so's he can scrounge off me too, the way the rest of them do?' she said, not prepared to admit, even to Craig, that her father was in prison. 'No, I was just thinking, not having Maurice to turn to is going to be a bit like trying to swim the Channel with no backup boat. I might drown.'

Craig looked at her in surprise. 'It's not like you to doubt yourself,' he commented.

Sandy laughed. 'I doubt myself all the time,' she told him, 'I just try not to show it.' She allowed a few seconds to pass, then said, 'Promise not to tell anyone, but I'm nervous about seeing Michael tomorrow.'

Craig frowned. 'For any reason?' he asked. 'I mean, you're not normally – are you?'

'A bit. But more today. I suppose because Maurice has gone and I'm feeling much more vulnerable without him than I'd ever imagined I would. You know, just in case anything goes wrong.'

Craig was incredulous. 'What on earth can go wrong?' he cried. 'You said it yourself at the meeting just now, things couldn't be going better, and since Michael's got the best part of everything he owns invested in World Wide, including his share of McCann Paull, he's likely to start offering you obeisance when he finds out what you managed to get from Deightons. So I can't see what you've got to feel nervous about. Besides, you don't know what Maurice might have left you in his will.'

'Nothing,' Sandy informed him. 'We talked about it before he died. He gave me enough in his lifetime and I truly didn't want to spend the next however many years fighting it out in the courts with his children. So we agreed. He gave me the apartment and my success. I did very well.'

'Do his family know you're going to be at the funeral?' Craig asked.

She shook her head. 'I'll just do the movie-star bit, you know, low-profile background, soak up all the scorn, lower my hat brim, look tragic, then leave the way I came – alone.'

Craig was grinning, but when he looked at her he was concerned to see that she didn't seem to be joking. For a moment her eyes met his, and there was still no smile when she looked away.

'Are you all right?' he said, speeding up to overtake a bus. 'Maybe this has hit you harder than I realized.'

'I think it has,' she said, swallowing hard.

'Listen, if you want me to come in with you,' he said, 'I can always call Guy and reschedule.'

'No, it's OK. I'm just feeling sorry for myself. I'll get over it.'

They drove on in silence, passing the brewery in Chiswick where roadworks held them up for a while, then turning at the Hogarth Roundabout towards

Mortlake. It was unlike Sandy to be depressed, or quiet, and Craig wasn't entirely sure how to handle it.

'When are you actually seeing Michael?' he asked, for want of anything else to say.

Sandy felt her heart contract. 'Tomorrow night,' she answered. 'We're having dinner.' She began to rummage in her bag and said something Craig didn't catch.

'Sorry?' he said.

'I said, it'll be the first time I've been on a date since I left the escort business.'

To his dismay Craig was once again stuck for words, since he didn't imagine for one minute that Michael was viewing tomorrow night as a date.

After a while Sandy gave a dry, empty laugh. 'I don't suppose you're the person to ask if there's something wrong with me,' she said. 'Anyway, there must be if nobody's asked me out in all this time. Not that there's been anyone I've particularly fancied, but well, you know . . .' She glanced at him, then looked out at the barren trees and flat, colourless acres that stretched south of Chiswick. 'It's a horrible feeling finding out that you can't get a date the way everyone else gets one. You know, the normal route of someone asking you out because they want to get to know you better. Or even because they want to screw you. Seems the only way I can get someone is to be paid for it. Like a whore. Well, that's what I was, I suppose. At least sometimes. I didn't always sleep with them.' She took a breath. 'Michael's the only man I've slept with since coming to London who I didn't meet through the escort business.'

'You're always working, that's why you never meet anyone,' Craig insisted.

A few minutes ticked by.

'I've tried to get over him,' Sandy said, her eyes still averted. 'But what do you do when in your heart you just know someone is right for you? I mean, I can't help

139

feeling that way, can I? It's not something I asked for, it just happened. And it certainly doesn't make me happy, especially not when he's over there in LA with another woman who he's planning to marry in a couple of months. Things are better between us now, though. We get on well together. I think he actually likes me, which is a definite improvement on the way he felt when he fired me.' She turned to Craig as he stopped at a pedestrian crossing. 'What would you do if you were me?'

'In what way?' he asked awkwardly.

Sandy turned away and sighed. 'Never mind,' she said.

Neither of them spoke again until they were pulling up outside the cemetery.

'Are you OK for getting back?' Craig asked.

'Stacy's already booked me a cab,' she answered, flicking up the sun-visor after checking her make-up. She smiled briefly. 'Sorry if I burdened you with my problems.'

'No burden,' he said. 'We're friends. It's just sometimes I don't know if I'm the right one to advise you.'

'Where Michael's concerned I don't think anyone can,' she confessed. 'I mean, it's not something I understand myself, the way I feel about him, so how can I expect anyone else to?'

Craig looked at her and thought how young and sometimes painfully naïve she still was, despite her success. She had so many qualities, and leadership was definitely amongst them, yet where Michael was concerned she was like a whole other person.

Seeing her bite her lip and realizing it was probably nerves about going to this funeral, he reached out for her hand and gave it a squeeze. He could only admire her for the courage it was taking to go in there now, and in his heart he felt the ache of her loneliness. With Maurice dying and Michael about to get married, he could easily imagine how bewildered and at sea she was feeling, probably even more than she realized.

'Are you sure you don't want me to come in with you?' he said.

She nodded. 'Sure. But thanks for offering.'

He tightened his hold on her hand. 'I'm going to be honest with you,' he said gently. 'Aside from the work issue, I think another reason you never get asked out on a date is that you just don't give any other man a chance.'

She turned to look at him, an amused, though slightly sad expression in her turquoise eyes. '*Is* there any other man?' she said, and with a quick smile that only suggested she might be joking, she opened the door and got out.

Ellen ran into her office, yelled out 'OK,' and snatched up the phone as Maggie put the call through. 'Matty, hi, at last,' she cried, dumping her briefcase and shrugging off her jacket. 'Sorry I didn't get back to you before, but it's so crazy here, and now with Michael flying off to England . . . Anyway, how are you? How did it go with Tom when he drove you home the other night?'

'Well, we talked about you, and then about you, and then some more about you,' Matty answered.

'What do you mean?' Ellen said, stopping what she was doing.

'Oh come on,' Matty laughed, 'you've got to have noticed, the man doesn't have eyes for anyone else. Oh, he's polite enough, but it's pretty plain he'd rather be talking to you, and if he can't talk *to* you, seems he's just as happy talking *about* you.'

'Matty, you're completely wrong,' Ellen informed her, going to the computer screen and calling up her messages. 'The only reason he talked to you about me was that I'm all you've got in common right now. Didn't you bring up about the script?'

'Sure, and you're doing a great job, he tells me. He really admires how professional and insightful you are and thinks, when the time comes, you should get first billing on the writer's credit. Of course, that's not all he wants to offer you, but we didn't get that far. Now answer me this, how the hell do you stand to be alone with him, in the same room, and keep your hands off him? He's so damned gorgeous.'

Ellen was laughing. 'He and Michael are good friends,' she reminded her cousin. 'And whereas I grant you Tom is an extremely attractive man, I happen to be very much in love with Michael. Hang on.' She put a hand over the mouthpiece and spoke quickly to Maggie who'd just come in the door. 'Get the proofs over to the Four Seasons for Tom to see,' she said, 'and then courier a set over to England for Michael. Are they any good?' she added, as Maggie dropped a large package on the corner of her desk.

'Haven't seen them,' she answered. 'The messenger just brought them in. Ted Forgon's in his office. Said he'd like to see you if you've got a moment to pop in.'

Ellen looked at her watch. 'I'll try,' she said. 'Matty, you still there?'

'Still here. So when's Michael back?'

'Friday. Great timing on Clodagh's part to go and fall over now. I mean, this isn't exactly my idea of fun being left alone with Michelle and Robbie. Tom joined us for dinner last night, so we reminisced about Rio and Sarajevo, at least they did and I listened. Then we talked about Pakistan and the refugee camps and all the problems the Afghan women and children are facing there right now. You can imagine how much I had to contribute to that. Then we caught up with all the gossip on their fellow let's-risk-our-lives-to-do-good-ers. That was particularly fascinating, as I just love hearing all about people I've never even met and am never likely to. In the end I went to bed and left them to it. So let me put you right about something, Matty, if Tom's got a thing for anyone round here, it's very definitely Michelle.'

'What about Michael's brother? Where's he while all this is going on?' Matty wanted to know. 'Aren't he and Michelle supposed to be an item?'

'Cavan? He's still in Pakistan. I expect Michael'll have to rush off to rescue him from a guerilla kidnapping or political imprisonment any time now. In fact, my money's on the week of the wedding, what say you?'

'Boy, you do sound stressed,' Matty remarked. 'What are you doing for lunch? My treat.'

'Matty, I'd spring for champagne cocktails and three courses at the Ivy right now, given half a chance. Instead, I've just sent Olivia to get me a chicken burrito which I know is disgusting, but I feel like indulging myself even though I won't have time to eat it before I go pick up Robbie to take him to the dentist. And does any kid stay in school for an entire day any more, is what I want to know?'

'I thought the dentist was yesterday?'

'So did I. I got it wrong. Yesterday was tetanus and whooping-cough shots. Today is the dentist. And Michelle can't take him, because she's got an important lunch with the charity officials, then she's got to go shopping to buy herself something to wear for the big night. Meanwhile, Tom is helping her work on her speech, so I get an extra couple of hours back in my schedule because he can't see me until Michelle's speech is done and delivered. What's more, in Michael's absence, Tom will be escorting her to the charity gala on Thursday night while I stay at home and babysit Robbie, because it's Lucina's night off. I didn't actually know that Michael was supposed to be escorting her, that was obviously something he forgot to mention. Hang on, Maggie's back.'

'Mark Gladley's on the line,' Maggie told her, 'he said he can reschedule the screening for Tuesday week if that suits you better. He needs an answer now though.'

'Well?' Ellen said. 'Does it suit me better?'

'It could, but I'll need to check with Ken at Glitz and Glamour,' she said, referring to the company that was organizing the wedding. 'And I need the diary of your dress fittings.'

'It's right here,' Ellen said, delving into her briefcase and bringing out an untidy stack of notes.

'And Michelle just called,' Maggie continued. 'She said to let you know that she's sent flowers to Michael's mother on your behalf, just in case you'd forgotten.'

Ellen's eyes widened with amazement. Outrage was a beat behind it.

Maggie winced. 'She also said, as she doesn't know LA very well she'd really appreciate some company when she goes shopping this afternoon, if you can make it. I said you'd call her back.'

Ellen looked about to explode. 'What is it with that woman?' she seethed. 'Call her back and tell her she's got more cheek than a Sumo's backside, and enough goddamned people running around after her, so the hell does she get me too. And while you're at it, ask her if she understands that other people have schedules. Or is it that hers is so full up with worthy causes that no-one else's counts?'

'What about the flowers?' Matty said down the phone. 'You're surely not letting her get away with that?'

'Like hell I am!' Ellen raged. 'Maggie, find out which florist she used, get on to them and cancel the flowers she sent for me. Tell her I organized mine and Michael's when I took Michael to the airport.'

'Did you?' Matty asked.

'No, but she doesn't need to know that,' Ellen retorted. 'I'll just remind Michael to do it while he's in London. With any luck he'll manage it before Michelle's get there.'

'Anything else?' Maggie enquired.

'No,' Ellen snapped.

Maggie exited quickly, leaving Ellen to wonder exactly what she would say to Michelle on the phone, though not really caring. 'Do you see what I have to put up with?' she said to Matty. 'Now tell me I'm not overreacting here, the way Michael thinks I am. I mean, would you stand for this kind of shit?'

'Not a chance,' Matty assured her. 'But I'm not about to become Michael's wife and Robbie's stepmother, so you're going to have to find some way of dealing with her. Which reminds me, is everything OK between you and Robbie? He seemed kind of distant the other night.'

'With me, not you,' Ellen pointed out and sighed. 'I guess it's kind of tough having me and his mother under the same roof, and his mother is a novelty these days, whereas I'm just the one who reminds him to brush his teeth and forgets to pack his favourite cookies for lunch. The latest, this morning, is that he doesn't want me and Michael to get married. I tell you, if she weren't so goddamned holy and decent, I'd swear Michelle had put him up to it, but even I, who would like to see the woman on the fastest jet plane out of here, find it hard to suspect her of something like that.'

'What did you say to Robbie?' Matty asked.

'What could I say? I ignored it. It was probably the wrong thing to do, but we were right outside the school gates and I was already late for a nine o'clock with the site managers at Paramount.'

'How's that going?'

'OK. We could be moving the production offices over there some time in the next couple of weeks.'

'What about you and Michael?'

'We're staying here. Listen, I've got to go. I daren't be late for Robbie again, and Ted Forgon's just asked me to pop in and see him.'

'How is the old goat?' Matty enquired.

'Getting more active now that the statute of

limitations has started its countdown,' Ellen answered. 'Oh my God! I've just had a brilliant idea. Maybe I could get him on my side over the casting of Rachel. Michael might be running the show, but Ted's the majority shareholder, he's going to want an executive credit, and maybe even an executive input . . . I need to think about this, I'll get back to you.'

An hour later, having performing some excellent groundwork on Ted Forgon's ego ready for when she might need it, Ellen was leading Robbie across the schoolyard towards the car. All the other kids were back in class, ready for the afternoon session, and she was wondering if she could somehow work it for her and Robbie to take the rest of the day off and spend some time together. But with having to cover for Michael, as well as keeping up with her own hectic commitments, she was insane even to think it, for she didn't even have time to be here now, much less to start treading the delicate path it would take to deal with Robbie.

'Honey, don't scuff your shoes,' she said, as he dragged his feet round to the passenger side of the car.

Ignoring her he carried on scuffing, then flung his school bag rudely into the back before climbing in after it.

'You going to get on your booster seat?' she asked.

'Don't want to,' he replied.

'You're not going to be able to see where we're going,' she reminded him.

He stayed silent.

'OK, then put your seat-belt on,' she said.

He didn't move.

Leaning in, Ellen took the seat-belt, fastened it around him then got into the driver's seat. 'What did you do this morning?' she asked, reversing the car out of its parking space.

'Boring stuff,' he answered.

Ellen glanced in the rearview mirror, but he was too

146

low for her to see his face. She didn't need to, though, she'd already seen his scowl and didn't imagine it had disappeared. Despite her impatience her heart fluttered with misgiving, for the last thing she wanted was him to suffer the kind of confusion his behaviour was indicating.

'Can we make friends?' she said after a while.

No answer.

'How about we go to the movies tonight?' she suggested.

'Mummy's already taking me.'

They didn't speak again all the way over to Sherman Oaks where the dentist had his office. And while they were there the only words Robbie addressed to her were, 'I can do it myself,' as she made to help him up in the chair.

As she watched the dentist checking him over she could feel her heart aching, for despite his awkwardness with her he was such a good boy really, did everything the dentist told him and gazed up at the man with such wide and fearful eyes that she wanted desperately to hug him. Right now though, that would be the last thing he'd want, and even though his shirt was hanging out and his socks were falling down when he got out of the chair, she didn't dare to point it out.

'Do you feel like going to the juice bar?' she asked, as they got back in the car. Until lately this had been a Saturday morning treat when the three of them went grocery shopping together.

'No, Dad's not here,' he said sullenly.

Ellen nodded and watched him climb up onto his booster seat for the return journey to school.

'How about giving Spot ten minutes in the dog park?' she said.

This time he nodded, and though it was going to make her horribly late for a meeting with the set designers, and then in turn for a script session with Tom, the house was on the way back to school, and if need be she'd take Spot on to the office with her rather than use up any valuable time returning him home.

The minute Spot got sight of the other dogs he was off on his usual mad social round, plunging right into the heart of a big-dog group and wagging his tail so hard it almost lifted his back legs off the ground. Ellen waved to a couple of people they knew, then carried her phone over to one of the picnic tables and began making the long list of returns Maggie had given her just before she'd left. She was about to start on the fourth call when she noticed Robbie sitting at another table, head bowed, legs dangling and looking for all the world as though he'd been abandoned.

Quickly clicking off the line, she picked up Spot's lead and walked over to where Robbie was. The park was surprisingly full for the time of day, with every imaginable breed of dog strutting its stuff around the water trough, running to fetch frisbees and balls, or attempting to hump each other fast before their owners could intervene. It was Spot's overactive libido that had got him into so much trouble in the past, especially as he had no particular care as to the size, sex, or even which end, of the other dog he assailed. Today, however, as though sensing Robbie's despair, he soon came trotting out of the fray and took up position at his young master's feet, where he kept a beady eye on park proceedings.

'Do you want to talk?' Ellen said.

Robbie shook his head.

She waited a moment, then said, 'Well, I feel like you're kind of mad at me, and if you don't tell me what I did, I can't say sorry, can I?'

After a while he mumbled something that she didn't quite catch.

'I didn't hear you,' she said gently.

He started to swing his legs back and forth. 'I want you to go,' he told her.

148

Ellen's heart contracted. 'You mean you want me to leave you here?' she said, knowing that wasn't what he meant.

'No!' he almost shouted. 'I want you to go away and leave me and Spot and Mummy and Daddy alone.'

As her chest tightened Ellen lifted her eyes to the steep hills surrounding the park. It seemed like a different world all of a sudden, remote and impervious to the helplessness she was feeling.

'If you go away then Mummy'll stay,' he declared.

'Oh darling,' Ellen said, 'that's not true. Mummy's got her work . . .'

'It *is* true,' he cried, slamming his hands on the bench. 'You're only saying that because you don't want her to stay.'

Ellen looked at his hurt and angry little face that was so like Michael's, yet so like Michelle's too.

'Who said I didn't want Mummy to stay?' she asked softly.

'You did!' he accused. 'You told Daddy you didn't want Mummy in the same house as you. But Daddy wants her to be there, I know because he told me. And if you went away then Mummy wouldn't have to go back to where Uncle Cavan is, she could stay here with me and Daddy.'

Ellen was at such a loss she barely knew what she was saying. 'But Daddy and I are getting married, sweetheart,' she said. 'You know that and I thought . . .'

'I don't want you to get married,' he raged.

'Did you tell Daddy that?' she asked, wondering if that was the reason Michael had been so distant with her lately – except it wasn't really Michael who was being distant, it was her, but only because she didn't know how to handle this godawful situation with Michelle. 'Did you tell Daddy you didn't want me and him to get married?' she asked again.

He shook his head, and her heart went out to him as

she realized he was probably afraid to say it to Michael, because his five-year-old instincts were already telling him that Michael wouldn't do as he wanted.

'Did you talk to Daddy at all about the way you're feeling?' she said.

'He just says he loves you, but that's because you're there and Mummy isn't. If Mummy was there all the time he'd love Mummy, not you.'

So he had said something to Michael, but probably not much by the sound of it, which meant that the cruel perversity of all this was that she was the only one he felt close enough to confide in, and the only one he trusted enough to give him what he wanted. Of course, that was much too complex for him to understand: all he knew was what his little boy's logic was telling him, that she was the reason his mummy and daddy weren't married. And for all she knew he was right, because seeing Michael and Michelle together these past few days had shown her how very close they still were. In fact, she suddenly realized, it was probably seeing that closeness that had given Robbie the confidence to speak up now.

'Come on,' she said, standing up, 'let's get you back to school.'

Chapter 9

Even though she'd seen him earlier, when he'd called into the office on his way from the airport, Sandy still felt a jolt in her heart the moment she spotted Michael sitting at a corner table studying the menu. Knowing he was waiting for her was so pleasing she just couldn't keep down her smile, and she felt tremendously glad that she'd devoted so much time and care to getting ready for the evening.

After handing her coat to the hostess she followed the maître d' across the quiet, subtly-lit restaurant, leaving a lingering trail of perfume in her wake, and causing a few heads to turn to watch the striking young woman with neatly-cut, ash-blonde hair and appealingly childlike features pass by. As always she was wearing high heels to raise her from her meagre five foot four, as she hated being towered over by anyone, especially other women. In Michael's honour she was wearing a stylishly low-cut bronze satin dress, with thin gold chain straps over her shoulders and a hemline that was short enough to show her slender legs to advantage, but not too short to invite a wrong impression. In fact, the dress wasn't dissimilar to the one Ellen had worn the night she and Michael had first met – a night Sandy remembered well and would like nothing more than to forget.

'Hi,' she said, as the maître d' pulled out a chair for her to sit down.

Michael looked up, and quickly got to his feet. 'Wow,' he said, 'you look sensational.'

Pleasure eddied through her, causing a faint colour to rise to her cheeks, as she put her purse on the table and sat down.

'Can I bring madame an aperitif?' the maître d' offered.

Sandy looked at Michael.

'Bring us two glasses of champagne,' he said.

The maître d' bowed and went away.

'I thought we'd celebrate the Deighton investment,' Michael said. 'You've really saved the day with that one, and I honestly can't thank you enough.'

She smiled. 'It only came through this morning,' she told him. 'I was afraid we might not make it in time. How are things looking your end now?'

'They're improving. We should have a much better cash flow by the middle of next month, when the money's due to come in from Granger Fielding. Did I tell you how the old man called me up and told me straight out that if it weren't for Richard Conway he wouldn't touch me with a barge pole?'

Sandy laughed. 'Well, there's nothing like giving it to you straight,' she commented.

Michael's eyes were glinting with irony. 'I've got to tell you,' he said, 'that old man Fielding's not the only one who feels that way. The Yanks truly don't like giving out money to anyone who doesn't have a US track record. They're really making me sweat over this.'

'But you're getting there.'

'Yeah, I'm getting there. Miramax have a soft spot for the Brits, and I've got a situation going with them and Fox Searchlight right now that has them both vying for a US distribution deal. Obviously that's good news, but the problem is, these things take time and we're in need of the cash right now.'

'So how much did Granger Fielding come up with?' she asked.

'Three and a half million. Which means we're still looking for another ten, minimum. Twelve would be better. Mark Bergin's getting some promising noises out of his guys in Sydney, he tells me, and Chris is doing well in New York.'

'And I'm off on a whistle-stop tour of Europe next week,' she added, 'for meetings with everyone from BMW to Moët and Chandon. So I think we should remain optimistic for twelve.'

Michael smiled, and after the waiter had put down their drinks he raised his glass to hers. 'Here's to you,' he said softly. His eyes were looking closely into hers, and as she felt the subtle change in mood she smiled too, and watched him sip his drink.

'Craig told me about Maurice,' he said. 'I'm sorry.'

Sandy lowered her eyes, embarrassed and surprised by the lump that rose in her throat. The humiliation she had suffered at the funeral would take a long time to forget, but she'd gone for Maurice, not for the relatives who were so afraid he'd left everything to her. They would find out soon enough, though how she'd managed to stop herself screaming it in their faces when they'd treated her so shabbily and called her such cruel names, she still didn't know. She looked at Michael and realized this was the first time he'd ever mentioned Maurice.

'He was an unusual man,' she said, then laughed. 'I don't suppose you'd argue with that, when he was responsible for backing my efforts to finish you off.'

Michael's eyebrows rose.

'You'd have liked him,' she said. 'He was very unassuming, asked for nothing, but always knew how to get what he wanted.'

'Then I hope he taught you well,' Michael said, a light of mischief in his eyes.

Sandy's heart tightened as she wondered if that was some kind of invite. Then she grinned as he stifled a yawn. 'No matter how boring you're finding me already,' she said, 'I'm going to put that down to jet lag. Now tell me, how's your mother? Did she get my flowers? Forget it, I expect she got so many you'd never know.'

Michael chuckled. 'Believe me, she got them. She made me sit there and listen to every blessed card she'd received and sniff every flower she'd stuffed in a vase, and all to make me suffer for being the only living person in her vast sphere of family, friends and acquaintances who forgot to send some. Ellen, of course, who should have sent some with me, gets no blame for this, because Ellen can do no wrong in my mother's eyes, whereas I have yet, in my miserable thirty-four years, to do anything right.'

Sandy laughed. 'What about Cavan? Did he manage to send some from Pakistan?'

'He didn't have to, Michelle did it for him.'

Sandy smiled. Though there was no hint of a criticism that Ellen hadn't done the same for him, she couldn't help wondering if there was one there all the same. 'Did you see Zelda today?' she said. 'She tells me Michelle's in LA. That must be nice for Robbie.'

At the mention of his son Michael's eyes instantly softened. 'He's obviously missed her a lot more than we'd realized,' he said. 'He's really happy to see her. I just hope it's not going to be too much of a problem when she goes back.'

'When will that be?'

'The middle of next week. But then she'll be back again for the wedding, so it won't be too long for him to wait. She's staying with him while we're on honeymoon. I think my mother's intending to be there too, so he's going to be thoroughly spoiled, which'll end up making things doubly difficult for me and Ellen when we get back, but I guess we just cross that bridge when we come to it. You're coming, aren't you? To the wedding? You got your invitation?'

Sandy's smile was still in place. 'Yes, I got it,' she said, wondering if he had any idea what it felt like to be sitting there with someone you wanted so much, discussing their upcoming wedding to somebody else. 'And I'll be there. I don't know who's supposed to be running the office, since you've invited us all, but I guess that's another bridge that'll have to be crossed when we come to it.'

As they drank again their eyes remained on each other, until Michael looked down as he put his glass back on the table.

'How are things going with Tom Chambers's script?' she asked.

'Pretty good,' he answered. 'Ellen and Tom are giving it a lot of time now, and Vic Warren's in daily touch by phone or e-mail, so things like minor casting and set design are already well under way.'

'What about the end?' she asked. 'Have they decided what they're going to do about that?'

'There's talk of wrapping it up in LA,' he answered, and grinned as she pulled a face. 'It could work,' he assured her.

'So what's the aim of this film?' she said. 'Is it to bring Rachel's killers to justice? Or is it to get World Wide some awards?'

'Both,' Michael answered without hesitation.

'Did he manage to find out who the killers are?'

'Yes.'

Though she was interested, she knew better than to ask, for the revelation was going to be one of the major publicity hooks when it came time for the movie's release.

'I'd like to see some of the rewrites, if they're available,' she said.

Michael glanced up at the waiter as he approached to take their orders. 'Give us a couple of minutes,' Michael said, opening his menu.

After they'd chosen he looked back at Sandy and said, 'Listen, I'll have to come clean here. I haven't told Ellen yet that I'm going to make you a producer on this, so would you mind keeping it to yourself until I've had a chance to?'

'Of course not,' Sandy assured him. 'But why? Do you think she'll have a problem with it?'

'I don't know,' he answered. Then, clearly wanting to change direction, he said, 'She couriered over the proofs of a publicity package today. I'll bring it into the office tomorrow for you to take a look at. It's good material for potential investors, should help when you go to Europe next week.'

Sandy was surprised. 'A publicity package?' she said. 'Does that mean you've cast the part of Rachel? Or are we still just going on Conway's name?'

'For the moment, yes we're still going on Conway's name,' he answered. 'But we've cast Rachel, it was just too late to get Michelle's name on to the proofs.'

Sandy's eyes widened. 'Michelle, as in Michelle Rowe?' she said, immediately gaining some insight into the tension she'd sensed between Ellen and Michael over the casting. 'I thought she'd given up acting.'

'She's making an exception for this,' he responded. 'She and Tom are very good friends.'

He was watching her closely, and Sandy realized that he was trying to gauge her opinion on the choice of Michelle, which suggested it might not be quite a done deal yet. However, before she committed she wanted to weigh up precisely how she might benefit from this. It could be she'd be better off siding with Ellen, who was no doubt completely opposed to the idea – and in any other circumstances Sandy would be too, for the mere fact that Rachel was American would have been enough to persuade Sandy that an American actress should play the part. On the other hand – in other words, on a personal level – if this was causing a rift between

Michael and Ellen, which it had to be, then she certainly didn't want to find herself in Ellen's camp should things start turning ugly.

'Would I be right in thinking,' she said, deciding she should have Ellen's position completely spelled out before she moved on, 'that Ellen isn't happy with Michelle's casting?'

The irony in Michael's eyes was confirmation enough.

'Who's got final say?' she asked.

'Tom. But only for the part of Rachel.'

Sandy smiled and stored that away. 'You gave me the impression a while ago,' she said, 'that Ellen wasn't happy about the project, full stop.'

'Let's say she's had her reservations,' he replied. 'But meeting Tom's helped. He's very persuasive, and there's nothing like coming face to face with someone who's been through what he has to make you change your mind.'

Sandy picked up her glass and stared at it thoughtfully. Though she gave no outward sign of it, her heart was thudding harshly and her nerves were fluttering like crazy. She wasn't even sure she had the courage to do what was in her mind, until, in a voice that she managed to keep perfectly calm, and with a smile that was wholly benign, she heard herself say, 'Well, I suppose when you're as power-hungry as Ellen, it's probably not easy to be *told* what your next big project's going to be. I'm sure she'd much rather have been consulted.' She laughed. 'And in charge.'

Michael was frowning. 'Power-hungry?' he echoed. 'Is that how you see her?'

Sandy's eyes came quickly up to his. 'Oh, well, perhaps I've got it wrong,' she said. 'It was just the impression I got when we first met. I don't suppose I've seen so many signs of it since, except over this, of course. But then I'm not there every day, so I don't really know what's going on.' She laughed and waved a hand. 'And who am I to accuse someone of being power-hungry, when I've done the kind of things I have to get where I am.'

He was still looking pensive, which surprised Sandy, for she hadn't expected him to take the bait quite so readily. But he had, and for the moment it seemed he wasn't going to let go.

'Tell me, what gave you that impression?' he asked.

Sandy pondered for a moment, then said, 'Well, I suppose it was what she said about Ted Forgon. You know, the day she and I had lunch at the Café Roma in LA. God, that was ages ago now, before you were even living over there.'

'I remember the occasion,' he said.

Sandy smiled. 'Well, I don't know what Ellen told you about that lunch,' she said, 'but I don't imagine it's any secret now that she was the one who told me what stage you were all at in setting up World Wide. It was how I was able to give Ted Forgon what he needed to buy into the company.'

Michael's face was looking strained. 'Ellen gave you that information?' he said, clearly bemused, but not yet angry. 'I don't understand. Why would she do that?'

'Oh God, I thought you knew all this,' Sandy said.

'No,' he corrected her, 'but I'd like to.'

Sandy looked trapped, as though she really didn't want to go on. 'Well, to be honest,' she began, 'I wasn't really sure why she did it myself at the time. It was only later, when I really thought about it, that it started to make sense. It was her way of getting you to go to LA. She knew if Forgon got himself a majority share in World Wide that you'd fight to get it back, and that you could only do that if you were there on the ground. So she had to arrange for Forgon to take over, and the best way of doing that was to send me in for her.' Her eyes danced, as though this were merely mischief they were discussing rather than outright betrayal and deceit. 'I've

158

got to admit, she played it brilliantly,' she said, 'and everything was on her side, including the fact that it was *me* who'd invited *her* to lunch, rather than the other way round. I can tell you, I wouldn't mind those kind of breaks whenever I'm trying to manoeuvre things to work in my favour. Oh God, I'm sorry, this really is all news to you, isn't it?' she said.

'You're right, it is,' he confirmed. 'I'm just wondering what made you think she'd have told me.'

Sandy looked incredulous. 'Well, I suppose because you got control back from Forgon virtually the minute you arrived in the States. God only knows how Ellen managed that, but I assumed it was something the two of you had worked out together. There again, why tell you about her involvement when she can heap all the blame on me? I'm sure I'd have done the same in her shoes and I'm sorry now that I even brought it up.'

He said nothing as he absorbed her words, though it was very clear that he didn't like what he was hearing at all.

'Listen,' she said, after a while, 'as you know, I'm the last person Ellen would ever confide in, so I'm only surmising here. I could have it totally wrong. All I know is what she told me over that lunch, and what happened as a result. And let's face it, it all worked out pretty well, so there's no reason to get upset about anything.'

It was a while before Michael's eyes came up to hers. He gazed at her for a few seconds, searching her face, then suddenly he smiled. 'You're right,' he said, 'it did work out, for all of us, including you.'

Sandy laughed with relief. 'Maybe you'll tell me one of these days,' she said, 'exactly how you managed to get back control.'

'Maybe I will,' he said. 'But now, what I want you to tell me is whether or not you've managed to contact Vic Warren.'

Satisfied with the change of subject, Sandy finished

her champagne and updated him on her latest conversation with Vic Warren, who would be flying over to London the following evening with a mass of notes he'd made for script changes, casting, crewing and a hundred other concerns that needed his input. The seeds of Ellen's treachery had been sown: to overwater them now would be simply to drown them. The fact that she was lying bothered her not a bit, for it was her word against Ellen's, and with a certain friction already developing between Ellen and Michael this was unlikely to be dealt with in a particularly rational manner.

The rest of the meal passed in a friendly way, with lots of business to discuss that frequently made them laugh and plunged them into some good-natured banter, as well as seeming to draw them physically closer to each other across the table.

It was after they'd ordered coffee and she'd returned from the Ladies that he unwittingly opened up another channel for her to feed in more doubt about Ellen. Not having seen it coming Sandy knew she must tread carefully, for planting the suggestion that Ellen might have slept with Ted Forgon at some point in her career certainly wasn't the direction Michael was expecting the conversation to take. On the contrary, unless Sandy was greatly mistaken, what he was trying to find out was whether or not *she* had ever slept with Forgon. She was curious to know why he'd be interested in that, but there would be time later to fathom out his motive. For the moment she was happy enough to go the route of misunderstanding.

'You know, I think you're wrong, Michael,' she said, unwrapping the dark chocolate that arrived with her coffee. 'I know there were rumours at the time that Ellen was sleeping with Ted Forgon, but I honestly don't think she did. To be frank, I'm surprised you even suspect it.'

Michael looked at her in amazement. 'No, that's not what I was saying,' he laughed. 'I'm convinced she never slept with him, it's just not her style.'

Sandy smiled. 'Whereas it would be mine,' she said.

He had the good grace to look embarrassed, before saying, 'I'm sorry. I'm not sure how we stumbled onto this subject, but maybe it would be safer to get off it.'

'Whatever you say,' she responded, her eyes shining with mirth. She hadn't felt this good in so long that were there not still a half-bottle of wine on the table, she might have considered herself drunk. 'But plenty of women do use their bodies to get what they want,' she told him. 'Whether it be promotion, a new coat, an exotic holiday, a peaceful life, or simply to make a decision go their way.' She gave that a moment to sink in, thinking now of Tom Chambers and the casting of Michelle – a decision Ellen would very much like to go her way. The allusion was probably too subtle for Michael to pick up right now, but it was something she could easily come back to another time. 'Or,' she continued, looking him right in the eyes, 'depending on the man, it could be to achieve unsurpassable pleasure in bed.' She dropped her gaze to his lips, then returned to his eyes. 'Most women want that,' she told him softly.

She hadn't flirted so outrageously since the days she'd been paid to, in truth she'd thought she'd lost the ability, but right now, looking at him across the table and remembering that one night he had made love to her, she was prepared to do almost anything to make it happen again. What was more, from the way he was looking at her, she could tell she had aroused him.

'When do you plan on coming into the office again?' she asked.

'In the . . .' He cleared his throat. 'In the morning,' he answered. He picked up his coffee, and was very quickly back in control. 'I've got a stack of phone calls I need to make. I don't really want anyone to know I'm here though, I won't have time to see them all. If Vic's getting in at five, I'll meet with him at Heathrow so he can fly back again when we've finished. I promised my mother I'd take her out to dinner tomorrow night. Maybe you'd like to join us?'

Sandy's hand stopped in mid-air. She was so stunned that for a moment she couldn't answer. 'Well, yes, I'd love to,' she said, putting her coffee down. 'I'll have to check my diary, but I'm sure I can reschedule if necessary.'

'Good,' he smiled. 'The others are all coming too.'

She had no idea if he knew how badly he had crushed her with that, or even if he'd intended to, but it didn't matter. She'd made sufficient headway tonight in creating some doubt about Ellen; she'd also discovered that she still had the power to turn him on. It was enough for now.

Thanks to a lingering jet lag Michael woke at four in the morning with an erection that was so hard it was almost painful to move. He had no clear recollection what he'd been dreaming of, all he knew was that Ellen wasn't in the bed beside him and he wanted her badly.

He looked at the clock and groaned. Then, remembering it would only be eight in the evening in LA, he pulled on his dressing-gown and went downstairs to get the phone. By the time he returned to the bedroom he was thinking about the suspicion Sandy had put in his mind earlier, that at some point in her career Ellen might have slept with Ted Forgon. He was certain it wasn't true, nor could he make himself believe that Ellen had discussed his plans for World Wide with Sandy at a time when the whole project was so vulnerable, especially not when Ellen had known very well that Sandy was out to finish him. No, he didn't believe any of it, though he could wish it wasn't bothering him the way it was seeming to.

He started to dial their number in LA. He was halfway through when he abruptly rang off. From out of nowhere the way Sandy had looked last night when

162

she'd spoken of women wanting pleasure in bed had come back to him, and for a moment all he could think of was the night he had taken her to his apartment and screwed her half senseless. He'd be lying if he tried to tell himself he didn't want to do it again, it made him hard just to think of it.

But despite how gratifying the whole thing might be, there was also something vaguely disturbing in the way he wanted Sandy. Even though she had changed a great deal since he'd first known her, it was still his basest instincts she appealed to, arousing surges of violence in his lust and a desire to abuse and humiliate her in ways that appalled him even to think of.

Quickly he dialled again. 'Hi darling, it's me,' he said when Ellen answered.

'Michael? What time is it over there?'

'Just after four in the morning,' he answered. 'Jet lag.' He turned onto his side and rested the phone more comfortably into his shoulder. 'I miss you,' he murmured.

'Sorry? What did you say? How's Clodagh?'

'I said I miss you, and Clodagh's just fine. A bit bruised, but she'll live.'

'Did you get any flowers?'

'I did, but they were later than everyone else's so they don't count as much. How's Robbie?'

There was a short silence before she answered. 'I think Michelle's just putting him to bed,' she said. 'Would you like to speak to him?'

'Sure, when I've finished speaking to you.'

'Honey, I'm sorry, but I'm right in the middle of getting changed. I've got a dinner tonight at the Hillcrest. Ted Forgon needs a partner for some function they're having and I said I'd fill in. Oh, and Tom's escorting Michelle tomorrow night at the charity gala, so you don't need to worry about that either.'

Michael's eyes closed. The last thing he wanted was a

fight, so he said, 'Put me onto Robbie if he's awake. If not I'll speak to Michelle.'

Michelle was lying on her bed in the semi-darkness, Robbie beside her and an unfinished book resting on her chest, when Ellen tapped lightly on the half-open door.

'Can I come in?' Ellen said, peering round.

'Sssh, he's asleep,' Michelle whispered.

Ellen looked at Robbie's sleeping face and felt her heart ache. 'It's Michael,' she said, holding up the phone.

'I'll speak to him,' Michelle smiled. 'Suffering with jet lag, is he?'

Ellen nodded and after handing the phone over, she gently smoothed Robbie's face before leaving the room.

'Michael?' Michelle said into the phone.

'Hi, how are you?' he asked.

'Fine. How about you? And Clodagh?'

'We're OK. Robbie asleep?'

'Just. He misses you.'

'I miss him too.'

Michelle paused and wondered if Ellen might be listening outside. 'Michael, we need to talk,' she said softly.

It was a moment before he answered. 'I know,' he said. 'Is he OK?'

'Of course he is. And he loves her, but . . . Look, let's do this when you get back.'

'OK. By the way, good luck tomorrow night. I hear Tom's taking you.'

'It would have been nice if we could've all gone, but it wasn't to be.' She paused, then said, 'I miss you too, Michael. Come back safely.' She waited for him to answer, but he didn't, so she quietly clicked off the line.

Laying the phone down on the bed she turned to look at her son, tracing the gentle curve of his inky dark eyebrows, the small nose, his parted lips, the flush of his cheeks. There was no love in the world to compare to the way she felt about this boy. It was so powerful it could tear her to pieces, so commanding it could swallow her up in its might. If need be she would kill for him, so what in God's name had made her abandon him to the care of another woman?

A single tear rolled across her cheek and dropped onto the pillow. She'd never been able to understand what had made her do it, and not a single day went by that she didn't deeply regret it. But at the time when she and Michael had tried to work things out, it hadn't taken her long to realize they were destined to fail. Michael had loved Ellen and had wanted to be with her, so Michelle had decided to let him go and take Robbie too. She'd felt she owed Michael that, after depriving him of the first four years of their son's life. It was the hardest thing she had ever done, and maybe, if the kind of life she was offering hadn't been so fraught with hardship and danger, she would never have found it in herself to be so noble.

Hearing Ellen call out that she was leaving, she swung her legs off the bed and went to say goodbye. But by the time she reached the sitting-room Ellen had already gone, so, turning off the lights, Michelle returned to her bedroom and lay down again next to Robbie.

She could understand Ellen's resentment of her, God knew she'd feel the same were she in Ellen's shoes, but sadly there was nothing she could do to make Ellen feel any better. After all, Robbie was her son, and none of them could do anything to change that. Nor would she, even if she could, for despite the anguish it was causing her now, there was nothing in this world that could ever make her wish he wasn't hers.

Nor was she ever going to stop loving Michael, despite how deeply she cared for his brother. She hated to admit it, but Cavan was really only a substitute for Michael, and she just didn't want to go on pretending any more. Now all she wanted was for her and Robbie to be with Michael, to be a family as they should be, and would have been, had she not gone off the way she had. But with the wedding only eight weeks away, she just couldn't see how that was ever going to happen.

Chapter 10

'Stop!' Ellen gasped. She was laughing so hard she could barely catch her breath. 'Just stop! I'll never be able to take this scene seriously again.'

'But I'm only doing what's written here on the page,' Tom protested, his grey eyes simmering with humour, and Ellen collapsed again as he mimed the removal and throwing into the air of his head.

'It says here,' he pointed out, '"Chambers tosses his head."' He looked at her and shrugged. 'I'm just trying to give you some idea of how this is going to look when it gets to the screen.'

'Stop it,' she cried, wiping tears from under her eyes. 'Oh, God, what are you doing now?'

He was groping blindly around the floor, as though searching for something. 'It says "Chambers drops his eyes,"' he explained.

Ellen's head fell back as she exploded into laughter again, then she shrieked and swung her legs onto the couch as he began crawling towards her. 'There's nothing about you being on your knees,' she protested.

'Correction. It says "Chambers doggedly pursues his aim."'

Ellen's ribs were aching. 'No more,' she pleaded. 'I'm in pain.'

He sank back on his heels and looked across at her face, eyes bright with tears, cheeks flushed with laughter. 'OK, a definite improvement on the way you came in here,' he decided. 'Because, I've got to tell you, I was pretty scared when you walked in the door. I thought I'd done something *real* bad.'

Ellen's laughter was rising again. 'You know, I kind of like the idea of scaring you,' she teased.

His eyes reflected her humour. 'Oh, you certainly do that,' he said dryly.

She held his gaze for a moment, then, feeling herself starting to blush, she turned back to the script on her lap. The first thing she read was 'Chambers drops his eyes,' and her lips began to tremble again. 'I told you,' she said, 'I'm never going to be able to take this scene seriously now.'

'But it's not a serious scene!'

'It is so! It's the point at which you challenge the editor of the *Washington Post* to print your story about FBI abuses on the Mexican border. *And* to name names.'

'Which has got nothing to do with anything that came after,' he pointed out.

'Not true. It shows us at an early stage how committed you are to your work. It also shows us how things do or don't get coverage in the press. And getting turned down makes you so mad and frustrated it causes your first major fight with Rachel, which in turn convinces her to give up her desk job and join you in the field. So I'd say it's a pretty important scene.'

Chambers was grinning. 'You've got all the answers,' he said, stretching his long legs out on the floor and resting his back against the couch facing hers. 'So, it's an important scene, but the way it's written, it's dumb as hell.'

'That may be so. Excuse me, did you just yawn?' she challenged.

'Who, me?' he replied, still stifling.

She was grinning. 'So how did it go last night?' she asked. 'Did Michelle get through her speech OK?'

'She's a pro,' he answered. 'And it was so brilliantly written, she could hardly fail.'

Since he'd more or less written it for her, Ellen threw a pen at him, which he caught and looked over with some interest.

'What are you doing now?' she demanded.

'Looking at a pen,' he answered, seeming surprised she didn't know.

As her laughter bubbled up again she felt the ease and euphoria of these wonderfully light-hearted moments stealing warmly through her. 'You're in a crazy mood today,' she accused.

His eyes met hers, and feeling her colour rising again she looked away.

'It must have been a good night,' she remarked.

He shrugged. 'It was OK. These things can get a bit dreary, but it was good catching up with old friends.'

'Were there many there?'

'Yeah, a few. Not a good show by the press, which was a shame.'

Ellen's guilt immediately flared, as the publicist they'd hired for the movie had suggested they use the event to get some early coverage for Michelle in the role of Rachel, but Ellen had vetoed the idea. She wondered if Tom or Michelle knew that, though she was pretty sure they didn't. She just hoped to God Michael didn't find out, or it was going to mean yet another fight, which was all they ever seemed to be doing lately.

He'd wanted her to go pick him up from the airport this afternoon, but she'd had this meeting scheduled with Tom, which she might have cancelled had she not still been so angry with Michael for agreeing to escort Michelle to the gala. That he'd been unable to make it in the end didn't matter, it was the fact that he'd agreed to do it in the first place, and hadn't even mentioned it to her. However, she had offered to send a car to meet him, but, just before leaving the office to come here, she'd been informed by Maggie that Michelle was stepping into the breach. It was why she'd been in such a foul mood when she'd arrived, and the fact that she'd also been told that Michelle had gone to get Robbie from school so he could go to the airport too, had infuriated her to such a degree that she still wasn't too sure exactly when she'd be ready to leave here and go home.

'You've gone serious on me again,' Chambers accused.

Ellen's eyes came up to his and she couldn't help but smile.

'I'm not going to ask if you want to talk about it,' he said, 'because you might say yes.'

Ellen spluttered with laughter. 'Do you think we're going to get any work done here today?' she enquired.

'Sure,' he answered. 'You agreed the scene was dumb, so let's talk about what we should change while I open a bottle of wine and pour us both a glass.'

'But it's only . . .' she began, looking at her watch, 'five thirty! My God, I had no idea it had gotten so late. Where did the time go?'

Chambers was at the refrigerator. 'White?' he said, taking out an expensive bottle of Chardonnay.

'I guess I ought to call home to remind someone that Robbie has karate tonight,' she said and, picking up the phone beside her, she got halfway through dialling before cutting herself off. 'Let them sort it out,' she said, as Chambers uncorked the bottle.

'What time's Michael back?' he asked, as he passed her a glass.

'His plane was getting in at three thirty,' she answered, avoiding his eyes as she took her drink. Her heart was starting up an unsteady beat, and she didn't really want to think about why. She couldn't help but wonder, though, if letting him know that Michael was already home was sending signals she wasn't even sure she wanted to send. But whether or not he was picking up on them was impossible to say, as his back was turned while he fixed his own drink.

Sipping her wine, she allowed her eyes to travel the length of his body in a way she'd almost rather die than let him see. But it wasn't the first time she'd looked at him that way, because Matty was right, there really was something about him, and he had such an amazing physique that it was impossible to stop her imagination moving right through his clothes and conjuring up an image that was much more to her liking than it should be.

Lowering her eyes to her glass, she took another sip and wished Matty had never suggested that he might be interested in her, because it had been on her mind a lot since, and she had to admit that were it not for Michael she'd be finding him very hard to resist. But, in truth, no matter how angry she was at Michael, nor how attracted she was to Tom, she loved Michael far too much to put what they had at risk.

'Oh God, here we go again,' she groaned, as her cellphone started to ring. 'If it's Jackie I could be a while.'

It was Jackie Bott, one of the producers, but the call didn't take as long as Ellen expected, as Jackie and the rest of the team were in the process of staking out their new offices over at Paramount. However, she'd barely finished before another call came in from Maggie, then another from the accountants, then another from Billy Christopher. Each conversation turned out to be as hilarious as the next, as Tom kept insisting on joining in and there weren't many on the team who didn't rise to the occasion of his wit.

It was after seven by the time she finally got up to leave. By then they'd managed to hack out half a dozen more scenes and had almost finished the bottle of wine. She knew she'd probably had too much to drive, but she was feeling much more mellow towards Michael now, and a little sorry that she had stayed here so long as another means of punishing him.

171

Chambers walked her to the door, and opening it turned to give her the peck on the cheek that had become their custom. But somehow it didn't quite work, as they both made to lean the same way and entirely by accident their lips touched.

Ellen started to apologize, but as her mouth opened beneath his neither of them pulled away. The desire that suddenly flared through her was so intense it was like a pain, and as his lips lingered on hers she could feel her body's urgent demand for more.

'Sorry,' he said, pulling away.

'No, uh, I'm sorry,' she said, unable to meet his eyes. Then, forcing a smile, 'I'll see you tomorrow, yes?'

'Tomorrow,' he repeated.

She passed him and started down the corridor. 'Uh, tomorrow's Saturday,' she said, turning back.

He nodded and grinned, and rolling her eyes she made like she was firing a gun and went on to the elevator.

Despite the fact it was getting dark by the time she arrived home, the temperature still hadn't dropped below eighty, even in the hills, and the moment she stepped out of her air-conditioned car she could feel the heat smothering her. She had deliberately thought no more about Tom, except to convince herself that it had been nothing more than a moment's aberration and had little, if anything, to do with the real picture of her life. That belonged only to Michael.

As she started towards the house she could feel some nervousness mounting, though she wasn't entirely sure why. Maybe it was because he might be angry with her for not going to the airport, or annoyed that she hadn't called to check he'd got back OK. Of course, he could have called her, and the fact that he hadn't could well be a sign that his mood wasn't good, at least not with her. She guessed he was probably OK with Michelle though:

after all, she'd been there to meet him, and had thought to take their son along too.

Swallowing hard on her resentment, Ellen foraged in her purse for her keys and opened the front door. She hesitated a moment as the sprinklers started up in the rocky flower-beds across the front of the house. It could have been the wine, or it could have been just the fact she had missed him so much, but right then, more than anything else she wanted all this tension to go away and to feel Michael's arms around her as he told her he still loved her every bit as much as she loved him. Even thinking about it brought a lump to her throat, and, making a quick resolve to keep her jealousy and misgivings over Michelle in check, she pushed open the door and went inside.

Robbie was due back from karate any time so she guessed the empty house was down to Michelle, or Michael, or both, having gone to pick him up. She dropped her briefcase outside the study and, half hoping that Michael might be taking a nap after his long flight, she went on through to the bedroom. Though his suitcase was next to the bed, there was no sign of him, so, deciding to take a shower before he got back, she started towards the bathroom. It was a shame, she was thinking, that she couldn't swim naked in the pool and let him find her that way, but with any luck he'd come back in time to join her in the shower.

Hearing a strange noise outside she stopped and frowned, not sure what it was or exactly where it had come from. She turned round, feeling glad that she hadn't switched on the lights, instead allowing those from the garden to illuminate the room. That way, if there was an intruder, she could see, but hopefully not be seen.

Her heart was beating fast as she moved tentatively towards the window. The security system was off, but there was a phone next to the bed, and if there really was someone outside in the garden she stood a good chance of escaping through the front before they managed to get in. But there was no sign of anyone. The shadows were still, the pool was empty, and all the windows appeared to be closed.

She was about to turn back into the room when she suddenly noticed two half-empty glasses on one of the tables next to the pool. And then a horribly familiar movement caught her eye and as she looked deeper into the shadows she saw Michael's and Michelle's naked, moonlit bodies making fast, urgent love on one of the thickly padded loungers.

For a long and agonizing moment Ellen couldn't move. She simply stood there, staring, unseen in the darkness, unthought-of in the deceit. In those few, mindless seconds, she told herself it wasn't Michael she was watching, it was someone else. Then she thought it was Michael, but that she was dreaming. It was a nightmare and she'd wake up any second. She even thought that if she carried on into the bathroom, as though she hadn't seen it, it would be like it had never happened.

Then she started to shake, and seconds later some of the horror of what this meant began to reach her. She tried to resist it, to push it away as though it could be erased by sheer will of denial. Her head began to swim. She looked around and felt so strange and liquid inside she thought she might faint. She moved towards the bathroom then turned away. She barely knew what she was doing as she returned to the sitting-room, picked up her briefcase and went out of the front door.

As she got into her car she had no clear idea where she was going. She guessed it must be to Matty's. She was numb, unable to connect her thoughts to the pain, or the betrayal to belief. The image of their intimately entwined bodies was trying to take over her mind, but she closed it out. It was too much to deal with. The devastation of her dreams, the total crushing of her heart, were a reality she was unable to face.

She turned into Benedict Canyon and the car rocked as she took the corner too fast. She pressed a foot on the brake and slowed right down. It was as if, by doing that, she might slow the beat of her heart and decelerate the rise of her panic. The road twisted down over the hill-side, cutting a route in the darkness between the huge, glossy mansions of movie stars and moguls. Palm fronds etched black across the face of the moon, spotlights glowed from porticoed porches, traffic sped past her. She reached Sunset and drove on to Santa Monica. Minutes later she was heading along Melrose to Doheny. The streets were so familiar; but the lights seemed dazzling as a strange, enervating emotion engulfed her. It was as though she were driving through a space that had no connection with time; that had lost its recognizable features of normality. The edges of her mind were blurred, the feelings inside her were like a force that had detached itself from her soul and was seeking to devastate her heart.

She left her car with the valet and rode up to the fourteenth floor. Her heart was thumping, all her senses, as distant and alien as they seemed, were now honed on what she was doing. She had left the world that she knew and was walking into another that would lead her along paths she was afraid to tread, but was refusing to resist.

'Hi,' she said as Chambers opened the door, and she heard herself laugh at his surprise.

'Did you forget something?' he asked, clearly bemused.

'No.' She smiled.

He watched her walk past him, then he closed the door and followed her inside.

She turned to look at him, her eyes slowly scanning his face, until they finally came to rest on his lips. She felt no need of words, for the air between them was suddenly thick with the desire that had overcome them earlier, and the fire in her loins was a power she had no wish to control. She knew he could read her thoughts, could feel him picking up her need and silently she willed him to use it, even abuse it, any way he saw fit.

Neither of them moved, until finally she began to unfasten the buttons of her shirt. His eyes remained on hers as she peeled the fabric from her skin and let it fall to the floor. Then she removed her bra and let that fall too. He looked at her breasts, taking in their full, creamy smoothness, the large, tight buds of her nipples, moving his eyes over them lingeringly, caressingly, then returning them to hers. She began to unzip her trousers, but moving forward he stopped her. And, taking over, he undressed her himself, while kissing her mouth, deeply, erotically, demandingly, before making a descent over her body to the aching moistness between her legs.

She moaned softly as his tongue sent sensation after sensation flying through her, then she watched as he undressed himself. His body was as large and powerful as she'd expected, his arousal was immense. She moved into his arms and opened her mouth to his tongue. Then slowly she slid down his body, kissing his neck, his shoulders, until reaching for his penis she took him deep into her mouth.

'Oh Christ,' he moaned as her fingers raked his legs, found his balls and dug hard into his buttocks. He sank back against the wall, allowing her to bite him, suck him, squeeze him, until he could bear no more. Quickly he pulled her to her feet, scooped her up in his arms and carried her through to the bedroom.

He laid her down on the bed, then stood over her, gazing at her wild chestnut hair spread out on the pillows, her beautiful mouth so soft and red and inviting. Then he looked at her body, and the way her legs were opening to let in his eyes. He leaned over her and gently inserted his fingers. 'I've wanted to do this since the moment I saw you,' he whispered.

She looked up at him, then her eyes fluttered closed as he began to move his fingers back and forth.

'Are you sure this is what you want?' he asked.

'Yes, I'm sure,' she responded. Desire was pulling through her with such a force that even the thought of him entering her was arousing her to a point where she'd never be able to turn back, and as he lay over her she opened her legs wide ready to receive him. And then he was there, pushing into her, filling her, pulling her to him, and plunging the huge, commanding power of his erection to the very heart of her.

His mouth found hers and his tongue moved into her too. His movements were so skilled that as he played her she could feel her entire body giving way to sensation. He knew what she wanted, where to touch her, and when to increase his motion so that she cried out in shock and rapture. He held her to him, pressing her to his chest, and carrying her to a place that she couldn't avoid. Then he was moving there with her, holding her tighter and tighter as he rammed himself into her and felt the harshly breaking spasms of her climax gripping him like a soft, hungry mouth.

A while later she sank into the bed and he lay over her, his heartbeat pounding against her, his penis still hard and not yet ready to leave her. Her head was turned away, but he could feel her breath on his hand, then the wetness of her tears. He held her closer, then let her go as, sobbing, she pulled herself away and got up from the bed.

'I'm sorry,' she gasped, 'I'm so sorry . . .'

'Ellen . . .'

'No, don't say anything.' She was crying so hard it wasn't easy to speak. 'I should never have come back here. I shouldn't have done this. I wasn't . . . I wasn't thinking straight . . .'

'Ellen, listen . . .'

'No. You don't understand,' she sobbed. 'Michael and Michelle . . . I saw them . . . Oh God, I should never have done this to you.' She looked at him and a sudden rage and confusion began to tear her apart inside. 'Why do you want her here?' she pleaded. 'Why does she have to be the one to play Rachel? She's ruining my life. She's taking Michael and Robbie . . . Oh God . . .' She looked frantically around the room as though trying to find a way out of her pain. 'I have to go,' she choked.

'Ellen! Wait!' he cried as she ran into the other room and began pulling on her clothes.

'No, no, don't touch me,' she begged as he came in after her. 'I didn't mean for this to happen. I love Michael. Please understand that. It's Michael I love.' Then the memory of him on the lounger with Michelle suddenly swamped her and she almost collapsed. 'He still loves Michelle,' she sobbed as fresh tears streamed down her face. 'I saw them together . . . He was . . . They were . . .'

'It's OK,' he said, grabbing her shoulders. 'Just take a breath. That's it. Now, are you telling me you found him with Michelle? Making love to Michelle? Is that what you're saying?'

Ellen nodded and closed her eyes as the pain seared through her. 'Make her go away, Tom. Please! Please!' she begged. 'Let someone else play Rachel. Oh God, what am I saying? It's not going to stop him. Nothing is. They've got Robbie. He's holding them together and . . . I can't bear it.' She covered her face with her hands. 'What have I done?' she choked. 'Oh God, what have I done?'

'It's all right. No-one need ever know,' he assured her. 'Ellen! Are you listening to me?'

'I'm sorry,' she said. 'I've got to go. Please forgive me. Please try to forget I ever came back here tonight,' and before he could stop her she'd grabbed up her purse and was running out of the room.

By the time she arrived at Matty's the pain and horror was taking her over completely. Her car phone kept ringing, but she didn't pick up. She was too afraid to speak to Michael, and too ashamed to speak to Tom. It was as though her entire life had suddenly plunged into the depths of a nightmare with no possible way out.

'My God! What happened to you?' Matty cried as she opened the door. 'You look terrible.'

'I walked in on Michael and Michelle,' Ellen answered, going past her to the kitchen. 'Where's the wine? I've got to have a drink. Are you on your way out?'

'Yes, but it can wait,' Matty responded. 'What do you mean, you walked in on Michael and Michelle? Like, they were . . . ?'

'Yes,' Ellen confirmed. 'Next to the pool. They didn't know I was there. They still don't know.'

'Michael called here earlier, looking for you.'

Ellen's heart contracted as she turned to face her. 'He was looking for me?' she said, holding on to the words as though they were some kind of lifeline. 'What time was it?'

Matty shrugged. 'I don't know. About an hour ago, I guess. Pour me one of those. I'll just make a quick call then I'm at your disposal.'

Ten minutes later they were sitting either end of the sofa, drinks in hand and the total travesty of the past two hours now fully revealed. Matty's face was pale with shock, while Ellen looked at her and wanted only to die.

'I don't know what to do, Matty,' she said. 'I mean, I can't go back home, not while Michelle's there, and how the hell am I ever going to face Tom again?'

'Well, I guess we'd better deal with first things first,' Matty responded, 'and that's where you're going to spend tonight. It'll have to be here, apart from anything else you're in no fit state to get back in a car, but you'll

179

have to call Michael and let him know where you are.'

Ellen's eyes closed as the dread of speaking to him closed around her heart.

'When does Michelle leave?' Matty asked.

'The day after tomorrow. Or that's when she's scheduled to go. Things may have changed by now. Oh God, Matty, I was so afraid something like this would happen, and now it has I've gone and made it so much worse. What the hell was I thinking? What was I trying to prove?'

'It's not so abnormal to do what you did,' Matty informed her. 'You were probably in shock, or denial. Does Tom know about Michael and Michelle? Did you tell him?'

Ellen nodded. 'After we made love I just went to pieces. I made such a fool of myself, but yes, I told him.'

'Must have done wonders for his ego,' Matty murmured. 'Anyway, do you think he's likely to tell Michael what happened – between the two of you?'

Ellen shook her head. 'He said he wouldn't.' Then suddenly she stiffened. 'Oh God, Matty,' she breathed. 'I've got to speak to him. I don't want him to tell Michael I know about him and Michelle either.'

'Why?' Matty asked as Ellen snatched up the phone.

'I don't know. I guess because everything's so complicated and I need time to think.' She asked for Tom's room number, then passed the phone to Matty. 'You do it,' she said. 'I know I'm a coward, but I can't face speaking to him again yet.'

Matty took the phone and put it to her ear. 'Hi,' she said when Chambers answered. 'It's Matty Shelby here, Ellen's cousin.'

'Hi Matty,' he said. 'Is Ellen with you?'

'Yes,' she answered. 'She's here.' She paused, then said, 'Try to understand, she doesn't feel up to speaking to you right now, but she wanted me to ask you . . . Well, if you speak to Michael . . . She doesn't want him to know that she walked in on him and Michelle, so would you mind . . .?'

'Tell her I'll do whatever she wants,' he responded. 'How is she?'

'Kind of shaken up, but she'll be OK.'

'Michael's looking for her,' he said. 'He called here about fifteen minutes ago. I told him we'd been working all that time and she'd just left, so he's going to be expecting her home pretty soon.'

'OK. I'll tell her. And thanks.'

Ellen listened as Matty relayed what had been said. She felt sickeningly light-headed, displaced, unconnected, bewildered and afraid. She wanted Michael so desperately it was like she was drowning. She belonged wherever he was, not here where he wasn't. She wanted the clocks turned back, the last scenes of her life unplayed out, the terror of her future never to come into being. 'He just got back today,' she said, pressing her fingers to her eyes. 'I should have gone to the airport, then none of this would have happened.' She looked up at Matty's face. 'How can I tell him I'm staying here for the night when he's only just got back? What excuse can I give?'

Matty was at a loss.

'I'll have to tell him that I've decided to stay here until Michelle goes,' Ellen said finally. 'It's going to make things worse . . .' She laughed bitterly. 'How much worse can they get? And for all I know it'll be what he wants, me out of the way so they can all be a family again.' She turned to look out at the night and by the time she turned back her eyes were submerged in hopelessness and pain. 'I don't suppose there'll be a wedding now,' she said, barely able to get the words past the terrible ache in her heart.

'OK, don't let's start jumping to conclusions,' Matty chided. 'We don't know what really went on there tonight. Nor do we . . .'

'Matty! They were making love!' Ellen broke in. 'What more do we need to know?'

'All I'm saying is sometimes these things, well, they just happen. They don't mean anything, they just . . .'

'No, Matty,' Ellen said. 'The woman's Robbie's mother, so whichever way you look at it, it means something.'

They sat quietly for a while, both absorbing the irrefutable truth of the last words.

'You know what I keep thinking,' Ellen said after a while. 'I keep thinking that he wanted me to find out. That something in him wanted me to walk in and find them like that.'

'Oh come on!' Matty protested.

'But he knew I'd be home any time,' Ellen insisted, 'so he had to know what a risk he was running, and they were right there, next to the pool. They weren't even in her bedroom where I might never have found them.'

'But why would he want you to know? It doesn't make any sense.'

'It does if he wants us to break up,' Ellen answered.

Not sure how to argue that, Matty fell silent again.

Ellen looked at her and felt the pain of what was happening plunge to the very depths of her heart. She'd so desperately wanted Matty to protest, to point out how she had got it wrong and how everything was going to turn out all right. But Matty couldn't, and as the far-reaching effects of the past two hours started to close in on her it was as though she was being swallowed into a vacuum of despair.

'Why did I go back to the hotel?' she said, almost to herself. 'Why the hell did I do that?' She looked at Matty. 'I keep wondering was it really a tit for tat, or was there something much deeper and more calculating that was driving me, something I'm not really in touch with?'

'What do you mean?' Matty asked.

Ellen shook her head. 'I'm not sure,' she answered. 'I

guess I'm just thinking about all the strange and frightening things that go on in the subconscious, things we're not even aware of . . . Like Michael wanting me to find him with Michelle, like me running to Tom . . .' She paused for a moment, then getting up and going to the window she said, 'If Michael wants out of our relationship then it could mean the end of everything for me – or certainly as far as this movie's concerned. So was there something in me that knew that, and made me go to Tom in an effort to get the movie out of Michael's hands and into mine? At least then I'd have something . . .' She turned back to Matty. 'Something he wants as much as I want him. Maybe I could use it to bring him back to me.'

Matty was looking at her with narrowed, baffled eyes. 'Is that what you think?' she said. 'That you'd do something like that?'

Ellen shrugged. 'I think I just did,' she answered. 'But I don't know if I meant to.' She sighed deeply and her breath shook on a sob. 'I had dinner with Ted Forgon the other night,' she said. 'I told him what was going on with the movie, you know, about the casting and Michelle playing the part of Rachel, and you know what he said? He told me to get Tom on my side. There was no point working on Michael, he said, Tom was the one to give me what I wanted, so I had to do what I could to change his mind.' She looked at Matty with a grim, almost baleful smile. 'Maybe that's why I did it,' she said. 'Maybe it was always in my mind to sleep with him in order to get what I wanted, and finding Michael with Michelle gave me all the justification and excuses I needed.'

'This isn't you talking,' Matty said. 'You're in post-trauma shock and analysing your motives like this is only going to screw you up even more. I think you should get on the phone to Michael now and tell him where you are.'

183

Ellen's heart lurched, but even as she recoiled from the prospect of speaking to him, she was longing for him with a desperation that felt it might explode from her heart. It all seemed so wrong, so utterly out of kilter with their lives and how very deeply they loved each other. In just over seven weeks they were supposed to be married. He had wanted that so much. The honeymoon was arranged. The church was booked. All their families' flights were reserved. They couldn't back out now, and surely to God they didn't want to. Despite what had happened she couldn't make herself believe he didn't love her any more, even though there was every chance he didn't. But she didn't want to consider that, she wanted only to see his eyes as they gazed deep into hers, to feel his arms around her, as in her heart she relived the joy and laughter they had shared, the intimacy, the dreams, the power and strength of their love. It wasn't all over. It couldn't be. They were so much a part of each other's lives now, had built so much, come so far. They would get past this, they had to, because neither of them wanted the alternative.

Her head went down as she felt herself slipping into the comforting realms of denial, but even there she could find no escape from the pain. It was filling her up, crushing her, scaring her. Even if she could she didn't want to take the movie away from him, she wanted to make it with him, and if it meant having Michelle in the lead she'd live with it, just as long as they stayed together.

She was about to pick up the phone when it suddenly rang. She looked at Matty and felt her heart begin a slow, fearful throb as Matty reached for the receiver.

'Hello?' Matty said.

'Matty, it's Michael again. I'm really worried about Ellen. Tom says she left the Four Seasons almost an hour ago, but she's not answering her phone. Has she called you since we spoke?'

184

Matty's eyes went to Ellen. 'She's right here,' she said, 'I'll pass you over.'

Ellen's face was deathly pale as she took the phone. 'Hello?' she said.

'Darling, are you OK?' he said. 'I've been going half out of my mind wondering where you are. Are you coming home?'

Tears were stinging Ellen's eyes at the love and confusion in his voice. 'Honey, I've . . . I've had a little too much wine to drive,' she said. 'I think I better stay the night with Matty.'

'I'll come and get you,' he said.

'No. Don't do that.'

'Ellen, I've missed you. I want to see you.'

Her throat was locked with emotion, and though she wanted to scream at him for what he had done, she also desperately wanted to carry on as though it had never happened.

'I want to see you too,' she whispered, 'but Michael . . .'

'Yes?' he said when she didn't continue.

She looked out at the starry night sky and envisaged him standing in their study, his belovedly handsome face creased with concern. 'Honey, I think it's better if I stay with Matty until Michelle leaves. Please don't think I'm trying to pick a fight,' she rushed on as he started to protest, 'I just think it would be a good idea for you three to spend some time together. I'll see you at the office.'

'Ellen, I can't agree to this,' he said. 'I want to see you, *now*.'

'No, Michael,' she said. 'Please, just do as I ask and don't insist I come home until after Michelle has gone. Is she still leaving the day after tomorrow?'

'Yes.'

'Then it's not long to wait, is it?' She paused. 'Do it for Robbie,' she said. 'Let him have some time with his mommy and daddy.'

He was silent, and Ellen could feel her heart breaking

as she tried to figure out what he was thinking. He had to be wondering if she knew what had happened, guilt alone would make him think that. But short of asking her right out there was nothing he could say, and the fact that he didn't argue any further was a horrible confirmation that what she had seen really had taken place. But now she was just as guilty as he was, for she had made love with another man and were he ever to find out about that it would be an end to his friendship with Tom – and how the hell could they carry on with the movie if that were to happen? Though somehow they'd have to, because with so much investment already in place, or spent, there was no backing out either.

'Do you have a breakfast meeting in the morning?' he asked.

'No.'

'Then meet me at seven thirty in your office. I'll bring coffee and bagels.'

She said nothing.

'Ellen?'

'Yes?'

'I love you.'

'I love you too,' she whispered, and barely able to hold back the tears she abruptly ended the call. 'Then why did you screw her, you bastard?' she sobbed. 'Why the hell did you do it if you love me so much?' She turned to look at Matty. 'I don't even have the luxury of getting mad at him,' she raged, 'not unless I want him to know I'm as guilty as he is.'

Matty sat quietly, waiting for her to calm down. It was a while before she spoke. 'I was just wondering,' she said, 'you know, about Tom, and what he was like? I mean, he's kind of cute and . . . All right, I'm sorry, I should never have asked,' she finished hastily as Ellen looked at her in disbelief.

A few seconds ticked by.

'I just had the feeling that he'd be kind of good,' Matty said, 'but no big deal.'

'OK, he was,' Ellen confessed. 'But it wasn't like it is with Michael.'

'Did he make you come?'

'I don't *know*.'

'Well you were there, weren't you?'

'OK, yeah, I guess he did. But none of this is relevant, Matty. It's only Michael who counts.'

'As far as you're concerned. And as far as he's concerned you're the only one who counts. But Michelle and Tom have feelings too. One of them could be seriously in love with one of you guys.'

A cold dread opened up in Ellen's heart. 'I hope to God it's not Michelle,' she said. 'If it is, then there's every chance this could happen again.'

'And if it's Tom?'

Ellen sat with that for a while, then finally raised her eyes to Matty's.

'If he is in love with you, you could use it to persuade him out of casting Michelle,' Matty said, slightly awed by the machiavellian slant to her own suggestion.

Ellen's eyes widened. 'In favour of you?' she said.

Matty shrugged. 'If Michelle's no longer in the running for Rachel, then as far as I can see it, we can both only win. Better still, after what he did tonight, I can't see Michael putting up much of a fight to keep her. Not if it's you he still wants, which it certainly seems to be.'

Ellen was thoughtful again, then finally shook her head. 'I know what you're saying,' she responded, 'but I could never use Tom like that.' Then her eyes came back round to Matty as she added, 'Except I already might have.'

Chapter 11

There were now only three weeks to go before the wedding and though there wasn't a single shred of doubt in Michael's mind about how much he loved Ellen, or how much he wanted her to be his wife, he wished to God they weren't having to go through all this fuss. The main problem was the religious orientation of both their families, meaning that there was just no way they could avoid the church, the motherly input, the endless list of guests, or the thousand and one other things that went into making up the crushingly expensive circus of a Catholic wedding.

Still, apart from being rushed off their feet, and having far too little time to spend together, they seemed to be coping with it all, and whatever it was that had forced Ellen to spend a couple of days with Matty before Michelle had returned to Asia didn't appear to have left any lasting damage. At least he didn't think it had, but in truth it was hard to tell when there was so much going on around them. Occasionally he got the sense that Ellen was avoiding him, but then, during the times they did manage to spend together, she was as loving and receptive as ever, unless she was putting on an act. But she seemed excited about the wedding, and kept insisting how much she was looking forward to the honeymoon and being able to relax and spend two whole weeks just enjoying each other.

It was of course what he wanted too, but whether it was guilt that was taking the edge off his own excitement, or whether it was the way Ellen seemed to be putting on an act, he couldn't really say. All he knew was that something wasn't right. Of course, there was nothing like a guilty conscience to breed paranoia, so maybe it was all in his head, and as her oddness of behaviour had only started about a week ago, it was easy to persuade himself that it had nothing to do with Michelle at all.

But it wasn't easy living the lie, unable to explain why he'd done what he had, or to swear it would never happen again. Though nothing would ever induce him to confess, when the only one it would really hurt was Ellen. Of course it would never have happened if she'd come to the airport that day, for there would have been neither the opportunity, nor the inclination. Not that it was her fault, things had just turned out that way, but there was no doubt that he'd been seriously pissed off when he'd discovered that it was a meeting with Chambers that had taken priority.

Sure he wanted the script in shape, but he wasn't unaware of the way those two flirted with each other, and it wasn't something he liked too much. He'd never said anything, because the last thing he wanted was to come on like some paranoid, insecure jackass, but there was no getting away from the fact that that was partly what had driven him to make love to Michelle that night, but only partly – and though he really didn't like to think about it at all, he couldn't help wondering what had driven Michelle.

At first he'd thought it was something that had just happened, one of those situations that had arisen and they had both got carried away. But he was far from being certain about that now, not only because of what had been going on in his own mind at the time, but because of the whole way it had come about.

After Michelle and Robbie had collected him from the airport they'd returned to the house, and almost immediately he had gone out again to take Robbie to his karate lesson. Michelle had stayed behind and when he'd returned she was swimming in the pool.

'Hi,' she'd called, as he'd come out onto the patio. 'Any chance of a drink?'

Feeling in need of one too, he'd gone back inside to mix two large Martinis. Despite the darkness and being so high in the hills, it was as hot as hell, so when he took the drinks outside and Michelle suggested he take a dip too, he stripped down to his boxers and dived in with her.

As they swam they talked, but his mind was barely on what they were saying, for he was thinking about Ellen and just exactly what she and Chambers might be doing down there in the privacy of Chambers's hotel room. The fact that she was so late getting back, and that she hadn't bothered to call either, was making him think the worst.

'Mmm, that feels so much better,' Michelle said, climbing up the steps of the pool and reaching for a towel. She was wearing a black one-piece bathing suit, cut high on the leg, and plunging almost to the waist at the front. She had always had an excellent body and Michael couldn't help noticing just how good she looked as she strode over to where he had left their drinks.

'You look tense,' she smiled as he came to join her.

'I guess I've got a lot on my mind,' he answered, picking up his drink and going to sit on one of the loungers. 'Do you want to talk about Robbie?'

'Not now,' she said. 'You're too tired.'

A few minutes ticked by. Even the sounds of the night seemed to be stilled by the heat.

'If you don't mind, I'm going to take my swimsuit off,' Michelle said.

Her words were like an instant charge through his

190

body, though he neither spoke nor moved. He knew this was a situation he shouldn't be getting into, but instead of forcing himself to go inside he merely stared down at his glass and listened as she rolled the tight wet lycra down over her body.

Still he didn't look at her, for he knew only too well how beautiful she was, and how easy it would be for him to give in to the demands of his own body.

It was only as she moved behind him and began to rub his back that he started to speak, but even then all he said was, 'We shouldn't be doing this.'

'Sssh,' she whispered, pressing her fingers into his shoulders and beginning gently to massage.

It felt so unbelievably good that he merely closed his eyes and allowed his head to fall forward. The pressure of her hands and proximity of her naked body was too potent to resist.

'Lie down,' she said, and taking the glass from his hand she put it on the table next to hers.

She was in front of him again and as he looked up at the slender beauty of her body, the erect buds of her nipples and careless fall of her hair, he lifted a hand and placed it on her hip. The scent of her was so powerful that he could feel the erection almost bursting from his shorts, and as she eased herself gently towards him he'd buried his face in the damp, curling thatch of her pubic hair almost without thinking.

The taste of her was so hot and familiar that he tightened his grip on her, and pushed his tongue deeper and faster into her. He could hear her panting and groaning, and felt the harsh dig of her fingers in his shoulders. She leaned over him and he reached up for her breasts, squeezing her nipples and sucking even harder with his mouth.

Then he was on his feet, lowering his shorts, and pushing her down on the lounger he lay over her and entered her as she enclosed him in the circle of her arms and legs. He had a brief vision of Chambers doing the same to Ellen, and Ellen receiving him as willingly as Michelle was receiving him now. A sudden anger fired his passion and as he rammed harder and harder into Michelle he thought of Ellen and hated himself for what he was doing, though he was unable to stop.

When it was over he excused himself and went inside. As he showered he tried to blot what he had done from his mind, but already the guilt was claiming him and all he could do was thank God Ellen hadn't come back. Not even the fact that she could be making love with Chambers lessened his guilt, for he knew it was jealousy which caused him to imagine it.

Now, as he steered his car from La Cienega onto Sunset, he could only thank God that Michelle wasn't the type given to hysterics, or any horrendous notions of blackmail. For sure, she'd been upset when he'd asked her to forget what had happened. She'd even asked him to delay the wedding to give them all some more time to think, but in the end she had accepted that it truly was Ellen he loved and that to do what Robbie wanted just wasn't going to work.

Pulling into the parking lot behind Café Med, he waited for someone to vacate a space, then eased his car in. As he locked up and walked over to the restaurant he was wondering, not for the first time, what had happened to change Tom's mind about the casting of Michelle. Or, more to the point, how Ellen had managed to talk him round, since she had to be behind the change of heart, especially as Tom was now considering Matty. Not that Michael had any objection to Matty, she was a damned good actress and was in truth much better suited to the part than Michelle. It was simply that Tom had been so decided, it was the only 'final say' he had insisted upon, and now he had done a complete about-turn.

Though Michael couldn't help suspecting the worst,

he wasn't going to give rein to it, though he couldn't help wondering who was going to break the news to Michelle, and how, once someone did, he was going to convince her that it had nothing to do with what had happened between them.

Still, his main concern right now was for Ellen, which was why he had invited Matty to lunch in the hope that she might be able to throw some light on the way Ellen had been this past week.

The restaurant, on the corner of Sunset Plaza Drive, with its shady terrace and red check tablecloths, was a lunch-time favourite for the industry, which was presumably why Matty had chosen it. She'd want to be seen with Michael, since he was definitely becoming one of the people to be seen with.

He found her sitting at a secluded outside table, olive oil and bread already served and a glass of iced tea in need of a top-up.

'Sorry I'm late,' he said, kissing her on both cheeks. 'Did you get my message?'

'No, but it doesn't matter,' she answered, as he slid into the seat opposite her. 'So, how are you? Three weeks to go. Not getting second thoughts, I hope.'

He laughed. 'Not me,' he answered, signalling to a waiter. 'Bring me an espresso,' he said, 'and more iced tea.' He looked at Matty again. She was a strikingly attractive woman with more than a passing resemblance to Rachel, which made him wonder if maybe she and Chambers had something going. It could account for Chambers's change of heart on the casting. But if there were anything romantic going on Ellen would have been sure to mention it.

'Have you seen much of Ellen lately?' he asked.

Matty looked at him in amazement. 'Are you kidding?' she answered. 'You've got to have an appointment weeks in advance to get near my cousin these days; even the dressmaker's complaining.'

Michael smiled. 'It's a pretty hectic time,' he said. 'What about Tom? Have you seen him at all?'

'A couple of times,' she said, and felt her cheeks starting to colour as she tore off a piece of bread and dipped it in oil. She didn't eat, instead she forced her eyes back to Michael's. 'You obviously know he's considering me for the part of Rachel,' she said. 'So are you trying to tell me you have a problem with that? Is that what this lunch is about?'

He shook his head, and hid his irritation. It was so typical of an actress to think everything was about her, but he was fond of Matty, and knowing what a break this would be for her, he realized he was being too harsh. 'No, I don't have a problem with it at all,' he assured her. 'I've got to admit, I was surprised when Ellen told me, but it'll be good to have you on board.'

'Thanks.' Matty's dark eyes showed her appreciation. 'So,' she said, after a while, 'I could flatter myself that it's my scintillating company that got me this invite, but I know you're too busy for such personal luxuries.'

Michael's espresso arrived with a waiter who was keen to take their order, so after scanning the menu quickly, Michael ordered a seared tuna for himself and a chicken Caesar for Matty, then handed the menu back. 'I'm worried about Ellen,' he said frankly.

Matty looked at him, showing no surprise or concern as she waited for him to continue.

He glanced awkwardly around, feeling the midsummer heat burn through his shirt and the noise of the other diners drum through his ears. 'She's not herself,' he said. 'I don't know what it is, I just know that something's not right.'

'In what way?' Matty asked.

He looked more awkward than ever. 'In the way she is with me,' he said.

'You mean . . .?'

'I mean in every way.'

194

Matty thoughtfully sucked in her lips. 'Did you talk to her about it?' she said.

He nodded. 'She says there's nothing. I asked her if she was sure she still wanted to go ahead with the wedding, and she accused me of being the one who wanted to back out. I think we got past that, but I've caught her crying several times since, and she's so uptight and hostile towards me that I . . .' He looked down at his coffee, clearly having a difficult time putting all this into words. 'Is there anything I should know?' he said, returning his eyes to Matty's. 'I mean, did something happen she isn't telling me about?'

'Like what?' Matty asked.

Michael looked at her and wondered if there really was any chance of learning the truth here. She was Ellen's cousin and would stand by her no matter what. So if Ellen did know about him and Michelle, but didn't want to discuss it, there wasn't much hope of Matty breaking her trust. Nevertheless he had to try, though exactly what he was going to do if Ellen had managed to find out, he had no clear idea. 'I don't know,' he said. 'Like anything. Does she seem upset to you, when you speak to her?'

Matty smiled. 'No more than any other bride three weeks before her wedding,' she told him.

Michael smiled too. 'Do you think that's all it is?' he said. 'Stress?'

'I'm positive that's all it is,' she answered. 'I didn't know she was crying a lot, but from what I hear that's pretty normal too.' She hesitated a moment, then said, 'How are things with Robbie? Is he accepting her more now?'

Michael sighed and shook his head. 'He's being pretty obnoxious,' he confessed. 'He's trying hard not to be, but just the way he's counting the days to Michelle's return has got to be tough on Ellen. She's great with him, which is more than he deserves, but the poor kid's only five, we

195

can't expect him to understand what goes on in the world of grown-ups. I smacked him last night. It was the first time and I don't know who was more shocked, me or him, but he backchatted Ellen in a way I wasn't going to accept.' He forced a smile, then, swallowing hard, he turned to look out at the passing traffic. 'Of course, he wants to leave home now and go to live with his mother,' he said.

Matty studied his pale, handsome face and her heart went out to him in his pain, for it was so clear how much he was suffering, not only because of Robbie, or because of his guilt for sleeping with Michelle, but with all the stress that he too was undergoing in the build-up to the wedding. But his concern wasn't in any way for himself, it was wholly for Ellen, which only went to prove how deeply he loved her, and how vital it was that he never found out about Tom, or that Ellen knew about Michelle. They didn't need to deal with history when they had so much to look forward to. All that mattered now was how much they loved each other, and it would be just plain crazy to let the madness of a single night in any way damage that.

At least that was what she was telling herself, for no matter how much she wanted to help Michael through this, there was just no way she could be the one to tell him what had gone on the night he had flown in from London. It simply wasn't her place, nor, in the end, would he thank her for it. 'You know what I think?' she said.

Michael turned back to look at her.

'I think that honeymoon is just what you two need right now. It's been a tough call for you both, you know, since you came to LA and Ellen moved in with you. I mean, you didn't have much practice at being together like that before, and she's not used to being a mom, nor are you to being a dad. And with the way the movie's really taking off now, and all the pressure you're both under because of that, to be frank, I find it amazing either of you are still sane.'

Michael smiled.

'And what's more,' she continued, 'there's nothing like a wedding to bring out the worst in people, even those who are about to get married. What am I saying, *especially* those who are about to get married,' she corrected with a laugh. 'And if you're looking for reassurance that she still loves you, I can give it unreservedly, wholeheartedly, with passion, conviction and total knowledge that it's absolutely true.'

Michael laughed. 'I guess that's what I was looking for,' he said, glancing up as a waiter hovered with their food.

Matty waited for their plates to be put down, then, picking up a fork, she said, 'Just tell me something, when Michelle comes back for the wedding, is your brother coming too?'

Michael looked surprised. 'Of course,' he answered. 'He's the best man.'

Matty smiled. 'Good, because I'm going to be honest with you, it was hard on Ellen having Michelle around. I think she needs to see her and your brother together to be convinced that everything between you and Michelle is really over.' She paused. 'I guess it is, isn't it?'

Michael's eyes darkened with intensity. If she knew, this was probably the closest he was going to get to her admitting it, so it was his only chance of letting Ellen know how truly sorry he was. 'Matty,' he said, 'I love Ellen more than I've ever loved anyone in my life. I always thought, after Michelle, that nothing could ever be that strong again. But I was wrong, because what I feel for Ellen goes beyond anything I can put into words.' He stopped, but Matty could see he wasn't finished. 'I'll be honest with you,' he said, 'it's taken some mistakes on my part to find out just how much she means to me, but they're not mistakes I'll ever make

197

again.' His eyes were suddenly boring into hers. 'I don't want to lose her, Matty,' he said. 'I really don't.'

Matty smiled, and reaching across the table she covered his hand with hers. 'Believe me,' she said, 'she doesn't want to lose you either. Which is precisely why it isn't going to happen.'

Sandy had checked into the Four Seasons Hotel on Doheny, made a couple of phone calls back to the UK, then gone straight on to a meeting with Michael and a group of executives from CBS. Though *Rachel's Story* was taking up most of their time now, there was still other World Wide business to attend to, like the twenty-six-part TV series, based on the Shirley Whitfield novel *Too Many Barriers*, that Michael had commissioned while still in London.

So officially she had flown to LA a week earlier than everyone else in order to join Michael for the big sell on *Barriers*. Unofficially, she was here to get the lie of the land before the wedding actually took place.

Since Michael's recent trip to London she'd been waiting for the repercussions of her revelation that Ellen had betrayed him over World Wide. As their relationship had appeared to be going through a rocky phase anyway, Sandy had been extremely hopeful that her news would help drive an even bigger wedge between them, but so far that didn't seem to have happened. But having not yet seen them together it was impossible to know exactly how things were progressing this close to the wedding, though common sense was telling her that there was every chance she was going to be turning up at that church on Saturday 15th along with everyone else.

But nothing was over until it was over, and as she had a dinner scheduled with Ted Forgon the following night, she hadn't yet given up hope of preventing the wedding from ever taking place. That had to be her goal for now, difficult though it was, she had at last been forced to accept that it wasn't going to be for love of her that Michael would end his relationship with Ellen. At least, not right now he wouldn't. He would only do it because he either couldn't, or didn't, love Ellen any more. And bringing that about obviously wasn't going to be anywhere near as straightforward as Sandy had hoped. But it wasn't in her to give up, especially not when she knew Michael still desired her, nor when there was Tom Chambers's sudden change of heart on the casting of Rachel to explore. Of course there might be nothing sinister in that at all, but on the other hand her instincts were telling her that it would certainly be worth a small investigation.

Seeming to sense her tiredness after the long flight, Michael took over the meeting and managed to bring the CBS team much closer to signing up a twenty-six-part TV drama than they'd probably ever been in their lives. It was the suggestion that NBC had called World Wide back for a fifth meeting that had done it, which was of course a ruse, but Hollywood thrived on the paranoia of executives who lived in dread of passing on the big one, but were even more terrified of committing.

'It's definitely a no-go,' Michael laughed, as he opened the passenger door of his Land Cruiser for Sandy to get in. 'But it feels pretty good getting them on the hop like that. Sam Beckers at Showtime is going to be a whole different ball game. We're seeing him tomorrow. I'm quietly optimistic on that front.'

Sandy waited as he walked round the car and climbed up into the driver's seat. 'What time are we supposed to be having dinner with Tom tonight?' she yawned.

Michael grinned. 'Eight, at the hotel,' he answered, 'but I don't think you're going to make it.'

She looked at her watch. 'Right now it's two in the morning for me,' she informed him. 'But if I can nap for an hour I should be OK for this evening. Is Ellen joining us?'

'I hope so,' he said, steering the car out of the parking lot onto one of the streets that joined up with Ventura.

'I read the rewrites of the first forty scenes,' Sandy said, looking around at the startling profusion of restaurants, banks, dry-cleaners, yoghurt stops, supermarkets, music and video stores, and of course the ubiquitous McDonald's. 'They're good. I mean, really good.' She turned to look at him. 'What do you think?'

'The same,' he answered. 'It seems Ellen's got something of a feel for Rachel, or so Tom tells me, that's why it's working out so well.'

'Have they done anything with the ending yet?'

'We discussed it briefly the other night, but they're not planning to start work on that until Ellen and I come back from honeymoon.'

Sandy turned away. It made her sick just to think of them together, never mind in the throes of a honeymoon. 'Where are you going?' she asked through the dryness in her throat. 'Or is it a secret?'

He smiled. 'Ellen thinks we're going to Hawaii,' he answered. 'I'm not sure how she figured that out, but she's wrong.'

'Won't she be disappointed? Hawaii sounds pretty exotic to me.'

'It's OK,' he said. 'Or so they tell me.'

'So where are you going?'

'We've got a house in the Caribbean, I'm taking her there. After all the craziness of getting the movie up and running we need to be alone for a while, and a hotel isn't going to offer that in quite the same way as the house will. It's what she wants too, but she thinks I haven't picked up on the hints.'

Sandy could feel her face tightening and she wondered if Ellen had any idea how lucky she was to be so loved. 'So what happened about Michelle?' she asked. 'I hear she's no longer in the running for Rachel.'

Michael turned his head sharply. 'How did you hear

that?' he asked. 'It's supposed to be under wraps, at least until Michelle's been told.'

'Actually, Ellen told me,' Sandy said. 'I spoke to her last week about something else, and she mentioned that Tom was now considering an American actress for the part.'

Michael's eyebrows went up. 'For American actress read Matty Shelby, Ellen's cousin,' he informed her. 'But she's right for the part, which was why Ellen fought so hard for her.'

Sandy gazed out at the largely unrecognizable assortment of cars with their crazy number-plates and witty or spiritual bumper stickers. She was suddenly so tired she could hardly think, never mind speak, which couldn't have been more frustrating when they were right on the subject she wanted to be on. 'So you agree with the new casting?' she said, stifling another yawn.

'Nothing's in stone yet,' he responded, 'but yes, in principle, I think Matty could work out well in the role. Why, you don't anticipate it having any adverse effect on the European investors, do you?'

She shook her head. 'No, I don't think so,' she answered. Then, laughing, she said, 'You know, I feel quite humbled by all the responses I got while I was travelling around. Mind-blown at first, then incredibly humbled. I shouldn't think that as many as half of the companies I spoke to had ever even heard of me, or you, yet somehow I managed to come out of that trip with over five million dollars.' She turned to look at him. 'It's amazing how personally involved you start to feel with these guys after they've given you their trust like that, isn't it? I really want this to work out now, for them as much as for us. Is that how you feel too?'

He laughed. 'It's exactly how I feel, especially when we've got so many friends and family with their money tied up in it too. Did I tell you my mother gave me twenty thousand pounds – virtually the whole of her life savings – when I was last in London? Seems no-one's prepared to believe we can fail.'

'We can't,' Sandy said, fishing around in her bag for a throat sweet. 'Except I have to say I thought you'd be keen to have another big name in the role of Rachel, when the movie's actually about her, rather than Tom.'

'But Rachel gets killed two-thirds of the way through, so that makes Tom's the bigger part.'

'Of course,' she said and yawned again.

By the time they arrived back at the hotel she was fast asleep in the seat next to him, and woke only when the car valet opened the door and Michael spoke her name. For a moment she was confused, wondering where she was, and as though reading her mind Michael smiled and said, 'The Four Seasons. Los Angeles. Heading fast towards the end of the second millennium.'

Laughing, Sandy unfastened her seat-belt and allowed the valet to help her down.

'I'm coming in to see Tom,' Michael told her, as he walked round the car to join her. 'Ellen's tied up with the wedding organizers for the next couple of hours and Robbie's staying the night at a friend's.'

'Would you like to come and have a drink with me?' Sandy offered, as they walked past the uncannily lifelike statues at the entrance and went into the crowded lobby.

He laughed. 'Sandy, you're so tired you can't even walk a straight line,' he said.

'We could go to my room,' she suggested.

He looked at her, and despite everything that had happened these past few weeks, and all the guilt and self-recrimination that had followed, he still felt the stirrings of a response to the promise in her eyes. 'Get some sleep,' he said. 'I'll call you at eight to see if you're fit to come and join us.'

Though her cheeks coloured at his rejection, her eyes lingered a moment longer on his, before she pressed the button for the elevator and stepped inside.

Going into the bar Michael ordered himself a neat Scotch from the waitress, and sat down at a dark corner table hoping not to be recognized. He wanted a few minutes alone, and though the Four Seasons was hardly the place to get it, he was here now and due to meet Tom in fifteen minutes. He looked at his watch, then taking out his cellphone he dialled Ellen's number.

'Hi,' he said, when she answered. 'How's it going over there?'

'OK,' she said. 'We're just talking flowers. We should be through in about an hour. Matty's with me, shall I invite her to join us for dinner?'

'Sure.'

There was silence for a moment, until Ellen said, 'Did you call for a particular reason?'

He laughed. 'No. Just to hear your voice. I wish we could get out of tonight. With Robbie at Jeremy's we could have the evening to ourselves. Shall I cancel?'

'No,' she said. 'We're going to have all the time we need in a couple of weeks. Did Sandy arrive OK?'

'Yeah. She's taking a nap. I don't think we got anywhere with CBS.'

'You didn't expect to. Listen honey, we're kind of busy here, do you mind if I ring off?'

'Sure. I'll see you later. Love you.'

Not for the first time she didn't say it back, and as the line went dead he could feel the anxieties that had forced him to speak to Matty a week ago starting up again. She was so cold with him lately, or perhaps not cold, just not the way she usually was. And, unless it was his imagination, she wasn't at all keen to be alone with him, for this was the second time in as many days that she had turned down the opportunity. So what was going on? Was it really just the wedding that was taking up all her time? Or was there something else she wasn't telling him about?

His drink arrived along with a dish of olives and

pistachios. He watched the waitress walk away, her long, willowy legs moving gracefully through the tables. He guessed she was an actress, most of them were, and the slinky movements were no doubt for his benefit, since she'd called him by name, so obviously knew who he was. She turned and glanced back over her shoulder and, catching him watching her, treated him to a smile that offered all he could ever want. He looked quickly away. Christ, there was so much sex on offer in this town it could drive a man to celibacy.

Clicking on his phone as it rang, he took a call from Maggie telling him to get in touch with the World Wide lawyers right away. Guessing from the tone of her voice what the call would be about, he rapidly dialled the number and was put straight through to George Cohen.

'OK, Michael,' the spirited eighty-year-old lawyer began, 'fasten your seat-belt, because this ride's about to really take off.'

'Miramax?' Michael said, feeling the excitement start to pound.

'If you're prepared to sign by midday tomorrow,' Cohen said, 'then they'll go two higher than Fox Searchlight.'

'You're kidding me,' Michael gasped. 'They're offering ten million dollars?'

'You got it. So what do I tell them?'

'That they've got themselves a deal,' Michael laughed. 'Jesus Christ, George. How did this happen?'

'Oh, I guess the fact that I know one of the Weinstein brothers might have helped a bit,' he said modestly. 'And they believe in the project, son. And after what I told them about you, they believe in you too.'

Michael was momentarily too overcome to speak. He hadn't known this man for more than six months, yet Cohen was prepared to do this for him.

'So, I'm filling up the pen with ink,' Cohen said. 'I'll expect you at eleven tomorrow.'

'It's a date,' Michael told him, and rang off.

He sat for a moment, taking in exactly what this massive investment was going to mean. To begin with, they could go ahead with the building of the sets, lay down provisional shoot dates, start searching for locations, offer pay or play contracts and hire themselves a major publicity firm to start work on the pre-release promotions. In fact there were a thousand things they could set in motion now, and he could barely take in how eminently possible it had all become. Then it started to feel overwhelming, even a little unnerving. There would be no backing out now, not that he had any intention of that, but being this locked in was much more sobering than he'd expected.

Picking up the phone he quickly dialled Ellen's number again. She was going to be every bit as excited – and stunned – as he was, and there was no-one else in the world he wanted to share this moment with more than her. But she'd turned her phone off, and when he tried the wedding organizer's number he was told she'd already left.

He tried to think who else he should call, but for some reason he could no longer get his mind to focus on this, as, out of nowhere, he was recalling what Sandy had told him about Ellen during his recent trip to London. He hadn't given it much thought since, for the idea of Ellen as some kind of aspiring megalomaniac had seemed just too absurd. But lately it was starting to appear much less so. After all, she was pretty much in charge of the movie now, was getting the final say on the script, and had managed to change Tom's mind about Michelle. She was also the one who was in contact with Richard Conway's people, who attended most of the meetings with the producers, showed up for a lot of the castings and talked daily on the phone with Vic Warren. Added to that she was as involved as he was with the running of ATI, so had a hand in just about all the packaging that was going on in the agency, and as far as the wedding was concerned he couldn't think of a single decision that had been his. So maybe Sandy was right, she was some kind of control freak, and because of it she was coming pretty close to burning herself out. It would certainly account for the emotional outbursts and loss of appetite lately, in fact it could easily provide the answers to a whole lot of things that were going on right now.

Sighing, he took another sip of his drink. It was pretty sobering to be finding out you didn't know the woman you loved right on the eve of your wedding. Not that he was considering calling it off; everything was arranged now, and, goddamnit, he loved her no matter what her faults. But if it carried on this way, with Ellen struggling to gain more and more control, instead of husband and wife they would be arch-rivals for a company whose majority shareholder was a man Ellen had lately been seeing a great deal of.

Just the thought of Ted Forgon made him uneasy, for the statute of limitations was fast winding down, and Michael couldn't be certain which way the old man would go when he finally came out from under the threat of jail. One thing was certain, he wasn't going to view Michael as his very best chum, nor was he likely to knuckle under and take some kind of consultancy role. Forgon was used to being the boss, and the minute that limitation ran dry, the driver's seat would be right where he was heading. And there would be a few old scores to settle then, so just what was Ellen doing making up to the old boy now, when, of all people, she was the one Michael was going to need on his side?

Chapter 12

For the moment Ellen and Tom were the only ones at the table, as Matty had gone to the ladies' room, while Michael went to wake up Sandy with the good news about Miramax. This was far from being the first time they'd been alone since the night they'd made love, for they'd had several script sessions in the past few weeks – which they'd now relocated to one of the ATI conference rooms – and Tom often stopped by the office to pick Ellen up and take her over to Paramount for the endless number of production meetings they were both required to attend.

So the early awkwardness had already been dealt with and Ellen would forever be grateful to him for the way he had handled things, assuring her that Michael would never learn what had happened from him, and that as far as he was concerned it was already forgotten. She'd laughed at that, and, realizing how ungallant it must have sounded, he'd winked and told her that were the circumstances any different there was just no way he'd be giving her the benefit of his selective amnesia.

Since that day they'd never spoken of it again, and though the attraction she'd felt before seemed to have gone, she sometimes wondered if it was the same for him. But that wasn't something she was going to get into, for it could simply be her ego at work, still wanting to be admired even though she had no desire whatsoever to be unfaithful to Michael again.

But despite how loving and attentive Michael had been since that night, or how euphoric they both were now, knowing that the movie was going to go ahead much sooner than they'd even dared to hope, there was no getting away from the fact that things between them had changed. And in her bleaker moments she was terrified they would never be the same again. The problem was, the trust had gone. Perhaps if he'd confessed what had happened with Michelle she'd be finding it easier to deal with, except that was crazy, for the last thing she wanted was to be forced into confessing herself. So what the hell she was supposed to do about the way things were she had no idea, for though she desperately wanted everything to be right again, there was a very strong part of her that was still so damned angry that she almost took pleasure in pushing him away. She'd even considered calling off the wedding, though the thought of it filled her with panic. But it was there, on her mind, every minute of the day, and after what had happened with Robbie earlier, she wondered if she wasn't a whole lot closer to leaving than she'd realized.

Michael didn't know about it, and she didn't want to tell him, for the last time Robbie had backchatted her Michael had smacked him, which had done nothing at all to help matters. Robbie saw her as the enemy now, the horrible, evil woman who was coming between his mom and dad and ruining all their lives. He'd told her that this evening, right after he'd told her how much he hated her and that he never wanted her coming into his room again. And he wasn't coming to the wedding, he was going to stay here with his mom, because she was the only one who loved him. After that he'd slammed his door in her face and though she'd heard him sobbing into his pillow, she'd known that she couldn't be the one to comfort him. So Lucina had gone in, and it had hurt

Ellen terribly to hear him pleading with Lucina to make Ellen go away so that his dad could marry his mom.

'Listen, I don't want to get personal here,' Chambers said, breaking into her thoughts, 'but you haven't heard a word I've been saying, and frankly, you look terrible. Beautiful,' he smiled, 'but terrible.'

Ellen forced a smile too. 'Thank you,' she said.

He looked into her eyes and let the humour fade as he saw how troubled she really was.

She turned sharply away. 'It's OK,' she said. 'I'm just tired, and stressed with the wedding.'

His eyes stayed with her, though she refused to meet them. It went much deeper than that, he could tell, but he didn't blame her for not wanting to open up to him. Besides, now was hardly the time, as Michael and Sandy were heading towards the table and finding Ellen with tears in her eyes was going to look odd enough, without encouraging her to break down.

Getting to his feet he watched Sandy as she looked first at Ellen, then at him. Had she noticed the tears, he wondered, or had Ellen managed to blink them away?

'Tom, this is Sandy Paull,' Michael said, as Tom reached out to shake Sandy's hand.

'It's good to meet you, Sandy,' he said. 'I've heard a lot about you,' but no-one, he was thinking to himself, had told him how young she was.

Her turquoise eyes were shining with interest as she looked back at him. 'Probably not as much as I've heard about you,' she smiled.

'Hi Sandy,' Ellen said, getting up to embrace her. 'How are you? Exhausted, I imagine.'

'Better now I've had a sleep,' Sandy assured her, tearing her eyes from Tom. 'And thrilled about the Miramax news. I'm wondering if you and Michael have got time for a wedding now, with all that's going to start coming up?'

Ellen glanced at Michael and, seeing how doubtful he

was of her answer, she just wanted to put her arms around him and ask him to take her home. 'It's our first priority,' she said, sitting down again as Matty joined them. 'This is my cousin, Matty Shelby.'

'It's nice to meet you, Matty,' Sandy said. 'I expect you're up to your ears in wedding plans too.'

'Oh, it went past my ears days ago,' Matty laughed. 'Hi, and welcome to LA. This isn't your first time though, is it?'

'No,' Sandy answered, as she sat in the chair Michael was holding out for her. She glanced up to thank him, but his eyes were on Ellen and Sandy watched as he sat down next to her and covered her hand with his. When she looked up again it was straight into Tom Chambers's eyes and she felt herself colour at what he might have deduced from the way she'd watched Michael and Ellen. But there was no way he could detect the envy in her heart, and as she was still smiling there was a chance she'd shown nothing more than a distracted kind of interest.

'I read the latest rewrites, coming over on the plane,' she said, glancing at Ellen then back at Tom. 'It's really starting to take shape. I'm intrigued to know how you're going to end it.'

Ellen was frowning. 'I didn't know you'd read the script,' she said, turning to Michael.

Sandy looked at Michael too. Obviously he hadn't told her, but she'd thought it was just her producership they were keeping under wraps, had no idea she wasn't supposed to have read the script either. Still, Ellen had to find out some time, and Sandy was pleased to be here to witness the response.

'I'm keeping Sandy up to date with it,' Michael said, 'so that she's got some idea what she's talking about when she goes about raising money in Europe.'

'But you had the publicity package,' Ellen protested. 'It gives a full synopsis, biographies of Tom and Rachel, who's playing the lead . . .'

210

'It's not the same as seeing the script,' he told her, obviously annoyed at being put on the defensive, and desperate to get off the subject.

Ellen looked at Tom.

Tom shrugged. 'Well, since Sandy likes it so much,' he said, 'I guess there's no harm done.'

Sandy smiled and sensed immediately how furious Ellen was that Tom had taken her side. Then she looked at Michael who was clearly still annoyed. 'I'm sorry,' she said, 'I didn't realize I wasn't supposed to have read the script.'

'No, don't apologize,' he told her. 'As one of the executive directors of World Wide, you had every right to. And as one of the movie's producers it would have been very strange if you hadn't.'

Sandy's eyes returned to Ellen who was looking at Michael as though he'd just slapped her. 'I'm sorry,' she said, 'but I didn't know that Sandy was one of the producers.'

'Since she's helping to raise the finance,' Michael responded, 'I think a producer's credit is the very least we can give her.'

It was clear that Ellen was having a hard time controlling her temper. 'Does that mean Mark Bergin in Sydney, and Chris Ruskin in New York are also getting producer credits?' she asked.

'Of course,' he answered. 'Why would I give it to Sandy and not to them, when they're bringing in finance too?'

'Why would you give it to anyone without discussing it with me?' she retorted.

Michael looked awkwardly around the table. 'I don't think now's the time for this,' he said.

'Where's the waiter?' Tom said. 'Is everyone up for champagne, after all, we're supposed to be celebrating.'

'Excuse me,' Ellen said, and got abruptly to her feet.

Matty watched her walk away, then looking across at

Michael she felt her heart go out to him, for as angry as he was, she could see how horribly perplexed he was too. And, she had to confess, so was she, for she'd spent the past couple of hours at the wedding arranger's with Ellen, and it was clear to Matty that Ellen was in a terrible way. There hadn't really been any opportunity to talk, but after the way she had snapped at the organizer, the emotional state she had worked herself into on the way here, and now seeing how angry she was with Michael, Matty resolved to get to the bottom of what was eating her. Of course, Michael making love to Michelle had to be featuring in there somewhere, so must the way Ellen had hit back with Tom, but if Ellen was having such a hard time holding it in like this, then it seemed they were going to have to find a way of dealing with it, instead of just pretending it hadn't happened.

As Ellen came back Sandy happened to glance over at Chambers. The tears in Ellen's eyes hadn't escaped her when she'd first arrived, and now, unless she was imagining things, Tom's concern went some way beyond mere politeness. In fact, for a moment there, he seemed genuinely worried, and given how pale and exhausted Ellen looked, Sandy wasn't having too much trouble coming to a conclusion that was pleasing her immensely. Something was going on between those two, and with any luck it was of a pretty serious nature.

By the time their food was ordered and brought Ellen was feeling much calmer and was actually starting to enjoy herself. The talk now was mainly of the wedding, and finding herself able, if only briefly, to let go of her nerves, she was making them all laugh with the chaos that had taken over her days. As she talked she entwined her fingers through Michael's, probably drank a little too much wine, and avoided eating any real amount of food. Her appetite had been erratic for a couple of weeks now, which she knew was normal before a wedding, and she'd certainly had no objection to her dress being taken in another inch earlier that day. She just knew how much Michael would love the dress, and what she was planning to wear underneath, and the thought of how much pleasure she was going to give him suddenly filled up her heart and pushed tears to her eyes.

'Oh God, I've been like this for days,' she laughed, using a napkin to dab her cheeks.

'Weeks,' Michael corrected.

'It just suddenly comes over me,' she said, turning to kiss him. 'It's not that I'm depressed, I'm just . . . emotional, I guess.' Then lowering her voice she said, 'I can't wait till we're on honeymoon.'

'Then don't let's,' he murmured.

Smiling, she leaned against him and turned back to the others, listening as Sandy and Matty questioned Tom about his work as a journalist, wanting to know all about the different wars he had covered, the hardships, massacres, tyrannies and famines. She guessed that he was embroidering some of his tales to make for better listening, and then she started to think of how terribly sad it was that he had lost Rachel and never loved again since. But after watching Sandy for a while, she could at least be sure that he wasn't going to be short of a bed partner for the next couple of weeks.

Though the thought of that didn't make Ellen jealous exactly, she wasn't as happy about it as she might have been, for she didn't like Sandy, and certainly didn't think she was good enough for Tom. But if it kept her out of Michael's way, then Ellen guessed that was fine by her. And Tom could look after himself. He'd soon see through Sandy, if he hadn't already, for she was just a scheming little bitch who would screw anyone in an effort to get what she wanted. And, unless Ellen was greatly mistaken, she was about to make Tom her next target in order to gain more control of the movie. Well, that was going to happen over Ellen's dead body.

213

Turning back to Michael she looked up at him, scanning his face and squeezing harder on his hand. There seemed to be so much going round in her head at the moment that she couldn't cope with all the added stress Sandy was bringing, and suddenly wanting desperately to be alone with Michael she quietly suggested they leave.

They weren't far from the Four Seasons when Ellen asked him to pull over.

He glanced at her in surprise. 'Are you OK?' he asked.

'I just want you to hold me,' she answered.

Immediately he steered the car over to the kerb and pulled her into his arms. 'Are you sure you're OK?' he said, holding her tight.

'Sure.' Her eyes were closed and once again she could feel her heart flooding with emotion. 'Do you love me?' she whispered. 'I mean really, really love me?'

'Oh God, you know I do,' he told her.

'You won't let anything come between us?'

'Never,' he swore.

She pulled back to look into his eyes. 'Are you sure you want to marry me?'

'Sure,' he smiled, stroking her hair back from her face.

'You don't love anyone else?'

'No. Only you.'

'Not Michelle?'

'Not Michelle.'

'Or Sandy?'

He laughed. 'Or Sandy.'

She gazed at him anxiously, as though searching for something she was unable to find. In the end he lifted her mouth to his and kissed her deeply.

'In less than a fortnight this circus'll be over,' he said, 'and then for two whole weeks it'll be just us.'

Her head went down. 'I wish it could be over now,' she whispered.

Putting his fingers under her chin he raised her eyes

back to his. 'We can get on a plane and go to Vegas right now,' he said. 'Or I guess we should wait until we've signed with Miramax tomorrow, but after that we can get married right away, if that's what you want, and let everyone have a party next Saturday while we're a thousand miles away.'

She looked at him and he could see she was tempted, but in the end she sighed and shook her head. 'We can't disappoint our mothers now,' she said, 'especially not mine when I'm the only daughter she has.'

'Ellen, this is about us,' he reminded her. 'Not about anyone else.'

'I know, but whichever way we do this we're still going to have each other, so perhaps we should do it their way, if only to keep the peace.'

'Then keep that in mind,' he said. 'We're going to have each other no matter what. OK?'

'Do you promise?' she said, thinking of Robbie and Michelle and Tom – and so many other things that would take too many words and too much heartache to tell. 'No matter what?'

'It's what I said, and it's what I mean,' he vowed, but as he kissed her again she knew in her heart that she was asking too much.

This was Sandy's fourth day in Los Angeles, and though the schedule wasn't really any more hectic than she was used to, she was exhausted, and appeared to be coming down with a cold, if not flu. She felt so dreadful it was all she could do to drag herself through the meeting she and Michael were at with Warners, and the minute it was over, sensing how much she was struggling Michael ignored her protests and insisted on taking her back to the hotel.

As he drove she tried hard to concentrate on what he was saying, but her throat was horribly sore, and she was so groggy and tired she could barely keep her eyes

215

open. Breathing was difficult too, and it was only when he brought the car to a standstill and gently shook her awake that she realized she'd dozed off with her mouth open.

She tried to remember what he'd been saying, but it was escaping her, and though there were a hundred things she wanted to say to him they were such a jumble inside her head she just couldn't grasp them. Except there was something she wanted to tell him about the dinner she'd had with Tom Chambers last night. He'd taken her to the Chaya Brasserie in West Hollywood, which apparently was one of the places to be seen at – or was it something she wanted to tell Tom about Michael? For a fleeting moment she remembered that last night had felt a bit like a date, which had been wonderful at the time. It was ages since anyone had teased and flirted with her like that, and she had to admit she really quite fancied Tom, though today the effort it took even to think of it was simply beyond her.

'You'll feel better after you've had a sleep,' Michael told her as he helped her from the car. 'It's so damned hot out, and with all this air-conditioning – it takes some getting used to.'

Sandy looked around, blinked a couple of times and felt vaguely bemused. The sun was like a white-hot fire on her skin, even though she could feel herself shivering. 'Where are we?' she said.

'At my house. I hope you don't mind, but by the time I get you back to the hotel, I'll be late for the lawyers.'

'No, that's fine,' she said, wanting only to put her head on a pillow and tug the sheet around her like a child. And minutes later, after slipping out of her dress while Michael waited outside, that was exactly what she did.

'Are you OK?' he asked, putting his head round the door.

'Mmm,' she murmured, snuggling in deeper.

'I'm sorry it has to be Robbie's room, but Ellen's

parents are in one of the guest-rooms, and my mother's in the other. I don't know where everyone is right now, but no-one should disturb you. Here,' he said, leaning over her and flicking off the intercom, 'you won't want your snores echoing all over the house.'

She smiled, and watched as he went to pull the curtains.

'I'll come back for you in a couple of hours,' he said, and as he closed the door gently behind him she could already feel herself drifting into sleep.

It was late afternoon when Matty pulled into the driveway of Ellen and Michael's house. There were no other cars around, not even the Geo Ellen's parents had rented. But the garage doors were closed, so there was no telling who was at home without going to check.

Though everything looked locked-up and deserted, to Matty's surprise, when she knocked on the front door it came open. This unnerved her a little, as the last thing she wanted was to walk in on burglars, but since Ellen wasn't at the office, the dressmaker's, the caterer's, or any other meeting Maggie knew about, there was a chance she was here at home. If she was, she wasn't answering the phone, but maybe she'd only just got here.

'Ellen!' she called, looking through the huge sliding picture windows to the garden as she crossed to the study. 'Ellen!'

After checking the kitchen and den she walked back across the sitting-room and opened the door that led to the master suite. 'Ellen!' she called again.

Still no reply.

She glanced up the stairs to the guest suite. Ellen's parents were staying there until after the wedding, but there were no sounds to say anyone was around, so Matty continued along the narrow hall and into the vast muslin-draped bedroom that overlooked the garden and pool. She felt a quick jolt of unease as she noticed Ellen's purse on the bed – if she was here, why wasn't she answering?

'Ellen? Are you there?' she said, going to the bathroom. Her heart was starting to thud as she pushed open the door, then she gasped as she saw Ellen standing in front of the mirror.

'Oh God, there you are,' she said with a laugh of relief. 'You had me worried. What are . . .' She stopped as she realized Ellen hadn't moved, then, following Ellen's eyes to the narrow white tube lying on the marble counter in front of her, she felt her heart turn inside out.

'Oh my God,' she murmured. 'Please tell me that's not what I think it is.'

Ellen didn't answer, and for a moment Matty could only stare at her. It was true she'd had her suspicions, but she guessed, like Ellen, she hadn't wanted even to think them. But now here was the evidence, staring them right in the face, and even Matty could feel the world starting to fold.

Going to Ellen she turned her round and held her fiercely in her arms. 'It's all right,' she said. 'It's going to be all right. We'll work it out.'

Ellen didn't move. Her arms hung limply at her sides, her eyes stared vacantly ahead.

'Ellen, listen to me. Listen,' Matty said, shaking her gently. 'We're going to work this out, OK? It's going to be all right.'

Ellen's eyes drew focus, but as she looked at Matty she smiled the saddest smile Matty had ever seen. Matty wrapped her in her arms again and as she felt her body shake with sobs, she looked at the pregnancy test and felt the whole horrible nightmare of what it meant start to engulf her. Of course, it explained why Ellen had been the way she had these past few weeks – she'd suspected this, but hadn't had the courage to face it. And who could blame her for that, when she was just days away from getting married and had no way of knowing whether the father was Michael or Tom.

'Matty, what am I going to do?' she choked. 'Oh God, what am I going to do?'

'Come and sit down,' Matty said, leading her towards the bed. 'Come on. You're going to be OK. We're going to figure this out.'

'I can't get married now,' Ellen said, her voice racked with pain. 'I love Michael too much to . . .' She took a breath. 'Oh God, maybe this . . . this is God's way of making me let him go so he can be with Michelle and Robbie and I won't be in the way any more.'

'Sssh,' Matty said. 'That's not true. For all we know the baby's his, and if it is that doesn't make any sense. When were you ovulating? Do you know?'

Ellen nodded and bit down hard on her lips as fresh tears filled her eyes. 'It was right around the time I slept with Tom,' she answered, her voice high-pitched with misery. 'I slept with Michael the Sunday before, then again the Sunday after. And the Friday in between was when I slept with Tom.'

'It would be foolish to ask if you used contraception,' Matty said.

Ellen closed her eyes. 'Do you think I'd be in this state if I had?' she said. 'Oh God, what am I going to do? It's going to break his heart. He'll never forgive me, I know he won't. But it's not fair, Matty. It's just not fair. He sleeps with Michelle and gets away with it. And I only slept with Tom out of some ridiculous fit of pique and look what a mess I'm in now. It's just not fair.'

'I know,' Matty soothed. 'But there are ways out of it, Ellen. I mean, you could always . . .' Her eyes dropped to Ellen's stomach.

'Have an abortion?' Ellen finished. 'Matty, I'm getting married in five days. How the hell am I going to get an abortion between now and then without Michael finding out? And besides, it's just not an option. It can't be. The baby could be his and . . .' She started to shake her head. 'No, I couldn't do it, Matty. I just couldn't.'

Matty's eyes went down. As far as she could see it was the only way out. Not that she really approved either, but when needs must and all that. But Ellen was right, she couldn't get it done before the wedding now, and even if she could, there wouldn't be any hiding it from Michael.

'His mother's so thrilled about us getting married,' Ellen wept. 'She's been so wonderful ever since she arrived. She's been dealing with Robbie and trying to make things better there and . . . Oh, Matty, you've met her. She's so lovely and sweet and adores Michael and Robbie so much. She told me this morning how happy she was to be getting me as a daughter. She hardly knows me, Matty, but she's prepared to accept me . . . She's even been talking about going to spend some time with Mom and Dad on the farm in Nebraska before she goes back to England. They're all getting along so well.' She laughed through her tears. 'Well, you know the Irish. Dad's taken them all out in the car now. They've gone down to the church to get a look at where they're going to sit on Saturday. They're so excited. Matty, how can I let them down? And how the hell can I put Michael through the shame of anyone knowing why we've called everything off? I can't do it, Matty. I just can't do it.'

Matty sat quietly thinking, trying to imagine what she would do were she in Ellen's shoes. In the end she had to agree with Ellen, she couldn't call it off, so maybe the answer was to deal with it all after the wedding.

Ellen's eyes were steeped in pain. 'But it'll be like trapping him,' she said. 'And the deceit . . . I can't do that to him either, Matty.'

Matty looked at her helplessly, for no matter how hard she tried she knew she had no more chance of coming up with the right answer than Ellen did. 'Then I think,' she said finally, 'you're going to have to talk to him now and let him make the decision whether you go ahead or not.'

Ellen blanched. 'Oh God, no,' she murmured, a terrible fear darkening her eyes. 'Not now. I can't do it now.'

'Well, it's either before or after,' Matty said gently.

Ellen looked frantically around the room, a hand pressed to her head as she tried to make herself think. 'Not today,' she said. 'I can't do it today. Michelle and Cavan are arriving tonight . . .' She stopped as her heart caught on the thought of Michelle.

'Tell me they're not staying here,' Matty said.

Ellen shook her head. 'Vic Warren's got a house just along the road. They're staying with him.' Her face suddenly showed all the torment she was feeling inside. 'It's where Michael's supposed to be staying on Friday night,' she added brokenly.

Matty inhaled deeply and wished to God she knew what to say.

'I'd better get rid of it,' Ellen said.

Matty looked at her in amazement.

'The test,' Ellen said, getting up from the bed. 'I'd better throw it away.'

Matty followed her into the bathroom. 'Where are you going to put it?' she asked.

Ellen looked at her helplessly. 'I don't know,' she answered.

Matty held out her hand. 'I'll see to it,' she said.

Ellen handed it over, then turned to splash cold water on her face. 'I'm meeting everyone at Ed Debevick's in half an hour,' she said. 'You know, the diner where the staff sing and dance on the tables.'

'I used to be one of the staff,' Matty reminded her.

Ellen nodded absently. 'We're eating there before we go to the airport for Michelle,' she said. 'Michael's meeting us there.' Her face started to crumple. 'How am I going to face him?'

221

'You'll do it,' Matty said firmly.

Ellen looked anything but convinced.

'You'll do it because you love him and because you have to,' Matty told her. 'Now come on, dry your face, brush your hair and I'll come down to Ed's with you.'

Sandy, lying quietly in Robbie' bed, had heard every word of Ellen and Matty's conversation. It seemed that the intercom Michael thought he'd turned off had somehow managed to switch to two-way transmission.

For a long time after their cars had left the drive Sandy lay where she was, stunned, not only by what she had heard, but by the fact that she had heard it at all. It was so utterly beyond belief that she could hardly take it in. Yet the fortuitousness of it, as well as everything it meant, was already working so fast in her mind she could barely keep up with it.

There was no doubt now that she had the means to put an end to the wedding, and were it not for the fact that she actually felt sorry for Ellen, she might have laughed out loud. Instead she made do with a smile and marvelled again at the way fate had delivered the solution right into her lap when she'd all but given up hope of ever finding one. Indeed, all those attempts at poisoning Michael's mind against Ellen, the lies, the deceit, even the self-delusion now seemed so pathetic in light of what life itself had cooked up. So it just went to prove, if something was meant to be, life would most assuredly deliver.

Her eyes closed as a surge of euphoria welled up from her heart. It wasn't until she got up from the bed and a dizzy spell overtook her that she remembered she was ill. But whether it was the sleep that had helped her, or this earth-shattering piece of providence, she had no idea. All she knew was that she no longer felt even half as bad as she had when Michael dropped her off, and now she could hardly wait for him to come back.

Or maybe now wasn't the time to tell him. She

222

couldn't say why she felt that, except her instincts seemed to be warning her not to act too hastily. There were five days between now and the wedding . . . She stopped at the sudden notion of standing up in church as the priest asked if anyone knew of just cause or impediment, and announcing Ellen's secret to the world. Her heart started to race. The very idea of it was so shocking and dramatic that she seriously doubted she had the courage to do it. But it certainly had its appeal, and after giving all her other options some thought she might find herself right back at this one, so she wasn't discarding it yet.

She soon realized that there were any number of different ways she could play this, but after giving them all a quick run-through, trying out her words, second-guessing reactions, trying to foresee the outcomes, she still wasn't convinced she'd hit on the right one yet. Then quite suddenly the perfect answer presented itself with such ease and certitude that not even a trace of doubt shadowed its formation. It was so obvious and so simple she was surprised it had taken her this long to get there, which only went to show that she probably wasn't over her small bout of flu after all.

Looking at her watch she wondered if she'd catch Tom at the hotel before he went to have drinks with the director, Vic Warren. Not that she had any intention of breaking the news on the phone, but maybe he'd be free later, for dinner. The very idea of spending another evening with Tom was exciting enough, without the added bonus of what might come after.

Chambers's expression was unreadable, which, for some bizarre reason, seemed to be making him even more attractive. And the anger she sensed in him, which she knew was directed at her, was increasing his appeal no end.

They were in the garden of the Four Seasons hotel,

two cocktails on the table in front of them, and the occasional stroller passing by. The evening sun was dazzling, which gave her a good excuse to mask her failing nerve with sunglasses. This was an extremely delicate manoeuvre, trying to get him to break the news of Ellen's pregnancy to Michael, she just hoped to God it wasn't going to backfire.

When at last he spoke, his words did nothing to reassure her. 'I want you to forget everything you overheard,' he said, 'and I don't want you ever to mention it again, not even to me.'

'But what if it's your child?' Sandy protested. 'Surely you'd want to know that.'

His eyes became discomfitingly intense, and for a weirdly horrible moment she got the impression he was seeing a lot more than just her face.

'Do you want Michael to bring up your child thinking it's his?' she persisted. 'Would you really do that to him? Or to the child? Surely it has the right to know its own father.'

'Listen to me,' he said, speaking in a way that made her cheeks heat up, 'if Ellen says that baby is Michael's then it's Michael's.' His eyes were boring into hers. 'Do you understand what I'm saying? Are you getting the message?'

'Yes, but are you?'

A bitter smile crossed his lips. 'Oh, I'm getting it all right,' he answered. 'I'm getting it loud and clear.'

Brushing past that, she said, 'If you won't speak to Michael then I think you should at least speak to Ellen. It might help her to know you're prepared to stand by her . . . I mean, if she needs it. After all, this is a terrible thing she's going through, and she obviously cares about you or she'd never have slept with you.'

He looked away for a moment, and sensing she might be making some headway with this line of approach she pressed on.

224

'I've seen the way she looks at you, and if you ask me she's more serious about you than she's letting on. You're an attractive man, Tom, I can completely understand why Ellen did what she did. But unlike Ellen I'm not about to marry Michael, and nor would I if I were carrying another man's child.'

His face turned hard again. 'We don't know that for certain.'

'But surely the doubt alone should be enough to postpone the wedding – at least until the whole thing can be settled. And think about it, it's a pretty rotten thing to do to a man, marry him when you don't know if the child you're carrying is his or not. Come to that, it's not a particularly pleasant thing to do to you. Not that I'm blaming her, she's obviously in such a state she doesn't know what to do, which is why, if you talked to her, it might at least help her come to a decision.'

There was a long and difficult silence, until finally Sandy put a hand on his and said, 'I know this can't be easy for you, and believe me . . .' She stopped as he suddenly got to his feet.

'Have the waiter put the drinks on my tab,' he said, and throwing a five-dollar bill on the table to cover the tip he walked back inside the hotel. To call Ellen? Sandy wondered, or Michael?

Chapter 13

The organist was playing Handel's organ concerto No. 4 as the wedding guests filed into the Church of the Good Shepherd on Santa Monica Boulevard in Beverly Hills. Already sixty or more were gathered, many dipping their fingers in holy water and crossing themselves as they bowed towards the altar before moving into the pews. Outside the entertainment press was gathering, reporters and camera crews eager to grab as many celebrities as they could before they disappeared inside the church. Fashion correspondents and gossip columnists were out in force too, for there were as many designer creations floating up the wide brick steps as there were potentials for rumour and speculation.

It was a beautiful hot June day; the sky was crystal clear and the luscious green of the palms stood out vividly against the blue of the heavens. Cars were filling up the surrounding streets and as the clock ticked towards twelve the bride and groom's closest friends and relatives began to arrive.

Ellen's and Michael's mothers came together, chauffeured in a long black limousine and escorted by Vic Warren and Craig Everett. The rest of the McCann Paull agents were in the limo behind: Sandy, Zelda, Harry, Janey, Diana and a couple of assistants. Soon after Michael's sister, Colleen, and her husband Dan arrived, with their two sons, Charlie and Ben. Their five-year-old daughter, Tierney, was back at the house with Ellen, realizing all her wildest dreams as she showed off her cream taffeta bridesmaid's dress and headband of small white flowers. There was a quick flurry of activity from the press as they learned who the chic raven-haired woman and her family were, then suddenly all attention was focused on another black limousine that was pulling up at the kerb.

As he stepped out Michael was laughing, and made a comic show of trying to protect himself from the sudden thrust of cameras and microphones. Cavan, who was so like his older brother there could be no mistaking who he was, watched in fascination and tried not to laugh at the way their mother was scowling from the door of the church. It was reminiscent of the days they'd hung back from bedtime, or started messing about with the other kids when they'd been told to come inside.

Though they and the ushers were all dressed in long black tailcoats and charcoal grey trousers, Michael's was the only blue cravat and grey Paisley waistcoat. The others wore lemon cravats and burgundy waistcoats. As Tom was amongst the ushers he was suitably attired, and was busy showing Ellen's friends and family to their seats as Michael and Cavan made their way in behind them.

The irony of being chosen to take care of Ellen's side wasn't lost on Tom, but he showed only humour and consideration as he went about his duties. From where she was sitting in the sixth row of Michael's side he could feel Sandy's eyes watching him, but he studiously avoided them until the moment Michael stopped halfway up the aisle to exchange some good-natured banter before moving on to the front. That was when Tom finally looked at Sandy, then turned away.

He knew she didn't understand why he was letting this happen; he knew too that she'd wanted him to

227

confront either Ellen or Michael, so that no blame or bad feeling would attach itself to her as it often did to a messenger. But she stood about as much chance of manipulating him like that as she did of Michael actually dumping Ellen for her. No-one had ever told him about her crush on Michael, but as it was as obvious as her methods of flirtation, which, in their way, he found kind of amusing, no-one had had to.

'Hey Tom,' he heard someone behind him call, and he turned to find a couple of old photographer friends he hadn't been aware Michael knew, sliding into one of the back rows. He waved out, then glancing at his watch he saw that it was already a couple of minutes past the time Ellen was due to arrive. But that was OK, it was traditional for the bride to be late, and besides, not all the guests were seated yet.

At the front of the church Michael glanced at his watch too. Next to him Cavan, looking like a rock star with his long hair and three-day beard, started to grin.

'I reckon she's going to stand you up,' he teased, and immediately flinched as his mother clipped him round the ear.

'Don't be making jokes in church,' she whispered loudly.

Michael was laughing. 'Great hat, Ma,' he told her.

'She said no jokes,' Cavan reminded him, and promptly received another swift clout.

'Uncle Michael, can I have a ride on your shoulders?' his nephew Ben wanted to know.

'Since when did you ride shoulders in church?' his mother demanded.

Ben looked up at her in confusion, his little three-year-old face a virtual replica of her own. 'Is Tierney wearing that silly dress today?' he asked.

'You know she is,' Colleen answered. 'And it's not silly, it's lovely.'

'It's silly isn't it Dad?' he said, turning to his father. 'You said it was silly.'

'I said it was pretty,' he corrected hastily as his wife turned her flashing blue eyes upon him.

'Is this our family?' Cavan whispered to Michael.

'We could be at the wrong wedding,' Michael responded.

'You could be right,' Cavan said. 'It would account for Ellen not being here.'

Though Michael kept smiling his insides were tensing up. She was almost ten minutes late by now. He cast his mind back to the night before, when he'd left her at the house to go and stay at Vic Warren's. She'd seemed fine then. Distracted, it was true, but with all that was going on around her, and so much to think about, it was hardly surprising. And when he'd called later to tell her he loved her, she'd cried and told him how much she loved him too. She'd even said she couldn't wait for tomorrow to be over – presumably because she was looking forward to them being alone together at last. But maybe that wasn't what she'd meant.

Resisting the urge to look at his watch again, he felt himself turn cold as the organist restarted the pre-wedding repertoire and behind him the guests continued to murmur. He didn't even want to think about what they were saying, for they too must be starting to wonder what was happening. Maybe Robbie had kicked up a fuss, refusing to be a page, or to get into the car. But Michelle was with him, and if need be she'd surely tell Ellen to go on ahead while she stayed back to deal with Robbie. Then suddenly his blood turned to ice. Michelle! What if he'd misjudged her? What if she hadn't accepted that it was never going to work for them, and had decided to tell Ellen what had happened between them? Jesus Christ almighty, that was it! For some unknown reason Michelle had got it into her head to choose today, of all days, to ruin his life.

He glanced at Cavan, but there was no way he could voice his fears to his brother, not when Cavan was so crazy about Michelle – it would tear the boy to pieces to find out she still wanted Michael. And he had to stop thinking of Cavan as a boy. He was twenty-three now – fifteen years younger than Michelle, and ten years younger than Michael, but that still didn't make him a boy. He thought of the time, six years ago, when he and Cavan had spent five long weeks sailing the high seas while he, Michael, had tried to come to terms with the way Michelle had left him. She'd been pregnant with Robbie, but her work, her vocation as she'd called it, had still come first. Never, not even in his worst nightmares, had he dreamt that he would go through that kind of hell again. It had taken him so long to get over it that not until he met Ellen had he even started believing he could.

Sandy glanced at Tom who was now sitting beside her. He was looking straight ahead, his hands clasped loosely in his lap. He showed no signs of tension, but he had to be wondering where Ellen was – unless he already knew. Somehow she didn't think so, for he surely wouldn't be letting Michael go through this agonizing wait if he'd known that Ellen wasn't going to show. Or maybe he would. He was so damned inscrutable there was just no knowing what he might do.

She glanced at him again. He really was something else. So dark and mysterious, and kind of intimidating, at least while he was being like this. It was impossible not to wonder what he'd be like in bed, fantastic, she imagined, maybe even as good as Michael.

Suppressing a sigh, she turned her eyes to the front of the church. She could only see the back of his head, but it was enough to fill her up with sadness - and a bitter envy of Ellen. It seemed whichever way Ellen turned she was going to get one of them, Michael or Tom, so she just couldn't lose. And to Sandy's mind no-one, but no-one, deserved to be in that position, least of all a woman who had betrayed Michael.

In the end, as the time continued to tick by and everyone in the church became increasingly restless, Sandy couldn't hold back any longer. She had to know if Tom had spoken to Ellen; she needed to know if Michael was about to be humiliated in the worst possible way, by a woman who didn't even love him enough to remain faithful.

She'd already drawn breath to ask when there was a sudden commotion at the back, and the news that Ellen had finally arrived swept through the church in an audible murmur of relief. She was almost fifteen minutes late and Sandy's disappointment was crushing.

Tom turned to her then and spoke so softly she only just caught what he was saying. 'If you utter as much as one word during this ceremony,' he said with a smile, 'I'll kill you.'

Sandy's eyebrows shot up, even as the colour suffused her cheeks. Not for a minute did she think he meant it, at least not literally, but the fact that he'd come to Ellen's defence like that sent her resentment and hatred of Ellen soaring to totally new levels.

At the back of the church, holding tightly to her father's arm, her face hidden by a veil, Ellen waited for Matty and Michelle to finish fussing at her train. Having got word of her arrival the guests were starting to turn, all of them smiling, some waving. Then one of the ushers signalled the solo trumpet and organist, and, as the triumphant strains of Charpentier's Te Deum filled the church, she began the long walk up the aisle to Michael.

As she moved past the pews her heart was so full it was difficult to breathe; she had never felt so much love, nor so much guilt and fear. She tried to concentrate on her bridesmaids, Matty and Tierney, or on Robbie who looked so handsome as a page-boy, even though he didn't think so. He'd seen her crying earlier and had been meek as a lamb ever since. There had been so many tears that by the time she'd got into the car with her father she'd felt utterly drained. But, having made the decision to go through with it, she wasn't going to ruin the day for Michael, so she forced herself to smile while silently praying to God for forgiveness.

She was halfway up the aisle when she finally saw Michael, and a moment's panic tore through her. But she kept on going, and as he turned to watch her she felt the love in her heart eclipse everything and everyone around them. She'd known he would adore her dress, as it fully revealed her shoulders and hugged her figure all the way to her knees, where it fish-tailed out around her ankles. But she could tell from his eyes that it wasn't the dress he was seeing, it was her, and in there with his familiar mix of irony and love she could see the relief. It was at that moment that she knew she had done the right thing in coming, for the pain she'd have caused him by staying away would have been so much greater than anything that might follow.

At last she was standing beside him and they were facing the priest. Her veil was pulled back and her flowers were with Matty. She listened as the priest spoke, felt oddly faint, but willed herself to stay calm. That morning, for the first time, she'd thrown up, though whether it was anxiety and nerves that had caused it, or the baby, she had no idea.

The priest continued to speak. Then Michael turned to take her hand and as she looked up into his eyes he began to repeat his vows. The only time she looked away was to watch the diamond-clustered band sliding onto her finger, then it came time for her to repeat her vows too. Her voice was thin and shaky, but as her lips started to tremble she saw the humour in Michael's eyes. It was his way of giving her strength and she took it.

Then everyone was singing the first hymn; the lessons were read, mass was held and the priest gave his sermon. One of Michael's nephews complained he wanted to go to the toilet, and someone at the back had a coughing fit.

At last the final words of the service were spoken, then turning to look up at Michael she felt herself fill with emotion as his lips came gently down on hers and he kissed her with all the love in his heart. Then he was leading her back down the aisle, and everyone was smiling and laughing, taking photographs and shooting videotape, and she was looking at them and laughing too, holding Michael's arm and feeling the euphoria starting to wash over her. But the moment she saw Tom it stopped, and as her smile began to wane she looked at Sandy and felt suddenly afraid.

She turned away quickly, reminding herself that she was Michael's wife now, and no matter how much Sandy hated her, or wanted Michael, it wasn't that that was ever going to come between her and Michael.

The reception, which was being held in one of the magnificent ballrooms of the Four Seasons hotel, had been going on for some time now. The buffet luncheon was over, the toasts and speeches had been made and Michael and Ellen had taken the floor. The band was inundated with requests from the two hundred guests and as the dancing became faster and more outrageous, and the champagne continued to flow, many new and sworn-for-eternity friendships were getting under way.

Ellen and Michael danced and danced, until finally to a bawdy chorus of howls, catcalls and laughter they disappeared upstairs to change, and lookouts were posted ready to inform everyone when the happy couple were ready to depart for the airport.

Certain his absence wouldn't be noticed, Tom slipped quietly away from the party and headed upstairs to his room. He didn't need to be a part of the group that saw Ellen and Michael off, nor did he want to be there as any kind of reminder to Ellen.

As he rode the elevator to the fourteenth floor he was picturing the way she had danced in Michael's arms and thinking of how lovely she had looked – lovelier than he had ever seen her. The rich, honey-coloured skin of her shoulders and the desire in her eyes when she'd looked at Michael had reminded him of the night he had made love to her himself, a night it seemed he was now destined never to forget.

Unlocking the door to his room, he flicked on the lights and crossed to the mini-bar. Instead of opening it he stood with his hands on the top and stared absently out at the night. He was thinking of Rachel now, and how different his life would be had she lived. Certainly he wouldn't be here, reliving almost every day they had spent together for the sake of a movie. In fact he couldn't imagine Hollywood ever even touching their lives, they were so much a part of another world. But he was here, and as painful as the reasons were, and as much pleasure as he took in the time he spent with Ellen, he was under no illusion about his feelings for her. He liked her, deeply admired her and desired her a great deal, but he wasn't in love with her.

If the circumstances had been any different there was every chance he might be, but he was in no doubt about her feelings for Michael, and despite what had happened between them that night he had no wish for it to be any other way. Except now it was possible she was carrying his child, and no matter what he tried to tell himself, it did make a difference. At this stage he wasn't going to explore what kind of difference, as he doubted he could come up with an answer. What he suspected, however, was that she probably hated him now for being a part of the terrible dilemma she was in. Certainly she had gone out of her way to avoid him these past few hours, dancing and chatting with everyone, and only pausing briefly to thank him for taking care of her family at the church.

He returned his thoughts to Rachel, and wondered what was going to happen to the movie now. God only knew when, or even if, Ellen was planning to tell Michael about the problem with the baby, but if she did and it turned out to be sooner, rather than later, then Tom didn't even want to think about what kind of nightmare it was going to be for the three of them working together. And there didn't seem much choice but to go ahead with it now, for they were simply too far in to back out. Were it possible, he would probably pull out himself, and leave it to Michael and Ellen to produce. But this was Rachel's story, and though he knew Michael would never turn it into some kind of testosterone-triumph-over-crack for the likes of Stallone or Segal, there was simply no way he could allow himself to walk away from it. It would be like letting Rachel down all over again.

Reaching inside the mini-bar he took out a bottle of chilled champagne and a couple of glasses from the shelf above. He'd noticed Sandy leaving the party long before he had and guessed she was alone in her room, trying to deal with what was probably one of the first truly crushing blows of her life. As blows went Tom didn't rate it particularly highly, but she hadn't experienced the world the way he had, nor had she caused the death of someone she loved. But that wasn't to say this was easy for her, and considering how reluctant he was to spend the evening alone, he reckoned they could at least have a shot at cheering each other up. Besides, tonight wasn't a night he wanted to be dealing with any more of the phone calls from Bogotá that had lately been coming his way, so out of here was going to be the best place to be.

Sandy had stayed only until the speeches were over, then, having other matters to attend to, she had slipped quietly from the reception and up to her room. It had been such a relief to get away, as being forced to watch the way Michael was so attentive to his bride, so witty and involved with everyone else, and so far from her reach, had been almost impossible to endure. Her single, burning hope now was that this baby would blow it all apart. But it would only do that if it were Tom's, and no-one would know that for certain until the child was born. Which meant that the big question hanging over them now was, would Ellen wait until the birth to break the bad news to Michael – if indeed there were any bad news to break – or would the pressure of not knowing force her to break down and confess long before that?

At first Sandy had considered it to be more in her interests for Ellen to confess now, but after taking some time to think about it she was starting to realize the disastrous effect it would have on the movie, which was something, as a businesswoman, she didn't want at all. A lot of people had put a great deal of trust in her over this project, and as she had no more wish to let them down than she did to see World Wide suffer, she realized she would have to think more carefully about how she was going to play this.

It hadn't taken long for an alternative route to present itself, and when it did she could only feel amazed that she hadn't seen it sooner. Indeed she might have done had Ted Forgon not been forced to cancel dinner the other night, for it was seeing him at the wedding that had reminded her what a perfect ally he would make. It was just a shame she hadn't thought of him before, since there was no doubt he'd have stepped in with pleasure to tell Michael about the baby, then this galling spectacle of a wedding might never have taken place. But perhaps it was better this way, for if anyone had the power to force Ellen and Michael to continue with the movie, despite their personal problems, it was Forgon.

Today was the first time Sandy had seen Forgon in a couple of months and the first thing she'd noticed was that he'd definitely put on weight. Obviously the overindulgence in Martinis and lack of executive stress was finally kicking in, but at seventy-one he could still, at a stretch, be considered a handsome man – though slightly ridiculous with his woven mahogany hair and dazzling capped teeth. The only accoutrement that was missing was the bimbo - indeed it had surprised Sandy a lot to see him with a woman who was at least his own age. She'd soon found out that it was his sister from Florida, the one who had nursed him back to health after the major heart attack he'd suffered a couple of years ago, when in true Hollywood fashion he'd almost taken off to his maker while in the throes of giving it to some secretary or starlet.

Getting him to meet her upstairs in her room had only been difficult insofar as she hadn't wanted anyone to see them leave, or to connect their absences. However, it was unlikely anyone would as all the focus was on Ellen and Michael, and a considerable amount of champagne had been consumed by then. What they'd had to discuss hadn't taken long: a few minutes for the imparting of the information she had; a few more for what she wanted in return, then a small added incentive for him to play it her way.

They were at the incentive now, meaning that he was sitting on the edge of the bed, trousers undone, while she knelt in front of him and gave him the kind of satisfaction he craved. She'd guessed there'd be a price, and considered herself fortunate to be getting away with this, as she'd desperately not wanted to go the whole way. If it had come to that, she wasn't sure what she'd have done, as it was well over a year since she'd last had sex and she certainly didn't want to end that unhappy state with Ted Forgon. As it was, the very idea that she was up here doing this, while Michael was downstairs celebrating his marriage, was so depressing she could have wept. But that wasn't going to get rid of Forgon, so, blocking all else from her mind, she threw herself into the task with the same practised vigour she had used during her days as an escort.

At last it was over and as he zipped himself up she turned discreetly away and offered him a drink.

He laughed. 'Don't think I don't know you want me out of here now,' he told her. 'And there's a wedding going on downstairs. Let's get back to it.'

She shook her head. 'You go,' she said, closing the mini-bar and turning to face him.

He cocked a single eyebrow and gave her a look that suggested he might prefer to stay a while longer.

Beneath her pastel pink Dior suit Sandy could feel her skin crawling. She glared at him, as though daring him to ask for more, certain now that she would blow the entire deal they'd just made rather than allow him to put a hand on her again.

As though sensing this he laughed, and taking out his wallet he dropped a ten-dollar bill on the bed.

She looked at it, then at him.

'In the States, hookers get paid,' he explained.

Her eyes remained on his. Not for a single second did she show how deeply the insult had cut, but she did have the satisfaction of glimpsing a momentary discomfort as he very nearly squirmed beneath the contempt in her eyes.

Tucking his wallet back inside his jacket he said, 'Right, I'm out of here.'

She watched him walk to the door. 'Before you go,' she said, 'you never did answer the question – how come you let Michael take control of World Wide when you had it, and him, sitting in the palm of your hand? Or should I say, what does he have on you?'

Forgon's shrewd brown eyes were sparkling with humour. 'You've got to be crazy if you think I'm going to tell you that,' he responded. 'But I will tell you this, it isn't going to be worth diddly a couple of weeks from now, so the information you just gave me couldn't have been better timed.'

She looked at him and suddenly wished she could take everything back.

His pointed white teeth showed in a grin. Then rubbing his crotch he said, 'Great head, by the way.'

As the door closed behind him Sandy continued to stand where she was, staring at it and fighting hard to hold back the anger and humiliation that was tightening her throat. It was hard to know whom she hated the most, him or the woman whose heart was thudding inside her skin. He had no right to treat her like that, but nor had she been compelled to behave like that. The truth was he hadn't even suggested the incentive, she had, though God only knew why when she loathed the very idea of what she'd done almost as much as she detested whatever it was that had made her do it.

It was as though she didn't trust any man to give her what she wanted, without giving them something in return. Yet she *had* given something to Forgon – the information that Ellen didn't know who the father of her baby was – and in return Forgon had promised to do everything in his power to make sure Michael continued to work on the movie. So there had been no need for what had followed; no good reason for her to debase herself like that, nor to have subjected herself to his contempt.

Pushing herself away from the mini-bar she unbuttoned her jacket and walked to the bed. The ten-dollar bill was still lying there. Throwing her jacket over it, she turned back to one of the armchairs beside the desk. As she passed the mirror she stopped and gazed at her reflection in the pale orange light cast from a floor lamp. Her blonde hair was slightly mussed, though immaculately cut and highlighted; her turquoise eyes glimmered darkly in their circles of sky-blue kohl and her lips appeared pale and thin without their usual coating of gloss. She wondered what people saw when they looked at that face, and tried to work out what there was to see. Some days she felt so displaced and alone, and horribly cowed by the coldly determined woman she had become. She almost laughed at that, for it was odd indeed to think she intimidated herself – it was like a dog running away from its bark, or a bully cringing from his own fist.

Turning away she sank into the sumptuous armchair and pulling her feet in under her she tucked her hands inside the white silk straps of her bodysuit. Her skin felt soft and cool and she tried not to think of the last time it had been touched by a man. But there was no escaping that longing, for the memory still lived so vividly in her mind. Michael had made love to her in a way no other man ever had. There had been no payment for her services then, there had been only passion and longing and an almost insatiable need for more and yet more. It was why she had never slept with anyone since, for she knew in her heart that no-one could live up to Michael, or make her feel the way he had.

Hearing a knock on the door she instantly froze. Forgon had come back to test the slut again. How much would he pay her this time? Twenty dollars for the whole way? Fifty to do it from behind? She was cheap, so cheap. Not even during the days when she'd done it to survive had she been so cheap. So why now? Why was she allowing this to happen when she had risen so far and achieved so much? Was there something in her that needed this, that thrived on the humiliation and indignity? Wasn't she worthy of real love and consideration? Didn't she deserve what other women had? For her everything was a fight; a ceaseless challenge to win, a bitter confusion of morals, and conflict of conscience. It was as though she was on a lone and complicated journey to an end that would never come.

Tom knocked again and glanced along the hall as someone came out of a door further down. He was sure she was in there, but didn't want to call out until the couple coming towards him had passed and taken the elevator to a place that no longer abutted his life.

They moved so slowly he could feel an irrational anger mounting inside him, making him want to yell at them to speed up for God's sake. It was rare for him to feel such fury towards something so trivial, which perhaps went to show how trying today had been – much more than he'd want to admit.

Turning his mind from the couple he thought about Sandy and wondered what she was doing in there. Sitting alone in the darkness; sobbing into her pillow; staring out at the night; or maybe just taking a bath? He was vaguely intrigued, and even a little uncomfortable with his decision to seek her out, though he assumed it was because she was on her own too. She was also, apart from Matty and Ellen, the only other living soul who knew about the baby, and certainly the only one he could talk to. Except he had no desire to discuss, or even think about, the unholy mess they were all now in. Nor did he want to talk about Rachel, or the movie, or anything to do with his life. So quite why he was here was eluding him, unless the reason was no more complicated than a simple need to communicate with another human being.

'Sandy!' he called, knocking again as the elevator doors closed. 'It's Tom. Are you in there?'

He waited, but there was still no answer, nor a single sound from inside. So it looked like he had it wrong, she wasn't there after all. Dropping his head, he started back down the hall, and tried to decide whether he should hit the bar or return to the wedding. He guessed the wedding was the polite way to go, and as it surely couldn't be much longer before Michael and Ellen left, he shouldn't have too long to wait to make his reappearance.

He'd already called the elevator when he heard Sandy's door open. It was a moment or two before she stepped out into the hall, and when she did he felt himself starting to smile. Gone were the expensive high heels, the designer jacket, and greasy coating of lipstick; in their place was a strikingly lovely young woman with an amateur kind of finesse, an endearingly unpractised mystique and a truly great pair of shoulders.

Seeing the antagonism in her eyes his smile widened and he held out the champagne and glasses. 'I thought maybe you could use some company,' he said, taking a step away from the elevator as the doors swept open.

She continued to glare at him, hard enough to stop him coming any further, but not so hard that he turned and got into the lift.

'OK, it's me who's looking for the company,' he confessed, letting his arms drop to his sides. He shrugged. 'I guess I'm being too presumptuous . . .'

He assumed his best forlorn and abandoned expression, then peered at her from under his lids to see what effect he was having.

Catching him looking she struggled not to smile.

'I can sing,' he offered, and promptly broke into a bawdy little ditty that caused her to laugh.

'You'd better come in before the men in white coats find you,' she said, and turning back into her room she held the door open for him to follow.

Returning to the chair she'd been sitting in, she pulled her legs under her again and looked up at him in the warm amber light. He was standing at the foot of the bed, apparently assessing the room.

'Great place you've got here,' he told her.

She rolled her eyes and tried again to stop herself

smiling. 'It certainly beats the first room I lived in,' she responded, thinking of the damp, grimy little bedsit she'd rented when she'd first arrived in London. 'Not quite up to your suite though,' she added.

'Ah, but I'm living here, you're just staying,' he replied, by way of justification. 'So, are you going to help me with this?'

Sandy looked at the bottle of champagne, then returning her eyes to his she nodded. 'OK,' she said.

After popping the cork he handed her a glass and was about to propose a toast when some kind of commotion started up outside. He guessed the time had arrived for Ellen and Michael to leave.

Going to the window he pulled aside the drapes and looked down at the champagne-crazed euphoria. Sandy came to stand beside him, and together they watched the wedding guests swarm around the decorated limousine, clamouring to get one final embrace or photograph with the happy couple. More rice was thrown, so was confetti, and the single women of the crowd called for Ellen to send her gorgeous bouquet of white flowers their way. At last she flung it high in the air, so high that at one point it was closer to Sandy and Tom than it was to the ground. Then it started to fall, and as three dozen arms reached out to catch it, Ellen and Michael quickly got into the car.

The bouquet was caught by a young girl neither Tom nor Sandy recognized but whoever she was, even from where they were standing they could see her flush of pleasure. Then all the attention was once again on the white limousine as it started to pull away, dragging a colourful and noisy arrangement of cans, ribbons, boots and black cats behind it. Because of the tinted windows Ellen and Michael were already lost from view, but Sandy and Tom, just like the rest of the crowd who trailed the car to the road, stood watching as it entered the traffic on Doheny, waited for the red lights to turn green, then began heading south along the lamplit, palm-lined street towards the international airport.

Tom turned to look down at Sandy. Her features were lost in shadow, so it was impossible to read her expression. Tapping his glass against hers he said, 'Let's drink a toast to me.'

Sandy blinked. 'To you?' she queried.

He shrugged. 'Why not? Do you have a better idea?'

She nodded. 'Yes. Let's drink one to me,' she said.

'To you?' he responded, as though amazed by the notion.

She grinned. 'OK then, to you,' she conceded, and lifted her glass.

'To you,' he chimed in, and waggled his eyebrows comically as she started to laugh.

After taking a sip she moved back to the chair and watched as he made himself comfortable on the bed. He was sitting with his back against the headboard, his elbows resting on his knees and his cravat hanging loosely down his shirt-front. He'd left his jacket in his own room, and his shoes he'd kicked off before climbing on to the bed. It was really too dark over that side of the room for her to see him clearly, but she knew very well how good-looking he was. An image of Ted Forgon suddenly flashed through her mind, and she felt her soul sink at the knowledge of what had happened less than an hour ago, right there on the bed. What on earth would Tom think if he knew? Which would appal him more: what she had done, or why she had done it?

'So what shall we talk about?' he said.

She shrugged. 'I don't mind. You choose.'

He thought for a while, and was about to speak when she said, 'Aren't you even interested to know if that baby is yours? I mean, doesn't it piss you off just a little bit to think that she's gone off on honeymoon with another man, while carrying your child?'

He didn't answer right away – instead he thought of

244

the way she had phrased her question, and how swiftly she had gone from the possibility of the baby being his, to the certainty that it must be. Another indication of the way she tried to make things the truth simply by declaring that they were. It was a strategy that many a spiritualist would claim to have almost foolproof results; though in this instance he doubted Sandy's self-delusions had much to do with affirmations and Universal feedback.

'Have you ever made a study of metaphysics?' he asked.

Sandy's eyes immediately went down, but as she sipped her champagne, stalling for time, he knew from the faint colour in her cheeks that she didn't understand the term.

'It's a subject that fascinates me,' he said. 'You know, what it is that draws us together as human beings. Whether there is some kind of supernatural force that weaves its magic on us all, taking us through time, linking us to the planets, the galaxy, the entire universe, before reintroducing us to each other in future lives, other guises, other conflicts or resolutions . . . I guess I'm getting into karma now, but why not? Doesn't it interest you to know if we've ever met before? Or what the purpose is of us being here, now, in this room? Do we have some unfinished business from a previous existence? I wonder if you knew me when I was a Vietnamese pirate; or if it was when I was a Parisian whore?'

A wary humour was creeping into Sandy's eyes. Was he teasing her, or had he already had too much to drink?

'It could be you had the pad next to mine on Mars, a couple of dozen millennia ago,' he mused. 'Or maybe you were the cat I chased when I was a dog in South Carolina. I don't know, I just get the feeling that there's more to us, here tonight, than the mere escape of a wedding. Don't you?'

By now Sandy was grinning. 'If you say so,' she answered. She knew, from the dinner conversation they'd had a few nights ago, that she was out of her depth with Chambers, for his humour was so much more sophisticated, his world so much wider and knowledge so much greater, than the narrow horizons imposed by Hollywood and showbiz. But oddly she wasn't feeling daunted by the enormity of his experience, nor cowed by his superiority of intellect. Instead she was feeling vaguely intrigued by all he could teach her, and definitely flattered that he would choose to spend an evening with someone like her.

'I've got to hand it to you,' she said, reaching out for the champagne to refill her glass, 'you've got a pretty neat way of changing the subject.'

He nodded as he thought about that. 'Yeah, I guess you're right,' he finally agreed.

'So what about the baby?' she said.

He drained his glass, then looked at her. 'What about Michael?' he responded.

Again she flushed. 'What about him?' she said.

'As far as you're concerned, what about him?'

'I don't know what you mean.'

'Sure you do. When are you going to let it go? He's married to Ellen now . . .'

'Who's carrying your child.'

He shrugged. 'Maybe, maybe not. The only definite carrying around here is your torch for Michael, which is nowhere near as bright or as pure as you like to think it is.'

Her face started to tighten. 'What . . .?' she began.

He held up a hand. 'Getting it wrong isn't a sin,' he told her. 'We all do it, and then we move on.'

'You mean like you did after Rachel?' she snapped.

His eyes seemed hard for a moment, but she didn't look away. 'Touché,' he responded, and getting up from the bed he went to replenish his own glass. As he poured he

246

glanced down at her and noticed the delicate points of her nipples through the sheer silk of her top. But he was more interested in her vulnerability than her sexuality.

Returning to the bed he sat down again and looked at her in the semi-darkness. She was staring at her drink, but he guessed she knew he was watching her. 'Tell me the three most important things about Sandy,' he said.

Her head came up.

He smiled and saluted her with his glass.

'Are you serious?' she said. 'You want to know the three most important things about me?'

'It's why I asked.'

Though obviously still surprised, he could see how pleased she was to be asked. He waited quietly as she put her head to one side and thought. 'Well,' she began, 'there's my job. That's important.'

He nodded.

'Then there's . . . Let me see, well I suppose there's . . .' She started to chew on her top lip. 'There's um, the money I make.' She looked at him as though seeking his approval.

Again he nodded.

Several more minutes ticked by, until finally her eyes returned to his, telling him she couldn't think of anything else.

He smiled. 'A lot of people don't even get past one,' he told her.

She took a large sip of champagne and felt some trickle down her chin. Using her fingers to wipe it away, she looked at him again waiting for him to say more. 'You're in love with Michael, aren't you?' he said. 'At least you think you are.'

'Why don't you believe it?' she retorted, failing to keep the edge from her voice.

He shrugged. 'You wouldn't be trying to inflict all this misery on him if you cared about him,' he answered.

'What misery?' she demanded, her guilty conscience

making her wonder for one horrible moment if he'd spoken to Forgon.

He looked surprised. 'You're trying to break up his relationship with Ellen, when any fool can see how much he loves her.'

Her eyes moved away, but he could see she was stung by his words. 'She was unfaithful to Michael,' she suddenly blurted, 'so now she's going to get what she deserves.'

'And you honestly think that's going to result in giving you what you want?' he said.

Again she looked away. Her expression was mutinous, but he had no doubt he was reaching her. 'We don't always realize what we want,' she said finally.

'Bingo,' he grinned.

Her eyes were flashing as she looked at him. 'I meant Michael, not me,' she snapped.

'Why should it be the case for Michael, yet not for you?' he replied. 'But you're right, we don't always realize what we want, and most of us are guilty of wishing for things that aren't in our best interests at all. Often we don't know that until we've got them, so it's probably best to heed that old warning about being careful of what you wish for, because you might just get it. And believe you me, wishing the worst for Ellen isn't going to work for you, no matter how it all comes out in the end. Besides, you don't wish the worst for her really, what you're wishing for is the best for you, and you think that can only come if her life falls apart.'

Sandy was staring up at him. Her barriers were still up, but he could sense them shifting. 'This is beginning to sound like a lecture,' she grumbled.

He shrugged. 'Yeah, I guess it does,' he responded. 'And all I was trying to do was make you understand what a wonderful woman you really are. Of course *you* don't think so, but you can't fool me.'

She sat quietly with that, enjoying the fact that he

thought so, even though she wasn't sure that he meant it. She glanced at him once or twice, then, just for the hell of it, she said, 'I used to sleep with men for money, or whatever else I could get out of them. How wonderful do you rate that?'

His eyebrows went up. 'We're not talking about what you do, we're talking about who you are,' he answered.

'Aren't we what we do?'

'As long as what we do isn't a lie. You sleeping with men for some kind of gain wasn't true to the person you are.'

'How do you know that? Maybe I liked it.'

'Did you?'

She was about to lie and say she did, but then realized she was just being childish. 'No,' she said quietly. 'I didn't.'

'Tell me,' he said, 'how much do you like yourself? A little, a lot, or not at all?'

'What kind of question is that?' she scoffed. 'I can hardly say I like myself a lot, can I?'

Laughing, he said, 'I detected some kind of accent then. Where are you from?'

'The Midlands,' she answered. 'Do you know England?'

'Very well.' He paused and drank some champagne. 'When are you planning on going back?'

'Next Wednesday. I've got a few things to do for Michael here before I can leave.'

He nodded, compressed his lips and frowned. 'You know, I think I'll come with you,' he said.

To his surprise she actually jumped. 'What, to London?' she said.

'Yeah, I haven't been there in a while, and I've got a couple of weeks to kill before Ellen and I get back to work, so where better to spend them than London? With you.'

'You want to come to London to spend some time

249

with *me*?' She shook her head in bewildered suspicion.

He smiled. 'I wasn't planning on staying with you,' he told her. 'Just on getting to know you. I could catch up with a few old friends, there's a couple up in Scotland I'm particularly fond of who I haven't seen for ages. And maybe I could see Vic Warren while I'm over. He's flying back on Monday to start the sound edit for his latest movie, but I'm sure he could fit me in somewhere.'

Sandy said, 'Maybe you could meet some of the investors too. I think they'd appreciate that. I'll call the World Wide business managers on Monday and get them to set up some meetings.'

'Sure,' he said, noting how the confidence had crept back into her voice now she was on familiar ground.

She smiled, then lowered her eyes as he continued to look at her. She wasn't entirely sure how she was feeling right now, except excited that he was coming to London. She wondered if it meant he wanted to sleep with her, and if he did, whether he planned to wait until they got to London, or do it now. She looked up, and finding him still watching her she wondered with alarm if he was reading her mind.

'When was the last time you had yourself some fun?' he said.

A hint of wariness crept into her eyes. 'What do you mean?' she asked.

He laughed. 'How old are you? Twenty-five? Twenty-six?'

'Twenty-six.'

'And when was the last time you went to a disco? Took a vacation? Screamed at a rock concert? Looked round a museum? Went for a picnic? Or did anything that didn't involve work?'

She blinked.

'It's time you loosened up a bit, Sandy,' he said. 'You're getting old before your time, and there's nothing in the rule book that says it has to be all work and no play, no matter how ambitious you are. Nor did I ever see it written anywhere that you have to dress like a forty-year-old executive before you're even thirty.'

Her eyes widened in amazement. 'This suit is a Christian Dior,' she protested.

'And perfect for a wedding,' he conceded. 'But I've seen you all dressed up in that stuffy designer rubbish ever since you arrived. It's for women twice your age, and believe me, no-one's going to think any the less of you if you tone down the make-up. In fact, you look gorgeous without it, so I've got to wonder why you're trying to hide your own beauty?'

He waited, but she didn't answer.

'So I guess we're back to you not liking yourself too much,' he said.

'I never said that,' she protested.

'You don't have to say it,' he smiled. 'You've just got to change it. You know, I think I'll take you shopping myself. I'm no expert, but I reckon we could have ourselves some fun.'

'My name's not Eliza Doolittle,' she grumbled, though secretly she was delighted by the suggestion.

'God forbid that an American should ever presume to teach a Brit how to talk,' he laughed.

She looked confused.

'Wasn't that what Henry Higgins did for Eliza Doolittle?' he reminded her.

She nodded.

He glanced at his watch. 'It's seven thirty,' he said. 'The stores don't close until nine, so what do you say we go get you something entirely different to anything you've got in that trussed-up, expensive wardrobe of yours, then go paint this crazy town red?'

Her heart was racing with pleasure. No-one had ever taken this kind of interest in her before, and that it was Tom was blowing her mind. The trouble was, she wasn't entirely sure how to handle it. In a way she'd have

251

preferred to have sex. She'd feel more comfortable with that. A bit more in control. Though something told her she might not be in control where he was concerned, so maybe the idea of shopping and clubbing was safer than she thought. In fact, the very idea of shopping with a man, which wasn't something she'd ever done before, was extremely appealing.

'What shall I wear to go shopping?' she asked.

His grin widened and she felt her heart catch on how devastatingly handsome he was. 'Do you have any jeans?' he asked.

She shook her head. 'Not with me.'

'Then show me what you do have, and if you as much as reach for the make-up, the date's off.'

'Date?' she echoed.

'Don't tell me you never heard of a date?' he cried.

She laughed. 'Of course I have, I just didn't realize that was what we were doing.' She paused.

'Well, get used to the idea,' he said, swinging his legs off the bed, 'because that's what we're going to be doing for at least the next eight hours, and if you tell me you don't dance I'm going to sign you up for therapy. Now, let's take a look at this wardrobe.'

It wasn't until well after midnight, as she twisted and whirled and laughed and clapped in the flashing lights of some overcrowded nightclub, that she realized how many hours had passed since she'd last thought about Michael. But despite the way her heart sank as she did, she was having far too much fun to give in to it now. Never having felt so good in her new short black petticoat dress and knee-high, three-inch-heel black leather boots, she gyrated brazenly towards Tom, arms high in the air, then shrieked with delight as he scooped her up and swung her round in a circle. For the moment it didn't matter that it wasn't Michael she was with, when the time was right it would be, and until then all she could do was thank God she wasn't in Ellen's shoes.

Chapter 14

Gazing down at the gentle, persistent motion of the waves was like gazing into her own heart. Each time courage reached her, it was sucked away again by an undertow of fear, a pressing need for escape. She was two people now: the new bride who adored her husband, laughed with him, played with him and made love with him so willingly and passionately it was as though they were discovering each other for the very first time. And then there was the other her: the woman whose deceit was eating her up inside, whose fear watched the 'new bride' so jealously that she knew it was only a matter of time now before it swept on to the stage and took control.

It astonished her to find she could put on such a show, that she could detach herself so completely from the truth and pretend to be the woman she'd always been. She'd done it at the church, throughout the reception and now, for the past five days, here on her honeymoon. Guilt stalked her constantly, but if it ever came too close she reminded herself that all she was doing was living her life the way it should have been – and would have been had she not taken that single, insane act of revenge that was now about to take its revenge on her. And it would, because there was no way of avoiding it, no way at all.

But why shouldn't she and Michael have these two

weeks of happiness? What was wrong with giving him that when she was going to take so much away? Even if the baby turned out to be his she knew how hard it was going to be for him to forgive the doubt, and wondered if in the end they would ever get past it. She hoped desperately that the fact no-one else knew would help, but even if it did, she just couldn't get rid of the dread that once she told him the truth he was never going to feel the same way about her again.

Right now she was standing in the small patio garden of their Caribbean home, looking down at the white, empty beach and glittering aquamarine sea. To one side of her was the double hammock that Michael had tied between two palms, where they often lay in each other's arms gazing up at the sky. Because of the time of year the humidity was intense, but this was where they'd wanted to be, away from the rest of the world, yet still in their own home. She looked down at the sun loungers that were strewn with towels, tanning oil and the books they were reading. For a horrible moment the image came to her of him making love to Michelle on a lounger beside their pool in LA. She pushed it quickly away. She had no right to be jealous now, nor to use his betrayal to justify her own. She had wanted Tom Chambers and when faced with an excuse to seduce him, she had done just that.

Walking across the red brick tiles and under the flower-covered pergola, she stopped at a tub of geraniums and began to pull off the dead leaves. As she worked she almost smiled at the unusual spectacle she would present, dressed as she was, to anyone able to see her. But their small two-bedroomed villa in a secluded bay on the west of the island was overlooked by no-one, except maybe the pilot of a descending plane. Occasionally strollers found their way onto the beach below, but the hillside between was covered in giant cacti and other trees and shrubs, enough to obstruct the view up to the house. They were very private here.

Hearing the car come to a stop at the side of the house, she left the geraniums and walked across the grass to the two tallest palms in the garden that grew in a giant V from the ground and soared so high in the sky that on a bad day their green feathery tops were lost in cloud. Standing between them she turned so that she could see Michael coming, and leaning her shoulder against one tree she reached out to rest her hand on the other. He had taken many photographs of her here, striking just this kind of pose, but none while she was dressed like this.

As he came round the corner of the house, carrying two bags of groceries, she felt her heart swell, then weigh so heavily inside her it was as though she could no longer support it. She loved him so much it went beyond anything she could ever fathom or maybe even, in the end, endure. And knowing how much he loved her too turned the ache inside her to a terrible, wrenching pain. She watched him, knowing he hadn't yet seen her, almost afraid of what she would see in his eyes when he did. Yet it was what she wanted, his desire, his passion, his urgency and love.

Pressing down the handle with his elbow he opened the door to the kitchen and disappeared inside. She heard him call her name, then saw him return to the door and look out. It was a moment or two before he found her, but when he did it was as though the space between them no longer existed, for the immediacy and power of his response leapt through her veins too.

He came towards her, his intense blue eyes drinking in the sight of her. This was the sexiest underwear she had ever owned, and the very first time she'd worn it. She wasn't sure why she'd chosen now, today, to put it on, except she wanted to do anything and everything in her power to please him – and from the way he was looking at her now, there was no doubt in the world she was doing that. The white stretch-satin bodysuit went right up to her neck, where it folded over in a neat little lace collar. The shoulders were cut away, so were the cups of the bra, leaving her breasts completely exposed. From the waist down there was no more to the suit than the long thin triangle that barely covered her pubic hair. The white garter-belt was made of the same white satin, the stockings were also white.

As he reached her he stood looking down at her, his eyes burning with all the emotion she had feared, yet craved. His desire was so intense she could feel it knifing through her too, and the need for him to touch her was growing to a pitch she was finding hard to bear.

Resting his hands on the trees he lowered his head to her breasts and taking first one, then the other nipple into his mouth, he began to suck and pull and bite until he had drawn them out so far they were throbbing. Her eyes were closed, her breath was coming in short, ragged gasps. He stood up and looked at her again, then his mouth came crushing down on hers as he drew her harshly against his erection, and ripped off his shirt so he could feel the hardness of her nipples on his skin. Her fingers were fumbling with his shorts, frantic to get to his penis, wanting it in her hand, in her mouth, and deep inside her. As she found him he groaned, and drew back quickly as a sudden climax threatened to claim him.

She looked up at him, waited for him to steady, then turned so he could see her from behind. Her back was totally covered, her buttocks were totally bare. He ran his hands over the soft, firm flesh, down to her stocking tops and around to the front of her. Kicking off his shorts he pulled her back against him, placing his penis along the narrow thong of her bodysuit. Her head fell back on his shoulder, and, as she looked up at him, he cupped her face in one hand and brought her mouth to his. His other hand had returned to her breasts, lifting them, squeezing them and grazing the nipples over his palm.

Their tongues were as entwined as their hearts as he continued to kiss her, until finally he lifted his head and looked into her eyes.

'Do you have any idea how much I love you?' he whispered.

'I love you too,' she said, then moaned softly as he lowered his hands to ease open her legs. Obediently she parted them, then gasped as he suddenly tore open the bottom of her suit and pushed his fingers inside her.

'Oh God, Michael,' she murmured, as he began to stroke her. 'Oh God, don't stop. Please don't stop.'

He quickened his fingers, while with his other hand he pushed his penis down between her legs and began slowly to penetrate her.

'Oh Michael,' she cried as he filled her. 'Yes, oh God, yes.'

Her final yes was more of a scream as he rammed himself into her. Very slowly he pulled back, then rammed himself in again. She bent forward, using the trees to balance, but almost lost it as she felt the full length of him plunge right up inside her. His hands circled her waist as he slammed himself in, harder and faster. The sensations were so fierce her knees were turning weak. He held her tight, keeping her against him as he soared towards climax. Then suddenly he pulled out, turned her round and took her in his arms.

She lifted her mouth to his and only broke away to pull the bodysuit over her head. She wanted to feel his skin against hers, the coarse dark hair, the hard muscle and sweat. She could feel the strength of his thighs pressing through the silk of her stockings and wanted them against her too. Quickly she peeled the stockings off, unhooked the garter-belt and returned to his arms.

Naked, they lay down in the grass, eyes locked together, as he entered her again and began to make love to her with such tenderness and skill it brought tears to her eyes. He knew everything about her, where to touch her, when to kiss her and how to surprise her. She watched him and touched him and yearned to become part of him. Knowing she was going to lose him filled her with such longing it was as though there was nothing else in her. She looked into his eyes and seeing him smile, she smiled too. She pulled his face to hers and kissed him deeply. Then she rolled him onto his back and sat over him.

His hands came up to her breasts, caressing them and holding them, before descending to her waist, to her hips and round to her buttocks. He ran them along the insides of her thighs until he reached her and pulled her wide open. Then his thumb was on her, rotating, rubbing and pressing. She fell over him and clung to him with her arms and legs as he laid her on her side and came into her for a long, long time.

Later that evening Michael was on the phone to his mother, then Michelle and Robbie, while Ellen cleared away the remains of dinner and emptied what was left of a bottle of Chianti into the glasses she'd left on the table. They'd eaten outside on the patio, cocooned in the darkness by the burnished glow of citronella candles to keep the mosquitoes at bay. The moon was high and dramatically clear in a black, starry sky and the sound of the waves, soughing up from the shore, swept through the perpetual buzz of crickets and seemed to merge with the wonderfully romantic songs that were playing on the CD.

As she sat down at the table, propping her feet up on a chair, Michael said goodbye to his mother and waited for Robbie to come on the line. Turning to look at Ellen he winked, and pulled a sofa cushion out from behind him. She looked lovely sitting there in the candlelight, her hair clipped carelessly on top of her head, her lightly tanned skin glowing more darkly against the pale peach shades of her shorts and top.

She smiled back at him, then carried in his drink. He was gently biting her thigh and making her laugh as Robbie suddenly exploded onto the line.

'Dad!' he shouted. 'Dad, guess what?'

'And what would that be?' Michael said, glancing up at Ellen.

Brushing her fingers lightly over his face she wandered back out to the table and sat down again.

'I got a commendation for my maths today. That's the second one this week. And if I get another before the end of next week I can win a red badge. I've got a blue one now, because I've got two. And Mummy said if I get a red badge we can go to Big Bear camping and I can wear my badge.' He grabbed a quick breath. 'And Dad,' he pressed on, 'guess what? I've got a new poster in my bedroom. Maggie sent it over from the office. It's really cool. You can see it when you come home. When are you coming home?'

'At the end of next week,' Michael laughed. 'And well done getting the commendation. I'm proud of you. If you get the red badge then Ellen and I should be back in time to come to Big Bear with you.'

'Oh yeah!' Robbie cheered. 'Mum! Dad says he might come to Big Bear too.'

'How're Gran and Uncle Cavan?' Michael asked.

'They're OK. Uncle Cavan's teaching Gran to drive your car and they nearly had an accident today, but they're all right. Gran said it was Uncle Cavan's fault because he shouted at her, and Uncle Cavan said he wouldn't dare to shout at her, because she would hit him. So she hit him anyway. It was really funny.'

Michael was laughing. 'Just as long as my car is still in one piece,' he said, 'or I'll hit them both.'

'Oh, got to go now, Dad, *South Park* has just started.'

'Hey! Do you want to say hello to Ellen? She's right here?'

Michael's heart sank at the silence. 'Robbie? Are you

still there?' he said, wishing to God he'd never made the suggestion in Ellen's hearing.

'Yes,' came a small, sullen voice.

Repressing a sigh, Michael said, 'I love you, son.'

'Love you too, Dad,' he replied. 'Can I go now?'

'Sure. I'll call again in a couple of days.'

Putting the phone back on the hook Michael wandered out to the patio and sat down. 'Sorry,' he said, looking at Ellen across the table.

She smiled. 'It's OK,' she answered, hurting as much for him as she did for herself.

'We'll work something out,' he said, circling his fingers round the stem of his wineglass.

Ellen looked at him and longed to put her arms around him, as though to protect him from all the pain that was coming – pain that was so much bigger than this it couldn't even begin to compare.

He lifted his eyes to hers and gazed at the candlelight reflected in her pupils. 'I thought,' he began, then took a breath. 'I wondered, you know, when you threw up a couple of times before the wedding . . .'

Guilt hit her heart like a stone.

'Nerves?' he said and gave a humourless laugh. 'I guessed, but, you know.' He looked at his drink again, then picking it up he took a sip. 'I don't know if having any more would be the answer for Robbie. At least not right now. What do you think?'

She tried to swallow, but her throat was too tight. 'It might not be,' she said in a whisper.

Again his eyes were gazing deep into hers. 'But it's not all about Robbie,' he said softly. 'It's about us too, and . . .' He stopped and wiped a hand over his unshaven face. 'Maybe it's too soon,' he said. 'Maybe we should wait a bit longer, you know, with the movie coming up.'

'Is that what you want?' she said, barely able to speak.

'I want whatever you want,' he told her. 'I guess I was just wondering, you know, with it not happening, if

260

maybe, when we get back, we should go and get ourselves checked out. I mean, I know I've got Robbie, but that doesn't mean it couldn't be me. Something might have gone wrong between now and then. Something, you know, that's going to be easy to fix.'

Her eyes were burning, as she drew in her lips to stop them from trembling. He was trying so hard not to offend her, or to make her feel responsible, or inadequate. She looked at him in the softly flickering candlelight and loved him with every fibre of her being. 'There's nothing wrong with you,' she said, her voice barely more than a croak.

He watched her, waiting for her to continue, but she couldn't. Dread was taking over everything inside her, rendering her incapable of anything more than the effort to breathe.

'Are you trying to tell me there's something wrong with you?' he said, a sudden fear in his eyes. 'Something not to do with . . . Something more serious?'

She shook her head. 'No,' she said brokenly. 'There's nothing wrong with me either.'

As he waited she could sense his confusion, and wondered why this was happening now when she had tried so hard to avoid it. Two weeks was all she had wanted, and then she'd have told him. She wasn't ready to do it now. But the moment was here and no matter how desperately she longed to escape it, she knew she no longer could.

'What is it?' he said. 'Ellen, what are you trying to tell me?'

The tightness of her heart was so intense she could feel every beat as it throbbed through her chest. 'I . . .' She reached for her glass, but didn't pick it up. 'You recall the night you came back from London? You know, after your last trip?'

She almost felt him become still and knew exactly what was going through his mind.

She tried to smile. 'I came home,' she said, her voice faltering on the words. 'I saw you with Michelle.'

'Oh my God,' he murmured. He turned to look out at the night, as though somewhere there, in the darkness, he would find what he needed to say. Then his eyes returned to hers, and she could see his remorse as clearly as she could see the unease. 'I know I should have told you,' he said, 'but . . . Oh Christ, Ellen, I'm sorry. You've got to know it didn't mean anything. It would never have happened, but . . .'

'No, Michael, please, I just want you to listen,' she interrupted.

He watched her face and started to reach out for her hand, but she shook her head and drew her hand back. She could see how much that hurt him, but it just wasn't possible for her to tell him while he was touching her.

'After I saw you,' she said, 'I got back in my car and started to drive. I'm not sure whether I knew where I was going . . . All I can remember is trying to blot out what I had seen, and it was like, if I went back over the route I'd just come then maybe it would roll back the time. I'd been with Tom at the Four Seasons, so that was where I ended up.' She looked at him. 'I slept with him,' she whispered, 'and now I'm pregnant.'

As the blood drained from his face she could feel the world slipping away. The sounds of the night dipped and rose, the hot, humid air closed around her face like a suffocating sponge. She watched him and felt the brutal tearing of the bond between them as though it were happening as a real and physical wrench. Her hands started to move as though they could somehow put it back together, but there was nothing to touch. They were drifting away from each other, having nothing now to pull them back. She could almost hear the ramifications of what she'd said as they began to crowd in on him, and sensed his bitter struggle for understanding as it sought the steady ground of reason or logic. For one awful and strangely light-headed moment, it all felt like a dream, one in which she knew she would wake up any minute, but just couldn't make herself.

At last he moved, putting his hands to his head and pressing down hard.

'Oh God, Michael, I'm sorry,' she said, tears spilling unchecked from her eyes. 'I'm so sorry. I didn't . . .' She jumped as he got abruptly up from the table.

'You're *sorry*?' he seethed. 'What, do you think that makes it all right? Because you're sorry?'

'Michael, please,' she begged, 'let's at least try to talk . . .'

'Talk! Are you out of your mind? You're carrying another man's child . . .'

'I don't know that for certain,' she cried. 'It could be yours.'

He stared down at her, his face so hard with anger she could barely make herself look back.

'It could be yours,' she repeated.

His nostrils were flared, his lips were bloodless and thin. 'No,' he said, shaking his head. 'Oh, no.'

'Don't say that,' she choked. 'You don't know . . .'

'Nor do you,' he responded, 'that's the whole point,' and turning away he started into the house.

Panic brought her to her feet. 'Michael, don't walk away,' she cried, grabbing his arm. 'Please, not like this.'

He looked down at where she was holding him, then returned his stony eyes to hers.

'Michael, listen,' she gasped. 'Please try to under-stand . . .'

'I do understand,' he said, and prising her off he went on into the house.

Ellen stayed where she was, her whole body shaking as she put a hand to her head and began to look around in despair. She tried to remind herself that she'd known he would react like this, that she was prepared for it and would be able to reason it through. But it didn't help, for she knew now that despite her very worst fears she had managed, in some kind of foolish delusion, to retain the whisper of a hope that somehow it would be all right. God only knew how it could be, because she'd never been able to imagine it – it was just something, like the blind faith of a child, that had stayed with her, but was now being crushed so completely she was afraid it would never come back.

He slept in the spare room that night. Unable to face their bed alone, Ellen closed up the house and curled up on a sofa. Hour after hour ticked by as she lay there, marooned in the hell of her own pain, tormented by the merest thought of his. She tried to make herself think about the future and what they would do, but her mind was locked in the moment, unable to move past the anguish and despair. So many lives would be affected now, but most of all theirs, and though she knew she would find it in her somewhere to handle it, right now the dread of going back to LA was almost overwhelming.

It was during those dark and frightening early-morning hours that she began to consider abortion, no longer as an option, but as an answer. The thought of it scalded her eyes with more tears and sent denial surging through her heart. She could consider it all she liked, but it wasn't an answer and never could be, for no matter who the father was, she was the mother and it was to her that tiny little life would be looking for all the love and protection it deserved. So how could she kill it because of a mistake she had made? What right did she have to make it pay for something it didn't even understand?

When dawn finally came she looked out at the lightening sky and felt exhaustion steal over her. She resisted the thought of a new day, but no matter what she did time was always going to move on – the sun would rise, night would fall and life and its disasters would have to be faced. But not now, please not now, when she had cried so many tears and suffered so much guilt and remorse she no longer had the energy even to keep her eyes open.

Though she slept, strange and doleful nightmares swooped around her, taunting her with images that scared her and pushed her fiercely to the surface of sleep, but never through to the other side. She murmured and tossed, and finally woke with a start to find her limbs bruised and aching and her head throbbing a blinding tattoo. Immediately she remembered why she was there and felt a gulf opening in her heart. She longed for more sleep, but was afraid of that too, not wanting to return to the peculiarly heartless world of her subconscious.

Forcing herself to her feet she went through to the bathroom and cleaned her teeth. Then she looked at herself in the mirror and saw the reflection of a pale, haunted woman. She brushed her hair and snapped it into a slide, then splashed cold water on her face to try to bring back some colour. With each move she could feel her reluctance to breathe. It was as though the slightest breath might bring in more pain.

Trying to shake off her fears, she went back to the kitchen to put on some coffee. Then she saw Michael standing at the edge of the garden staring down at the sea. Her heart somersaulted. She wanted so desperately to go to him and might have done so, were it not for the instinct that was warning her against it. She stood where she was, allowing many minutes to tick by. She remembered him once telling her where he had been when Michelle had told him she was pregnant and leaving – somewhere on the south coast of England, on a cliff, overlooking the sea. She wondered if he was thinking of that now, and smarting at the bitter irony of the similitude.

She watched as he turned and came towards the house. A cowardly streak tried to make her shrink back and go hide in the bedroom, but she forced herself to remain where she was. Hiding from each other wasn't going to help, if anything it would only make things worse.

As he came closer she could see he hadn't slept, nor had he shaved or changed his clothes. She'd have given anything in her power to spare him this, and silently berated the cruelty of fate that had driven her to cause so much hurt to someone she loved so much. He was looking at her now, and her heart was thudding as he came to the open door.

'Just tell me this,' he said, his face hard with anger, his eyes suffused with confusion and pain. 'Why did you choose now to tell me, when you could have done it last week, before the wedding?'

She wished she knew what he wanted her to say so she could give him that comfort, but all she had was the truth. 'I wanted to . . .' she began. 'But I couldn't find the courage and . . .' Her voice faltered and despite how determined she was to hold herself together, she could feel herself starting to break. 'I didn't know how to tell you and . . . and everyone was there . . . They were all looking forward so much to the wedding, so were you . . . I didn't know what to do . . . And I love you, Michael . . .'

'But you had to know I wouldn't have married you if I'd known about this,' he spat.

His words cut through her heart. 'No, I didn't know,' she said.

'Like hell!' he raged. 'You knew all right, it's why you kept it to yourself. Because you had it all worked out, didn't you? You knew what you were doing and to hell with the rest of us. Jesus Christ, what kind of woman are you?'

'Michael, please . . .'

'You know what's really galling me right now?' he cut

266

in. 'It's that Sandy Paull was right about you. God knows, I didn't want to believe her, but boy was she right? And what a goddamned, mindless fucking moron I was not to have seen it for myself. She had you sussed from the word go . . .'

'I can't believe you're saying this!' she cried. 'Sandy Paull's got nothing . . .'

'She told me about the lunch you had with her,' he shouted across her. 'The lunch you told me you never understood. You remember that one, don't you? The one back before I moved to LA? Sure you remember it. How could you ever forget when it proved such a triumph?'

'I don't know what you're talking about. Michael, you're . . .'

His head came forward as his eyes blazed with fury. 'It was at that lunch,' he spat, 'that you gave her all the information she needed on World Wide so she could pass it on to Forgon. You were helping her to bring me down in London so's you could get me to the States. It was what Forgon set you up to do, and you had, how many grand was it, resting on your success? So tell me, did you get it? Did he pay you? I mean, I came, didn't I? You got me there. So did the bastard cough up?' He hit a hand to his head. 'What a fucking asshole,' he seethed, ''cos I've got to tell you, Ellen, I had no idea. See, I thought you loved me. I thought I was coming to the US so's you and I could be together and make something of World Wide – together. I thought we were going to get married and have a fam–' He stopped, and she could see from the way his mouth was pinched how close he was to tears.

'I didn't realize what a fucking power freak you are,' he suddenly shouted. 'I never even guessed it, until Sandy told me. And even then I wouldn't let myself believe it. Jesus Holy Christ, how blind can a man be?'

'Michael, stop! You're wrong about all this,' she said, her voice choked with tears. 'I don't know what Sandy told you, but she's lying. You know she's a liar . . .'

'What I know is what you told me last night,' he seethed. 'And it all fits together. You want control, don't you, Ellen? Of me. The movie. World Wide. Where the fuck is it going to end? Is there anything, or any of us, that you don't want to control? You're all chummy chummy with Forgon again lately, and what a coincidence that is, now the statute of limitations is about to expire on him screwing an underage girl. He'll be back in charge any time now, so where are you? In his fucking pocket again, that's where. So tell me, what kind of bargain are you striking up this time? You want my job? Is that it? Are you sleeping with Forgon to get it, the way you slept with Chambers to get rid of Michelle?'

'Michael, you don't mean any of this! You know it's not true . . .'

'You slept with Chambers to get rid of Michelle,' he yelled. 'And now you're carrying his child . . .'

'No! I slept with him because I caught you screwing Michelle!' she yelled back. 'So face some responsibility here. We both made mistakes . . .'

'Responsibility!' he laughed incredulously. 'I didn't sleep with the man, and I'm not the one who's pregnant. So if there's any responsibility around here it's all yours. In fact, as far as I can see, catching me with Michelle turned out to be a pretty convenient excuse for you, because God knows you've had the hots for that man ever since you laid eyes on him. So how long has it been going on? Just what kind of a jackass were you trying to make of me? I mean you got me to marry you . . .'

'I love you!' she yelled furiously. 'And I've never been unfaithful to you except that one time, after I caught you screwing Michelle in *our* house, when you had to know I would walk in any minute. So what the hell was going on inside your head that night? Were you thinking about me? Were you hell! You were thinking about you and how you still can't get over the woman who walked out on you all those years ago. It makes you feel big to screw her, doesn't it? It puts you back on top. And who the hell am I while you're doing it? I begged you not to let her stay in the house, but you overruled me. It wasn't going to suit you for her to stay somewhere else, was it? You had to show her you had another woman now, and her son, and we were all getting along just fine without her. Except we're not, because you still want her, and so does Robbie. So where do I fit in? There's no room in there for me. And answer me this, what if Michelle was the one who was pregnant right now? You'd have left me at the altar, wouldn't you? You wouldn't have cared less about me.'

'But Michelle's not the one who's pregnant, is she?' he shot back. 'You are. And unless I'm gravely mistaken you're expecting me to pass another man's child off as if it were mine. Well, dream on, Ellen, because it's just not going to happen.'

As she watched him walk away she felt her stomach starting to churn, and knowing she was about to throw up she ran back to the bathroom. As she bent over the sink she prayed to God that he wouldn't hear her, it would be too cruel a reminder, too harsh a proof, for right now.

A few minutes later she was sitting on the edge of the bath, wiping the sweat from her face and waiting for her heartbeat to slow. This was the first time she'd been sick since the morning of the wedding, and she could only hope that it wasn't going to turn into a daily event. She had yet to see a doctor to confirm how far along she was, but as she knew already that it was either eight or nine weeks she hadn't seen the point in getting the nightmare confirmed. But of course she'd have to, when they got back, and knowing that she would be going alone was too horrible to bear.

She looked at her wedding band and felt her heart recoil from the jolt of emotion. This was how it was going to be from now on, trying to deal with the pain and self-pity, the terrible regret and inability to change things. It wasn't something that was going to go away, or get solved in a matter of days, or cured by the right medication. She was going to have to live with this, day in, day out, with no escape and no way of knowing until the baby was born exactly who the father was. She thought of Tom and how he would take it when she told him. It wasn't hard to imagine him supporting her and standing by her in a way Michael couldn't, after all he wasn't the one she'd betrayed, but already she could feel herself rejecting him, because even if he was the father, he wasn't the man she loved.

Hoping a shower might make her feel stronger, she turned on the water and stripped off the clothes she'd worn all night. As she soaped herself she tried not to wonder if she and Michael would ever shower together again, or make love, or kiss or even sleep in the same bed, for the dread they might not was too hard to face. But surely to God he wasn't just going to leave her. He was angry now, and hurt and confused, but once he calmed down he would see how wrong he was in the conclusions he had drawn: that she wasn't the power-crazed manipulator Sandy Paull had accused her of being, that she had *never* given Sandy any information on World Wide, nor had she slept with Tom in order to get Michelle off the movie. It was exactly what Ted Forgon had advised her to do, but that was Forgon's answer to everything. It was a bitter pill to accept that it had worked, but no matter what was going on in her subconscious that night, getting rid of Michelle hadn't been her driving reason for sleeping with Tom.

But what did it matter what her reasons were? It was done, and the consequences must now be lived with. There wasn't only their marriage to think of, there was the movie too, and as deeply as she feared the direction Michael might now take, she knew that however much it was going to hurt her she had somehow to persuade him to talk so that decisions could be made.

The sun was high in the sky when she finally went in search of him. He was nowhere in the house, nor was he down on the beach, but the car was still there, so she guessed he must have gone for a walk. She hoped it would calm him, and give him the chance to see that their marriage wasn't only about their love for each other, but many other things as well, and most particularly of all right now, to work out how they were going to overcome the mistakes they had made that had resulted in this.

She'd been standing at the edge of the sea watching the waves lap over her feet for some time before she sensed Michael's presence. She turned round and looked up at the house. He was standing close to the V-shaped palms, too far away for her to see his expression, but the way her heart was suddenly thumping seemed to be telling her that maybe there was some room now for hope. The fire had probably gone from his temper, and it could be that he needed her now to show him the way through this, to give him something to hold on to that would help to make it all right. She didn't yet know what that could be, but as she started back up the hill she knew in her heart that the mere desire to work it out was all it would take to enable them to make the first step.

By the time she reached the garden he had gone inside. She walked over to the patio, then stopped as he appeared in the doorway. As she looked at his face a cold dread began to smother her hope and as he spoke she could feel each word crushing her.

'We can't stay here,' he said, 'so I'm flying back to LA tonight. You can come with me if you want, but when we get back I want you to move out of the house.'

'But Michael . . .' she protested.

'I don't want to discuss it,' he barked. 'No amount of talking's going to change things, so let's not waste our time trying. As far as the movie's concerned I want you off it. Vic Warren's on board now, he's the director, so he's the one to work on the script with Chambers. You've got other projects going, they'll need your attention, unless, of course, you choose to resign. It's all the same to me, but as of now, our marriage, our relationship, is over.'

Despite the terrible hurt he was inflicting her eyes suddenly flashed with anger. 'I thought you were made of stronger stuff than this,' she spat. 'You're just going to give up because you can't have all the answers you want right now. Is that it? Well, what if this child does turn out to be Tom's? It's mine as well, or doesn't that count? I mean, it was me, wasn't it, who you were swearing you loved all this time, who you could never get enough of, who you never wanted to live without? I haven't changed. I haven't suddenly become the monster you, or Sandy Paull, are trying to make me out to be. I'm the woman you loved enough to marry, the woman who still loves you despite the fact you screwed Michelle which was what started this whole nightmare rolling. And I love your son too, because he's yours, because he's a part of you and I love you too much to let the fact that he's another woman's son get in the way. So where's your love for me, Michael? What happened to the for better, for worse? Can't you see how much this is tearing me apart? Don't you care that it's hurting me too? That I need you now more than I've ever needed you? Are you really going to turn your back on me and leave me alone to face the gossip and the humiliation when this could very easily be your child I'm carrying? Is that how much you love me?'

She could see the pain in his eyes and knew that, even if only in a small way, she was starting to reach him. It meant he still loved her, which she hadn't really doubted, but loving wasn't always enough to overcome the resisting. And he was still resisting, she could sense it as surely as if his hands were against her, pushing her away.

'Speak to me, Michael,' she urged. 'Please. Tell me I'm not wrong about how much you love me. Tell me you're there for me, that you're not going to shut me out, and make us both suffer in ways we probably can't even imagine.' She paused and forced back the emotion that was weakening her voice. 'I need you, Michael,' she said.

Though his face was still strained, she wondered if she hadn't seen his eyes soften before he turned to look out at the glorious tropical expanse that surrounded them. She was certain now that she was getting through to him, that she was showing him how much their love meant to them both, and how damaging his pride could be if he let it. She thought of Robbie and how that very same pride had stopped him seeing his own son for the first four years of his life, and her heart turned over, for it was a harsh reminder of just how stubborn he could be. She wondered if she should mention it, use it to show him what pain he caused himself by refusing to let it go, but as she started to speak he turned back and as his eyes met hers the words died in her throat.

'I don't think I can make love to you again,' he said.

Ellen looked at him, swallowing hard on the pain as it rose up from her heart and fighting the terrible urge to beg him not to mean what he'd said. 'Then at least let's carry on living together,' she responded. 'We don't have to sleep together, not until you feel right about it, but if we're still under the same roof we'll at least have a chance of working things out.'

His eyes remained on hers, but though he didn't agree, he didn't disagree either.

'Michael, please, just think about it,' she said, 'and ask yourself, do you really want to deal with all the gossip and innuendo it would cause if I moved out? Can't you see what a nightmare that would be, for us both? And how's it going to look, us breaking up just as I get pregnant? Do you really want to live through that kind of publicity? God knows, it's bad enough having to deal with this now, when it's just between us, think how much worse it would be with the whole world knowing. We should at least try to make things look normal, and if you make me leave the house and then stop me working with Tom, it's not going to take very long for some bright spark to put two and two together . . . Michael, stop! Where are you going?'

He turned round, and she instantly drew back from the contempt that was blazing in his eyes. 'You know, you almost had me for a minute,' he snarled. 'I was this close to falling for your bullshit, and believing this was really about us. But it's not, is it? It's all about you, and the fact that, even now, you don't want to give him up any more than you want to lose control. Well, go to him, Ellen. Go tell him about his baby, and while you're at it you can tell him that as of right now you're off the movie. And if Tom Chambers doesn't like it, then that's just too bad, because I don't give a fuck whether this movie gets made or not.'

'Michael! Michael!' she cried, going after him as he walked towards the bedroom. 'You know you don't mean that. You've put everything of yourself into this movie. It's why I'm behind it too. Michael! Stop! Listen to me, please,' she begged, as he dragged his suitcase from under the bed. 'What about us? Please tell me you're not giving up. I know you love me, Michael . . .'

'Wrong tense,' he snapped. 'It's over, Ellen. You, me, the movie, it's all history, and as far as I'm concerned you and Chambers can take your script, and your kid and your goddamned ghosts and get the fucking hell out of my life.'

Chapter 15

The taxi was going much too fast, randomly switching from one lane to the other, as they sped over the Chiswick flyover heading out of West London towards the M4. Considering it was July the weather was disgusting, rain drizzling down from a pewter sky, while riotous winds gusted through barbecue parties and picnic plans. It had been like this for three days now, and was forecast to continue for another three.

Tom's stay in London had passed too swiftly, and it was frustrating Sandy no end that they were now on their way back to the airport where he was taking the three thirty flight to LA. They'd had a fabulous time, and her only regret was that she'd been unable to see him every day, but the demands of her job had forbidden it. Besides he'd gone to stay with friends in Scotland for a couple of days, then to Brussels to meet up with a group of reporters who were working on a story about the new international link-up between the Colombian drug cartels and the Russian and Italian Mafias. But he'd called her while he was away, and had taken her to dinner the night he got back, despite not flying in until gone ten o'clock.

And now, here it was, over already, and she so desperately didn't want him to go that she had even said so last night, which had made him grin and tweak her nose, a kind of intimacy he'd fallen into these past couple of weeks. They'd been at an after-show party at the Shaftesbury at the time, along with several other agents from McCanns whose clients were in the play. It was such a thrill for Sandy to have a partner for the occasion, and that it should be someone as striking and eligible as Tom Chambers was almost too good to be true. Of course everyone thought they were having an affair, which she was more than happy for them to think, though she'd have been a whole lot happier if they really were.

'So when did you say you were planning on coming out to LA again?' he asked, turning his gaze away from the damp and misty landscape they were racing through.

'I think at the end of the month,' she answered. 'It depends on how things go here, but I should be able to get away again by then.'

Was he hoping the trip would be to see him, or was he just assuming it was business that would bring her? It was another of the zillion ambiguities she'd failed to sort out during the time he'd been here, and she wasn't going to ask now for fear of him insisting she didn't fly all that way on his account. Of course, there would be plenty of business for her to attend to while she was there, but the main reason she was going was in the hope they could spend some more time together.

After a while he looked at her again and smiled. 'You look great,' he said. 'The way I imagined you would once we got you out of those solidly constructed designer suits and into something . . . well, something like this.'

The compliment made Sandy's eyes shine, for the retro Seventies outfit she was wearing today – beige bootleg pants, a short cream sleeveless shirt and a pair of white Hobbs platform sandals – was one of the few she had chosen herself. Most of the rest of her new wardrobe, as well as the soft shaggy hair and subtle make-up, was down to him, for, true to the promise he had made in LA, he had thrown himself fully into restoring her to youth and introducing her to style. They'd had an hysterical – and fiercely expensive – time doing it, especially as he was no connoisseur, which meant they'd relied pretty heavily on fashion magazines and sales assistants, and on the whole, as long as it pleased him, it pleased Sandy too. She'd even tried, one time in Selfridges, to get him to help choose her underwear, but he'd backed off, laughing and insisting he'd be way out of his depth with that.

It really had been the oddest time, for in every other way they were just like a couple – calling each other two or three times a day, taking each other to parties and discos and concerts, and laughing and giggling over all kinds of secrets they swore they'd never told anyone else. They seemed so close, behaved like they were, and even talked like they were, but not once had he even attempted to kiss her, much less anything else. And it wasn't as if he could be thinking she was the one holding back, not when she'd practically told him right out that she wouldn't mind sleeping with him, and had acted as sexily and suggestively as she knew how.

Were it not for the fact that she knew he'd slept with Ellen his resistance might not have rankled so much, but just the thought of him making love to Ellen, who already had Michael, was a horrible and totally insufferable truth to have to deal with. What, she wanted to know, was so damned fantastic about Ellen Shelby that made her irresistible to the men Sandy wanted? It might not have been so bad if they wanted Sandy too, but whereas she did everything in her power to attract them, it seemed all Ellen had to do was exist. Of course, her existence might not be such a brilliant one now, considering what lay ahead.

'I had a call from Michelle last night,' Tom said.

Sandy turned to look at him. 'Oh?'

277

He glanced at her briefly. 'Ellen and Michael got back the night before last.'

'Oh,' she repeated, in a much darker tone. 'A week early. Did she say any more than that?'

'Apparently Ellen's moved out. She's gone to stay with Matty.'

Though Sandy's heart was starting to beat faster, she wasn't entirely sure how she felt about that. 'Did Michelle mention anything about the baby?'

'No. She didn't seem to know what was going on.'

They were both quiet for a moment. Sandy wondered what he was thinking, how the news had really affected him. For her it seemed slightly unreal. Though it was what she had wanted, to break Michael and Ellen up, the fact that it had now happened wasn't giving her quite the satisfaction she'd expected.

'The press are going to give them a hard time over this,' Tom commented.

Sandy shot him a look. 'Are you going to tell Ellen you know about the baby?' she asked.

He shook his head. 'I don't know. I doubt it. I'll need to get the lie of the land, see how she wants to play it. This is going to be real tough for her.'

Sandy couldn't help resenting the fact that he cared, but she said nothing. Spending this time with him had given her some insight on a quite different approach to her responses, one that was less hostile and defensive than the way she would normally react. And though she wasn't absolutely in tune with it yet, in this instance she found that she could feel herself holding back for a moment, and instead of seeing the situation for how it was affecting her, she was giving some consideration to how it was affecting him. And looking at it from where he was, she realized what a struggle of conscience he must be having, for he probably really valued his friendship with Michael and would be as sorry to lose that as he would to lose the movie. What he might gain, though, was Ellen and a child, and having only just found him herself Sandy felt devastated by the idea of having to let him go.

Of course it could turn out that Michael would be free, but it wasn't Michael she wanted any more, it was Tom. No-one had ever taken this much interest in her before, or bothered to make her feel this special, and though in some ways it seemed to weaken her, in others it was lending her an inner-strength that was so much easier to deal with than the massive chip she'd always had on her shoulder. But now the fact that he was soon going to be in the same city as Ellen, the same building, the same room and maybe even the same bed, was starting to eat her up so badly she had to force herself not to think about it for fear of all the violent things she wanted to do.

'Will you marry her, if it's yours?' she asked.

He laughed in surprise. 'I think we're getting a bit ahead of ourselves,' he said. 'Remember, she's married to Michael and my guess is, despite all this, that's the way they both want it to stay.'

'What about Michael?' she said. 'Obviously he knows now, so how are you going to face him? What are you going to say?'

'God knows,' he answered. 'But I can tell you this, it's not a meeting I'm looking forward to, on any level.'

Lifting her head to look at him, she said, 'The movie's safe. World Wide will be making it, come what may. I made sure of that before we left LA.'

His eyes were widening. 'How did you do that?' he asked.

'I talked to Ted Forgon. He's the boss, remember? And as he's about to take over the reins again, or so he tells me, he's the one who'll be making the decisions. And I happen to know that he wants Michael to executive produce your movie.'

Tom looked sceptical. 'It might be what he wants,' he

279

said, 'but I don't hold out much hope of Michael staying with it, not now. Except, with all the money he's raised, the loyalty . . .'

Sandy smiled. 'I promise you, Ted Forgon'll make it in Michael's best interests to continue.'

Tom frowned as he thought about that, not appearing to like the sound of it. 'And what about Ellen?' he said.

Sandy shrugged. 'What about her? It can happen much more easily without her than it can without Michael, especially now Vic Warren's about to join. And besides, Ellen's going to be too busy going off to the doctor's, or putting her feet up, or knitting, or whatever pregnant women do.'

The lines around his eyes deepened as he smiled. 'Not quite the image I have of a pregnant Ellen,' he responded, 'but I take your point. And with the way things are there's every chance she won't want to stay on the movie.'

'Precisely,' Sandy agreed, knowing full well that what Ellen did or didn't want was going to count for nothing now that she, Sandy, had done a deal with Forgon. Of course there was every chance that Michael would want Ellen off the movie too, considering her involvement meant spending so much time with Tom. So, it was a pretty safe bet that Ellen Shelby was already history where *Rachel's Story* was concerned, and as she, Sandy, had already been named a producer, there didn't seem to be any reason for her not to be in LA as often as she liked in the forthcoming months.

Michael looked from Robbie to Michelle and back again. They were in Robbie's bedroom and in the flickering grey-blue light of the silent TV they appeared almost dreamlike. Michael wondered if there was anything he wouldn't give for this to be just a dream.

'Do you understand what we're saying, sweetheart?' Michelle said, smoothing Robbie's hair.

Robbie nodded. He was sitting up in bed, fiddling with the hanging cord of his Batman lamp. Spot was next to him, snuffling in his sleep.

From where he was sitting on a beanbag next to the bed Michael looked up at his son's confused and worried face and fought back a surge of emotion.

Michelle spoke again. 'We understand how difficult this is for you, darling,' she said, 'and you don't have to give us an answer straight away, OK?'

Robbie looked at her with his wide blue eyes. 'I want you to stay here with me and Daddy and Spot,' he said, his lips starting to tremble.

'I know you do, darling,' she said, and Michael could see how hard it was for her not to draw him into her arms. 'But we just tried to explain why that can't happen. It's not that Mummy and Daddy don't love each other, because we do, it's just that we love other people too. Most of all though we love you, which is why you get to choose which one of us you want to live with.'

Robbie turned to his father, and though Michael met his gaze the possibility of losing this child, whom he loved more than his own life, was tearing him apart so badly that he didn't know how much longer he could hold on.

'Mummy has to go back to Pakistan for a while,' he said, repeating what Michelle had already told him. 'But after, in a few weeks, if you decide you want to live with her, she and Uncle Cavan will fly back here to get you and take you to live in London. You'll be near Gran and Auntie Colleen and all your cousins.'

'Can't you come too?' he said.

Michael shook his head, then followed Robbie's eyes to Spot as the shaggy little black bundle shifted and groaned. He hadn't asked about the dog yet, probably just assumed that wherever he went the dog would go too. The truth of it was, though, that at any time now it was likely to be just Michael and Spot in this great big house, for Britain's quarantine laws would prevent Robbie taking his beloved pet with him.

'I want to go to sleep now,' Robbie said abruptly, and snuggling down into his sheet he put an arm around Spot and buried his face.

Michelle's eyes came up to Michael, then without saying any more they quietly left the room.

'He's too young to make this decision,' Michelle whispered after closing the door behind them.

'I know,' Michael answered, 'but what else can we do?'

Michelle looked blindly out at the lamplit garden and pool. Her heart was almost exploding with the need to beg him to make a go of it. She could come here and he could continue with World Wide. That way they could be the family Robbie wanted. It was what she wanted too, more than anything else, but with the way things stood between Michael and Ellen she knew that now wasn't the time to discuss it. In truth there would probably never be a time, because despite the terrible dilemma he and Ellen were now facing, in her heart Michelle knew that he was never again going to feel the same way about her that he once had.

Turning to look at him, she smiled and gave his hand a quick squeeze, before starting back to the sitting-room.

Michael followed and went to the bar to fix them a drink, while Michelle sat down with Cavan and Clodagh.

'We've left it with him,' Michelle said, slipping a hand into Cavan's.

Clodagh looked over at Michael and felt his pain clawing into her heart. This had to be harder on him than he was ever going to admit, and she blamed herself for the way he was unable to share it. She wished to God she knew what had happened between him and Ellen. Whatever it was, he obviously didn't want to discuss it and until he did she knew she was never going to get this break-up to make sense. One minute they were the happiest couple alive, living it up at the wedding of the year, the next they were back from honeymoon, separated and barely speaking. What on earth could have gone so wrong in such a short space of time?

'Here you are,' he said, passing her a small brandy.

Taking it, she looked over at Michelle whose head was resting on Cavan's shoulder. She'd always cared for Michelle, ever since she'd come into Michael's life; it was taking some getting used to seeing her with Cavan though, especially with the difference in their ages. Not that it was any of Clodagh's business, but she would dearly love to see Michelle and Michael back together, if only for the sake of their son. She was a realist, however, so knew that wasn't going to happen, not even in the face of this mysterious rift.

'Aren't you having one?' Clodagh said, as Michael handed drinks to Cavan and Michelle.

He shook his head. 'No, I'm going to take a shower, then I've got some reading to do before I go into the office tomorrow.'

Knowing that meant he wanted to be alone, Clodagh squeezed his hand as he kissed her, then listened for the door closing behind him. When it did, she looked at Michelle.

'I know he's confided in you what happened between him and Ellen,' she said, 'and I'm not going to ask you to break his trust, but is there nothing you can do to make any of this any easier for him?'

Michelle swallowed hard. 'I swear to you, Clodagh,' she said, 'if I could, I would.'

Clodagh's face seemed to collapse, and looking down at her brandy she felt her son's despair as though it were her own.

'It's good you're staying on, Ma,' Cavan said, recognizing her need to help. 'If nothing else he's going to want you here for Robbie – at least until Robbie decides what he's going to do.'

After taking a shower Michael towelled himself dry, searched out some clean shorts and resisted the urge to call Ellen. He had nothing to say to her, he guessed he just wanted to hear her voice, but he could live without it. Somewhere, deep down inside, he knew he was still angry, but he had it in much better control now and imagined it would stay that way, just as long as he didn't have to spend too much time around his mother whose kindness and concern were driving him nuts. Still, he'd have to get used to it, as Michelle and Cavan, the buffers, were leaving tomorrow, so with Lucina having made an abrupt return to Mexico, it was going to be just him, Clodagh and Robbie for a while.

Feeling bad at his resentment towards his mother, he was almost tempted to go back out there, but knowing he was too on edge to deal with much else today, he stayed where he was.

From a different emotional perspective, losing Robbie was going to be every bit as bad as losing Ellen, and with it coming at the same time he had to accept that he was going to be dealing with the most difficult time he would probably ever have to face. Nothing was going to make it easy, but not for the first time in his life a sixth sense was telling him he was handling it all wrong. But no matter which way he looked at the problems, he just couldn't figure out a way that felt right.

Knowing he was in danger of going round and round in circles if he didn't at least try to focus on something else for a while, he took a stack of contracts from his briefcase and got into bed. As there was no particular urgency attached to them, nor any real need for his scrutiny, it wasn't long before he found himself reaching for the latest scenes Tom had given him for *Rachel's Story* – scenes Tom and Ellen had worked on prior to the wedding.

Knowing that the child Ellen was carrying had very probably been conceived along with these scenes wasn't exactly helping him give them a fair reading, and as they contained some tender moments between Rachel and Tom, it was proving about as pleasurable as a kick in the face. However, he had determined to go on with the movie, for far too many people had put their trust in him for him to let them down now and as it was a project he had believed in from the start, he wasn't prepared to let his personal feelings get in the way.

With Vic Warren about to take over the script, there was no reason for Ellen to remain involved, and when he and Tom had met the day before Tom had shown no signs of insisting. In fact, Ellen had hardly been mentioned, and certainly the baby hadn't, for as far as Michael was aware Tom didn't even know, and he had no intention of being the one to tell him. Nevertheless, their meeting had been strained and awkward: the unspoken fact that Tom had slept with Ellen was right there between them.

Obviously, it would help matters considerably if Ellen were to resign, though it certainly wasn't what Michael wanted, even if it was causing him problems seeing her every day in the office. That was going to get harder once her pregnancy started to show, and God only knew what the press were going to do then, as they were bad enough now with their sly innuendos, ludicrous speculation and blatant untruths. But that was something they would have to deal with when the time came – for now all that mattered was getting the movie ready to shoot and watching his back every minute of the day in readiness for Ted Forgon's knife.

He had a meeting scheduled with Forgon at the end of the week. It would be the first time they'd talked, privately at least, since Forgon had raised the flag of his comeback. He didn't imagine the meeting would be pleasant, few dealings with Forgon ever were, but there was no way of avoiding it, and in some ways he was actually looking forward to it. After all, Forgon now had what he wanted, Michael McCann in his power, and it was going to be interesting to find out exactly how the old man was planning to finish him.

Hearing Michelle and Cavan climb the stairs to the guest suite above, he turned out his own light and lay in the darkness. The intensity with which he missed Ellen was cruel, but he knew even if she were there he would be unable to hold her, or make love to her, or deceive himself even for a minute that the child was his. Michelle had been as shocked as he was when he'd confided in her, had felt guilty and responsible and desperately sorry for Ellen. He wondered if she'd told Cavan, but doubted it, as the entire truth would entail confessing her own part in the betrayal. Were it not for the fact that he still loved Ellen so much, he knew it would have been very easy for him to turn to Michelle right now, for he had felt much closer to her lately than he had to anyone else. Indeed his admiration and love for her had grown considerably these past few days for the way she'd coped, not just with Robbie and the break-up of his marriage, but with the fact that she was no longer going to play the part of Rachel. As far as he knew no-one had ever told her that her casting was in jeopardy, so the decision not to play Rachel had been entirely hers. Having seen what problems it had caused already with her being here, she had judged it in everyone's best interests for her to withdraw. It was a truly noble gesture, and one that was very typical of her.

Rearranging his pillows, he put his hands behind his head and stared out at the moon. He doubted he would sleep much, he hadn't since Ellen had gone. God only knew how much worse it was going to be if Robbie went too, and he ached for the decision his son's little five-year-old heart was having to reach. No child should be forced to choose between his parents, but neither he nor

Michelle had seen any way round it. He had to know that they both loved and wanted him, that whatever he decided was fine by them.

It was around two in the morning when he heard his bedroom door creak open. Sitting up he saw Robbie standing in the moonlight, Spot right behind him, and not for the first time Michael realized that if his son knew there was a chance he'd have to leave his precious dog then he would almost undoubtedly stay.

'Hey there,' Michael whispered, 'couldn't you sleep?'

'Can I come in with you, Dad?' he asked.

'Sure, come on.'

Michael flipped back the covers and gave him a hand up onto the bed. Spot waited for an invitation, but when none was forthcoming he hopped up anyway.

The three of them lay quietly for a while, Robbie's head on his father's shoulder, his hand idly toying with Spot's ears.

'Daddy?' he said after a while.

'Yes?'

'Did Ellen go because of me?'

'No,' Michael answered, hugging him. 'It had nothing to do with you, I promise.'

'Then why did she go?'

Michael inhaled deeply. 'It's kind of hard to explain,' he said.

'Will she come back?'

Michael's throat was suddenly tight. 'I don't know,' he said.

Robbie turned his head and gazed up into Michael's shadowy face. 'I want to stay here with you, Daddy,' he said.

Michael's eyes closed and he had to swallow hard before he could speak. Even then he found he couldn't, so he just held his son close and thanked God that, for the moment at least, this was one loss he didn't have to endure.

Chapter 16

They'd been back from honeymoon for just over a week and already pre-production for *Rachel's Story* had gone into top gear, with casting, crewing, costume design and set-building all well under way, and provisional shoot dates being discussed for September. Nothing had yet been mentioned, or apparently changed, regarding Ellen's role as executive producer, but she sensed it soon would be. She knew through Maggie that Michael had spoken to Tom a couple of days after they'd returned from Barbados, but she had yet to learn what decisions had been reached. If Michael was still expecting her to resign, he was giving no sign of it, nor was there anything to suggest that he was backing out either. But, just in case, she was starting to wind down her role, and was concentrating more now on World Wide's other projects. Not that she was happy about that, in fact it was proving a terrible wrench letting go of the movie, but since Michael had so much more invested in it than she did, it only seemed right that she should be the one to give way.

She'd left the office early today, for a doctor's appointment at the medical centre in Santa Monica. Just before leaving she'd run into Michael, which hadn't been easy, but though she knew he was finding it every bit as difficult as she was, so far they seemed to be dealing with it surprisingly well. At least on the surface they were, but it was still early days so there was no knowing how long they could keep this up. Considering the news she'd received today, it was probably going to be a lot easier for her than it was for him.

'Hey, what's all this?' Matty cried, coming in the door of the apartment and finding herself assailed by the delicious aroma of something cooking. 'Candles, soft music, fancy napkins. Are you expecting someone?'

Ellen smiled, and ground more pepper into the pan. 'Just you.'

'Mmm, what's cooking? It smells so good.'

'Shrimp with garlic, ginger and soy sauce.'

'My God, it's my birthday and I forgot,' Matty declared.

Ellen laughed and passed her a glass of wine.

'What *is* all this?' Matty said, confused. 'I mean not that I don't appreciate it, you can cook for me any time, but I am not looking at the same woman I left at the crack of dawn this morning.'

'You are looking,' Ellen declared, 'at a woman who is pregnant by the man she is married to.'

Matty stared at her in blank amazement. 'I'm sorry,' she said. 'You've lost me. Is there some new miracle predictor or something that I never heard of, because I could swear you were in a state of total ambiguity when I left here this morning.'

'I was,' Ellen confirmed, 'but no longer am. And no, there's no miracle diviner, just the tried and trusty old calendar.'

Matty blinked. 'Humour me,' she said.

Ellen turned back to the stove, whisked the pan from the heat and emptied the shrimp into a serving dish.

'Just a minute,' Matty said excitedly, 'you were going to see the doctor today, right?'

Ellen grinned.

'So?'

'So, I am thirteen weeks pregnant.'

Matty's face dropped in astonishment, then suddenly she too was grinning like the proverbial Cheshire cat. 'You're kidding me,' she said. 'No you're not, you wouldn't over something like this. Oh my God, Ellen. Oh my God, this is so wonderful. Did you tell Michael yet? Oh God, I can't believe . . . But hang on, how come you got it so wrong? I mean, you're not even showing and thirteen weeks is a lot.'

'I am showing – a bit,' Ellen protested.

'But did you miss a period? You must have known if you missed a period?'

'Yeah, I think I did miss one, but there was so much going on, with the build-up to the wedding, things being as crazy as they always are at the office, and everything else, I just didn't notice. Then, after what happened with Tom,' she shrugged, 'I jumped to conclusions and got it wonderfully, fantastically and mercifully wrong. This is Michael's baby. Michael's and mine.'

'Oh Ellen,' Matty murmured, embracing her. 'This is just such wonderful news. I'm so happy for you I could cry. I guess you didn't tell Michael yet, or you wouldn't still be here.'

'No, I didn't tell him yet,' Ellen confirmed, and, having strained the rice, she picked up the loaded tray and carried it out to the veranda. 'I hope it's OK with you that we eat right away,' she said. 'I'm famished and as I've hardly eaten this past month I just couldn't wait.'

'Fine by me,' Matty said, sliding into a chair and putting her wine down. 'It'll be a relief to see you getting fatter, instead of thinner, given your condition.'

Ellen smiled. 'So did you have a good day?' she asked. 'Did those script changes work out?'

Matty sighed. 'Selling a script change to Dorothy the Dictator is like selling contraception to the Pope,' she responded. 'But we don't want to talk about that, it'll get sorted one way or another, and as it doesn't rate too well alongside global warming, world famine, or holy wars, I can't even claim it has any importance. Whereas your news does. OK, not in a Save the Planet sense, but definitely in a save the marriage sense. So when are you planning on telling Michael?'

Ellen was chewing a mouthful of food so it was a moment before she answered. 'I'm not,' she said when she was able.

Matty's shrimp remained in mid-air. 'Excuse me, did I just hear you say you're not?' she said.

Ellen nodded and carried on eating.

'Well you can't just leave it there,' Matty protested.

Ellen looked over the railing as someone splashed into the pool below. 'I'm not telling him,' she said.

'But you have to. I mean, surely you want to . . .'

She waited, but Ellen merely shook her head.

'OK, there's obviously something here that I'm not getting,' Matty said. 'Why the hell wouldn't you want to tell him? You do want him back, don't you?'

'Of course I do,' Ellen replied. 'I just don't want him back this way.'

Matty shook her head, then rubbed her eyes as though she was having a hard time understanding. 'You're really making me work here,' she said, 'and it's been a long day, so could you just give me this straight?'

Ellen ate some more shrimp, then putting down her fork she sat back in her chair and looked out at the softly darkening sky. 'I don't know if I can explain,' she finally answered. 'I guess it's just instinct. It doesn't feel right to tell him now, so I'm not going to.' She turned back and looked at Matty. 'I love him,' she said, 'and I want him more than anything, but I can't forget the way he was prepared to let me go through this alone. OK, I know he was hurting too, that he was probably reacting to shock, and given time he might have come round. Well, I guess I'm going to give him that time, because if he really loves me and wants me too, then he'll find a way of working things out for us. Besides, even if I were to tell him now,

I don't think he's ready to forgive me yet.'

Matty was quiet as she sipped her wine. 'I understand what you're saying,' she began, 'but . . .'

'My mind's made up,' Ellen interrupted, 'so please, don't try to plead his case.'

Matty looked at her in the candlelight and experienced a quiet admiration for her strength. 'Did you find out anything yet about what happened when Michael and Tom met last week?'

Ellen shook her head. 'I can hardly ask Michael and I haven't spoken to Tom. The truth is, I've been avoiding Tom, but there's no reason for me to now. Except in Michael's eyes, of course.'

'I'm not sure what you're doing is right,' Matty said after a pause. 'He really loves you, Ellen, and this has got to be tearing him apart. Even if it takes him a while to get past it all, I think he deserves to know the truth.'

Ellen was shaking her head. 'No, Matty. He's got to learn that he can't just walk away from the people he loves when things go wrong. He did it with Michelle when she went off to Sarajevo pregnant with Robbie, and now he's done it to me. OK, I understand that he's feeling betrayed, but he's got to accept some responsibility for what happened, because no matter what he wants to tell himself, it's not all mine.'

'I guess you're right,' Matty said.

'I am,' Ellen replied firmly. 'We just have to be grateful that no-one else ever got to find out, because that's something I don't think either of us could deal with.'

Michael looked up from his desk as the outer door to the executive suite opened and Ellen came in. She appeared slightly breathless and flushed, and he wanted to think that it was because her arms were full and her briefcase was heavy, rather than that it had anything to do with the baby.

'Oh Maggie,' she said to their assistant, 'there's a pile

of videos for me downstairs, could you get someone to bring them up? Good morning, by the way. Did Oscar Weinberg call yet? I need to speak to him before ten.'

'He called a few minutes ago,' Maggie confirmed. 'He's in his office. I've got to take this down to the mail room, before the courier turns up. I'll get someone on to the videos. Coffee's made, the others are running errands, but should be back any second.'

As the door closed behind her Ellen dumped her stack of files and went to pour some coffee.

'Hi,' Michael said, coming to stand in the doorway of his office.

Ellen spun round. 'Oh, hi,' she said, feeling her heart twist. 'I didn't realize you were here.'

He watched her pour. 'How are you?' he said.

'Yeah, OK. I'm fine. How are you?'

She looked so alive, so vibrant and happy that he couldn't help being surprised. It wasn't that he wanted to see her fall apart, but he just hadn't expected her to be dealing with their break-up quite as well as this. Maybe she and Tom were getting it on again, and now he was out of the way they could . . . No, he wasn't going that route, self-pity was never an answer and despite the impressive show she'd been putting on the past couple of days, he was convinced she wasn't finding this any easier than he was.

'I need to know,' he said, 'if you've told Tom about the baby.'

Her surprise showed. 'No,' she answered. 'Why?'

'Are you going to?'

'No.'

He guessed it was the response he'd been hoping for, though exactly what it proved he wasn't entirely sure. Right now, though, it was the fact that she seemed so unemotional that was throwing him.

'We've been getting some pretty positive feedback on

the twenty-six-part series,' he said, making for safer ground. 'The one Sandy was dealing with, just prior to the wed–' He stopped abruptly, then continued. 'I was hoping you'd take it over. Sam Field at Fox is interested to know more, so's Elaine Wade at Prime Time.'

'Great,' Ellen responded enthusiastically. 'Can I take a look at the figures?'

'They're on the computer. I'll give you the code. Uh, I guess we need to schedule a meeting so we can catch up with what's going on.'

'I'll talk to Maggie,' she said. 'It should probably be some time this week, before things start getting out of hand.'

He hated the idea of having to book some time with her, but she seemed to be accepting it like it was the most natural thing in the world.

'Are you OK about taking on this project with Sandy?' he said. 'I mean, I could always pass it on to someone else . . .'

'No, it's great,' Ellen assured him. 'I've read the first three scripts, it's something I'd like to be involved in.' She glanced at her watch. 'Aren't you seeing Ted this morning?'

He wondered how she knew that, if Forgon had told her. 'Yes,' he said. 'He's coming here.'

Ellen's eyebrows went up.

'I think I should tell you,' he said, 'that Michelle's decided not to play the part of Rachel. I know we were probably going to withdraw it anyway, but she doesn't know that, so I think it would be kinder if we let her think she turned it down.'

Once again it was impossible to read her expression, so he had no idea how she felt about his consideration of Michelle's feelings.

'I've told Tom,' he said. 'We should be in a position to make Matty a definite offer by the end of the week.'

Her eyes went down and it was only then that he

realized how much this was hurting, being so apart from her, so formal and removed.

'Would you like some coffee?' she said with a smile.

He shook his head.

'OK, well I guess I'd better be getting on.'

He watched her walk into her office, then turned back to his own.

The fact that she hadn't commented on Michelle's withdrawal, or Matty's casting, suggested that she no longer considered herself involved in the movie. Further proof of that was in her failure to turn up for a producers' meeting the day before, or even to ask how Vic and Tom's recent five-day field trip to Mexico had gone. She'd covered it well, but he knew that she had to be hurting over this, and feeling horribly shut out. But it was how she would have to stay, because there was just no way he could tolerate the thought of her working with Chambers again.

Having spent the past couple of weeks going over ATI and World Wide's figures and forecasts, Ted Forgon had filled the first hour of their meeting with questions, comments, the inevitable insults and typical brusque appreciation. He'd never doubted Michael knew what he was doing, and the facts were bearing him out, for the changes he and Ellen had made to ATI by introducing an official line of TV and movie packaging were already showing signs of paying off, and the number of agents as well as clients had increased more than Forgon had realized. Indeed, he could see from his past couple of weeks' study that his finger had wandered much further from the pulse than it should have, which no son-of-a-bitch executive or competitor better interpret as a sign that the old dog was losing his teeth. It was simply that he trusted McCann and had seen no reason not to heed his physician's advice to take things easy for a while. At least that was the official story.

But now he was back, and not only did he have the new and improved ATI to administer, he also had the genesis of a thriving production company in World Wide Entertainment. He couldn't say he was in total agreement with all the projects they were considering for development, but he didn't plan on taking issue with any, there were always going to be bombs, no matter how hard one strove to avoid them. God knew he'd suffered his share.

What he did want to address, however, was the current status of *Rachel's Story* from both a financial and production standpoint, which was why he had saved it for last.

Right now he was reviewing the configuration of the movie's investment commitments, the proposed returns, fund-release dates and costs of insurance. They were looking at a budget of around twenty-plus million, with a further ten-to-fifteen for marketing, promotion and publicity. For an independent, this was massive, possibly even delusional, except McCann sure as hell appeared to be pulling it off. And it seemed Sandy Paull had managed to bag an impressive number of backers, not to mention pre-sales, over there in Europe, which shouldn't have been as much of a surprise as it was. She was a ruthless little cookie, unburdened by morals or conscience, and apparently blessed by a planetary gestalt that always seemed to put her in the right place at the right time.

'OK,' he said finally, looking up, 'it all seems pretty much in shape.'

'It is,' Michael confirmed.

'This could prove a major event for Hollywood, as well as World Wide,' Forgon stated. 'Done well, we should clean up at the box office as well as the Oscars. How's the script looking?'

'It's about to enter its third draft. Tom doesn't foresee anything significant enough to affect casting or location.

The only remaining problem is how to end it. Vic Warren's on board now, so it could be he'll have something in mind on how to fix it. The names of the killers are still tightly under wraps.'

Forgon nodded. 'OK. You've done a good job of bringing it to a point where you can hand over without too many problems, which is what I imagine you're intending now I'm back in the driving seat. Problem is, it's not what I'm intending. You started out as one of the executive producers on this movie, and that's where you're going to stay. And just in case you're drawing breath to tell me which parts of my anatomy I can shove up other parts, I should make it clear to you right now that if you walk off this project I'll see to it that the world knows that the kid Ellen is carrying might not be yours.'

Michael's face turned pale. For a moment he could hardly believe what he'd heard. How the hell did he know? Surely to God Ellen wouldn't have told him?

'If you're thinking Ellen told me, you're wrong,' Forgon said, apparently reading his mind. 'I didn't learn it from her, nor from her cousin Matty either. I guess that about covers everyone you thought knew, so let this be a reminder to you never to underestimate me. If there's a secret to be found, I always know where to look. Now I can't imagine you wanting Ellen to suffer the humiliation of her little secret being made public, no matter how mad you are at her and Chambers – and let me tell you, I'm on your side here, 'cos I can't think of a worse way of finding out your little bit of pussy is getting stroked by another man's dick.'

Michael's fists were clenched, but even if he could find the words, there was no way he was going to dignify that with a response. What he was going to do was start working right away on regaining control. He wondered how fast he could pull it off – fast enough, he hoped, to prevent him from choking the bastard with his own foul-mouthed tongue.

'So I want you on this movie,' Forgon continued, 'and I think I've just provided you with a good incentive for respecting my wishes. Next: I want Ellen back on it too. She told me yesterday she was going to be concentrating on other things now that Vic Warren's on the scene, but I don't want this show being run by a bunch of fucked-up men. It needs her input and I'm going to insist she gives it. Or maybe I should get you to insist, she's more likely to listen to you.'

Michael continued to stare at him.

Forgon stared back.

Michael's eyes never wavered.

'This kind of shit don't work with me,' Forgon blustered. 'I got you so tight by the balls you can't even breathe, never mind speak, so don't think this silent stuff has got me a-trembling.'

Michael's smile was like ice. 'Is that what you think it was meant to do?' he said.

Forgon's shrewd eyes narrowed.

Michael settled back into silence. The fact that he'd had no intention of walking off the movie wasn't one he was going to share with Forgon, nor was he going to reveal his reluctance for Ellen to rejoin. Let the son of a bitch think what he wanted, he'd have plenty of time to ruminate on his mistakes when all this was over.

Forgon got to his feet.

Michael could see how pissed he was at not quite getting the measure of Michael's response. Michael waited, knowing there was no way he could walk out without having the last word.

'There's no statute of limitations on that kid's paternity,' he snarled. 'I could run with this for ever.'

Michael got up. As he walked round the desk, his eyes were lowered. He raised them only when he was right in front of Forgon, and had the momentary satisfaction of seeing the man shrink. 'Let me tell you this,' he said softly. 'If as much as a single whisper of doubt over that pregnancy ever gets made public I'll know where to come. Whether it was you who did the talking or anyone else, I'll hold you accountable, and believe you me, with your heart, you can't afford the price.'

After Forgon had gone Michael walked over to the window and stared down at the stream of traffic below. Inside he was shaking. He knew he was on quicksand and would have to act fast before the bastard pushed him under. Putting him at an emotional disadvantage, by returning Ellen to work with Chambers, was a smart move, and one Michael knew he was going to find hard to deal with. But he could and he would, he just needed a moment to think it through. Except there was no way he could foresee the outcome of that, nor, on reflection, was it something he was going to torment himself with. Of course, he could always ask Ellen to go against Forgon's wishes, but there was just no way his pride would allow that.

So the immediate question was, what to deal with first, getting Ellen back on board, or setting his legitimate takeover of World Wide in motion. He'd never been comfortable holding the gun of statutory rape to Forgon's head, it wasn't his style of doing things, and it made him about as low as Forgon for resorting to it. He hadn't had much choice at the time, however, and he was a damned fool for not organizing a takeover long before now. The trouble was, he didn't have the funds to do it, not with everything he had already tied up in World Wide, and with nothing to borrow against while his share of McCann Paull was standing surety for the loans he'd taken to get World Wide off the ground.

He needed to speak to the other shareholders, perhaps call a meeting. In the meantime he guessed he should get on with the business of reinstating Ellen, so picking up the phone he buzzed through to her.

'Ellen Shelby's office,' Maggie answered.

Michael hesitated. Obviously Maggie was in with Ellen, but that wasn't what had stalled him, it was hearing Ellen's name. They'd decided that after they were married she'd be known as Ellen Shelby McCann in the long form, and Ellen McCann in the short.

'Hello?'

'Uh, Maggie,' he said. 'Is Ellen there?'

'Sure, I'll pass you over.'

'Hi,' Ellen said a moment later. 'What can I do for you?'

Her apparent ability to handle their break-up was suddenly back in his face and this time, rather than confusing him, it irked him.

'Forgon's just left here,' he said.

'Oh? How did it go?'

'You're asking me? I thought you'd already know. You're back on the movie. He doesn't want it being run by a bunch of fucked-up men, so congratulations, you're getting it all your way. Michelle's pulled out, Forgon's reinstating you, and I guess it won't be too much longer before Chambers'll be saying he wants you as the senior executive.'

The line went dead and seconds later she was standing at his door.

'Are you trying to tell me that you think I went to Forgon and begged him to get me back on the movie?' she demanded, her brown eyes flashing with anger.

He stared at her hard, but though he didn't believe it, he couldn't bring himself to say so.

'You fool,' she spat. 'You goddamned fool.'

He said nothing, though once again he was acutely aware of how badly he was handling it all.

'Well, I'm not going to turn it down,' she said, 'which is what I imagine you were hoping for. I've done a lot of work on that movie and I happen to believe in it every bit as much as you do. But just in case you think I'm aiming to take over, or trying to use my incredible

300

powers over Forgon, or Tom Chambers, to get them to do things my way . . . Where are you going? Don't walk out . . . Michael!'

He closed the door, then turned to face her. 'Did you tell Forgon you were pregnant?' he demanded.

Her face instantly paled. 'Did I *what*? Are you crazy?'

'Well he knows, and I sure as hell didn't tell him. He also knows there's some doubt about the identity of the father.'

Ellen stared at him in disbelief. 'How do you know? What did he say?'

Ignoring the question Michael walked back behind his desk. 'Are you sure you didn't tell Tom?' he asked.

'Of course I'm sure.'

'What about Matty?'

'Yes, she knows, but if you seriously think that either she or I . . . No, I'm not getting into this. You believe what you want to believe, because I'm not about to start defending myself for something I didn't do. But if it's OK with Tom and Vic I am going to get involved with the script again, and if you're thinking that I'm going to use what influence I might have to talk Tom into committing to Matty, then you're right, I will, because she's right for that part and you know it.'

There was hardly any colour in Michael's face as he looked back at her, but anger was all he would allow himself to feel. 'Well, we all know that you've got quite a lot of influence over Chambers,' he said, 'so I guess Matty can consider herself cast.'

After she'd gone he remained standing where he was, bound by the shame of his sarcasm, the sound of the slamming door still ringing in his ears.

Ted Forgon looked up from the video he was watching as Glori, his latest secretary, put her head round the door. She wasn't a bad-looking kid, not a patch on Kerry Jo though, the ex-beauty queen from Dallas he'd had just prior to his temporary retirement. He'd spent a fortune on that one, getting her all fixed up with bigger tits, tighter ass, fuller lips (top and bottom) and a wardrobe that'd made Barbie's look scarce. If the truth be told he'd been planning on marrying Kerry Jo, maybe even having a kid, until he'd come home early one day and caught her screwing the Mexican gardener. Of course, no-one knew about that, they all thought he'd got sick of her and sent her back to Dallas.

'Sandy Paull's still on the line,' Glori said.

Forgon glanced at his watch. That made fifteen minutes she'd been holding, all the way from London. 'OK, put her on,' he said, pausing the tape and getting to his feet. He knew only too well what this was about and was in the mood now for getting it over with.

'Sandy,' he said into the receiver.

There was a moment as she took her phone off the speaker. 'We had a deal,' she spat.

'We did?' he drawled.

'You know damn well we did. I gave you what you needed to control Michael; in return you were taking Ellen Shelby off the movie.'

'Oh, that deal,' he said. 'Well, I guess it seems I changed my mind.'

'A deal is a deal,' she exploded. 'Now I want Ellen Shelby off that movie or you can start kissing goodbye to the European investors.'

Forgon chuckled. 'You know what?' he said. 'You're better at blow-jobs than you are at bluffing. Now do yourself a favour and get used to the idea of Ellen working with Chambers. I'm sure if Michael can handle it, you can too.'

There was silence at the other end, but he had no problem imagining the fury that was causing it. He thought of his majority shareholding and, realizing that was the one area she could hurt him in, he said, 'We just need her for some script refinements, once that kid starts showing she'll back off herself, you'll see.'

He didn't get the impression she was appeased, but there was no way he was kissing ass. 'You start planning anything fancy,' he growled, 'then Michael's going to find out who told me about the kid. Or maybe it'll be Chambers who finds out how you tried to get Ellen off the show. He seems like the kind of guy who'd appreciate a good blow-job. Wonder if he knows that yours come with a price tag?' He laughed. 'You know what? It's making me hard just thinking about what you might do to get me to keep my mouth shut, so be sure to drop by next time you're in town, won't you?' and still laughing he hung up and went back to the video.

Chapter 17

With casting and crewing now almost complete and provisional shoot dates being struck into calendars, both Ellen and Michael were becoming so tied up with their various commitments that even sharing an office suite wasn't bringing them into contact as much as they would have liked. Not that either of them was prepared to admit that, but Ellen was fairly certain that Michael was just as guilty as she was of searching out excuses for them to meet. And when they were together, instead of the incendiary clashes that had taken place over the last couple of weeks, there was an amazing light-heartedness to their encounters now, much like before they'd broken up, and it was highly entertaining to see how baffled everyone was by it. In truth, it baffled Ellen too, for though it was an act, it didn't always feel like one, and she didn't imagine it did for him either.

However, he had given no indication of wanting her to move back to the house, nor, more importantly, of being able to deal with her unfaithfulness and what had resulted. For her part it was becoming harder and harder to hold on to her principles, for she missed their physical closeness terribly, and hated the way they were constantly pretending there was no issue between them at all. But deep in her heart she knew she had to wait for him to come to her; it was the only way this could be resolved satisfactorily, and these past few days she was daring to believe that it might not be so long before it happened.

'Working late again?' he said, entering her office and finding her alone at her desk. She was still there in the hope that he would come to find her, having checked his diary and discovered that he had no meetings or dinners scheduled for the evening.

Putting on a good show of engrossment she made a drawn-out turn from the computer, which was displaying the Academy Players Directory. 'Mmm, just checking out these suggestions,' she said. 'Tom's adamant we can't use Mexicans to play Colombians, because they look nothing like each other. I've also got to go over the latest publicity hand-outs. Did you see them yet? The ones where we're starting to make a real issue out of revealing the killers' names at the end of the movie?'

'One of the best kept secrets of the year,' he commented. 'I just wonder how much longer we'll be able to keep them under wraps.'

'Have faith,' she told him. 'As far as I'm aware it's only me, you and Tom who know. Oh, and Sandy. Tom told her himself.'

Michael's eyebrows went up, but whatever he thought about Tom and Sandy's apparent friendship, he made no comment. 'Want me to go over the hand-outs with you?' he offered, going to sit on one of the sofas.

Ellen feigned surprise. 'You're not rushing off?' she said.

'No. Where are they?'

'Right there in front of you. I think some of the copy's a bit cheesy, but it's getting there.'

He picked one up and gave it a quick read through. 'What visuals are we using?' he asked.

'No decision yet,' she said. 'But it'll probably be Rachel and Tom – or Matty and Richard, I should say.'

Michael nodded thoughtfully. 'You know, it might

not be such a bad idea to use some shots of the actual Rachel and Tom,' he said. 'It could work better for this kind of publicity to show the woman who was really killed. Everyone'll remember her, and if we're using the revelation of the killers' names as a hook, there won't be much we can come up with that's more powerful than the image of the woman they killed.'

Ellen was smiling as she shook her head. 'You're a genius, do you know that?' she told him.

'Yeah,' he answered.

Laughing, she threw a pencil at him and said, 'Did you have any luck talking Tom into giving some pre-shoot interviews?'

'Now there my genius failed,' he conceded.

He watched her as she got up from the desk, his eyes instantly going to her waistline to see if there were any signs yet. It was hard to tell, for though she was wearing a short tight rust-coloured skirt, the thin cotton sweater she had over it was too long and too loose to reveal anything more than a hint of cleavage at the neckline. She came to sit next to him, her bare legs almost touching his as she leaned forward to pick up a hand-out.

'Let's go over this wording,' she said. 'I daresay the experts will come up with something better, but based on what we've got here, I'm not sure we're communicating quite the right message.'

They sat together for two hours or more, probably much longer than was necessary, dealing with everything from the publicity wording, to the cost of various sets, to the need for security once they were under way. She was acutely aware of his nearness, could feel him looking at her legs and noticing the brief glimpses of her breasts she was deliberately showing him each time she sat forward. There was even a moment, when they were laughing over a particularly tacky line in the hand-out, that he actually looked into

306

her face and allowed his smile to fade. Ellen's heart raced at the emotion that came into his eyes, but as she gazed back, feeling his tension and confusion, he suddenly looked away and returned to the subject of security.

But it wouldn't be long now, she was certain of it. He was finding a way through, and she prayed to God that it would be soon, for the last thing she wanted was to deprive him of these precious months before their baby was born.

More than eight weeks had gone by since Sandy was last in LA. She'd been too tied up in London to get away sooner, though she'd been in regular contact with Tom, and Michael and Ellen, and knew just about everything that was going on with World Wide and *Rachel's Story*.

In fact enormous progress had been made. Thanks to Vic Warren the script could now boast a pretty good ending, the major parts were cast and contracted, several of the sets were complete and nearly all of the finance was in place. Over at their offices at Paramount the production team was blazing ahead, and she'd heard yesterday that a start date for principal photography had been sealed for October 2nd. As the major location scenes were being shot in Mexico, Vic Warren had just returned there, along with the DOP, designer, associate producers and unit managers. Current estimates were that they'd need at least eight weeks in the Sierra Madre, though Michael had confided to her during their last conversation that they were budgeting for ten.

Sandy wondered how things were now between Michael and Ellen. She knew they were still living apart, but whether any steps had been taken towards divorce, or reconciliation, Tom had never said. She guessed he probably didn't know anyway, but it wasn't a subject she liked to press him on, as she was in no hurry to find out if he was planning to step into Michael's shoes.

It wasn't hard to work out that, despite his efforts to convince the world to the contrary, life must be pretty grim for Michael right now, as he was having to deal with not only the undecided state of his marriage and Ellen's condition, but also the fact that he was failing to take control of World Wide. In truth, he was a hell of a lot further from it now than he'd been eight weeks ago, when he'd first tested the waters to find out which of the shareholders might be willing to sell. Mark Bergin, the Australian industrialist who owned ten per cent of the stock, had turned him down flat. She'd heard that Chris Ruskin in New York wasn't keen to part with any of his eleven per cent either, though even if he were, it still wouldn't be enough for Michael to take the chair. Curiously, he hadn't approached her yet, though she guessed that was because even if she were prepared to sell some of her twenty-one per cent, he was going to find it hard to raise the capital to buy. More or less everything he had was already in World Wide, including the funds he had borrowed against his shares in McCann Paull, and the mortgages he had taken on his apartment in London, villa in the Caribbean and house in LA. He might have more stashed away, of course, but she doubted it would be enough to make a serious bid.

Of course, she could help him out by buying up his share in McCann Paull, which would give her outright ownership of the London agency. But as it was unlikely the other World Wide shareholders would be willing to sell, cash alone wasn't really going to do him much good. Besides, she couldn't see him letting go of the agency, no matter how tough he was finding it having Ted Forgon as a boss.

Stepping out of the shower she reached for a towel and wandered through to the bedroom. It felt good to be back at the Four Seasons, though it would feel a whole lot better to be sharing a room with Tom. She knew she was going to have to wait a while for that, however, and wished she could feel more confident that one day it really would happen. He'd already checked her in by the time she'd arrived, getting her a room next to his, and ensuring there were flowers and champagne waiting for her to make up for the fact that he hadn't managed to get out to the airport to meet her. He'd left a message to say he'd be back around seven, so she had half an hour now to get herself ready.

Though she was doing her best to stay calm, she was more nervous and excited about seeing him than she could properly handle. Phone calls and e-mails were so much easier, even if they were madly unsatisfying. But somehow, on the phone, she always managed to hold it together, sounding confident, interested, even witty, whereas the prospect of coming face to face with him in the next thirty minutes was making her feel ludicrously inept and out of her depth. If only she'd been able to get over to LA as often as she'd hoped, she'd be much more in the swing of seeing him then, and who could say, they might actually be having a relationship by now. As it was, pressure of business in London had kept her there, and with the way *Rachel's Story* had started to move ahead, she had needed to be on the ground to oversee the transfer of funds from the UK and European investors. The way things currently stood she was responsible for raising just under thirty per cent of the budget, an achievement that had not only sealed her producer's credit, but had won her something she prized even more than that, Tom's admiration and respect.

But that wasn't all she'd gained from Tom, for over the past two months, since he'd left England, she'd spent all the free time she had devouring whatever she could find on metaphysics and spirituality. Zelda had been a great help, for she knew all about that stuff, and though Sandy had started out with trepidation and scepticism, she knew now that her resistance had been based on the fear that she might not understand it all. But it really wasn't so difficult, and she was totally fascinated by the concepts, and the way this new knowledge was changing her. She was starting to feel much less defensive than she used to, less fraught and needful of control. By giving situations room to breathe and time to develop she was finding they were yielding up far greater rewards than before. She'd become more patient, and was trying to struggle less to prove herself in an arena where she already held centre stage. It wasn't that she was becoming passive, or even saintly, it was simply that she was beginning to understand some of the things Tom had told her about the Universe and its laws.

She sometimes discussed what she was reading with him, but was still rather shy about it, and afraid she would appear naïve or trite. Besides, it wasn't every day that she felt in tune with what the books called her higher self, and she was still a long way from finding a spiritual means of dealing with her envy of Ellen Shelby or loathing of Ted Forgon.

But it was neither Ellen nor Forgon who was concerning her now, it was Tom and what was happening in Colombia. She had no idea how he reconciled his anger and need for revenge with his metaphysical leanings, but since he was very far from being a saint she considered his outrage not only reasonable, but human. She was nervous of it though, for while they were in London he had told her about calls he'd been receiving from a British journalist who was based in Bogotá. It seemed that Hernán Galeano, the head of the Tolima Cartel, was making it known, from his prison cell, that he wasn't happy about some Hollywood movie that was planning on naming his two nephews as killers. Tom insisted that he didn't give a shit what made Galeano happy, the Zapata boys, along with Salvador Molina, had raped and murdered Rachel, and if this was the only way he could make them pay then he sure as hell wasn't going to back off just because Uncle Hernán didn't like it.

Sandy wondered if Tom had mentioned any of this to Michael yet. She suspected not, as Michael hadn't brought it up at all when they'd spoken, and she was certain he would have. She was equally certain that, despite the bluster, Tom still harboured a desire to go back there to settle the score in person, rather than leave it to the authorities who would be forced to take action once the movie was released. But even if he didn't go back, there were plenty of Colombians in the United States, all kinds of unscrupulous characters, who'd be only too willing to carry out an assassination for the great Hernán Galeano. In fact, it was how the script ended: its only scenes of fiction depicted the vendetta breaking out on the streets of LA where Tom was hunted down, trapped, and delivered up to Rachel's killers. Though in true Hollywood fashion they'd written it so that Tom managed to escape, as the very last thing any of them would want was for life to start imitating art in such dangerous and unpredictable circumstances.

But it could happen, and well she knew it, so the question she was asking herself now was, should she warn Michael about the calls Tom was getting, or should she wait a while longer and see how things developed?

'Hey!' Tom cried, coming in the door. 'How are you? You look great. How was the flight?'

'Fine,' Sandy answered, returning his embrace. He smelt so good, felt so big and strong as he held her that already she could feel herself slipping onto unsteady ground. 'Thanks for the flowers,' she smiled, 'they're lovely.'

'Not tired?' he asked. 'Sure you are. But you can make dinner? We'll stay right here in the hotel, that way if you keel over I won't have too far to carry you.'

She continued to smile and wondered if he'd noticed

311

the semi-transparency of her dress. If he had he showed no sign of it. 'Did you see the sets?' she asked, as he opened her mini-bar.

'Mmm,' he answered. 'They're pretty good. Rachel's office. Our Washington apartment. A foundation for young prostitutes. Newspaper offices. You name it, they're building it.' He held up the bottle of champagne. 'Shall I open?'

She nodded. 'As long as we're celebrating seeing each other again,' she said. 'I missed you.'

He laughed. 'I don't believe it, but I like hearing it. Did you speak to Michael, by the way? He's finally tied up the video deal. *And* he's got the bond company he wanted, so we're definitely on target for October 2nd.'

Sandy took the glass he was handing her. 'Sounds like another reason to celebrate,' she said.

They touched glasses and sipped, but when he smiled down into her eyes she found herself looking away. 'How is Michael?' she said, wondering why she no longer found it easy to flirt. 'Does he tell you anything about the way it's working out with Forgon at the helm?'

'He doesn't say much, but I don't think he likes it too well,' Chambers answered, going to sit down. 'So far though, the old man's keeping a pretty low profile. At least where this movie's concerned. He's getting involved in your twenty-six-parter, I hear?'

Sandy's spirits sank. 'Ellen told you,' she said.

He nodded.

She went to sit down too, facing him on an opposite armchair. 'Yes, he's showing an interest,' she said. 'Actually, he's been quite helpful, putting Ellen in touch with various investors and producers.' She paused. 'You know, I'm surprised she has time when she's so involved in the movie.'

He laughed. 'You know Ellen,' he said. 'She likes to keep busy.'

Sandy smiled. She wanted to ask if Ellen was showing

yet, or if there were any signs that she and Michael might be getting back together, but she wasn't sure she wanted to hear the answers.

She glanced at Tom again. 'Has Michael talked to you at all about trying to take back control of World Wide?' she asked.

He shrugged. 'He just mentioned it was on his agenda. I think the fact that Forgon's giving him a pretty free rein with the movie is making it all tolerable for now. Did he approach you yet, with an offer?'

She shook her head, then laughed. 'I've got to tell you, I could be tempted to give him all my shares just to see Forgon go flat on his face. I loathe that man.'

Chambers grinned. 'Fortunately, I don't have too many dealings with him,' he said, 'but I get the impression your assessment's pretty universal.'

'Except Ellen seems to get on well with him.'

'I don't think that means she likes him. By the way, did you catch Matty on *Access Hollywood*? It was on a half-hour early tonight.'

Sandy grimaced and put a hand to her head. 'Sorry, I forgot. How did she get on? Was she good?'

'They gave her all of four minutes, but yeah, she was good. You know, Ellen was right, she's great casting for Rachel, and since she's got a bit of a profile here, in the States, she's probably going to bring in a lot more publicity for the movie than I'd realized. Did I tell you I keep getting offers too?'

'You mean for interviews? No, you never said. Are you doing them?'

He shook his head. 'Not right now. Michael wants me to, obviously, but you know, I'm just not comfortable with the idea of having my and Rachel's lives picked apart. They're getting the movie, it's enough.'

Sandy noted how protective he still felt towards Rachel, and what they'd shared, but rather than jealousy she experienced a deepening of the tenderness she felt

313

for him. She'd have liked to call it love, because she was sure it was, but she was determined not to rush this, the way she had with Michael.

'Any more calls from Bogotá?' she asked.

Though his expression didn't change, she sensed the stirrings of tension. 'Just one,' he answered.

'From Alan Day?' she said, referring to the journalist who'd called him before.

He nodded. 'Galeano's still pissed off and still making noises,' he said.

'Does Alan think there's anything to worry about?'

He shook his head. 'No.'

Sandy wondered if he was telling the truth. If someone was making threats on his life she couldn't imagine him telling anyone, even though he'd be a damned fool not to. This was LA, not Bogotá, here the police responded, and protected.

'Do you think there's any chance that events could start mirroring the script?' she said. 'I mean, will they arrange for someone here to come after you?'

He laughed. 'I wouldn't think so,' he answered. 'No, what Galeano wants is me back in Colombia. On his own territory he can get away with a whole bunch of stuff he'd never get away with here.'

'But he's in prison.'

'That hasn't stopped him running the cartel. Oh sure, it slowed him up for a while, but his nephews have worked pretty hard to put him back on top, and if the Colombian Congress passes this latest bill, which they will because he's managed to buy more than half of them, he could be out any time.'

She was shaking her head in disbelief. 'What kind of country is it?' she said.

'One that's a bit different to the one you're used to,' he told her, a glint of humour in his eyes.

'You're not going to go back there, are you?' she said. 'Please tell me you never will.'

He laughed. 'I'll tell you this,' he said, 'if I do ever go back, it won't be because Galeano's trying to pull my strings.'

'Not good enough,' she said. 'I want to hear you say that you'll *never* go back, no matter what.'

At first he didn't answer and she wished she could read his mind. He'd once told her what kind of vengeance he'd planned for Rachel's killers. It was horrible, too horrible even to think about, yet in truth was no more violent or grotesque than what they had done to Rachel. How could anything be that bad?

She continued to look at him, and when his dark eyes at last came back to hers she stared into them as they slowly searched her face. 'Believe me,' he said, his voice so soft she could barely hear him, 'the last place on God's earth I ever want to go again is Colombia.'

She swallowed. 'Even to track down Salvador Molina?'

Though he didn't drop his gaze, his face was suddenly hard and she knew already that even if she got an answer it wouldn't be the one she wanted. In the end all he said was, 'I think we should change the subject.'

Michael's mood was good. He wasn't too sure why when his life was all but falling apart, but he guessed it had a lot to do with Robbie. His child's love was given so readily, and undemandingly, and his joy was so easily shared and infectious, that even the ache Michael felt for Ellen was sometimes soothed just by the sound of Robbie's laughter. He wished to God he could spend more time with him, but all too often the pressing demands of work got in the way. And it was only going to get worse now the movie was so close to starting. This was why he had made an effort to spend the entire weekend with his son, because there was no way of knowing when they'd be able to do it again.

So far they'd had a great time, riding their bikes along

the beach at Santa Monica; taking a boat trip around the marina and laughing uproariously when Clodagh's hat took off in the wind; watching two movies back to back and creeping several rows forward when Clodagh fell asleep; and hiding from her on Sunday morning in order to get out of going to church.

She was now back from mass and refusing to speak to them as she banged about in the kitchen, clearing up after lunch. Michael was sitting at a table next to the pool, shaded from the scorching sun by a mahogany-framed parasol, while Robbie tried to teach Spot to dive. Though he'd vowed not to do any work this weekend, he was using these quiet few minutes to go over the bond documents again, reading through clauses the World Wide lawyers either wanted added or clarified before Michael and Ted Forgon signed. As far as he could tell there was nothing to get excited about, it all looked pretty straightforward, and as the most important aspect, the completion guarantee, had all the right figures and conditions attached, he could see no reason not to go public now with the start date.

As calm and philosophical as he was attempting to be, in truth he was as nervous as hell about this movie, for it wasn't only his first major feature as an executive producer, it was by far and away the biggest budget he had ever handled. Added to that was the fact that, one way or another, virtually everything he owned was wrapped up in this film, and though he stood to make untold millions if it was a success, if anything were to go wrong it wouldn't only be his reputation and career on the line, it would be just about his entire life.

But nothing was going to go wrong. The script was in shape, the money was in place and the cast and crew were the best in their field. Matty was working out great, getting stacks of publicity already, and, from what Vic had been telling him, was so inside Rachel's skin it was spooky. Whether or not Tom agreed with that Michael had no idea, it wasn't the kind of thing they discussed, though Ellen had been at rehearsals a few days ago when Tom had gaped in astonishment, then growing discomfort, at the amazing impersonation Richard Conway had done of him.

Casting was virtually complete now, deals were being sewn up on the Mexican locations, and the sets, which were being built over at Paramount, were due to be finished any day. Sandy, who'd been in town for the past three weeks, had been over several times to look at them, and was regularly reporting back to her investors in Europe.

Thinking about Sandy, Michael couldn't help wondering about the changes in her lately. He couldn't put his finger on what they were exactly, except that there was a very subtle kind of difference in the way she approached things, and a quiet confidence and sophistication in her manner that was much more alluring than the aggressive sexuality she had once turned on him. Whether this was working for Chambers, though, was something of a mystery, because though the two of them seemed pretty close, his calls were always put through to separate rooms at the Four Seasons – and there was nothing, when he was with them, to suggest anything more than friendship. If he was right, then he just hoped to God that the reason Chambers was holding back had nothing to do with Ellen – but that wasn't something he could afford to dwell on if he wanted to get through the next few months with his sanity intact.

With his thoughts still on Sandy, he wondered again whether he should approach her about her shares in World Wide while she was here. He hadn't really been surprised when the others had turned him down, right now there was a very good chance that World Wide could strike Hollywood gold with *Rachel's Story*, so all of them were much more interested in buying than selling.

Besides, he hadn't yet worked out a way of raising the funds, and Sandy, perhaps more than anyone, was aware of how deeply in debt he already was, which was why he had so far held off approaching her. For all the delicate changes she was exhibiting in her personal life, she was still a damned shrewd businesswoman and he wasn't in much doubt that, even if she were prepared to sell, the price she would exact for her shares would be crippling.

For the time being though, he comforted himself with the fact that Forgon appeared to be keeping his nose out of the movie, and as long as it continued that way there was no immediate need for a takeover. Even so, he'd be a whole lot happier if he'd managed one, as he didn't for one moment relish the fact that Forgon had final say on what was turning into a near twenty-five-million-dollar budget – especially not when a good percentage of that figure was being supported by Michael's worldly possessions.

'Daddy?' Robbie said.

Michael looked up to find him sitting on the edge of the pool staring in.

'Yes?' Michael answered.

Robbie's head remained bowed, as he swung his feet back and forth in the water. 'You know what I told you about Alex's mum and dad?' he said.

'Yes,' Michael answered.

His feet did several more circles. 'Well,' he said, 'what's divorce, Dad?'

Michael looked at his son's bony little shoulders and felt the weight of his burden. He knew how deeply troubled Robbie was by all that was going on around him, and wished to God he could give him some answers that would help. 'It means that his mum and dad won't be married any more,' he said gently.

Robbie sat with that for a while, and Michael braced himself for what was coming next. They'd had this conversation about Alex's parents before, so he knew which line they were going to tread, and it never failed to cut.

'Are you still married to Ellen?' he said in a small, hollow voice.

'Yes,' Michael answered.

'Are you going to get divorced?'

Michael looked out to the spectacular swell of the mountains, and unblemished blue of the sky. The day was so clear, the air so still and hot, that the view seemed more like a painting, too garish, too vital to be real. In a way it was like the pain inside him, too vivid, too pressing to be true. He couldn't answer Robbie's question, for he had no answers where Ellen was concerned. All he knew was how hard he struggled to suppress the pain, how he fought not to miss her, yet continued to long for her in every imaginable way. But no matter how deeply he loved her, how desperate he was to have her back in his life, he just couldn't get past the fact that she could be carrying another man's child. Not even the doubt made it any easier to handle; he sometimes wondered if in some way it actually made it harder.

What he needed was to find a way of dealing with his pride, for he knew that it was what had robbed him of the first four years of Robbie's life. But though he'd rather die than do something like that again, each time he felt ready to speak to Ellen he would find himself thinking about the baby, and what he was going to do should it turn out to be Tom's. Try as he might, he just couldn't see himself accepting it as his, but even if he could, he had to face the fact that Tom was going to have some say in it then, and there was every chance Tom would want to be as hands-on with his child as Michael now was with Robbie.

Robbie turned round to look at him. 'Are you going to get divorced?' he repeated.

319

Michael lowered his eyes to his. 'I don't know,' he answered.

Robbie's face was wrought with confusion. 'Is Ellen angry with me?' he said. 'Is that why she won't live with us any more?'

Michael put down his papers and went to sit next to him. 'She's got nothing to be angry with you about,' he said, dangling his legs in the water. 'She loves you, and I know she'd love to see you, if you wanted to.'

Robbie's eyes came up to his.

Michael smiled past the turmoil. 'Why don't you let me drive you over there, then you two can spend some time together? She's not mad at you, I promise.'

It pained him so deeply to know that Robbie was blaming himself for the break-up that he had already mentioned it to Ellen in the hope she might know what to do. It was why he'd suggested that Robbie went over to see her now, for it had been her idea that he should, as soon as Robbie was ready.

'Shall we call her?' Michael prompted.

Robbie looked down at the pool again, his tender little body hunched with indecision. 'Can I take Spot?' he said finally.

Michael smiled. 'Of course,' he said.

Robbie called out to his dog, who leapt out of a quiet doze in the shade and trotted into the house after him.

'Do you want to speak to her yourself?' Michael offered, as he dialled the number.

Robbie shook his head. 'No, you do it,' he said.

Michael looked down at his worried little face and felt his throat tighten with emotion.

Matty answered on the fourth ring. 'Oh hi, Michael,' she said, disguising the surprise she must have felt. 'Ellen's not here, I'm afraid. She's gone over to take a look at one of the sets.'

Michael was still looking at Robbie. 'OK,' he said. 'I'll catch up with her later.'

As he rang off he could see that Robbie's disappointment was almost as great as his own. 'I know,' he suggested, after telling Robbie where she was, 'how about we go and take a look at the sets too?'

Robbie looked undecided. He was obviously having a difficult time with this. 'Will it be like the outer-space one we saw with all those monsters?' he said.

'Not really,' Michael answered, 'but we don't want to frighten Gran, do we?'

Robbie grinned, then with Spot barrelling along happily at his heels, he went off to get dressed.

An hour later the three of them, and Spot, were heading along Melrose towards Paramount. Clodagh, thoroughly approving of their mission, had forgiven them for being heathens and was getting as excited as Robbie at the possibility they might bump into the famous Richard Conway.

Michael was quiet as Robbie and his mother chattered on, steering the car through the traffic and trying to deal with what was going on inside him. He knew how much Robbie's visit was going to mean to Ellen, how much it meant to him too. They were still a family, albeit fractured right now, but maybe they were going to find a way of putting it back together. He had to remember that there was a chance the child was his, and even if it wasn't Ellen was still his wife. It was the way he wanted it to stay. The very idea of divorce was unthinkable, it simply wasn't an option, not when he loved her this much. He just had to come to terms with what had happened, and *why* it had happened, and, like she said, take some responsibility himself.

'OK, wait here,' he said, pulling the car into the parking lot. 'I'll just go and check she's still here, and see if there's any construction going on. If there is we might need some hard hats.'

He'd visited the soundstage several times before, so

knew his way through the maze of buildings and alleyways that finally led to the sets for *Rachel's Story*. A couple of trucks were parked outside, backs open as huge blocks of scenery and set dressing were transported in through the vast soundproofed doors. There was a lot of hammering going on inside, a radio blasting and builders and electricians swarming over scaffolding and along the gantries. Spotting a couple of the line producers in conference with the designer and art director, he skirted a disorderly pile of foliage and started heading their way.

'Is Ellen here?' he asked one of them as they turned to greet him.

'Yeah, at least she was five minutes ago,' he answered. 'She was over at the hostage set. Do you know where it is?'

Michael nodded, thanked him and walked off in the direction of a newspaper office. As he recalled, the hostage set was behind it. He was right, and from the look of it, as he rounded one of the walls, it was pretty near complete. There had been a lot of discussion about this set, as no-one actually knew where Rachel had been held during her three days in captivity, so it had been up to Tom and the designers to create something plausible. Since Tom had interviewed a number of ex-hostages in Colombia, he'd had a better idea than most of the kind of conditions she could have been held in, and since it wasn't a guerilla kidnapping they'd dispensed with the idea of a remote forest camp or mountain village. What they'd opted for was apparently more in keeping with a cartel-style kidnapping, a room in a large old house, with boarded-up windows, an old wooden bed and a menacing network of overhead beams.

It was odd how even the air in the set was giving off a vibe that was chilling. He knew there was still much more dressing to come, mirrors flecked with mould, chains on the bed, dingy paintings, cracked china, an incongruously cheerful rug, but already he was getting a sense of how it was going to look – and worse, how it must have felt.

He stood looking at it for some time, very quiet, and still, allowing himself to be drawn into the ambient menace. After a while he could almost hear the distant echoes of Rachel's screams. It was as though they were coming out of the walls, pulling him in to her nightmare, guiding him with silent, agonized cries to the terror she had known as she was raped and beaten, tossed from one man to the next, punched so hard in the face that her nose was broken and her teeth knocked loose. He felt his hands tighten at his sides, his muscles tense, as though there were something he could do to stop it. But it was over, finished, locked in the past, a brutal, irreversible moment in time.

His eyes remained on the bed as he considered again how it must have been for Chambers. But that kind of anguish was impossible to imagine. It was no surprise the man wanted revenge, because, God knew, if it had happened to Ellen there was nothing he wouldn't do to make those responsible pay for their crime. But still the killers lived, not only at liberty, but no doubt in some kind of perverted glory for sending one American to hell everlasting, while the other remained in hell on earth.

He turned away, knowing that whatever personal issues he and Chambers might have, he was right not to have let them get in the way of the film. This story needed to be told, those who had committed the rape and murder had to face justice.

As he walked away he was still bound in his thoughts, so affected by the last few minutes that he was only vaguely aware of what was going on around him. Gradually the sound of workmen began to reach him, as a distant square of daylight popped in over a graffiti-covered wall. He glanced off to his right, to a set that was almost lost in darkness. Then, without really knowing why, he felt his whole body turning slowly to ice. Maybe it was because of the shadow, or maybe it was because of the strangeness of his thoughts, whatever it was, it was a moment before he could really connect with what he was seeing. When he did so, his head started to spin and emotions sprang through his chest that shut down his breath. It seemed like an eternity that he was held there, looking at Ellen, so lost in the depth of Chambers's embrace that she hadn't even noticed Michael's presence.

He continued to watch her, bound by the refusal to believe, yet compelled by the fact that he must. His heartbeat was starting to pound – he felt his life falling apart. He wanted to reach out, tear them apart, stop whatever was between them from happening. But it was too late for that, she was carrying Chambers's child, so without uttering a word he turned and walked quietly away.

Chapter 18

As Ellen pulled back from Tom's arms she could feel her cheeks warming with colour. She looked up into his face and smiled, awkwardly, even shyly, then laughing she said, 'I guess it was me who needed that. I hope you don't mind.'

'It was my pleasure,' he told her, in the droll, self-mocking way he so often assumed.

Ellen laughed again. She'd intended the hug to be a comfort to him, but when he had put his arms around her she'd realized just how much she had needed it too. It had gone on perhaps a little longer than either of them had intended, but there had been such a warmth to it, such a shared yet unspoken understanding, that neither had been in a hurry to let go. It was the first physical contact they'd had since the night they'd made love, and though she still couldn't deny how attractive she found him, there wasn't a moment's doubt in her mind that the arms she really wanted to hold her were Michael's. She missed him so much, and some days, like today, were much harder to bear than others.

Glancing quickly around she said, 'I should be going. I've got a plan for this evening that I really hope is going to work out.'

His handsome face showed yet more irony. 'Then I wish you luck,' he responded.

Ellen knew it was a mask, one he hid behind rather

than let anyone see the anguish, or sadness, he was feeling. Or perhaps it was anger he was disguising, fury even, at the still unfinished business in Colombia. Though she didn't imagine he ever forgot it, seeing the hostage set had to have been the most brutal of reminders, and with the shoot date coming so close, he was surely thinking, wondering, how effective the movie would be. Would it be enough to bring Rachel's killers to justice, and in turn would that be enough for him?

Ellen hoped to God it would be, for the last thing she wanted was to see him returning to Colombia to try once again to take his revenge on the men who had destroyed his and Rachel's lives. Though she could certainly understand his need to do that, it wasn't the answer, for if he killed Molina and the Zapata brothers he would be allowed no future other than behind the bars of some godawful Colombian jail. However, one thing was for certain, he needed some closure on this or he was never going to get on with his life.

'Come on, I'll walk you to your car,' he said, starting back towards the newspaper office and general chaos that was going on beyond.

'What are you going to do now?' she asked, falling in beside him.

'Me?' he said, sounding surprised. 'I don't know. I'll probably catch a movie, or go over some of the stuff our estimable star is testing me with.'

Ellen smiled, for Richard Conway's attempt to get inside Tom's head for the purposes of his role wasn't an exercise that Tom was enjoying. 'Sandy not around?' she said.

He stopped to pick up a wrench that one of the builders had just dropped. 'She flew over to New York yesterday,' he answered, passing the wrench over. 'One of her clients is auditioning for some Broadway show next week, she's gone to lend some moral support. I think she's got other business while she's there, so she doesn't reckon on being back until the end of the week.'

'She's coming back here?' Ellen said, standing aside as a couple of drapers carried past a ladder. 'How's she managing to be out of London for so long?'

Tom glanced at her with comically raised brows and Ellen laughed.

'So there is something between you two?' she said.

'We're good friends,' he answered.

Though she longed to know more, she reined in her curiosity, sensing it wouldn't really be welcome. And why would it be when his love life was none of her business, nor was it a subject she'd be entirely comfortable discussing. Though she had to confess that she wouldn't be too happy to learn that he was getting it on with Sandy, for despite Sandy's recent morph into a reasonable and sane individual, she certainly wasn't Ellen's idea of the kind of woman Tom needed.

'Looks like Joe and the others left already,' she said, referring to the designer and line producers. 'I needed to speak to him, but I'll call him later. Are you going to be there for the press call tomorrow?'

Tom grinned. 'Can you see Michael letting me get out of it?' he responded.

Ellen laughed. 'And no more should he,' she replied. 'You're a major bonus in the publicity package, whether you like it or not. People are going to want to see you every bit as much as they're going to want to see Richard Conway.'

'I think that might be overdoing it a bit,' he commented. 'For a start he's younger and better-looking.'

'Younger maybe,' she teased. 'And you don't have a manager who's a royal pain in the butt.'

They'd reached her car by now and as she opened the door to get in, she said, 'Why don't you give Matty a call? I don't think she's doing anything later, maybe you could take in a movie together.'

He shrugged. 'OK, I might do that,' he answered.

Ellen looked up into his warm grey eyes and was fleetingly tempted to hug him again, for no other reason than she was feeling horribly anxious about her plans for the evening, and a squeeze from Tom might just help bolster her nerve.

As she pulled out of the parking lot a few minutes later a quick glance in her mirror showed him walking back towards the sound stage. Her heart sank, as she didn't want to think about him returning to the set and trying to deal with everything it must be evoking. It was why she had called him earlier and asked him to meet her there, so that she could be around when he first saw the re-creation of Rachel's final surroundings.

Though he'd hidden it well she knew it had shaken him deeply, but that was probably nothing to what he was going to feel when it came to the re-enactment of what had happened in that room. There had been extremely long and detailed discussions on how those scenes were going to be handled, discussions that Tom hadn't always taken part in, preferring to leave it to Vic Warren to decide. God, this had to be a difficult time for him, and Ellen could only feel dismayed at herself for depriving him of the one friendship he could probably really do with right now, the one with Michael.

But she was about to try and do something about that, for the way she and Michael were going on couldn't be allowed to continue.

Pulling down her sun-visor to block out the dazzling afternoon sun, she motored on for a while, swinging the car up onto Sunset, then continuing until she reached Chalet Gourmet, a pricey and exclusive grocery store not far from the Director's Guild. Despite being a Sunday, there were still precious few spaces in the parking lot and the guy in the car behind was so close on her tail that she was tempted to slam on her brakes just to annoy him. He'd been with her almost since she'd left the studio, and it seemed he was keen on staying there. She hated being hassled like this, but rather than get into a fight, she pulled over to let him pass. As he came up alongside her she was sorely tempted to give him the finger, but there were so many crazies in this town it probably wouldn't be wise, especially not as he was slowing right down.

Looking over at him she saw that he was like a hundred other Latinos who drove that kind of old Betsy, with rusted paintwork, balding tyres and no tax or insurance. What the hell he was doing in the parking lot of a place like Chalet Gourmet had to be a whole other story, except in his deluded state he was obviously trying to pick her up. She glared at him, then felt her skin crawl at the smile he gave back. It was a smile that was missing teeth and conveying lechery in such a repugnant way that she actually shivered. Men like that were so loathsome they should be locked up just for existing.

He was signalling for her to lower her window, and since she could go neither forward nor back, she pressed a button and complied. By now she was too angry to be afraid, which was probably exactly what he was getting off on, so in as pleasant a voice as she could muster she said, 'Drive on, buster. I'm due at the AIDS clinic by four.'

His eyes were hidden by shades, but she saw his smile broaden before he treated her to an obscene, masturbatory gesture, then finally drove on. He said something too, something that sounded familiar despite his accent, but it must have been her imagination for there was just no way he could know her name. Besides, not even she referred to herself as Mrs McCann, so it had to have been something Spanish that just sounded like that.

An hour later she was carrying her shopping into the apartment and exchanging a quick hello with Matty who was on her way out.

'Don't wait dinner for me,' Matty said, 'there's some kind of panic going on with a couple of the costumes. I'm going over there now, and God only knows how long it's going to take. Oh, and I've got wig fittings in the morning, Vic wants you and Tom to be there so we can get the look right. Pierre's going to do the cut, and he wants to know if we need any more hairdressing assistants. He's got four on stand by.'

'Tell him to talk to Lucy, she's in charge of all that,' Ellen responded, dumping her bags in the kitchen. 'What time's the wig fitting? Don't forget we've got a press call.'

'It's before. At nine. The press call's at eleven, so plenty of time. Oh, by the way, Michael called.'

Ellen turned round. 'When?' she said.

Matty shrugged. 'A couple of hours ago. No message. He just said he'd catch up with you later.'

Ellen's insides had gone watery. 'He didn't want me to call back?' she said.

'Mm, mm,' Matty answered, shaking her head as she popped a grape. 'Boy, these are good. But call him anyway, if you want to. He's your husband, after all.'

'He's also a co-exec. producer,' Ellen reminded her. 'Meaning the call will have been work-related.'

'But you were hoping otherwise,' Matty said. 'I could see it in your eyes. You know, if you ask me, this has gone on long enough . . .'

'Spare me the lecture,' Ellen said, holding up her hand. 'I'm in total agreement, which is why I've got all this food – I'm going to invite him – and Robbie and Clodagh – over for dinner tonight. I thought it would be a step in the right direction.'

'I won't argue with that,' Matty responded. 'Now I've got to fly. Have a good time, all of you, and save a couple of mouthfuls for me.'

'You mean you're eating?' Ellen called after her. 'What about dieting for those love scenes?'

Matty scowled at her menacingly, then, coming back for a handful of grapes, she kissed her on the cheek and left.

Ellen carried on with her unpacking, picking up the phone as it rang and tucking it into her shoulder. It was Sandy calling from New York, wanting to know if Ellen had the latest budget forecasts for the twenty-six-parter. As it happened there were copies in Ellen's briefcase, so they spent the next fifteen minutes going over them, in preparation for a meeting Sandy was having the next day.

When finally she rang off Ellen was even more perplexed and irritated by Sandy than usual. There was just no way she was taken in by this new, saintly persona, although she found herself responding to it as though she were. It was hard being frosty with someone who seemed so friendly, but as chatty and agreeable as she was being Ellen remained convinced that the woman was a bitch, and maybe an increasingly dangerous one now that she was finding more effective ways to hide it.

Going back to the kitchen she finished unpacking her bags, then, allowing herself no time for nerves or procrastination, she picked up the phone to call Michael. But before she could dial it rang, and for the next half-hour she was tied up again on all kinds of problems and decisions concerning the movie. Knowing it had taken over Michael's life too, she couldn't help wondering how he was feeling right now, just a week away from the cameras rolling. No doubt he was as nervous and apprehensive as she was – or perhaps terrified would be a more accurate description – that something might go wrong.

She didn't want to be thinking about all that now though, she wanted to put it to one side and let them have at least this one evening as a family before everything rolled past the start line. It would be their first time together for more than three months, since before the wedding, and before the bombshell that had all but torn their lives apart.

'Hi, it's me,' she said when he answered the phone.

She waited, feeling her heart trip on his silence, but reminding herself it was his pride again, she put a laugh in her voice as she said, 'I was in the mood for cooking and thought you all might like to come and join me.'

There was a moment's pause before he said, 'I don't think so.'

She was stunned. It hadn't even occurred to her that he might turn her down, so she wasn't at all prepared for what to say next. 'Why not?' she finally managed.

'I just don't,' he said.

She was trying hard to establish some sense here, as his manner was nothing like it had been these past few weeks in the office, when she'd started to believe that he might at last be coming round to the idea of working something out. She felt suddenly panicked, as though everything was slipping away from her, but pulling herself quickly together she said, 'You must have a reason.'

'You know the reason,' he told her. 'We can put on a front for other people, but the pretence ends there.'

'What pretence?' she said, feeling her head start to spin. 'I love you, Michael, there's no pretence about that.'

His answer was so harsh she could hardly believe he had said it. 'I don't know what your game is, Ellen,' he snapped, 'but if you think you can string us both along until you know who the father is, then think again.'

'What do you mean? What are you talking about?' she cried.

'You know what I'm talking about,' he responded, and before she could protest any further he hung up.

She gazed around the apartment, momentarily

stunned, then snatching up her bag, she took out her address book and rapidly started to dial. Joe, the designer, wasn't home, so she tried his mobile, while flicking through the pages to find a number for one of the line producers. No reply from Joe's mobile, and as she clicked off the line a call came in from one of the cast which she dealt with, then started to dial again.

She knew it was guilt that was driving her, that the chances of Michael knowing about that shared moment with Tom were minimal, but it was standing out so sharply in her mind that she had to find out if someone had seen, and then told him. At last she tracked down Ron Hubbard, one of the stage managers who'd been on the set earlier.

'No, I didn't speak to Michael today,' he said when Ellen asked. 'But I saw him.'

'Saw him?' she said, her heart starting to beat even faster. 'Where?'

'He was over at the set, looking for you. I guess he didn't find you, huh?'

'Oh my God,' Ellen breathed, then remembering who she was talking to she mumbled a quick goodbye and rang off. 'Oh my God,' she muttered again. 'What timing! What lousy rotten timing!'

The phone rang.

'Yes,' she barked into it.

'Ellen, I've got someone from *The Gossip Show* on the other line,' the senior publicist told her. 'They're asking if you want to comment on some rumour they've heard about a romance between you and Tom Chambers.'

Ellen's eyes were wide with shock, as a voice inside screamed out for this to stop. 'Are you insane?' she cried. 'There's no romance between me and Tom Chambers, and I want to know who the hell said there was.'

'The woman's not going to reveal her source,' the publicist told her. 'Do you want me to deny it, or do you want to go the "no comment" route?'

333

'Deny it,' Ellen snapped. 'Deny it categorically, and tell her if she goes public I'll sue.'

She slammed the phone down, was about to turn away when it rang again.

'Yes?'

'Hello Mrs McCann,' a soft, gravelly voice at the other end said, 'you don't know me, but I want you to know I'm a friend. And as a friend, I would advise you to pull out of the movie you are making . . .'

'Oh great! Just what I need, a whacko,' she seethed, and slamming down the receiver, she picked up her purse and keys and ran out the door.

Fifteen minutes later she was pulling up behind Michael's car where it was parked in the drive. Going over to the front door, she knocked hard.

Clodagh answered, her small, wrinkly face showing surprise, then pleasure, when she saw who it was. 'Oh my, how lovely it is to see you,' she said, giving Ellen a hug. 'We went over to the set to find you today, but you'd already left. Come along in now. Will you be staying for supper?'

Ellen didn't answer as she saw Michael getting up from the sofa where he'd been sitting with Robbie. His face showed no welcome at all, and she could feel her heart thumping as it struggled between anger and despair. She looked at Robbie who was watching her with big, uncertain eyes, and for one horrible moment she felt her nerve failing.

But she was quickly past it and looking at Michael again she said, 'I need to talk to you.'

If it had been in him to resist he must have decided against it, probably, she guessed, because he didn't want a showdown in front of Robbie. He turned towards their bedroom, and, glancing at Clodagh who gave her best reassuring smile, Ellen followed.

He was standing beside the bed as she closed the door behind her. She felt momentarily light-headed, as

334

though in some strange, undefinable way she was closing them off from reality, sealing them into a place where neither of them quite knew how to behave. She could see the hostility in his eyes, almost feel his efforts to keep her at bay, yet it was the very power of his resistance that was drawing her to him, enveloping her in the maelstrom of pride and anguish that was causing him so much pain.

She took a breath and said, 'I know you saw me with Tom, and I know what you must have thought, but you're wrong, Michael. It wasn't the way it might have looked. It was simply me trying to give him some comfort when he saw the set. It was nothing more than that, I swear. I love you, I've always loved you, and even the goddamned pride you're putting between us now isn't going to stop me loving you.'

His face didn't change, nor did he speak, but it was his silence that encouraged her to go on.

'Michael, please stop doing this,' she implored. 'I know you love me, and I know how much I hurt you, but don't you care what this is doing to me too? I want us to be together, to work through this and . . .' Words were starting to fail her, as she had no clear idea of what she wanted to say, whether she should tell him about the baby now, or what she should do. 'I know you feel you can't make love to me again,' she said, 'but you can, you know you can and I want you to. Michael, please. I can't bear this, wanting you so much and . . .' She hardly knew what she was doing, was giving herself no time to think, as she began taking off her clothes, shedding them as though they were veils around her emotions, until finally she stood naked before him.

His eyes didn't waver from hers, their fierceness seeming to see so far into her that even her nudity wasn't enough. She waited, willing him to move, to say something, even if it was to tell her to go. Each second that passed was more excruciating than the last. The air on her skin was a whisper of pain; the small swell of her child a heaviness that seemed minutely to grow. Though he wouldn't look she knew he could see it, a blur on the edge of his vision, a stone in the heart of his pain. She could feel her image in his eyes, as though he were smothering her with fear and anger and a growing need to hurt and love her.

It was hard to breathe. The air was static with feeling; sensations seared through her body with an intensity that burned and a need that curled into every hidden place. Her eyes were wide, her breasts were heavy and laden with desire. Her hands hung at her sides, wanting to reach, to feel, to bring him to her. Then he was coming towards her, reaching for her, pulling her harshly against him. His mouth came crushing down on hers, his tongue pushing between her lips, his hands cupping her buttocks and lifting her to him.

She tore at his shirt, returning his kisses with the urgency and passion that was inflaming them both. Very soon he was naked and she pressed herself to him, feeling his strength and hardness and sinking into the power of his need. Her fingers raked his hair, pulling his mouth down harder on hers, as his hands moved to her breasts, taking their weight and squeezing them, twisting her nipples, and kissing her harder than ever as his fingers pushed between her legs.

She was gasping and murmuring, holding him tightly as her desire became so intense that emotion was lost in its vastness. Yet it was only because of their love that they could take each other like this, devouring each other's lust with a hunger that knew no repletion.

She lay back on the bed and pulled him down with her. He came to her, swollen with urgency, hardened by the power of desire and love. Their eyes were on each other's, smouldering with need, drinking in the reflected wells of emotion. And then he was there, entering her, pushing into her, filling her until he could go no further.

He held himself there, looking down at her and feeling the invisible bonds that enclosed them, that locked them together despite all he did to keep them apart.

She raised her hands to his face, touching his lips with her thumbs, brushing his ears with her fingers. Then he pulled back and pushed into her again. His voice grunted from his lips as he rammed her again and again. She met his pounding with a magnificent force, rising up to take him, using her hips to mirror the frantic rhythm of his own. The muscles in his arms were straining as he continued to hold himself over her, and they watched the movement of their bodies seeking to scale the final barriers to release.

'Oh my God,' she cried, as suddenly he changed motion.

He grabbed her to him, taking her lips with his own and holding her so close it was as though they were one. He was still solid inside her, and could feel the pulsing beat of her climax as it tugged and clenched with a life of its own.

'Michael,' she murmured again, and again he was kissing her, emptying his heart through the movement of his body.

'I love you,' he whispered.

'I love you too. Oh Michael, don't let me go.'

His embrace tightened, and as he began kissing her again he felt the seed rushing from him, filling her, soaking her and shooting deep, deep inside her. Her moans of pleasure vibrated through his lips, her legs entwined his and her hands pressed him even more closely to her.

They lay that way for a long, long time, neither wanting to let go, dreading the moment their bodies would part. They could feel the quieting throb of each other's hearts, the stickiness of their sweat, the pull of their limbs. It was as though they were shielding themselves from the world, wanting to close out

337

encroaching reality as they were shutting out the air between them.

In the end Ellen was the first to move, pulling her head back to look into his face.

He kissed her softly on the mouth, and as her eyes closed she felt her heart fill up with hope. She wasn't sure if she could speak, if she dared to ask the questions in her heart, but then she heard herself saying, 'Please, Michael, tell me it's going to be all right. Say we can get past this.'

She looked into his eyes, waiting and willing, until finally he looked away and her breath stopped coming.

'Would it help,' she said, panic forcing the words from her lips, 'if I told you the baby was yours?'

Though he didn't move, she felt the effect of her words ripple through him. She hadn't intended to tell him like this, but the words had just come, so she watched his face and wished desperately that she could read his mind. The minutes ticked by and when still he didn't speak the chill of instinct began warning her that she wasn't going to receive the response she had hoped for.

'Even if you could tell me that now,' he said finally, 'I still can't tell you it would change anything. I wish to God it could, because I love you, we both know that, I just don't know if we can go back to where we were.'

'But who's talking about going back?' she cried. 'We need to go forward, to put it all behind us and build a life for our baby.'

His expression wasn't one to encourage her.

'Oh my God,' she murmured, drawing away. 'You do believe me, don't you? Tell me you believe it's yours.'

His eyes were steeped in anguish as he said, 'God knows I want to believe it, I just don't know if . . .'

'Then do the math!' she cried. 'You can work it out for yourself. I'm five and a half months pregnant. Michael, please! You can talk to the doctor, she'll tell you, the

338

baby's due in December, so it has to be yours.'

As he looked at her she could see how hard he was finding it to adjust, how afraid he was of accepting.

'Michael! Why are you doing this? I don't understand . . .'

'I'm sorry,' he said, 'the last thing I want is to hurt you, but I can't live a lie . . .'

'Where's the lie?' she shouted. 'The baby's yours, I swear it . . .'

He was shaking his head.

'Michael! Don't do this!' she cried. 'Why won't you believe it's yours?'

'Even if it is,' he cried, 'can you tell me honestly, in your heart, that you no longer want Tom?'

She looked at him in amazement. 'Of course I don't want Tom,' she replied. 'I love you. Why else do you think I'm here?'

He got up from the bed and going after him she spun him back to face her. 'Michael, listen to me,' she demanded. 'What happened, happened. You made love to Michelle, I made love to Tom. We were both at fault, we made mistakes and now we're paying. But for God's sake, don't make the baby pay too.'

'Do you think that's what I want?' he replied.

'No, I don't. But it's what's going to happen if you won't accept that I don't want Tom any more than you want Michelle.' She would have gone on, but the look that suddenly came into his eyes snatched the breath from her body.

'Oh my God,' she murmured, taking a step back, 'tell me I'm not reading this right. Please, tell me you're not using this as an excuse to go back to Michelle.' She was too appalled, too stricken by fear to go on.

Again he was shaking his head. 'This has got nothing to do with Michelle,' he said. 'It's to do with you and what I saw today. I don't know how many times you've slept with him, Ellen, and I don't want to know . . .'

'Michael, are you crazy? Didn't what we just did tell you anything? You were there, you felt it too, so don't you think it was the same for me? There's no-one else I want, *no-one*, do you hear me?' Tears were sliding down her face, but she was too distraught to feel them.

He started to speak, but suddenly her rage and frustration burst out of control. 'No!' she yelled. 'I'm not taking any more of this. If you can't deal with the fact that I slept with another man, if you can't forgive me when I'm prepared to forgive you, then you just don't deserve the way I feel about you.'

He watched as she picked up her clothes and began putting them on.

'You're a fool, Michael McCann,' she told him. 'You're so afraid to trust that you're screwing up both our lives and you don't even care. So, OK, Michelle walked out on you once, and OK, she was pregnant when she went, but that doesn't mean it's going to happen again.'

'It already is,' he reminded her.

'Because you're making it happen!' she almost screamed. 'You won't let me in, you keep shutting me out and telling me I want another man, when you're not even listening to what I'm telling you. Well, I've had it, do you know that? I'm through with trying to make you listen. So let's do this your way and see just how far we can really fuck this up.'

'There's always another option,' he said as she reached the door.

She turned back, eyes bright with tears, cheeks flushed with anger.

'Divorce,' he said.

Despite the pain she came forward, advancing on him with such intent it was as though she would strike him. 'If you really mean that,' she said, 'then you're not the man I thought you were. And if you're not the man I thought you were, then maybe we *should* get a divorce.'

After the door closed behind her he remained where

340

he was, too shaken by the cruelty of their words and stunned by the force of his feelings to make himself move. A turmoil of anger, jealousy and confusion was swelling inside him, battling his desire to hurt her, and filling him with despair. This was the woman he loved, the woman he cared for and wanted more than any other alive, so how could he have treated her that way? What the hell was wrong with him that he couldn't show the way he was feeling, couldn't let her close enough to understand the fear and jealousy that had all but controlled him since the day she'd told him about Tom? He had to go after her and try to take back what he'd said, but the problem was he had no idea what he could say in its place.

Chapter 19

There were just three days to go before principal photography was due to begin and Tom wasn't liking the way things were looking one bit. Alan Day, his colleague in Bogotá, was calling regularly now, warning him that Galeano's objections were becoming increasingly ominous. And it wasn't only Alan Day he was hearing from, it was several other reporters who were based in Colombia, as well as some lowlife hoods who claimed to be working here in LA for the Tolima Cartel. They very probably were, but as he'd already pointed out to one of them, planning his hasty, or even drawn-out despatch wasn't going to persuade anyone to stop the movie now. If anything, it would give the producers even more reason to make it. To his surprise the goon he was on the line to right now was agreeing with what he was saying, but as the man didn't give a damn, personally, whether the movie got made, he insisted he was concerning himself only with trying to save Chambers's skin.

'And why would you want to do that?' Chambers asked him.

'Because I'm that sort of a guy,' he was told. 'I don't want to see you getting blown away, *hombre*. I mean, I got nothing against you, so why would I? But I got my orders and right now I'm supposed to persuade you that it wouldn't be in your interests to go on with this film.'

'Well, thanks for the call,' Chambers said. 'Is there a number I can get back to you on?'

The voice chuckled. 'Now do I look that dumb, Mr Chambers?' he said.

'How would I know? I've never seen you,' Chambers replied. 'And with any luck, I never will.'

'I hope you don't either,' came the response. 'But certain people you're working with already have. I'm trying to do them the same favour I'm trying to do you. Seems they're not listening either.'

The line went dead. Chambers hung up and immediately redialled. 'Alan,' he said, making a quick connection to Bogotá, 'it's Tom. Any news?'

'Yeah. I put it on your e-mail,' the journalist at the other end answered.

'I didn't go on-line yet today,' Chambers said, feeling an unsteady rhythm starting in his chest. 'Tell me.'

'Well, we already know Galeano's not happy,' Day began. 'Members of the cartel have been in and out of the jail like punks in a whorehouse these past couple of days, and I got a message this morning on my e-mail that goes "We have repeatedly alerted Señor Chambers to the fact that certain businessmen in Bogotá have objections to the making of his movie. The names he is intending to reveal are false, and it is our duty now to inform him that unless production is cancelled by the end of today action will be taken to ensure the co-operation requested."'

Chambers's mouth was drying up. 'That it?' he said.

'You want more?' came the reply.

'So what do you reckon he's planning?'

'At a guess,' Day responded, 'it would entail measuring you up for a celestial suit.' He took a breath, and by the sound of it a slurp of coffee. 'This is serious, Tom,' he said. 'I don't think anyone gives a shit about Molina, but the Zapata boys are Galeano's flesh and blood – not to mention his insurance for life after Picota.

And, so rumour has it, they only did what Molina made them do.'

'Oh, give me a break!' Chambers spat in disgust. 'You saw those pictures, did it look to you like anyone was being forced – apart from Rachel?'

'I'm just passing on what I heard,' Day told him. There was a sharp noise at the other end, then Day said, 'Got the bastard. Damned bugs.'

It was a timely reminder to Chambers that in Bogotá all foreign journalists' phones were bugged, and no-one was ever entirely sure by whom. Could be the police, could be the military, could even be the *traficantes*. What was certain, though, was the roaring trade that went on in phone-tapped information.

'You know I can't stop the movie,' Chambers said, as much for the benefit of an eavesdropper as to state the truth. 'It's out of my hands. I mean, even if I wanted to, there's nothing I can do now.'

'The truth is, there was never anything you could do,' Day commented, 'not once the money started coming in. I know how Hollywood works. I bet you've got no more power now than a used-up dildo.'

'Less,' Chambers corrected. 'But I told you that weeks ago. Maybe these fuckheads just don't understand English. What do you say we try it in Spanish?'

'I think we already did that, didn't we, the last time we spoke?'

'Yeah, I think we did,' Chambers said. 'So I guess what they're telling us, with all these threats, is that the Zapata kids don't have much of a defence, once they've got all that fame.'

If a grin were audible Chambers would have heard one then. 'Can you get to a safe phone?' he said.

'Sure, no problem,' Day responded. 'I'll call you back within the hour.'

Chambers hung up, paced the room, then went to fix himself a drink. The fact that someone else on the unit could have been approached, or was receiving calls from Tolima agents, and he hadn't yet heard about it, was concerning and confusing him. He'd always assumed that it would be him the cartel would go after, because it just didn't add up for people in LA to get threatened. All that would do was take the vendetta straight to the Feds, which definitely wasn't a place Galeano would want it to be. Of course, it could be that the moron on the phone was bluffing, but that wasn't a risk Chambers was prepared to take. Trouble was, he wasn't too sure right now where to go with it, for there truly was nothing he could do to terminate the movie. A few months ago maybe, but definitely not now, when million-dollar pay or play contracts were signed, and Vic Warren and the crew were already down there in Mexico ready to start shooting.

Remembering the e-mail, he clicked on the modem and waited to be connected. It took only seconds before Day's message was in front of him. As he read it the phone started to ring.

'Tom?' It was Alan Day.

'Yep. I'm just looking at your e-mail. What about them going after someone else up here? Are you getting any vibes on that?'

Day was quiet for a moment, and Chambers could easily imagine the man's large, sharp-featured face and shock of black hair, as he attempted to join Chambers's new line of thinking. 'You mean like they did with Rachel?' he said finally.

Chambers's blood ran cold. Not even he had gone as far as to make that connection. But whether he liked it or not Day had a point, and his mind went instantly to the two women who currently featured most prominently in his life: Sandy and Ellen. Of the two he considered Ellen the likelier target, if indeed that was the route they were going.

'It's very possible,' Day continued. 'Very possible

345

indeed. And much more effective than threatening you. So why do you ask? Did you hear something?'

'The *cabrón* who's been calling me up was on the phone just now.'

'You mean the one who's claiming he doesn't want to kill you?'

'That's him. He says he's trying to do someone else the same favour.'

'Oh, a regular Robin Hood,' Day responded. 'But it doesn't sound too good. Have you got any idea who it might be?'

'No-one's said anything, so I'd only be guessing.'

'And who's your guess?'

'Ellen. As the executive producer, co-writer and close friend, she's an obvious choice.'

'You're forgetting her other qualification, she's also a woman. They got you on that once already, this time they're going to know you won't make the same mistake twice.'

'Jesus Christ,' Chambers muttered. His face had turned white and he could feel the same shaking in his limbs that he'd felt a hundred times before when dealing with the Colombian cartels.

'You're gonna have to talk to someone in charge,' Day told him. 'Someone who's got the power to pull that plug.'

Michael's face was so strained as he looked at Chambers across his desk that there could be no doubt of the fury he was trying to hold back. For the moment, however, he was struggling to get his mind past the relief that Ellen hadn't yet flown to Mexico. She was due to, in a couple of days, but she sure as hell wouldn't be going now.

'I know I should have told you about all this before,' Chambers was saying, 'but honest to God, it never occurred to me they'd go after anyone but me. And before we get ourselves in a panic here, let's remember

346

that I've got no evidence to say they're targeting Ellen. It's just a possible. Did she mention any calls, or anything unusual to you?'

Michael shook his head. This was crazy, insane. Everything was in fragments, broken up by the random chaos of all that he felt towards this man and what he was telling him. It wasn't only Ellen, though that was definitely the worst of it, it was also the chance of what this could do to the movie, to the company, their reputations, investments, futures . . .

'I'm waiting to hear from this guy in Bogotá,' Chambers went on. 'His name's Alan Day. He's a Brit. A freelance reporter. At the moment Galeano's goons are contacting him on the e-mail. There's a good chance they'll start getting more explicit with their ultimatums before anything actually happens, which should put us in better shape to know what to do.'

Michael picked up the phone and buzzed through to his assistant. 'Maggie, I want you to book my mother and Robbie on the next available flight to London, then get me Ross Sherman at the Police Department. Where's Ellen, do you know?'

'Gone to see her Ob/Gyn,' Maggie answered. 'She should be here any minute though.'

'Tell her I want to see her as soon as she gets in,' Michael said and rang off.

'What are the chances of stopping the movie?' Chambers said. He'd had to ask, even though he already knew the answer.

'None whatsoever,' Michael said.

Chambers nodded. He waited, hoping Michael might say more, but some kind of reaching out, joining together on this was too much to expect. 'I guess saying I'm sorry's not really going to do it, is it?' he said.

Michael got to his feet, and stuffing his hands in his pockets went to stand at the window. Chambers looked at him and wished to God there was something he could do to help ease the man's burden. Instead he was just piling on more trouble and danger, warning him of threats that could smash his life to pieces, while his marriage fell apart because his wife was carrying a child that might, or might not, be his. Were he any other man the load he was carrying now, coupled with the disaster that was looming, would very probably break him, but with Michael there was just no telling where his limits lay.

The silence went on, then without really knowing what prompted him, Chambers said, 'I think I should tell you, I know about the baby.'

Though he stiffened it was a while before Michael finally turned round. The look in his eyes was one Chambers knew he would never forget.

'I don't know what she told you,' Chambers said, 'but you should know that . . .'

'I don't want to discuss it,' Michael said, cutting him off.

'Maybe not,' Chambers responded, 'but she's your wife, man, and no matter what you're trying to tell yourself, no matter how hard you want to be on her, you've got to take her back now. If you don't . . .'

Michael's eyes were like granite. 'Just where the hell do you get off telling me about my marriage?' he spat.

'If you don't,' Chambers persisted, 'there's every chance you're going to find yourself in hell a whole lot quicker than you're due. Take it from someone who knows, someone who didn't do what he should have and ended up costing the woman he loved her life. Is that what you want? To spend the rest of your days with the kind of guilt that eats up your insides like a cancer, that tears you apart so's you can't even function the way other men function, because you're not fit to call yourself a man any more. I'm telling you, Michael, it cripples you from within, it gets you so's you can't sleep at night, can't think or breathe without remembering what you could have done, and didn't. It crushes you, makes you so's you might just as well stop living. Tell me, is that what you want, because it sure as hell is where you're heading.'

Even through the molten heat of his anger Michael was wondering if in some way that wasn't how he was already. He thought about the hostage set, and the way he had almost heard Rachel's screams and felt her torment. He'd thought then about the pain Chambers had been through, and had known how he'd have felt if it were Ellen. That hadn't changed, indeed, since the day she had come to him, had opened herself up to him and tried to make him see how much he was hurting them both, he had discovered a new depth to his feelings, a depth that had shown him just how incomplete he was without her. To admit that to himself was hard enough, to tell Ellen had been unthinkable, until he'd realized that it was just this kind of holding back that was tearing them apart. So he'd decided to tell her, he just needed to find the words, and he had been so close to doing that before Chambers had said just now that he knew she was pregnant. She'd sworn she'd never told him, but how else would he know?

'Can I use your computer?' Chambers asked, realizing they had to get off this personal ground. 'We should check the e-mail to see if there's been any more contact.'

Despite the regular calls between LA and Bogotá, and the hourly check on the Internet, over a week went by before there was any more contact from Galeano's people. In Mexico the cameras started to roll and in Beverly Hills the daily rushes started turning up for the executive producers to view. Taking a sudden interest now that shooting was under way, and there was less chance of his name being attached to a megalithic nearly-was, Ted Forgon came to the screenings, but though he grunted and clucked and snorted derision, he had yet to get seriously abusive or difficult about anything he'd seen.

After consulting the police, Michael had organized for security to be tightened both in LA and Los Mochis, and Ellen went nowhere now without a personal bodyguard. She'd returned to the house a few days ago, just after Robbie and Clodagh had flown back to London. She still wasn't entirely convinced that the call she had received, and barely even remembered, had been the threat Chambers was looking for, but as Michael wasn't prepared to take any chances she had gone along with his wishes. Not that her moving back to the house had really resolved anything between them, but it could surely only help, them living under the same roof. They were also sleeping in the same bed, but they never made love, and there seemed no sense of permanence to the arrangement, and nothing of any real consequence ever got discussed.

Knowing so few British people, it was hard for Ellen to understand the stubbornness and coldness that Michael was using to mask his feelings. She saw no need for it, and was so exasperated and frustrated that she'd all but given up trying to get past it. It wasn't that she didn't care any more, though he sure was making it hard to, it was simply that her pregnancy was now taking its toll on her energy and what little she had left she chose to pour into the movie. Where they would go and what might happen when it was all finally over wasn't something she could think about now, for there were still too many problems to be sorted, like Robbie and who he was going to live with, and whether Michael might even decide to go back to London with him. But even if Michael stayed, there remained his belief that she still wanted Tom, and she just didn't know what more she could do to persuade him that wasn't true. Maybe, if Sandy and Tom really did get involved . . .

In reality, that wasn't beyond the realms of hope, for

both Sandy and Tom had flown to Mexico earlier in the week and everyone knew how legendary film sets were for kick-starting romances.

The script hadn't called for rain, nor, Tom assured the director, had there been anything but clear blue skies the day Rachel was taken. But after a quick discussion under the drooping awning of a catering truck, it was decided that the kidnap would take place in a torrential downpour. Should the storm pass before the sequence was finished it would be down to the digital effects guy to sort it, and if it didn't match the exteriors of the hostage house they would just have to fix that digitally too. It was either that, or stand around this godforsaken hillside with a hundred or more people getting soaked to the skin, and not a frame of stock moving through the gate.

They began by rehearsing the stunts – three cars speeding along the steep, two-laned country road, and coming to a dangerous stop at the edge of a ditch. There was no-one but stuntmen in the cars right now, Matty and the actors who were playing the kidnappers were still warm and dry in their trailers.

The next couple of run-throughs entailed bringing on extra traffic, half a dozen trucks of varying size and cargo, Cartagena-plated saloon cars, a horse and trap and a bus. Numerous assistants and co-ordinators ran through the rain, shouting into radios and gesticulating madly, while Sandy and Tom watched squeezed together under a makeshift shelter that had been set up for Vic Warren and the video-feed monitors. It was easier to see the action from here, as the main camera was currently attached to 'Rachel's car' which was impossible to get close to, never mind into.

It wasn't until well into the afternoon that they were finally ready for a take, and though the light had faded quite grimly by then Vic Warren couldn't have been happier. It added great atmosphere, gave the entire scene a kind of sinisterness that bright sunlight just couldn't conjure. The fact that Matty's costume had to be changed, as thin white cotton pants and a short-sleeved top didn't do it in this kind of weather, was a minor consideration. However, it did mean another hour's wait while something suitable was found, altered and stressed down.

At last they were ready to roll, and as Matty and the other actors were called from their trailers the vehicles were set in their start positions, while the weapons experts began loading the AK47s and M16s. Since the weapon preparation was happening only a few feet from where Tom and Sandy were standing, they not only could see what the experts and stuntmen were doing, they could hear it too – and listening to the bragging and bluster Sandy felt a distinct distaste for how macho it seemed to make the men feel just to hold and handle those guns. She glanced up at Tom, whose face was partially hidden by a waterproof hat, but the glint in his eyes was enough to tell her that he was no more impressed by the manly display than she was. Perhaps even less so, since for him there was no forgetting that it was very likely these exact makes of guns that had been used in the original kidnap.

Sandy looked at the group again and noticed how unnerved Matty seemed to be as she watched them, and Sandy couldn't blame her, for they were the deadliest of weapons, even if they were loaded up with dummy rounds of ammunition. As one of the producers she could step in now and bring some order to the idiocy, especially as one of the stuntmen, who was doubling as a kidnapper, had just dropped to one knee and was making ludicrous chuff-chuffing sounds to simulate the machine-gun going off. Others were diving for cover, and making out as though they were blasting him back, while Vic Warren, unaware of what was happening, strode up the hillside with the DOP discussing at which points he would cut, so they had some idea where other shots would take over.

Sandy glanced around, hoping to find one of the set producers, or a unit manager, for she was unsure of her authority when no-one here really knew who she was. She had just spotted someone when she almost leapt from her skin at the sound of a deafening explosion. Matty screamed, and the stuntmen and male actors roared with laughter.

Sandy started forward, but Tom was already there, snatching the weapon from the stuntman who'd created the explosion. 'I don't know who you are,' he snarled, 'but as of now you don't ever touch one of these again on this set. Do you hear me? It's not a joke, man. These things kill.'

'And just who the fuck are you?' the stuntman demanded, sizing up for a more physical showdown.

'He's the writer,' Sandy responded. 'And I'm one of the producers and you're fired. Abbie!' she shouted to a runner.

Abbie was there in an instant.

'Get Roger Gaites, the stunt co-ordinator over here,' Sandy ordered. 'Then get someone from security to escort this person off the set. Are you OK?' she said to Matty.

Matty nodded, though she was pale and Sandy could almost feel her heart thudding.

'Take her back to her trailer,' she said to one of the dressers. 'Give her a brandy or something. I'll go and speak to Vic.'

'I'll take her back,' Tom said. 'Come and find us when you're done.'

Realizing how unsettled he was too by the incident, Sandy squeezed his hand, then ran off through the rain to catch up with Vic. Now she'd fired the stuntman they'd have to go through all the rehearsals again to prepare someone else for the role. That meant there was a good chance they'd get nothing in the can today, so Vic wasn't going to be happy. She just hoped he wasn't going to make her look foolish by overruling her on this.

But that was exactly what he did, though in as subtle a way as possible, by getting the fired stuntman back on the set to apologize to everyone concerned. It was probably the most sensible and diplomatic response, as the last thing they needed was any bad feeling festering in the ranks. Fortunately it all took a lot less time than Sandy had feared, and as the daylight had virtually gone Vic's mood improved no end, for he'd now decided this sequence always should have been shot at night – and a rainy, windy night was even better than just night.

Once again Matty was brought from her trailer, and finding Sandy nearby she went over to thank her for stepping in, almost having to shout to make herself heard above the rain. 'I probably overreacted, but I've got to tell you, I really haven't been looking forward to this scene,' she said. 'I guess it's because of what it's leading up to.'

'You'll be fine,' Sandy assured her, using a hand to wipe the rain from her face. 'Where's Tom?'

'Still in the trailer. You know, if you ask me this is a lot tougher on him than anyone realizes.'

Sandy nodded, then turned as someone called out for Matty to get in the car. She waited until Matty was in position, then running up the steps of the trailer she pulled open the door and disappeared inside.

The warmth enfolded her like an embrace, and peeling off her waterproof cape and hat, she stomped her boots, prised them off and took the towel Tom was handing her.

'Come here,' he said, as she began to rub at her hair, and pulling her to him he started to do it for her. 'You're soaked right through,' he told her. 'Why don't you go and take a shower, I'm sure Matty won't mind.'

Sandy looked up at him, then laughed at the face he pulled. 'Do I look that bad?' she challenged.

He nodded, and turned her to the mirror.

She groaned with embarrassment, for her hair was sticking out at angles, and her mascara, what little was left of it, was smudged over her cheeks in unsightly streaks. Her sweater and jeans were clinging to her like an oversized skin, but though she longed to strip them off, she wasn't sure about undressing in front of him.

She looked up, hoping he might give her some sign of what he wanted her to do, but he was already turning away and she could tell, from the way his head was bowed and his fingers were pressing his temples, that his thoughts were going in a very different direction from hers.

'I think we should fly back to LA tomorrow,' she said.

He looked up, seeming surprised, then realizing what she'd said, he nodded. 'You know,' he said, sinking down into the plush, hand-embroidered cushions of one of the sofas, 'I never thought it would get to me like this. I mean, I knew it would have an effect, it was bound to, but when I saw those guys messing about with those guns . . . It's the way the Colombians do it. They play with weapons like that, and who gives a shit if anyone gets killed? And it's not just men. You see kids carrying assault rifles or MGLs . . .'

'MGLs?' Sandy repeated.

'Multiple grenade launchers. Grown men are teaching kids of twelve or thirteen to use them. Girls too. They dress themselves up in combat gear and attach themselves to guerilla groups who coach them on how to blow up military targets and tear apart rich men's families by taking innocent folk hostage. More often than not they get killed themselves, because they don't know how to use the guns properly, or just because they've outlived their usefulness. It'll be kids like that who were paid to take Rachel. They wouldn't have known who she was. They wouldn't even have cared.'

His eyes came up to Sandy's but she knew he was barely seeing her.

'You know what I keep asking myself?' he said. 'I keep asking myself what was going through her head when they took her? Did she know what was happening? Did she put up a struggle? Or try to bargain? Chances are they used scopolamine. Do you know what that is?'

Sandy shook her head.

'It's a drug – locally they call it *burundanga*. Knocks a person out in seconds. I don't know if they used it, or even if I hope they did, because it sure as hell fucks up the body after. It's the stuff they use on tourists, what tourists that country ever sees now. They spike their drinks, wait for them to drop, then clear out their cash.' He was quiet for a moment, apparently still lost in his thoughts. 'You know, the crazy thing is, some of the kindest, most honest and generous people I've met in my life, I've met in Colombia. Rachel always used to say that too. She loved the people, the ordinary people who're trying to hack a decent living somewhere inside that hellish mess they call a country. She especially loved the kids, the ones she met on the streets. The teenage prostitutes who'd never known a normal life. All they know is the abuse they've suffered at the hands of their parents, or boyfriends, or pushers. They're kids with no childhood. No memories you'd ever want to visit. Yet the affection they give.' He laughed, humourlessly. 'Little faces peeping into yours, trying to make you laugh. Hands sneaking into yours, looking for warmth, ready for any amount of kindness. Rachel always used to take them candy – bubble gum or lollipops – and condoms. Some of them used to claim they got lucky on the condoms she gave them. I don't know what they really meant by that, but it's what they said. Maybe they got paid a few pesos more. Did I ever tell you, she had an exhibition once, of photographs

356

she'd taken of kids who worked the Zone. The Zone is an area of Bogotá that could make Dante's Inferno seem like a day at the beach. She took shots of them hooking, sniffing glue, cutting a deal, grinning their little faces off – they love to pose for a camera. Makes them feel special, but they'll only do it for someone they trust. Rachel knew them all by name, she cared about them and they knew it. She had a kind of connection with them . . . When the photographs were ready she gave them all copies, and put their names under their pictures at the exhibition. No-one really went to see it; but they were great shots, some of her best work.'

Once again his eyes returned to Sandy's. Seconds ticked by, as they sat in the scented warmth of the trailer, and vaguely heard the rain and commotion outside.

'I got an e-mail this morning,' he said, 'telling me that Galeano had seen that exhibition.'

Sandy looked confused. 'But isn't it over now?' she said.

He nodded. 'Oh yes. It finished four years ago, long before she died.'

'So what does it mean?' she said. 'Why would he tell you that?'

'I don't know,' Chambers answered. 'Or maybe I don't want to know.'

Not sure what to say, Sandy waited for him to go on.

'Just now,' he said, 'when I looked at the two actors, the ones playing the Zapata boys, who were messing about with those guns . . . Before that I was thinking, for everyone's sake, that maybe we should change the script. We could just hold Molina accountable for what happened to Rachel and be done with it. If we gave Galeano that reassurance he might call off his threats. But the Zapata boys were there. They raped her, butchered her and for all I know they were the ones who put the gun to her head and killed her. So tell me, am I wrong to feel the way I do? Am I allowing my own need

357

for revenge to put other people's lives at risk?'

Reaching out for his hand, Sandy held it between her own. 'We've done everything we can to make this set secure,' she said gently. 'And no, you're not wrong to feel the way you do. Anyone would, with any decency and morals.'

'Is it moral to want to kill a man? Doesn't that make me just as bad as those who killed her?'

'No. It makes you human. And you're doing the right thing, Tom. You're using this movie to bring her killers to justice, rather than do it yourself.'

'But what about Ellen?' he said. 'What if they harm her? How am I ever going to live with myself then?'

Sandy's eyes went down as his words grazed her heart. His concern wouldn't only be for Ellen, but for the child that might be his. 'We don't know for sure if they're targeting her,' she said softly. 'And Michael's doing everything he can to protect her. You know that.'

'But he's still so mad at her.'

'Maybe. But that doesn't mean he wants anything to happen to her.'

He sighed and brushed a hand through his hair. 'I guess not,' he said.

As she took in his angst she felt the unstoppable heat of envy stealing through her. Were it not for the baby then he might be remembering that she too could be in danger now, but she could see that that was a long way from his mind. And who could say, maybe she wasn't in danger, maybe she just didn't feature largely enough in his life for anyone outside to have noticed she was there. Not that she wanted the danger to fall on her, but if it did, maybe it would wake him up to the fact that he felt something more for her than he realized. But there were other ways of doing that, and if nothing else, he must surely crave the distraction that making love could offer.

'Tom,' she said softly.

He looked far into her eyes and she felt herself sinking

into the quiet charisma and power that was his. She wished now that she had taken off her clothes when she'd come in, that she could add her nakedness to the intimacy they were sharing, and use the vulnerability of it to show him how deeply she felt for his loneliness. Were he able to look upon her now she was sure he would understand how much he needed to be loved, and what strength he could draw from her willingness to give.

'I'm going to say something now,' she began, feeling herself grow warm with unease, 'something, well, that's not really easy for me to say. It might not be what you want, but I want you to know that it doesn't have to be anything special . . . It can just be between friends.' She laughed shortly. 'I mean, for me it will be special, but not so's I can't handle it, because I can . . .'

She stopped as his fingers touched her lips, and taking her eyes up to his she looked at him fearfully.

'I know what you're trying to say,' he told her gently, 'and I don't want you to think I don't appreciate it, or that I don't find you attractive, because it's not the case. You're a beautiful woman, Sandy, in more ways than you know.'

'But . . .'

'No, hear me out,' he interrupted. 'I care for you too much to use you the way you're suggesting, and no matter that you say you can handle it, it's not something I'm going to feel good about, when I know that it can't go any further.'

'How do you know that, unless you give it a chance?' she protested.

'I just know,' he responded.

She looked at him again and felt a rush of need engulf her. She wanted so desperately to make him understand that it was all right to love again, that it was the only thing that would heal him, but she just didn't know which words to use.

Then, as though he had read her mind, he said, 'Sandy, I know this is going to be hard for you to hear, but I need to tell you for your own good, and for reasons that are as true as the offer you are making.' Gently he touched her face again and smoothed the rosy softness of her cheeks. 'There can't ever be anything more than this between us,' he said, 'and not because of Rachel, or how I still feel about her, which is what I know you think. It's because of you and me, and who we both are and what our lives are about.' He stopped and looked sorrowfully, almost painfully, into her eyes. 'I don't love you, Sandy,' he said, 'and I'm not going to lie to you either. It would be the easiest thing in the world for me to take you to bed, to make love to you all night long and want even more in the morning. But it's not what you deserve. You deserve someone who can be with you and love you the way every woman should be loved. And I just don't have those feelings for you, Sandy. God knows, I wish I did, but I don't.'

As the burning heat of devastation enfolded her heart she hung her head and wished herself dead – or a mere few minutes back in time, before any of this had been said. She wanted to curl up in the shame of his rejection and have it smother her and choke her until she could no longer breathe the air that was a part of this pain. She'd done everything she could to make him want her, but in the end nothing had worked. She'd changed the way she looked, the way she dressed, even the way she thought, but still it wasn't enough. So just what was it going to take to make him want her? For a fleeting moment one of the recent lessons she had learned flashed her the answer: let go, stop wanting, and everything will be yours.

But that made no sense now, nor did it provide any comfort. All it did was make her want to hang on even tighter, so tight that she had to force herself to get up and leave before she fell to her knees and begged.

Chapter 20

They were now a full two weeks into the schedule, with a second unit operating on the streets of LA, picking up general driving and panorama shots with Richard Conway and three support cast, for the end of the movie. Every day new problems were arising and Ellen was so rushed off her feet, with viewings, meetings, interviews, phone calls and endless rounds of troubleshooting, that her bodyguard, Kris, was hard put to keep up with her. On the whole he managed, though he had several times to remind her that Michael had totally forbidden her to go anywhere – including the bathroom – without him. She did draw the line at that, however, but he was there the whole time in her office as she kept in contact with the main unit in Mexico, wanting a regular update on everything that was happening, and enjoying the gossip and slander as affairs began and egos bloomed. She should have been down there herself but Michael wouldn't budge on that, and in truth, as strained as things still were between them, she wasn't really that keen to be so far away from him.

Also, as her pregnancy was now entering its seventh month, there was no longer any hiding it, nor was she quite as mobile as she'd have liked. Kris had turned into something of a godsend, as he dealt rather efficiently with the small clutches of photographers and reporters who were being paid handsome sums for shots of the expectant producer. Speculation was once again running rife over her marriage, but as she and Michael were now living in the same house, rumours of rifts, divorce, abortion, other partners and even, in one mind-boggling broadcast, hoax weddings, weren't gaining much ground. In fact the entire circus of publicity was proving more ludicrous than harmful, and she probably wouldn't have minded it at all were it not for the fact that it was prompting so many weirdos and whackos to try calling her up. On the whole Maggie managed to stall them, but somehow this one had got through, and as Ellen listened to the voice at the other end she could at last feel Tom's and Michael's fears for her safety starting to fall on fertile ground.

The call had begun with her usual hurried hello as she flipped through the 'documentary' proposal that had just been faxed over from London. She wasn't really paying much attention, so it was a moment or two before she realized no-one had responded. 'Hello?' she said again, jotting a note on the fax to get that particular point clarified. '*Hello?*'

'Hello,' came the reply. 'I know you are busy, so I will come right to the point.'

Ellen frowned. The accented voice sounded just like those that were coming in on the dailies. 'That's good,' she said cheerfully, assuming she was speaking to one of the Latino actors. 'I didn't get your name though.'

'I am someone who wishes only to be your friend,' the voice told her calmly.

Immediately alarm bells started in her head, and letting go of the fax she leaned forward to buzz through for Kris who was outside talking to Maggie.

'I want you please to understand,' the man went on, 'that I have no grudge against you personally. But I have my instructions, which I shall be obliged to carry out.'

Ellen's throat was turning dry. 'What instructions?' she demanded, her finger still poised over the button, though not yet pressing. 'What are you talking about? Who are you?'

'I am to make you understand,' he replied, 'that the movie you are shooting is causing grave concern to certain people in my country. We have tried to explain this to Señor Chambers, but unfortunately he is not listening. So please, it is important that you stop this movie right now, today.'

Ellen was silent. Dimly she could feel her head starting to throb, and looking at her hand on the intercom she wondered why she hadn't yet pressed it.

'Do you understand what I'm telling you?' the voice said. 'Please, you need to understand how serious your position is.'

'Yes, I hear you,' she answered, her eyes moving about the office, as though somewhere, hidden amongst the piles of scripts and shelves of tapes and books, she might find the person behind the voice.

'You have the power to do what my people are asking,' he said. 'Please tell me you will do it.'

'But I can't,' she said, almost in a whisper.

There was a moment's silence before he said, 'Please be very clear about what I am saying. I wish you no harm. You are a very beautiful woman and I know that you have a baby soon to be born. Your husband will not want either of you to be hurt. I do not want either of you to be hurt. But the movie must be stopped. There are those who do not wish for it to be made and I will be forced to carry out my orders if you do not do as I tell you.'

'What are your orders?' she heard herself ask, her voice only just breaking through the tightness in her throat.

'You know what happened to Rachel Carmedi,' he answered.

Terror sank into her heart.

'Please,' he said, 'don't let the same thing happen to

363

you. Speak to your husband. Tell him the only way to save you is to stop the movie and forget all about the names Señor Chambers has told you.'

'But he can't do it,' she pleaded. 'It's not in his power.'

'*Please,*' the voice repeated, sounding so anxious it was as though he really did care.

The line was suddenly cut. Ellen flinched, then replacing the receiver she sat staring at it with wide, disbelieving eyes. After a moment she tried to get to her feet, but her legs were shaking too badly, her whole body felt weak. The voice was going round and round in her head, so soft, so mild and entreating; a voice it would be easy to trust, had it not belonged to a man who had been ordered to kill her.

Suddenly she snatched up the phone, needing to speak to Michael, but even before she began dialling she put it back down. She'd spoken the truth when she'd said there was nothing he could do, for the ultimate power wasn't his, it was Ted Forgon's – and the rest of the World Wide shareholders'. There would have to be a meeting, a vote, but with so many millions at stake, so many investors to consider, she knew already what Ted Forgon's answer would be.

'Out of the question!' he told her. 'Besides, they're bluffing. And you've got yourself a bodyguard, so what are you worrying about? Tell you what though, we'll get in touch with the police, tell them about the call, and from here on in you don't go anywhere without you got yourself an escort. OK?' He passed her a club soda with a wedge of lime. 'Just ain't any way I'm going to be pushed around by a bunch of Spics, specially not in my own town. So the next time this jerk calls, you put him on to me, do you hear? I'll sort the sucker out.'

It was no more and no less than Ellen had expected. But at least she'd passed the message on to the right quarter, which was what she'd been instructed to do. Surely they would understand now that there was nothing else she could do, for it would serve no purpose to tell Michael, when his hand would be as tied as hers, and when he had so much else to think of that she didn't want him to have to worry about her any more than he already was.

It was late the following afternoon that Michael drove up to the house and parked his car in the garage next to Ellen's. As it was a Saturday both units had stopped shooting at midday, which had calmed the phones for a while and given him a chance to catch up with other, slightly less pressing commitments. Ellen had left the office around four, taking a stack of work home with her, which she'd insisted she'd get down to after stealing a quick hour with her feet up. She'd looked tired, and pale, and he had been about to tell her they should cancel the dinner they were supposed to attend that evening, when the phone had interrupted. He guessed it was probably too late to back out now, but if she didn't look any better, he'd insist.

After dropping his keys in a fruit bowl he went to find her. It didn't take long, as she was standing in front of the pool, her back to the house, staring down at the clear blue water. Her hair was wet, and she wore a thick towelling robe, telling him she had probably just taken a swim.

He stood quietly watching her, wondering what she was thinking and if now was the time for him to start trying to prove what he finally understood she needed to know, that he loved her, no matter what. But that was easy to say now she had told him the baby was his – were there still any doubt would he really be standing here now, thinking this way? He had to believe he would, for the past few months had shown him how unable he was to let her go, how incapable he was of throwing it all away despite how much it hurt him to stay. Perhaps the hardest to understand had been how weakened he'd felt by the depth of his feelings, for they'd made him realize how out of control he was of his own life, and how dependent he was on her to make him feel whole. It had never before occurred to him that loving her so much would bring such problems, and though he hated himself for allowing his ego such power, he was still finding it hard to accept that he wasn't going to turn himself into some kind of besotted and gullible patsy by believing her just because he loved her. He'd seen so many men go that route, blind, pathetic fools that they were, and how humiliating and defeating it had been for them when finally they'd woken up to the truth.

But what was the truth? Was it really in the scenarios he tormented himself with, of Chambers turning her down, telling her he could never love her, that she should go back to her husband and let him think the child was his? With his air of tragedy and life fraught with danger Chambers had to be attractive to any woman, so how could he blame Ellen if she had fallen for him too? After all, where was the appeal and romance of his life and accomplishments as an agent and producer, when compared to the war zones and human despair that Chambers endured? But even if Ellen were still harbouring a secret longing for Chambers, in his heart of hearts he just couldn't make himself believe that she would lie to him over something as crucial as the identity of the baby's father.

But still there was that lingering doubt, upheld by his ego, and he knew he must do something to destroy it, and he must do it soon. After the birth would be too late, for then science would decree the father and she would know that he hadn't loved or trusted her enough to take her word.

As though sensing him standing behind her she turned, and seeing him she smiled. 'How long have you been there?' she said.

'A few minutes,' he answered. 'Where's Kris? I didn't see him outside.'

'He went into the study to use the phone,' she answered, pulling the robe tighter around her.

'It's too cold to swim,' he said.

She turned and looked back at the pool.

'What were you thinking?' he said. 'Just now, before you turned round.'

Her head went to one side as she continued to gaze into the water. 'I don't know,' she said. 'About the movie, I guess. And how precipitous it all feels. I mean, it's like we're all waiting for something to happen, something horrible and calamitous that's going to change our lives. Yet the whole thing just keeps moving along, cameras turning, actors whingeing, and nothing unusual's happening at all.' She looked at him and sighed. 'It just feels strange. Like waiting for a bomb to go off when you're not even sure there is a bomb.'

She hugged herself more deeply into the robe, and pulling her to him, he rubbed his hands over her back.

'You should take a bath to warm up,' he said.

She looked up at him, and making her laugh with the drollery in his eyes he led her back inside the house.

A few minutes later he was helping her out of her swimsuit and holding her hand as she stepped into the hot, scented water. She didn't sit down right away, but stood looking at him, uncertainly, even shyly, feeling the cloying steam swirling around her body.

She was hardly daring to breathe, for so many times in these past few weeks he had seemed to come so close, only to back away at the final moment, leaving her hurt and angry and despairing that he would ever get past his mistrust. In her heart she knew this wasn't the way he wanted it, but she knew too how difficult he was finding it to overcome.

Feeling the baby suddenly kick, she looked down at her tummy and was about to touch it when she saw that he was on the point of it too. She stood very still, watching, as he raised his hand and placed it gently over the protruding core of her navel. Then he moved it, gliding his fingers over the creamy softness of her skin.

It was the first time he'd touched her like this, and feeling almost overcome by the joy and relief it was giving her, she continued to watch, moving her eyes between his hand and his face, leaving her own hands hanging loosely at her sides, as though to permit him all the exploring he needed. He glanced up at her, then lifting his other hand he watched them both, following their slow, tentative sweep over the growing mound of the child.

There was no movement within, but still he felt strangely diffident, a little overawed, and totally intrigued. He looked at her swollen breasts with their large, distended nipples and small maps of blue veins. He touched them, kissed them gently, then touched them again.

At last his eyes returned to hers and, smiling as she saw his expression, she took his hand and brought it to her lips. 'Bathe me,' she said.

As she sat down in the water he knelt on the floor beside her, and began scooping handfuls of bubbles over her neck and shoulders. Then taking the soap he used it to massage her, making white, slippery patterns all over her breasts and belly.

She looked up into his face and seeing the wonder in his eyes, she reached out to touch him.

'I'm sorry,' he whispered.

She smiled and ran her thumb over his lips.

It was a while before he could make himself go on, until, laughing awkwardly at his reticence, he said, 'I'm not finding this easy, you know, getting in touch with my emotions. I mean,' he looked into her eyes, then turned to kiss the palm she had resting on his cheek. 'I always knew I loved you,' he said, 'but I never expected it to be put to the test like this, never dreamt I would come out so lacking – in courage and understanding.' He dropped his eyes for a moment, then, looking at her again, it was as though he could feel the strength of their love starting to flow past the fear he had harboured. 'I don't know if I can find the words to tell you how much you mean to me,' he said softly, 'but it's a whole lot more than I realized, more than I thought I could deal with for a while.' His voice suddenly gave out, and he smiled self-consciously at the way his emotions had tripped him. 'I love you,' he finally managed. 'I'm inept, I'm a fool and I don't deserve you at all, but I'm sure as hell never going to let you go. Either of you.'

Reaching out her arms she pulled him to her and kissed him with all the might of her love.

'Come in with us,' she said, when finally he raised his head to look into her eyes.

Stripping off his clothes, he got in beside her and lying down next to her he held her and stroked her and laughed as the baby kicked the soap from her belly.

Then he was kissing her again, more deeply and commandingly than before. Their needs and passions were aroused, but as she started to ask him to take her to bed, the phone beside them suddenly crashed into the moment.

'Do we have to answer it?' he said.

'I don't know. Do we?'

It continued to ring.

'I guess we should,' she said.

Scowling, he reached out and brought the phone to his ear. 'This better be good,' he said into the receiver.

'Michael? It's Tom.'

Michael's eyes closed. Of all the people . . . 'What can I do for you?' he said.

'I just checked my e-mail,' Chambers told him. 'We need to talk.'

'Where are you?' Michael said, reaching for a towel.

'In the air, about twenty minutes from LAX. Can you meet me?'

'If you think it's necessary.'

'If you're qualifying,' Chambers responded, 'I'd say it's vital.'

For the past twenty minutes, after he'd clicked off the phone to Michael and waited for the plane to land, Chambers had sat quietly in his seat knowing that there would be no more warnings now, no more procrastinating, the first person had already been killed, and he didn't even want to think how many more would die before he got the movie to stop.

Frustration, anger and impotence welled up in him. It mushroomed around him like a great shadowy monster. All he'd wanted was to make amends, to try somehow to show her, wherever she was, that he hadn't meant to let her down. That, were he given the time over, he would willingly sacrifice his own life in place of hers. But that wasn't possible, so making this movie, immortalizing her memory and bringing her killers to justice, was the only way he could think of to let the whole world, and her, know that he still loved her, still thought about her every day and still longed for her in a way he knew he would never long for any other woman.

He sat very still, showing nothing of the torment going on inside him. Sandy was beside him, allowing him the silence he needed. She had seen the e-mail too, and being unused to Colombian ways, her shock had been even more profound than his. He wished he hadn't shown her. There was no good reason to show anyone the terrible image that had been transmitted from Bogotá. They'd contacted him direct this time, obviously wanting no doubts about the message reaching him. There had been a message from Alan Day too – it seemed they had e-mailed him as a backup.

Chambers felt sick to his stomach, and afraid in a way

he hadn't been in a very long time. He knew the most important thing now was not to panic, or do anything rash that would end up causing more confusion and damage. He had to think about this as rationally as he was able, to sort out in his mind what he could do to stop the barbaric slaughter Galeano and his people had already set in motion.

By the time the plane landed and they were through customs, Michael was outside in the car. Seeing the Land Cruiser, Sandy pointed it out, then, stopping Tom as he made to go towards it, she said, 'You two need to talk. I'll take a taxi and see you back at the hotel.'

He nodded, kissed her hard on the forehead, and went to get in the car.

As Michael pulled away Chambers folded down the visor, attempting to see if they were being followed. There was so much traffic it was impossible to tell.

'I need to know,' he said abruptly, 'if Ellen has received any more calls.'

Michael glanced at him, then indicated to change lanes. 'No,' he said, narrowly avoiding a car rental bus.

Chambers allowed himself a moment's relief.

'Why?' Michael demanded. 'What's going on?'

'Something I wasn't expecting,' Chambers responded. 'It wasn't what they've been preparing us for. I guess the schmozo who's been calling me, the one who made out he was contacting someone else on the unit too, was just a decoy, someone to make us look the other way while they worked out the next best way to get to me. I say next best, because obviously going after Ellen would have been the worst. But if she hasn't received any more calls then we can probably assume the one she got, that she wasn't even sure was a threat, was benign.' He glanced over at Michael. 'We should keep on with the bodyguard though, just to make sure, but my guess is they don't want to bring the Feds down on their case, which is what it would mean if anything happened to her.'

371

Michael swallowed hard. 'You think just the threat of the Feds is enough to keep them away?' he said.

'I sure hope so,' Chambers replied. 'But what we're facing now has already become a reality. Find a place to pull over, you need to see this e-mail.'

They sped out of the airport, hanging a left down on to Sepulveda, and at the first hotel Michael pulled into the parking lot.

Chambers's laptop was already open, the image he had downloaded there on the screen. He passed it over to Michael.

'Jesus Christ!' Michael murmured, when he saw the mutilated body of a teenage boy. He felt his stomach rise and the air lock in his lungs. During all his years in the business he had seen a thousand pictures like this, but none had ever been real. There was no doubt in his mind that this one was. 'Who is it, do you know?' he said quietly.

'His name's Casto,' Chambers answered, his face totally devoid of colour, his words without tone. 'He's one of the kids Rachel photographed for her exhibition.' A stark bitterness crept into his voice. 'The exhibition we're due to start shooting at the end of the week.' He looked at the picture of the boy again, then looked away. 'His story's not unique,' he said. 'Sold by his mother, age five, for the price of a hit, taken in by a bunch of druggies who used him as a house-slave until he was ten. Then they put him into prostitution. He ran away, lived on the streets, continued his prostitution in order to survive. Sniffed glue, smoked basuco, got regularly abused in ways you don't even want to hear about. A street-smart, mischievous kid, with a wicked humour and a spirit that kept him alive when no doctor would even check him over. Not a handsome boy, which was why he was so badly abused – no pity for ugly gay boys in the macho world of Bogotá. Got his teeth smashed out by one of his tricks who thought it would make for a better blow-job.'

His eyes returned to the downloaded image of Casto's chubby, twisted little body lying in a doorway, neck so deeply cut his head was almost severed. 'He told me once he wanted to be a movie star and live in a big house with gates and bars and security guards so that no-one could ever get to him again,' Chambers murmured.

Michael was so appalled he could barely find any words. 'So what's the message?' he asked.

'The message,' Chambers responded, 'is that for every day the movie goes on one of these kids, the ones Rachel took shots of, is going to die.'

Michael's face drained as he stared at Chambers in disbelief. 'You can't be serious,' he said.

'No-one gives a fuck about any of these kids,' Chambers responded. 'They're *gamines*, *desechables* – gutter waste, disposable.'

With a horrible morbidity Michael looked at Casto's picture again and tried not to measure his own livelihood and reputation against the lives of children such as this. That was what it was now coming down to, because in order to save these kids he was going to have to jeopardize, and probably lose, everything he owned in the world – his agency in London, his stake in World Wide, his homes in London, Barbados and LA, not to mention all the hard-won commitments from investors – and bring the movie to a standstill. Not only a standstill, a total demise. And then he would have to look at the debts, the lawsuits, the bankruptcy and probable prison sentence that would inevitably follow. His brain began speeding, so fast he felt nauseous.

'Fuck,' he muttered. 'Fuck, fuck, and fuck.' He looked at Chambers.

Chambers looked back helplessly. He knew what this meant to Michael, so was under no illusion how much he was asking.

In the end Michael said, 'There's no choice, is there?'

'There's always a choice,' Chambers responded.

Michael sighed. 'You think I'd let them die?'

Chambers shook his head.

'Were it just me, I could try to do what you're asking,' Michael said. 'But there're the other shareholders, and I just can't see them going for this. Christ, I can hear Forgon already.'

Chambers remained silent.

Michael turned to look out of the window, his eyes unfocused on the passing rush of headlights. He thought of Robbie and knew there was no way in the world he could live with himself if he didn't do something to rescue these kids, no matter what the cost to himself. But still he felt sick, wishing to God he could think of something, anything, that would avert this disaster. He'd never dreamt that the day would come when Forgon would be his saviour, but right now that was exactly what he could turn out to be, for there was just no way Michael could see him agreeing to pull out of the movie. Too many stood to lose too much, including Forgon who personally was in to the tune of two million. And over twenty million more was already committed in ways it was impossible to back out of without facing bankruptcy and maybe prison.

His hand went to his head. The very idea of the bond company coughing up was so delusional it was laughable. The rest of the world had never cared about these kids before, and now with so much money at stake he could already hear the answers, that they were probably better off dead anyway.

Taking out his cellphone he started to dial.

'Who are you calling?' Chambers asked.

'Forgon. If he's home we'll go over there now.'

Forgon's leathery face was incredulous. In fact, he was so stunned by what Chambers and McCann had just shown him – and then told him – that he couldn't find a way to express his amazement. 'Let me get this straight,' he said, when finally he recovered his speech. 'You want me to turn tail on this movie because a bunch of badass Spics are threatening to off a few kids no-one's ever gonna miss, except the poor bastards they rob and contaminate with their foul diseases?' He looked at Michael. 'Did you get a brain bypass, boy? I mean, did you fuck up your wits with some shit drug, or something, because it's the only reason I can think of that you'd actually come here and ask me this, like I was going to give a fuck?'

Michael glanced at Chambers. He was about to speak when Chambers beat him to it.

'I think you should know that I've got a lot of powerful friends in the media,' he said, guessing blackmail was the language Forgon understood best, 'and they're just going to lap up the story of how Mr Bigshot Hollywood Producer let innocent kids die rather than lose a few million.'

'A few million!' Forgon exploded. 'You call what we've got invested here a few million? The last figures I saw we were in for over twenty, and I sure as hell don't call that a few. Now I suggest you go get yourselves a hit on reality, before you start believing anything you say is going to persuade me. We got some important people here who've put up as much as five million bucks each, do you seriously think they're going to give a fuck about a few kids in a city half of 'em probably never even heard of?'

'We need to take a vote on this,' Michael said. 'I've already called Maggie to get her to set up a shareholders' meeting.'

Forgon's eyes almost burst from his head. 'You're getting Mark Bergin over here from Sydney for *this*!' he spat. 'Did you lose your mind? The man's not going to vote with you on this. No-one in his right mind's going to vote with you on this.'

'Sandy will,' Chambers told him.

Forgon looked at him in astonishment. 'Is that so?' he responded sceptically. 'Did you ask her?'

Chambers couldn't lie.

Forgon started to laugh. 'Listen to me,' he said. 'If you think she's going to vote with you when she, personally, is answerable to at least half the investors, then you really are cruising with your lights out.'

Chambers looked at Michael.

'We'll let you know about the shareholders' meeting,' Michael said, and nodding to Chambers he led the way out of the room.

By six the following evening Chris Ruskin in New York and Mark Bergin in Sydney had agreed to fly to LA to attend a shareholders' meeting. Knowing what was on the agenda, Bergin had already warned Michael that he couldn't rely on him for support. Ruskin hadn't yet committed, either to Michael or to Forgon. Nor had Sandy, she'd wanted to speak to her investors first, which Michael had understood, but Chambers hadn't.

'These are children, Sandy,' he raged.

'I understand that!' she cried. 'And I swear, if it were my money I'd be prepared to do what you're asking. But it's not mine, and I owe these people, Tom. It wasn't only their money they gave me, it was their trust.'

'So you speak to them, and then what? You think they're going to sanction you voting with Michael?'

'No,' she said truthfully. 'I don't. But try to see this from my point of view. I *have* to consult them, not only morally, but very possibly legally.'

'You're the shareholder in World Wide. They have no say over how you vote there.'

'Of course they don't, but it's their investments that hang on the way I vote. Tom, please. I'd give anything for this to be just my decision, but we both have to face the fact . . .'

'That you don't care about the kids that are getting

killed,' he shouted, and before she could say any more he slammed out of the room.

The next morning Chambers downloaded the image of another child murder in Bogotá. This time the victim was a sixteen-year-old girl, whose broken, bullet-ridden body was slumped under a swing in a playground, a used syringe and a cuddly toy only inches from her outstretched hand. Her name was Priscilia. Chambers remembered her well, for many was the time she had tried to come onto him, using her then twelve-year-old body with a sophistication and guile it was tragic to behold in one so young. He guessed it was nothing short of a miracle that she had managed to stay alive this long, but that didn't change the fact that she didn't deserve to die like this.

It had been several hours now since he'd last heard from Alan Day, which could be either good or bad. Bad if anything had happened to the man, good if he was managing to get through to General Goméz – just about the only man on the ground who could help them with this. For the time being all Chambers could do was wait, and pray that the rest of Rachel's wretched child subjects were long gone from Bogotá – or even the world. It wasn't likely that many of them were surviving, most didn't last more than a few years on the streets, but as the hours ticked by and the cameras continued to roll he could only thank God that Rachel had never known what a terrible price her photographs were ultimately costing the children.

Ellen looked at Sandy's calm blue eyes and felt stunned. Not only stunned, but outraged and maddeningly confused. Were she talking to anyone else she might be thinking she hadn't heard quite right, but as it was Sandy she knew she had, though precisely how she felt about what she'd heard she just couldn't get a grip on.

377

'I'm sure you'd like some time to think this over,' Sandy said, 'but as you know, we don't have that luxury, so I'm going to have to ask you for an answer.'

Ellen blinked, looked away for a moment, then returned her eyes to Sandy. They were sitting in Ellen's office. Sandy was on one of the sofas, Ellen was squashed into a leather armchair. 'I'm sorry,' she said, 'but I just want to be clear about this. What you're saying is, that you'll give me *twelve* per cent of your shares in World Wide in return for me telling Michael this baby is his?'

'When it's born, yes.'

Ellen couldn't help but marvel at her nerve, and at how coolly she delivered her outrageous proposal, especially when it was only going to leave her with a nine per cent holding. But what was appalling her the most right now was how the hell Sandy knew there was some doubt over who the baby's father was. 'What on earth makes you think this baby could be anyone else's but Michael's?' she demanded.

Sandy explained how she had overheard Ellen telling Matty her fears that Tom was the father.

Ellen's shock hit another level, but at least it explained how Forgon knew. 'Does Tom know?' she asked.

Sandy nodded.

Ellen let go her breath and looked around the room.

Sandy continued. 'With your twelve per cent added to Michael's twenty-eight,' she said, 'there's a chance he'll be able to pull the plug on the movie. Providing, of course, Chris Ruskin votes with you.'

Ellen gazed at her in amazement. She was having a hard time taking all this in. 'Why don't you just vote with Michael?' she said.

Sandy merely looked at her, waiting for her to come up with the answer herself. It didn't take long.

'Because,' Ellen said, 'you want to be able to tell the European investors that you voted to keep the movie going.'

Sandy nodded.

If nothing else, Ellen was impressed by her honesty. 'And what are you going to tell them,' she said, 'when they ask why you signed twelve per cent of your shares over to me the day before the vote was due to be taken?'

'I'll think of something,' Sandy answered. 'Maybe I'll tell them you were blackmailing me and I had to pay up.' It wasn't funny and already Sandy wished she hadn't said it. 'The point is,' she went on, 'I can tell them that Chris Ruskin had assured me he was going to back Forgon, so with Mark Bergin's and my support too, Forgon would win hands down with seventy-two per cent of the vote. So me giving twelve per cent to the other side wasn't going to affect the outcome one way or the other.'

'Which it won't, if Chris does vote with Forgon,' Ellen pointed out.

Sandy nodded and Ellen stared at her hard as she tried to come up with the catch. She couldn't find one, except, of course, the condition of the transfer. 'And all I have to do for you to give me these shares is tell Michael the baby is his?' she repeated.

Sandy nodded.

Ellen looked at her youthful yet determined face, and suddenly felt the urge to laugh. 'And exactly how,' she said, controlling it, 'is all this going to benefit you?'

A faint colour rose in Sandy's cheeks. 'I'm trying to buy myself a little insurance for the future,' she answered.

Ellen waited for her to expand, wanting to see just how honest she would be.

'If the vote goes Michael's way and the movie is cancelled,' Sandy went on, 'there's a very good chance we're all going to be ruined, and if that happens . . . Well, you and Michael will at least have each other. What I'm trying to hang on to is a modicum of my reputation to help get me started again.'

'And there's also the chance,' Ellen added, 'that if Tom knows for certain the baby isn't his, he'll commit to you?'

Sandy said nothing.

Ellen was quiet as the full meaning of what she'd just said started to sink in. All this time Tom had known she might be carrying his child and had said nothing. But it seemed he'd kept himself available in case he had turned out to be the father, and, presumably, in case she had needed him too. At least, according to the way she was reading Sandy that appeared to be the case.

Keeping her eyes down she wondered about Sandy, and if she really did stand a chance with Tom if he no longer thought the child was his. She guessed she'd just have to let Tom answer that, for she was going to have no trouble telling Michael the baby was his, then the rest was going to be . . . Well, if nothing else, it was certainly going to be interesting.

'There's just one thing you seem to be forgetting,' she said, somehow knowing that Sandy hadn't, though how she was going to get round it was certainly beating Ellen. 'Under the terms and conditions of the company, you can't transfer any shares without first informing the majority shareholder.'

Sandy allowed herself a smile. 'If you read the terms and conditions,' she responded, 'which were originally drawn up by Michael and his lawyers when the company was getting started, you'll see that what it actually says is that Michael McCann is the one who has to be informed of any sale or transfer of shares, not the majority shareholder. Of course, it was expected back then that Michael would be the majority shareholder.' She paused, then smiled again. 'A very convenient oversight on the part of Ted Forgon, wouldn't you agree?'

Ellen was looking at her in amazement, and not a little respect. She really had done her homework. 'Does

Michael know that his name still figures that way?' she asked.

'I imagine so,' Sandy answered. 'But if he doesn't, he's about to find out. And if he agrees to the transfer, which I'm sure he will, I've already spoken to a notary whose office is in Century Plaza. He's expecting us sometime between three thirty and five.'

Ellen's eyes widened. 'You were so sure I'd do it?' she said.

'Let's just say I tried to stay optimistic.'

'And how do you know you can trust me?'

Sandy laughed. 'Oh, that's easy,' she said, 'you're not like me.'

Ellen looked at her, then she too started to laugh.

Despite the awfulness of what was happening to the children in Colombia, and the fact that they were now poised to lose just about everything they owned, Michael couldn't help but laugh when Ellen told him about the meeting she'd just had with Sandy.

'Did you know you were the one who had to be informed about share transfers or sales?' Ellen asked.

He nodded and she eyed him meaningfully. 'And you didn't even tell me,' she chided.

'Only because, when I found out, we weren't exactly seeing eye to eye.'

'And we are now?' she teased.

He smiled, and pulling her into his arms he kissed her. 'You know,' he said, his tone turning sober, 'whichever way we look at this we're going down. You realize that, don't you?'

Though the fear of it churned in Ellen's heart, her eyes were shining as she took his hand and placed it on the baby. 'As long as we all go down together,' she said.

Michael smiled, and kissed her again.

'What time's the meeting tomorrow?' she asked.

'Three thirty.'

She started to grin.

'What?' Michael asked.

'I just can't wait to see the look on Ted Forgon's face when we win,' she answered.

Michael laughed too, but this time not quite so heartily. The vote hadn't been taken yet, and still no-one knew which way Chris Ruskin would go.

Ellen and Sandy left the notary's office at five that afternoon. After congratulating each other, and recognizing a slight easing of their mutual antipathy, Ellen returned to the office, making a slight detour to drop Sandy off at the Four Seasons on the way. Sandy knew Tom would be there, waiting for a call or e-mail from Alan Day, while dreading another from the Tolima Cartel.

She hated how distant he had become with her, refusing to understand her obligation to her investors. She wanted to tell him now what she'd done to try to help him, but how could she when there was a very good chance she'd just sold his child to another man? She still couldn't quite believe that Ellen had gone for it so easily, but she guessed the mess Michael was in was so great that Ellen was prepared to do anything to help bail him out. Not that voting to cancel the movie was exactly going to achieve that; but whilst calculating it all out Sandy had considered it a pretty safe bet that Ellen would support Michael in trying to save the kids. Of course, like everyone else, Ellen might want to ignore their plight, but Ellen just didn't have what it took to detach herself that way. Sandy understood this, for not even she, who'd never felt much pity for anyone before, could reconcile herself to the idea of any child dying for the sake of a film. On the other hand, nor was she desperately attached to the thought of all those millions, as well as her career, going down the pan.

Right now though, Tom wanted the kids to come first,

so she had done what she could to support him whilst, at the same time, trying to secure at least something of her standing. And the fact that she was getting some payback on that bastard Forgon into the bargain was making her decision a whole lot easier to live with. She just couldn't wait to see his face the next day when he found out what she'd done, especially if Chris Ruskin voted with Michael. And considering how far back Chris and Michael went, she felt reasonably confident that Chris would.

Chapter 21

A third child was now dead. The latest victim was another boy, Manuel, who was just fourteen years old, had been put into prostitution by his stepfather at the age of ten, and had worked the streets and sleazy porn bars until he'd been found by an outreach worker and taken into a rehabilitation centre at thirteen. The update from Alan Day was that the boy had been making impressive progress towards one day becoming a chef – until Galeano's men had got to him yesterday, on his way back to the foundation from a mid-town restaurant, where he had started three weeks ago as an apprentice.

Chambers wept with rage and frustration, and for the young life that had been cruelly snuffed out at a time when he really might have had a chance. And for what? The sake of a movie that was supposed to bring justice for a woman who had once taken the boy's picture. This wasn't what she would want. God knew, she would have endured what she did a hundred times over rather than have these kids so brutally deprived of their lives. It wasn't what he wanted either, which was why, after a relentlessly sleepless night, he had decided that he simply couldn't wait for the shareholders' meeting to determine the fate of the movie.

It was just after nine in the morning when he picked up the phone to call Michael. Getting past Maggie wasn't easy, so in the end he left a message for Michael

to call back the instant he'd finished with Chris Ruskin.
He hoped to God that Michael could talk Ruskin round,
but even presuming for a moment that he did, and the
vote went their way, by the time the news was relayed to
Bogotá there was a very real chance another child would
already be dead. And as if that weren't bad enough, they
then had to ask themselves – again presuming Michael
got control – how long it would actually take to stop the
movie rolling? There was simply no knowing, for after
their lengthy meeting last night with attorneys, business
managers, accountants and two of the senior producers,
no-one could be in any doubt that a thousand lawsuits to
keep the show going would come flying their way the
instant the news had broken.

But all that was for later. For now, there was a lot he
had to get done in order to set his plan for the next few
days in motion, so picking up the other line he started on
the long list of calls that had to be made.

More than two hours had passed before he was finally
through, by which time he'd spoken to everyone from
his personal lawyer in Washington, to the film unit in
Mexico, at least half a dozen contacts in Colombia, even
more in the States and in Europe, and finally to Michael
and Ellen. The call to Ellen was the last, and after
confirming that she could meet him at two in the privacy
of Vic Warren's Mulholland home, he put the phone
down and went through to the bathroom to turn on the
shower.

In the next room Sandy was sitting alone, thinking about
what she had done. She had Ellen's word that she would
never betray the condition of the share transfer, and
knowing that it wouldn't be in Ellen's interest ever to
reveal it anyway, she had no problem trusting her. Even
so, this was a strange and bewildering situation she was
in, for there was a time, not so very long ago, when she
wouldn't have thought twice about the tactics she had

used, believing that the end always justified the means. But the way she had freed Tom from Ellen was troubling her, and she couldn't deal with it.

She tried to remind herself that it wasn't always possible to work things out in a way that made everyone feel good, and as she was very probably the only one who was ever going to feel bad over this, there wasn't really a problem. But for some reason it didn't feel that way, and she couldn't quite figure out why.

As the morning wore on she could feel herself starting to become nervous and agitated, almost afraid. Perhaps that wasn't so surprising when by four that afternoon the world as she knew it could come to an end. She kept trying to see beyond it, to envisage what might happen in any shape or form, but it was as though her mind had totally shut down on the future.

In the end, without thinking, or even planning what she would say, she tried to call Tom, but he was no longer in his room. She sat staring at the phone, then before she knew why she had dialled again and was asking to be put through to Ellen. But Ellen wasn't there either.

'Do you know where she is?' she asked Maggie.

'Sure. She went up to Vic Warren's place,' Maggie answered. 'She was due to meet Tom there at two, so you should get her if you try in a few minutes.'

Sandy suddenly felt very strange inside. It was as though a fog was dropping over her, filling her with noise and tensing her with fear. 'Thanks,' she mumbled to Maggie and put down the phone.

Her hands were trembling as she searched for Vic's number. She couldn't push through to the end of a thought. She felt panicked, then numbed, then horribly afraid. She couldn't say what she was afraid of, all she knew was that it was as though she were on the verge of doing something over which she had no control. She had lost connection with herself, had somehow cut loose from the normal constraints of behaviour and was being sucked into a compulsion she didn't understand.

She couldn't find Vic's number. Her eyes wouldn't focus, nor would her mind. Questions came at her, but no answers. Did she want to stop Ellen doing this? Did she want to confess to Tom what she had done? She gave a strangled sort of laugh. Was this what it was to develop a conscience?

Getting up she went into the bathroom and splashed cold water on her face. It sent a shock to her senses that helped calm her. She took a breath, let it out slowly, then took another.

It was several minutes before she realized what she must do, and as it reached her the sense of rightness that came with it flooded into her heart like a golden light. She looked at her reflection in the mirror and felt her eyes fill with tears as a small, lonely smile curved her mouth. Then going back into the room she called down to the concierge and ordered a hotel car to take her to Vic Warren's house.

It didn't take long to get there, fifteen, maybe twenty minutes, though it felt like an eternity. Every light was red, the world's slowest drivers were on the same route. Just past Michael's and Ellen's house the road was up, causing another wait that seemed to go on for ever. But she was sure they'd still be there, certain she would catch them and do what she must.

In the end she instructed her driver to ignore the red light and go on. A few minutes later they rounded a bend and the ornate, black-gated entrance to Vic Warren's house came into view. Sandy braced herself, and tried again to work out how she was going to do this. She wondered what they would think when they saw her, what she would do if she came upon them in a romantic embrace. But that wasn't going to happen, for when she looked up ahead she saw, with a sinking heart, that Tom's rental car was driving away in the distance.

And her car was still too far back to be noticed when Ellen's came sweeping out of the gates onto Mulholland Drive and turned right along the highway, heading after Tom.

Ellen was in the passenger seat, allowing Kris to drive while she tried to collect her thoughts and redirect them towards the shareholders' meeting, due to begin in under an hour. But it was hard thinking about anything else after the scene she'd just had with Tom, when he'd told her his plans for the future and what provisions he had made for the baby, should it turn out to be his.

Of course she'd told him straight away that it wasn't, but that hadn't proved anywhere near as easy as it should have, for it was only then that she'd realized he might actually have hoped that it was. She suspected that he hadn't realized it either, for the terrible disappointment that had come into his eyes was something she was sure he wouldn't have wanted her to see, had he known there was a chance he might respond that way. He'd covered it quickly with a typical, rueful kind of humour, but it had been so awful seeing him hurt like that that she had ended up making matters a thousand times worse by trying to hug him. His response had been as awkward as his embarrassment, which of course had embarrassed her too, and now she desperately wished she'd had the foresight, and the heart, to have handled it all with much more sensitivity and understanding. If she had, she might then have taken more time to talk to him about his plans, and to tell him how sorry she was he'd ever had to know there was a doubt over who the father was.

But it was too late now, and with the shareholders' meeting looming there probably wouldn't have been the time to talk much anyhow.

Remembering she'd promised to call Michael to tell him when she was on her way back, she was about to struggle past the baby to reach for the phone when she suddenly became aware of the way Kris was repeatedly glancing in the rear-view mirror. Her heart jumped, then her blood started to run cold as she noticed too how tightly his hands were gripping the wheel. 'What is it?' she said, glancing back over her shoulder. 'Is someone tailing us?'

'I'm not sure,' he answered. His tanned, rugged face was taut with concentration, his steely eyes flicked between mirror and road.

Ellen pulled down her visor and angled it so that she too could see behind. At first there was nothing, then a long black Mercedes appeared from around the bend and she felt a horrible heat spread through her body. 'This town is full of Mercedes,' she said, stating a truth that was as much to comfort herself as to try taking the edge off his tension.

'Sure,' he responded, noticing a smaller, saloon car coming up behind the limo.

They continued along the narrow twisting road that crested the Santa Monica mountains, catching glimpses of the Westside to the left, of the San Fernando Valley to the right. They raced past the flowery hedgerows and million-dollar homes, speeding up, slowing down and checking all the time on the car behind. By now Ellen's heart was thudding a loud, rapid beat, as she wondered what had happened to all the other traffic.

'Why don't we slow up and let him pass?' she suggested.

'That wouldn't be wise,' he answered, expertly righting the wheel after taking a bend too fast.

She looked back at the mirror, then stifled a scream as they suddenly swerved to the other side of the road.

'What is it?' she cried, grabbing the dash. 'What happened?'

'I think we lost a tyre,' he answered, struggling to regain control.

Suddenly the rear window smashed. She screamed and grabbed the wheel as they mounted the right bank and bounced off a barrier. 'Kris!' she yelled. 'What are you doing? For God's sake! Oh my God, no!' she cried, as he slumped lifelessly against her, blood spilling from the back of his head.

She fought frantically with the wheel, trying to keep the car on the road as it rocked from side to side and veered madly towards grassy banks and gates. Then the Mercedes was alongside her, forcing her over, pressing her closer and closer to the sheer drops that opened up between properties and parkland.

Adrenalin was rushing through her. Kris's foot was jammed on the gas. She looked at the Mercedes. Its passenger window was lowered. She saw the gun, then the face behind it. The world whizzed crazily by. She screamed, and spun the wheel. Sparks flew from the car as it scraped a wall. She turned the wheel again, then a searing pain tore through her chest and her eyes bulged in a split second of terror before the car slammed into a boulder, flipped to its side and flew wildly across the road, where it struck the bank, rolled onto its roof and skidded towards the cliff edge. It stopped only inches away, wheels still madly spinning, horn sounding as glass tumbled from its frames onto the grass. The Mercedes stopped, started to back up, then, spotting another car approaching from behind, the driver hit the gas and they disappeared fast.

It was dead on three thirty when Michael walked into the conference room with Maggie. Mark Bergin, the Australian partner, and Ted Forgon were already there, seated at one end of the long table looking like Hollywood's answer to hags at a hanging. Chris Ruskin had gone to make a quick call to New York. As yet there was no sign of Sandy, or Ellen.

Michael set down his files and spoke quietly to

Maggie, telling her to try Ellen's mobile again. He'd just heard from Chambers, who was already back at the Four Seasons, so he knew their meeting was over though he hadn't asked how it had gone. Nor had he asked what time they'd finished, or he might have been considerably more concerned than he was. He guessed she'd got caught up in traffic, and was annoyed that she hadn't bothered to call, or to turn on her phone. Still, she'd probably come rushing in any minute, hopefully with Sandy hard on her heels.

As Maggie left she passed Chris Ruskin in the doorway. He was a man of middling height, with a round face, grey curly hair and a dapper way of dressing. Normally his eyes glimmered with humour, but today the burden he was bearing had dimmed their light. Michael knew that after their meeting this morning he had gone on to another with Forgon and Bergin, and as this was the first time Michael had seen him since, apart from passing him briefly just now, Michael still had no idea which way he intended to vote. Looking at him now, it didn't seem like he did either – or maybe the way he was avoiding Michael's eyes was telling Michael all he didn't want to know.

Michael glanced at his watch, then sat down halfway along the table. Ruskin walked round the lower end of the table and took a seat facing him. Forgon and Bergin paused in their conversation, watched Ruskin sit down, then went back to whatever they were scheming.

Michael ignored them, and opened a file. Tucked just inside were all the documents he needed, which included several copies of the company's terms and conditions, and the notarized certificate showing that Ellen now owned twelve per cent of World Wide. Of necessity this bombshell needed to be first on the agenda. He wondered how Forgon was going to take it, and hoped to God, for several reasons, that when its full implication was realized it didn't bring on another coronary. But that wasn't likely, for the grim reality was whichever way the vote went Forgon was going to come out a winner, either because he'd managed to keep the movie rolling, or because, if he failed in that, he was going to get the satisfaction of seeing Michael's life in ruins.

Looking up from his paperwork, Michael gazed past Chris Ruskin and out the window to the upper storeys of the opposite building. He couldn't deny there was a part of him that wanted the vote to go Forgon's way, he wouldn't be human if he didn't, for then he would be absolved of responsibility for what was happening in Colombia by knowing that he had done what he could to stop it. And if he believed that he would believe Forgon had morals, for he knew already that in the event that he did lose, he would take the case to Vic Warren and the actors and appeal to them to stop anyway. Contractually, that would cause no end of problems, and no doubt end up making everyone's lawyers even richer than they already were, but it was either that or sit back, put up his hands and say, 'Hey, I tried.' But that kind of cop-out never had been an option, for as remote from his life as those poor, wretched kids seemed, there wasn't a single shred of his conscience that would allow him to ignore them.

He glanced at his watch again and was getting to his feet to go and see if Maggie had reached Ellen when he happened to catch Chris Ruskin's eye. It seemed Ruskin had been waiting, and Michael felt a jolt go through him as, almost imperceptibly, Ruskin gave him a nod.

Michael's expression said nothing as he turned away from the table and started out of the room.

'Hey, when are we going to get this show on the road?' Forgon called after him. 'Where's Randy Sandy, she's late.'

Inwardly Michael cringed at his coarseness. 'She'll be here,' he answered.

Forgon chuckled. He was a hundred per cent certain that take-care-of-herself-Sandy was going to vote his way.

After learning that there was still no sign of Ellen – or Sandy – Michael returned to the conference room and announced that they would get started, as the opening items on the agenda were ones Sandy was already familiar with.

'Ellen will also be joining the meeting when she gets here,' he told them.

Forgon immediately looked hostile, though he didn't actually protest, as she was one of the exec. producers after all.

Satisfied that Forgon wasn't going to speak, Michael opened the file in front of him and passed around copies of the document that showed Ellen to be a twelve per cent shareholder.

'What the fuck's this?' Forgon demanded.

'What it says it is,' Michael responded.

'So you gave her twelve per cent,' Forgon sneered. 'Are we supposed to be impressed?'

'No,' Michael answered, and passed around more photocopied documents. 'I gave her twenty-eight per cent,' he said. 'Now you're supposed to be impressed.'

'You gave her all your stock!' Forgon was clearly struggling to see where this was going.

Michael suppressed a smile. This was a move he had taken that morning in order to avoid a complication that even Sandy had managed to overlook – that according to the terms and conditions of the company there could never be an even number of shareholders. So now Ellen held forty per cent of the company, ten per cent more than Forgon.

Forgon's face was swelling. 'So where did this other twelve come from?' he wanted to know.

'From Sandy,' Michael replied.

He could almost hear the commotion going on in

Forgon's head as he tried to figure out what it all meant. If he had thirty per cent, Mark Bergin had ten and Sandy now had nine . . . His eyes flew to Ruskin. His was still the deciding vote. Then suddenly he remembered the clause about having to inform the majority shareholder before any share transaction took place. He couldn't have looked more smug as he cited it.

This time Michael went with the smile, and was on the point of handing over the relevant pages of the company contract when the door opened behind him. Assuming it was Ellen or Sandy, or both, and knowing that they would want to be party to this moment, he paused.

'Michael,' Maggie said softly.

Surprised, Michael turned round. Maggie's face was chalk white and she appeared to be shaking.

Michael suddenly felt very strange. *Ellen was late. There had been no call.*

'Sandy's on the phone,' Maggie said. 'I think you should come and talk to her.' *Sandy on the phone?*

Confused, Michael got to his feet. He could hear his heart pounding, and his limbs felt oddly light as he followed Maggie back to his office. Why was Sandy calling? Why wasn't she here? And why did Maggie look so awful? As he walked into the office Maggie's assistants looked up at him. They were deathly pale too.

'She's on your private line,' Maggie told him.

Michael went through and picked up the phone. 'Sandy?' he said. 'Where are you? Why aren't you here?' Then by way of a joke, as though to prevent what his subconscious already knew was coming, he said, 'We're just getting to the good bit.'

'Michael listen to me,' Sandy said, her voice choked with emotion. 'I'm at the hospital. It's Ellen.'

The fear hit him like a physical blow. His hand squeezed the phone so hard it would have hurt had he been capable of feeling it. 'What about her?' he said, hardly hearing himself speak.

Sandy was hesitant, as though trying to collect enough breath to continue. 'Something happened,' she said. 'Up on Mulholland. Her car went off the road.'

Horrible images flashed through his head. He couldn't get past the terror. 'Where is she now?' he managed.

'They brought her here, to Cedars Sinai,' Sandy answered, then she started to break down. 'She's in the operating room . . . The doctor just told me . . . I had to get hold of you fast . . . He said . . . he said, there may not be much time.'

Abandoning his car, Michael ran in through the Emergency Room doors and looked around.

Sandy was waiting. She ran towards him and took his hands as he tried to go by.

'Where is she?' he said.

'They're still operating.'

The smallest flicker of relief. She was still alive. He looked down at Sandy. There was mascara all over her face. Her skin was almost transparent.

'One of the doctors is going to come and talk to you,' she told him. 'We just need to let him know you're here.'

Michael waited where he was. Sandy went to the desk to inform the nurse he'd arrived. The nurse glanced his way, then after saying something to Sandy she disappeared through a set of automatic doors with opaque windows.

Sandy came back and they went to sit down. There was no-one else around. Michael felt himself suddenly swamped by despair, but moved quickly past it, knowing that he had to brace himself now for whatever the surgeon might tell him.

'There's something you should know,' Sandy said quietly. 'Kris is dead. He was shot while he was driving the car.'

Michael's eyes closed as his chest filled up with horrible emotion.

'I saw most of it,' Sandy said.

She waited to see if he wanted to hear more, but it was hard to get a sense of where his mind was. 'I was two cars behind,' she began, ready to stop in a moment. 'It looked as though Ellen tried to take the wheel. The car was going all over the place. I couldn't see who was in the Mercedes . . .' She stopped, swallowed and dabbed her eyes. 'The road is so twisty. So many bends.' She could feel herself being transported back to the scene, being gripped again by that horrendous impotence and terror.

She glanced up at Michael. He was still staring ahead.

'I didn't see the car go over,' she said. 'When we came round the corner it was already on its roof. Whoever was in the Mercedes must have seen us . . .'

'Us?' Michael said.

'I was in a hotel taxi,' she explained. 'The driver got on to the police as soon as he realized what was happening. That was even before the crash, so everyone arrived quite quickly after it happened.'

She wanted to say more, to tell him how horrible and terrifying it had been. How she had rushed up to Ellen's car and was dragged back at the last minute by her driver. If she'd touched it, it could have gone over. So she had to wait, sobbing and praying there on the grass next to Ellen, who was all twisted up in her seat-belt, head pressed against the roof of the car, face turned so that Sandy could see it. There was a thin line of blood coming from her mouth, what seemed like an ocean dripping from her chest. Sandy hadn't known whether she was alive or dead.

And around the other side of the silent, deadly tableau, Kris was half out the window, the lower part of his body trapped and crushed by the wheel, his gun back a way on the edge of the road.

But Sandy said no more, wanting to spare him her own feelings, for they weren't relevant now.

'What were you doing there?' Michael finally said.

Sandy's eyes moved about the Emergency Room. 'I don't know,' she said in a whisper. 'I knew they were meeting, Ellen and Tom, and I just . . . I don't know, I can't explain it. I just had this need to go and talk to them. But by the time I got there they were leaving. I saw Ellen and Kris coming out of the gates, and then this Mercedes pulled out of another drive further along and started to follow them.' She took a breath. 'I didn't think anything of it at first, you see so many limousines up around that way . . .'

'Mr McCann?' It was the nurse.

Michael looked at her kindly, oriental face, and felt the monstrous fear rise in him again.

'The doctor will be able to speak to you in a few minutes,' she told him. 'Please come this way.'

'How is she?' Michael said, getting to his feet. 'Is she going to come through?'

'The doctor will speak to you,' she told him, her gentle, almost funereal tone driving terror to the very roots of his heart.

'I'll wait here,' Sandy said.

Michael turned back. 'Get on the phone to Vic Warren and ask him to break the news to Matty,' he said. 'Then call my mother.'

'What about Ellen's parents?'

'I'll call them when we know . . .' He stopped, then started again. 'After I've spoken to the doctor.'

There was no scale by which he could measure his levels of fear or tension as he waited in a small side room for the doctor to come. Beyond it all he was trying desperately to connect with Ellen, but fear was a ghastly monster to control. Inconsequential thoughts flitted through his mind, like who might empty the wastebin beside him, or if the Hockney on the wall was an original. He looked at the other chairs and wondered about the hundreds of people who had sat in this room before him. For a long time he focused on a stain on the carpet, the block in his mind seeming as stubborn and unerasable.

Then he was thinking about the movie and the fact that it would have to stop now whether Forgon liked it or not – to begin with Matty would be on the next plane to LA, and to end with, there was a very good chance the police, or FBI, would halt it until investigations were complete.

He thought of Tom and how he had been right about them targeting Ellen, though not even Tom could have known that while he and Ellen were inside Vic Warren's house talking, Galeano's people were waiting outside. Later Michael would learn about the bogus roadworks that had closed down a two-mile stretch of Mulholland Drive and brought half of LA to a standstill. And about the bugs that had been planted in their home and on Ellen's phones at work. He even got to find out about the call Ellen had received and never told him about.

But as he sat there now, in a small room on the seventh floor of Cedars Sinai's north tower, less than fifty yards from the frantic efforts to save her life, he didn't know any of that. All he knew was the overpowering need to remain strong for her, to be able once again to tell her how much he loved her, and to ask her to forgive him for his stupidity and pride. He wanted her to know that he believed the baby was his, and that he wanted it with all his heart. But it would be too late now, for what were the chances of an unborn child surviving a crash like that? He thought of the moments in the bath, when he had touched her and the baby, and held them in his arms and felt them merge as one. And then he thought of how her body must look now, laid open to the rescuing hands of surgeons, while their baby . . .

Unable to stop himself he started to cry. The bitter irony of it all wasn't lost on him either, for he had agreed to her meeting Chambers in the privacy of Vic Warren's home as a way of showing her his trust, when really what he'd wanted was for her to be there when the lawyers had witnessed the transfer of his shares. Another gesture of trust.

But now wasn't the time to try reasoning with the curiously cruel quirks of fate, so he forced himself to think of Chambers again and how he was going to take it when he was told what had happened. It wasn't something Michael found easy to imagine, for his own guilt was reaching limits he could barely endure. How much worse it was going to be for Chambers, who had already lost the woman he loved, and would now no doubt hold himself responsible for what had happened to Ellen, and the children in Colombia too. How bitterly he was going to regret not putting his plan into action sooner. Had he known, of course he would have, but how could he have known?

The door opened and the surgeon came in.

Michael stood up.

'Mr McCann, I'm Dr Mills,' the surgeon said, holding out his hand. He was wearing aqua-colour scrubs and boots, his hair was covered by a cap and a mask hung loosely around his neck. His green eyes were giving nothing away.

Michael shook his hand. 'How is she?' His voice barely made a whisper.

The doctor's eyes remained firmly on his, as though trying to pass over some extra strength. 'I'm afraid not good,' he answered.

Michael suddenly wanted to hit him, pound him, throw him up against the wall and tell him to stop lying.

'The injuries she sustained from the crash are serious,' the doctor continued, 'but mainly thanks to her seat-belt, not life-threatening. It's the bullet she took in the chest that's causing the problem.'

Michael's eyes rounded with terror. No-one had told him she'd been shot.

'We've managed to remove it,' the surgeon was saying, 'but I'm afraid the damage it inflicted . . . It was very close to the heart . . . Her left lung has collapsed . . . We're working on stopping the bleeding . . . She's also sustained injury to her pulmonary arteries and oesophagus, and there is some serious contusion to the lung tissue which is causing bleeding directly into the lung.'

Michael's face was grey. He didn't want to imagine all the things he'd just heard, he didn't want them to be about Ellen. This was all just a nightmare. 'What are her chances?' he finally managed to ask.

The surgeon's eyes held firm. 'I'm sorry, Mr McCann,' he said, 'but I'm afraid I have to advise you to prepare yourself for the worst.'

'No!' Michael cried. The word had erupted from the core of his fear. He looked at the surgeon with fierce and desperate eyes. His skin seemed to be tightening over his bones, his insides were cowering from the truth. 'You've got to save her,' he said hoarsely. 'You've got to.'

'I promise you, we're doing our best.'

Michael nodded and bowed his head.

The surgeon waited a moment then said, 'The baby was delivered by C-section just after they got here. Your wife was already in labour.' He paused, waiting for Michael to ask, but he didn't. 'It's a boy,' he said.

Michael looked at him stupidly.

Mills permitted himself a small smile as he nodded. 'He made it,' he said. 'He's not a big guy, but he's doing just fine. He's in Neonatal ICU right now, but you should be able to see him later in the day.'

Michael nodded and pulled a hand over his face. He suddenly felt so exhausted he could barely continue to stand. 'What about my wife?' he said. 'When can I see her?'

'I'll let you know as soon as . . .' He stopped as the door opened and a nurse came in.

'Cardiac arrest.'

The doctor was out the door and along the corridor before Michael could make himself move. When finally he did he looked up to see Sandy standing in the corridor outside.

'The police are waiting to see me,' she said.

Michael nodded and swallowed the ocean of tears in his throat. Then turning around he went back to the chair.

Sandy came and sat next to him.

It was a long time before either of them spoke.

'The nurse told me about the baby,' she said. 'At least that's some good news.'

He sat forward, resting his arms on his knees and burying his face in his hands. 'It's mine,' he said, after a while. 'I know you thought it might not be, but the dates, they're . . . It could only be mine.'

Sandy sat quietly staring into space. The nurse had told her that already. Any earlier, she'd said, and the baby wouldn't have stood so much of a chance – seven months should be just fine though. Sandy had started to protest, then stopped as she realized the woman wouldn't have made such an error. And besides, it made sense, for why else would a woman with Ellen's morals have agreed to tell Michael the baby was his, unless it was the truth? So Ellen had taken the shares knowing that she wouldn't be lying to Michael. Which meant Sandy had been tricked. Played for a fool. How they must have laughed at her. But they weren't laughing now, nor was she feeling any bitterness or surprise – in fact right now nothing seemed to be reaching her at all.

'Your mother's coming over,' she told him, 'and Matty's on her way back.'

He didn't want to hear that, it was only confirming that the nightmare was real. 'I'd better call her parents,' he said.

He got up and started towards the door. When he

reached it he stopped and turned back. 'Did you get hold of Tom?' he asked.

Sandy shook her head. 'I don't know where he is,' she answered, looking suddenly very lost. 'He's checked out of the hotel.'

Michael put a hand to his head. 'I forgot,' he said. 'He's gone to Colombia.'

Sandy's face turned even whiter than it already was. 'But he can't,' she protested, 'they'll kill him.'

Michael looked at her and for a fleeting moment wondered how they had got to this place in their lives. Then, remembering that time was no longer on his side, he went to find a phone to call Ellen's parents.

Chapter 22

The heart monitor over the operating table flatlined at four forty-three in the afternoon.

By four forty-eight the five-man team had her back again and the urgent struggle to save Ellen's life continued. She'd now been undergoing surgery for the best part of two hours, and it was doubtful her body could sustain much more trauma. But her heart was stabilizing and for the moment at least they had managed to stop the bleeding.

Michael continued to wait. Rosa, one of the agents from ATI and a close friend to Ellen, had come to join him, bringing him coffee and doughnuts. The coffee he took. It made him feel better, though his body remained stiff, and the sense of unreality and exhaustion weighed heavily.

He'd seen the baby, tiny, helpless creature that it was, all tubed up and shut in a glass case to protect him from the world. He had no hair, and his skin was red and shiny, almost transparent. There was a problem with his lungs, though the obstetrician had said that was normal in prematures, and that there was very good reason to stay optimistic. Michael had stood looking at him for a long, long time, feeling emotions sway and catch in his heart, as he prayed desperately to God that Ellen would get to see him, and hold him, and be there as he grew strong and became ready to take his bow in the world.

So far he hadn't given him a name, though he had one ready if he had to. He just didn't want to do it without Ellen.

But for now all he could do was wait. It would be a few hours yet before either Matty or Ellen's parents got there, and he guessed that some time soon, probably when they'd finished with Sandy, the police would want to talk to him too.

As the movie was only a couple of weeks into shooting, and no vote had been taken to alter its course, Ted Forgon got on the phone to Vic Warren and told him he was recasting the part of Rachel. If Matty was going to be away for a while, they couldn't afford the delay.

Warren could hardly believe what he was hearing. Matty had only left the set a couple of hours ago, and as far as he knew Ellen was still in the operating room. He called Forgon every foul name he could think of, then refused to do anything until he'd heard from Michael. Forgon promptly fired him, then got straight on the phone to another director and told him to get himself down to Los Mochis, pronto. And while he was at it he called up a couple of screenwriters and told them to get themselves down there too, because the way things were going it was pretty certain a few changes would be needed.

'Give it some more blood and guts,' he told one of them. 'A couple of good chase scenes and some nice big tits up there for the love stuff. Go easy on the laughs though, this is supposed to be a serious piece. But forget about naming names, maybe you should elbow Colombia altogether. Turn it into a Russian spy piece if you have to, and do what you can to lighten it up a bit, or we're going to drive half the nation to Prozac.'

'Don't you think you should take a look at Tom Chambers's contract before you go ahead with that?' Chris Ruskin suggested. He'd just walked in on the end

404

of Forgon's call, and having no great love for Hollywood ethics, he had even less for Forgon.

'Fuck Chambers's contract!' Forgon responded. He was clearly really charged up by the idea of taking over.

Ruskin's face was impassive, though the contempt was only a layer away. 'I think you'll find he's got exclusive rights on the . . .'

'He gave up his rights the day he went into movies,' Forgon snarled. 'Now unless you're going to be some use around here, I suggest you get your fairy ass back to New York where it belongs.'

Sandy was the first to find out about Forgon's assumption of control. Having spent the past hour with the police she returned to the hotel to find a message from Vic Warren demanding someone get on Ted Forgon's case now or he, Warren, really would walk. There was another message from Chris Ruskin telling her to call him *immediately* she got back. There were still others from the set producers asking what they should do, and from at least half a dozen publicists saying they must have some kind of statement to give to the press. In fact it seemed as though the whole world was trying to get hold of her now that the news of Ellen's accident was out – and that was how everyone appeared to be referring to it, as an accident, for she could find no mention anywhere, either in her messages or on the few channels she quickly flicked through, of a shooting.

Exhausted though she was, she could feel a new energy starting to kick in. Obviously there was no way she could trouble Michael with any of it, nor was there any way she was going to stand by and let Forgon hijack this movie as though it were some vacuous thriller for the testosterone titans.

Picking up the phone she called Chris Ruskin first and asked him to come over to the Four Seasons right away. While she was waiting she tried calling Alan Day in

Colombia, but couldn't get a reply. By now Tom's flight would be halfway to Miami, where he would then make the connection to Bogotá. Quickly she got back on the phone and spoke to Maggie, Michael's assistant, telling her to put a message out at Miami airport for Tom to call the minute he landed. If nothing else, she should tell him about Ellen, and with any luck that alone would persuade him to turn around and come back. Forgon's attempts at sabotage would hopefully clinch it.

Chris Ruskin arrived, and over a fortifying few shots of brandy she told him what she intended to do if, for any reason, Tom didn't get the message and call back. She was still too beset by shock and the aftermath of all that had happened to calculate properly the size of the risk she would be taking, which was why she had wanted to run it by Ruskin to see how he responded. To her relief he was in total agreement, and even declared himself to be more than ready to share the responsibility should her plans backfire. From that Sandy realized he wasn't entirely in tune with how dangerous her plans could prove, but as they were really only a danger to her, she saw no reason to elaborate.

By five o'clock it was clear Tom wasn't going to ring. She tried not to take it personally, telling herself that he probably didn't get the message, rather than confronting the possibility that he still didn't want to speak to her. She got back on the phone to Maggie to see if maybe he'd called there, but he hadn't, nor was there any word from Michael. Sandy took that to be good news, for if Ellen hadn't made it she was sure they'd all know with a horrible speed.

Within an hour the movie's senior publicist had performed nothing less than a miracle, and Sandy was at CNN's Los Angeles studios preparing to do a live link-up with their studios in New York. She was to be the first guest of the evening on *Larry King Live*. The news of Ellen's accident was, for the moment at least, LA's top story. It would probably remain that way for one, possibly two hours, after that it would be lucky if it even got a mention again, which was why Sandy had to strike now, at a time when the incident already had attention. She'd told Larry King's researchers about the shooting, which was how she'd managed to get the top slot. They were thrilled – not only was this a great scoop for the show, but it was really going to get the American people going to discover that some Colombian drug lord was able to reach out from a prison cell and affect the lives of American citizens who were going about their business on American soil. Added to that, of course, was the fact that the woman who'd been shot was one of the executive producers on a movie about Rachel Carmedi, the American journalist who, most would remember, had been murdered in Colombia.

Somewhere, in the panicked rush of her mind, Sandy knew that if Tom were aware of what she was planning he would do everything he could to stop her. But he didn't know, and even if she was putting herself in danger something had to be done to stop Ted Forgon – and, maybe, to stop Tom Chambers too.

Fifteen minutes and a couple of commercial breaks later, her interview was over, and now the entire nation, and half the world, knew that Hernán Galeano's nephews, Gustavo and Julio Zapata, along with a Colombian lowlife by the name of Salvador Molina, had carried out the kidnap and murder of Rachel Carmedi. They also knew that Galeano had been hiring people to threaten those involved in the making of the movie; that Ellen Shelby McCann's accident had been a shooting carried out by Galeano's hit men; and about Galeano's instruction to murder a child a day as a means of getting the movie stopped, and of keeping his nephews, who were now instrumental in running the Tolima Cartel, out of jail. Sandy went on to describe the unspeakable arrogance of a man like Galeano who truly believed he

407

could get away with all this; and ended by revealing Tom Chambers's suicide mission to Colombia now, in a bid to save any more children from dying.

As she walked off the set Chris Ruskin and the publicist were waiting for her, took her shaking hands and congratulated her. She felt horribly faint, and in desperate need of some air. They took her outside, then Ruskin gave her his cellphone so she could call Rosa at the hospital to see if there was any news.

There was. Ellen was out of surgery and in Intensive Care. The next twenty-four hours were crucial, but if she managed to pull through them there was a chance she might make it. Michael was with her now, though she was still unconscious and expected to remain that way for a while yet.

Sandy returned to the hotel, leaving Chris Ruskin to go on to the production office with the publicist to sort out how they were going to handle the wave of publicity that was no doubt already heading their way. She needed to be alone now in order to carry out the rest of her plan, the part she hadn't mentioned to Chris.

Once inside her room she sat down at her laptop and began composing an e-mail which she then circulated to Michael, Tom, Alan Day, Chris Ruskin, Zelda Frey in London and her flatmate Nesta. 'After the interview I just did on *Larry King Live*,' it read, 'I know my life is now in danger. So I have gone away for a while, to a place where no-one will think to look for me. Please don't worry about me. I'll keep watching the news and when it is safe to come back, I will.' And to Tom she added, 'I don't know if what I did has made things more dangerous for you, but I am praying that it will force the Colombian and American authorities to stop the child killings, and to stop *you* carrying out your revenge.'

When she was finished she packed up her computer and put it, with several other of her possessions, in hotel storage and took a taxi to the airport. By nine o'clock that nigh she was no longer on American soil.

Ellen got through the next twenty-four hours, and the twenty-four after that. She remained in Intensive Care, connected up to so many machines it wasn't easy to get close to her. She was still unconscious and there were still no guarantees, but there was hope, and that was something Michael was clinging to, as hard as she was clinging to life.

He sat with her for hour after hour, holding her hand and gazing past the tape and tubes to her pale, scratched face with all its bruises and stitches. Her chest rose and fell in time with the pulsing pressure of the ventilator, and on the floor at his feet a small suction device, that was connected to a place somewhere behind her ribs, bubbled air through water. There was a tube in her nose to suck air and acid from her stomach; IVs were attached to her arms, and patches and snaps on her chest were wired up to yet more monitors.

He talked to her softly, insistently and lovingly. Sometimes he joked, sometimes he urged, occasionally he cried. He told her how sorry he was for all the heartache he had caused her; how desperately he wished he'd been man enough to stand by her when she'd first told him the baby might not be his. He rambled at length about his useless pride and the idiocy that had made him consider it a weakness to trust, or believe her, when she finally told him the baby was his. But because he knew that their son would matter to her the most, he spent long hours making up crazy and outlandish things the little rascal was thinking, all snugged up there in his private little playpen. The nurses had christened him Seven Leaguer because he was improving so fast, though Michael still hadn't been allowed to hold him yet, that would happen, the doctor said, as soon as he came off the ventilator. He recited long lists of names, asking Ellen to squeeze if he said one she liked, but so far there had been no response. He berated himself for being so inept that he couldn't even come up with a name she approved of, and told her he hoped they weren't going to fall out over this, because there were quite a few on that list that were OK by him.

On the third day the doctor pronounced her strong enough to try breathing alone. As she was still unconscious they had to leave the plastic tubing that ran down to her lungs in place. But she could still breathe with it there, the doctor insisted, they would simply turn off the machine.

When the time came the tiny room, with so many devices and strange, greenish light from the monitors, was full of doctors, and the tension was so great it was as though something might explode any second. They allowed Michael to stay, and he watched in frozen terror as the respiratory therapist did a final check before turning to the ventilator and putting a hand on the switch. He looked back at Ellen, then quietly shut down the machine. Everyone waited, watching her chest, willing her to breathe. The silence, now that the pneumatic pressure had gone, was horrible. Above her the heart monitor continued to bleep, but the waves were becoming erratic. Michael started to panic and was about to turn the machine back on, when the therapist put a hand on his arm and nodded for him to look. It was weak, very weak, but there was an unsteady rise and fall in her chest. She was doing it alone.

He felt ridiculous as tears poured down his cheeks and everyone, unable to touch Ellen, shook his hand and congratulated him instead. They were all so proud of her it made him want to break out the champagne. When they'd all gone he sat down with her again and leaning on the padded bed rail told her how much he loved her, how well she was doing and how happy she was going to make her parents, who were coming in later. Then, in a state of uncontainable euphoria, he expanded even further and told her how thrilled all the people who'd heard about her on *Larry King* were going to be when they heard how well she had done. He knew she didn't know about them, but they were the ones who were sending all the flowers that were filling up their home, as flowers weren't allowed in the ICU. Then he related the story of Sandy's interview, and how she had now disappeared before Galeano's men could get to her too. Obviously she didn't want to be yet another burden on Tom's conscience, though Michael didn't say that to Ellen.

Nor did he tell her that down in Mexico the movie was still under way, with a new director, new star and new writers. She didn't need to be troubled by the way Forgon was welcoming all the publicity with open arms, rubbing his hands in glee and telling anyone who cared to listen that this kind of exposure couldn't be bought at any price. The fact that he personally was the target of a national hate campaign, and had become the subject of every lampoonist from Leno to Letterman, bothered him not a bit. It was all about money and fuck everything else, including the bombardment of lawsuits that were coming his way. He didn't even give a damn about the Feds and their inquiries; not that he was being unhelpful, but so far he'd managed to get a judge to rule that the movie could keep going until the Federal Government could give good enough reason for it not to.

Needless to say a public and media outcry followed that ruling, everyone demanding to know how many children had to die or women be shot to provide good reason. And meanwhile Forgon just carried on lapping up all the publicity, and relishing the sour-grapes gossip of his industry peers who were either accusing him of staging the entire show, or hissing with envy at his great good fortune.

But Michael was going to put a stop to it all tomorrow. His lawyers had now gained him the necessary legal status to vote on Ellen's shares, so her forty per cent, together with Chris Ruskin's eleven per cent, gave them the necessary amount to stop Forgon dead in his tracks.

Michael just hoped it was going to be enough to stop Chambers's enemies too, for they had to be closing in on him by now, if they hadn't got to him already. There had been no word from him since he'd left, so Michael didn't even know if he was aware of Sandy's interview, or if it had had the desired effect of thwarting his suicidal mission. So far there had been a lot of hot air blowing out of Washington, though whether anyone was doing anything, either there or in Colombia, was impossible to tell. If the authorities had managed to cut in on him there was every chance that kind of news would have been made public by now. So it was Michael's guess that Chambers had either been able to give them the slip and was somewhere in hiding right now, or, God forbid, his enemies, having been tipped off by the interview, had been waiting for him when he got into Bogotá and had him exactly where they wanted him.

Chapter 23

The village was two hundred kilometres from Bogotá, down in a valley, remote from the world. From a small dusty window Chambers watched the square. It was dense with plane trees and magnolias that shaded the hot, cracked pavements and drooped low over the crumbling buildings around. Local traders were starting to open up for the day. The man who sold lotto tickets was taking coffee with a couple of ice-cream vendors in a dim, vinyl-clad café close to the church, their empty carts parked against the kerb outside. A vagrant lay asleep on a bench. Rowdy birds fluttered and flocked to the gutter where a beefy-looking woman was dumping the remains of stale *arepas de queso*.

The church clock tolled the first of the seven chimes it was due. Already the sun was seeking a thousand different trails through the wide canopy of trees. A dog scooted from the path of a fast-trotting horse that was carrying a slit-eyed *campesino* dressed in a handstitched *ruana* and fine calf-leather hat. He was quickly lost from view, disappearing along a side street from which the roar of two ancient, rusting Jeeps could be heard, crunching gears and revving up engines to get past any debris or stray humanity that obstructed their way.

The open-sided Jeeps came into view. The drivers were both wearing camouflage, M16s propped on the seats beside them. They drove at high speed, bouncing

413

over potholes and squealing round corners until they disappeared through the arch under Chambers's window. They'd be parking up now in the courtyard behind the *hospedaje* – the small, cheap hotel where Chambers had been almost since arriving in Colombia.

He knew now that he had Sandy – and Larry King – to thank for his detention, which was what General Gómez was calling it. Kidnap would be the word Chambers would've used, had he been asked, but Gómez wasn't interested in asking. Nor were the men who were guarding him – or holding him hostage, as he preferred to call it. He guessed he'd have to concede the point on guarding, however, since no-one was demanding any payment for his return. In fact, it wasn't certain they were going to return him at all, though he couldn't imagine what else Gómez was planning to do with him.

It was boredom that was making him fractious, for to be fair he knew he wasn't really a prisoner, as he'd been provided with a gun and was free to come and go as he wished – though not without escort. He was here for his own protection, as Sandy's interview had informed Gómez – possibly the only incorruptible police officer in Bogotá – that he was on his way, and why. The general had accordingly arranged for a welcome at the airport, sending a dozen of his handpicked men to board the plane and escort Chambers, much to the fascination of the other travellers, to a fleet of waiting cars, whereupon he was whisked off into the night. Had the general not done that, then Galeano's people would most certainly have afforded themselves the privilege of meeting Chambers, in which case there wasn't much chance he'd be sitting at this window today. And apart from the occasional stroll over to the café for a few games of *tejo*, or the couple of hikes through the hills he'd made in an effort to keep himself fit, about all he had done the past few days was sit at this window – and wait.

Gómez's men were not great conversationalists, nor

414

did they show much interest in what was going on in the world. This meant that Chambers still didn't know if the movie had been stopped, or if Ellen was managing to hold on. He'd have given a sizeable sum to be able to contact Michael, though even if he could, what the hell he'd have said he had no idea. Even with so many hours to think, Chambers was still unable to find adequate words to express how he felt about all that had happened, or how sorry he was that he had ever come into their lives only to bring them such pain. It was too late now to change it, though God knew he would if he could, but he could at least try to put an end to Galeano's monstrous control over their lives, which he knew amounted to little more than a game to the old man, something to keep him amused, and his enemies in tune with his power, during his ever-decreasing stretch in jail.

Deciding to go get himself a coffee, he tucked an old navy cotton shirt into his jeans, belted the Beretta automatic, and left the room. Carrying a lethal weapon in this village wasn't only normal, it was also an extremely wise thing to do, since the military base just down the road made an attractive target for every insurgent and *bandido* for miles around. There was also a pretty good chance that the price of his whereabouts was an especially high one, so Galeano's people could come riding in at any time.

Taking the back staircase he found his escorts in the quaint little courtyard, idling around the Jeeps and smoking *barillos*, the two newcomers about to check in before the other two checked out. Chambers didn't have a problem with the marijuana, but he didn't imagine Gómez would be too impressed were he to happen along.

'Ah, Señor Tom,' one of them greeted him. It was Valerio, at twenty-eight the oldest and also most senior-ranking among them. He had just arrived, so would be one of Chambers's companions for the day. Of them all,

Valerio was the most talkative, and probably the best-informed in matters not pertaining to their immediate surroundings. It had long since occurred to Chambers, however, that Valerio and his fellow officers had been carefully instructed in their ignorance of the outside world.

'I have a message for you,' Valerio declared, dropping the end of his cigarette on the ground and grinding it with a standard issue field-green Vietnam boot. 'The general sends his apologies that he has not come to see you sooner, but there have been important matters for him to attend to. However, he will be here in maybe an hour. He says you should be ready to leave.'

This unexpected piece of news surprised and cheered Chambers, until it occurred to him that he might be taken to the airport and deposited on the next plane out.

'No, that is not my intention,' Gómez informed him, when he finally showed up, some three hours later. 'I am taking you to La Picota to see Hernán Galeano.'

Chambers stared at him in amazement. He was a slight, impeccable man, with a handsome thatch of silvery hair and an impressive black moustache that framed his mouth like a horseshoe. He was well-known for the risks he took, and the fearless and impossible battle he waged against organized crime. He was also known as something of a joker, and it was to that side of his character that Chambers's suspicions immediately turned.

'I take it you do want to see the man?' Gómez barked.

'I don't know about see him,' Chambers responded. 'I'd like to kill him.'

'We'll need to discuss that,' Gómez replied, deadpan. 'But now you will come with me and we will drive to the prison. Galeano is expecting us. I did tell you, did I not, that the order for his release has been signed? He will be free by the end of the month.'

Though disgusted, Chambers wasn't surprised. It was

416

possible to buy anything here, including escape from a life sentence.

Minutes later they were speeding along the *autopista* in Gómez's grey armour-plated Mercedes. Though it was against regulations, he liked to drive himself once in a while, so the chauffeur had been banished to one of the gleaming black Jeep Cherokees – also armour-plated – that were providing the escort. The eight bodyguards inside the Jeeps were equipped with Uzi smgs and CAR-15 carbines, standard issue for the protection of high-ranking officers. The weapons were certainly necessary, for there had been at least two dozen attempts on Gómez's life that Chambers knew of, so the fact that he was still living was pretty convincing evidence that no-one went until their time was up. He'd come damned close on a few occasions, however, one of them not so long ago, hence the reason for his lengthy Spanish vacation, recuperating from a car-bomb attack outside his brother-in-law's country home.

'So why the visit?' Chambers asked.

'Galeano requested it,' Gómez answered. 'I thought you would have no objection. Did you ever visit La Picota before?'

Chambers nodded. 'There are a lot of people with a lot of information inside those walls,' he replied.

Gómez's eyebrows rose in agreement. 'Did you visit the rich guys, or the *lobos*?' he asked.

'Both.'

The forward Jeep was racing ahead. Gómez swerved out from behind a lumbering bus straight into the path of an oncoming truck. His foot hit the gas and he pulled off the pass with inches to spare. The men in the car in front, and the Jeep behind, appeared oblivious to their boss's close call with mortality, so intent were they in challenging their own.

'So, if you've already seen the rich guys, you know what to expect?' Gómez continued.

417

Chambers let go his breath. 'More or less,' he said. 'Why did he request the visit, do you know?'

'He wants to offer you a deal,' Gómez answered.

Chambers was immediately wary. 'What kind of a deal?'

'The kind where he gets to win and you get to lose,' Gómez answered with a grin. 'What other kind of deal is there, if you're Hernán Galeano?'

'He didn't tell you what it was?'

'No. By the way, did anyone tell you that the movie got cancelled?'

Chambers turned to look at him. 'No. When?'

'A couple of days ago. Everyone's flying back to LA, it was on the CNN news last night. They also said that the woman who was shot is making some progress.'

Chambers's relief to hear that Ellen was still alive momentarily swamped everything else. He thought of Michael and wished again that he could be there now, lending some support, doing whatever he could to help him through all this. He didn't imagine that Michael would welcome his presence, however, and it saddened him greatly to know that he had probably lost one of the most valued friends of his life.

Turning his thoughts abruptly away, he considered Galeano's victory in getting the movie stopped. That the man could wield such power from a prison cell was an outrage beyond any civilized level of tolerance, so too was the fact that Rachel's death remained unavenged. Bitterness welled in him with all the might of impotent fury – no-one, but no-one, should be allowed to get away with the hideous crimes and manipulation that Galeano was enjoying, though how to stop it, when the man owned half the Government, was a question with no easily detectable answer.

'What about the kids?' he asked. 'Did the list get any longer?'

Gómez kept his eyes on the road. 'Seven died that we

418

know of,' he answered. He glanced at Chambers. 'You want to know why I did nothing to stop it,' he said, 'so I will tell you. There was nothing I could do. The men he was using were all officers of the Metropolitan Police Command, which, as you know, covers the dope-dealing, gang areas of Calle del Cartucho and Olla de la Once. Not nice places. This is not my territory, nor are they my officers, so I was unable to get any news of the investigation.' He looked at Chambers again, then added, 'Until yesterday. I am still not sure there is anything I can do, the officer in charge of that area is notoriously corrupt and is known to encourage the death squads. He will do all he can to protect his men, and Galeano will pay him handsomely to do it.'

Chambers sat with that, knowing that nothing he said or felt would change the intolerable truth of this nation's horrifying corruption.

'There is also some other news you should know about,' Gómez told him. 'Your friend, Sandy Paull, has disappeared.'

Chambers's head spun round.

'Calm down,' Gómez chided, before he could speak. 'Alan Day informs me that she took herself into hiding right after the interview she gave. A very wise move, if you ask me. First she saves your life by letting me know you are coming, then she saves her own. Sounds like a pretty smart woman.' His eyes were twinkling, as he waited for his suspicions of a romance to be confirmed.

Chambers turned away, then immediately tensed as they rounded a bend and came right up on the tail of a horse-drawn cart.

Gómez was unruffled as he slammed on the brakes, then accelerated hard towards an upcoming bend.

This was by no means the first journey Chambers had made with Gómez behind the wheel, but, as always, he considered it could very likely be his last. Should that turn out to be the case, the irony of his last will and testament being called into play for a road accident would only be surpassed by the indubitably supreme irony that he had left all his worldly goods to a child who wasn't his.

But he wasn't losing any sleep over that, for he was well past the shock of his disappointment now, and, if he thought of it at all, was more intrigued by the discovery that he actually wanted to be a father. He could only feel glad that it wasn't going to happen with Ellen, however, for God knew he'd caused enough anguish in Michael's life without wanting to saddle the man with a thorn that could never be plucked. No, if he were ever going to have a child – and the chances of that were not looking good, considering where he was and the extreme likelihood he'd get blasted to kingdom come any second – he wanted it to be with a woman he loved, not one who loved somebody else.

Immediately Sandy came to his mind, not because he considered her to be that woman, but because he knew she did. However, he wasn't going to get into that now, it was neither the time nor the place. He'd deal with it later, if there ever came a later, when events in Colombia were no longer overshadowing the anger he still felt at the way she hadn't committed her vote to Michael; for her part in making him think Ellen's baby was his, and then for her decision to reveal publicly the purpose of his Bogotá mission. In truth, he already recognized the unreasonableness of blaming her for problems that were entirely his, but right now he would go no further than hoping she was OK wherever she was hiding, and had the common sense to stay there until all this was over.

It was mid-afternoon by the time they finally drove in through the electronically controlled gates of La Picota. Despite recognizing Gómez, the green-uniformed police guards who patrolled the entrance went through the usual drill of making every one of his party step out of their vehicles and running them over with metal detectors – which couldn't have been more absurd considering the small arsenal of hardware on full view inside the cars. Security cameras tracked their progress to the maximum security wing, where the bodyguards were told to wait outside while Chambers and Gómez were relieved of all visible weapons and escorted in.

Though Chambers had visited the prison before, so knew what to expect, this was going to be the first time he'd ever come face to face with Hernán Galeano. Already the proximity was stimulating his nerves and charging him up with more bitterness and vengeance than he'd felt in months. It was maybe just his imagination, but he was sure he could sense Rachel around him, moving along the corridors and stairwells with him, as though she were anxious, or maybe eager to be there when it came time to confront the man who had ordered her death.

Chambers's hatred was growing: the urge to annihilate the man who had ruined his life was starting to bind him up, gripping him with a force that was so strong it was moving out of his control. Quick images of Rachel's nightmare ordeal were flashing through his head, in a way he hadn't allowed them to in months. Once again he could hear her cries, see her terror, feel her pain. He cringed at the tearing, brutal force of the rapists, the hands that beat her, imprisoned her, violated her and finally killed her. He was becoming affected by the rousing air of violence creeping from the walls around him, sending a surging morass of rage rolling through his veins. Nothing had felt this intense since she'd died, and he knew beyond doubt that he wouldn't be leaving this place without laying hands on the son of a bitch who had ordered the abomination that had ended her life. Galeano wanted a deal, then he was going to get a deal, one he wasn't going to forget for the rest of his worthless existence.

At the end of a glaringly lit upper-level corridor with

no windows, nor visible signs of other human life, the blue-uniformed prison guard who was leading them told them to wait. He went in through a heavy iron door, leaving it to clang shut behind him. They could still hear the faint echo of his footsteps receding, and the muted sounds of prisoner activity that stained the bowels of this hell-hole.

Chambers knew Gómez was watching him – then he felt a firm hand on his shoulder. He didn't respond.

A few minutes later the guard was back. 'Come this way,' he told them.

They followed, passing through the metal door into the grotesque belly of the wing where the noise was a Kafkaesque symphony and the smell was a choking stench of ammonia mixed with a sweet drug concoction. They were led to a small unoccupied cell with nudes all over the walls, a couple of meagre bunks and a latrine in one corner.

'You will wait here,' the guard said. 'Señor Galeano will see you when he is ready.'

In a flash Chambers had him by the throat. 'You tell that son of a bitch he's going to see us right now,' he spat.

The guard's menacing eyes bored into his. His hand was reaching for his club. He was going to be real happy to smash this cocksucking *gringo*'s skull to pulp.

Gómez stepped in, putting a hand over the guard's, blocking the club. There was a moment's stand-off, then, with a grunt of disgust, Chambers shoved the man backwards and let go. Gómez held him steady.

'We don't wait for scum like Galeano,' Chambers snarled. 'So you tell that murdering bastard he either sees me *right* now, or he can go straight to fucking hell with whatever *deal* he's got cooked up in that corrupt fucking trash can he calls a head.'

The guard's eyes narrowed again. He wanted to waste this *cabrón* real bad.

Gómez spoke. 'Do as the man says,' he told the guard.

Very slowly the guard tore his eyes from Chambers and glared at Gómez.

Gómez nodded and smiled. 'You heard what he said. Go tell Galeano we know he's a big enchilada around you arse-licking scumbags, but to us he's got less worth than a used-up toilet roll. So we talk right now, or we're out of here.'

Venom blazed from the guard's eyes. He looked at Chambers again, then spat on the floor. He waited for Chambers to respond. Chambers merely looked at him. The guard's mouth twisted with contempt as, muttering obscenities, he started out of the cell.

A minute later Chambers and Gómez were being escorted by two more guards across an open landing. The inmates were tracking their progress, some silently, some whistling and jeering, others making lewd or violent gestures. Chambers and Gómez kept on going, heading for a plush leather door at the far end of the landing.

What they found the other side came as no surprise to Chambers, for he'd been in similar quarters right here in this prison, maybe had even been in these before. If he had, they had changed somewhat with their new owner, for he recalled none of the costly antiques or paintings that were placed gracefully around the freshly decorated walls, though he did recognize the huge picture window with its fancy bars and splendid view of the hills. There were computers, telephones, faxes, TV screens, a state-of-the-art CD player, Persian carpets on the floor, a matching set of three luxury sofas and a handsomely equipped open-plan kitchen where a clumsy-looking inmate was currently whipping up some delectable concoction. As they entered the cook glanced up, and Chambers was sure he detected a moment's recognition between the apron-clad thug and the ever-impassive Gómez.

'I will tell Señor Galeano you are here,' another toadying inmate said, looking and sounding like the finest of manservants. 'You can sit down.'

Chambers looked at Gómez, who appeared no more inclined to make himself cosy than he was. The manservant performed an obsequious bow, and turned towards the kitchen. Just past it, he knocked discreetly on a plain white door, then stood back abruptly as it opened and Hernán Galeano walked out.

Chambers's eyes were like flint as he looked the man over. He wasn't as tall as Chambers had expected, nor did he look particularly close to his fifty-nine years, but with his large, square-shaped head, hanging jowls and pencil-thin moustache, he was every bit as ugly as his pictures foretold. He was dressed in an expensive navy sweat suit, tennis socks and no shoes, and flashed more gold than a whore's secret stash.

He grinned. His teeth were big and false and ludicrously white. 'General Gómez, Señor Chambers,' he said, holding out his arms, 'welcome to my humble dwelling.'

As he came towards them Chambers could feel himself tensing. This was the slimeball son of a bitch who'd torn his entire life to shreds; who'd made billions of dollars exporting cocaine and heroin that ended up ruining the lives of so many innocent American kids; who'd ordered the hit on seven defenceless minors and paid the goddamned police to do it; who'd sent in his hit men to shoot and kill a pregnant woman and her bodyguard. And he sat here in this vamped-up jail cell, like some untouchable despot, with more privileges at his fingertips than a dozen fucked-up junkies had hours left to live.

'It was so good of you to come,' he said, holding a hand out to Chambers.

Chambers looked at the hand, then returning his eyes to the glassy blue orbs in Galeano's face, he pulled back his arm and before Galeano had time to blink he was doubled over in agony.

Chambers flexed his hand as the bodyguards rushed in, knives and iron bars coming out of thin air. Galeano crumpled to his knees.

Gómez looked at Chambers. 'Not clever,' he remarked.

Galeano was gasping for air, choking and trying to talk. 'Get back, get back,' he wheezed, waving for the bodyguards to back off. 'Just help me up.'

Gómez and Chambers watched and waited as the old man was set back on his feet, given a crisp linen handkerchief to dab his mouth and a glass of sparkling water. 'Bring my guests some drinks,' he managed after a while.

'Keep your drinks,' Chambers barked, stalling the rush to obey. 'What's your deal?'

Galeano grinned, then coughed. 'You're going to pay for what you just did,' he said breathlessly.

'The deal, Galeano,' Gómez pressed.

Galeano coughed again. 'I heard the movie was stopped,' he said. 'Is it true?'

'It's true,' Gómez confirmed.

'I want proof.'

'What the fuck!' Chambers spat incredulously.

'You heard the news,' Gómez told him.

'How do I know that's true? You guys, you can say anything on the TV. How do we know it's true?'

'You've got your people in the US,' Chambers seethed. 'The *sicarios* you send after pregnant women, you fucked-up son of a bitch. You can be extradited for that, and I'm going to make fucking sure it happens.'

Galeano chuckled. 'But I'm already in prison, thanks to you,' he said.

'He knows the papers are signed,' Gómez told him. 'So he knows you're going to be walking out of here any time now.' He started to grin. 'And do you know what's going to happen then?' he said, obviously relishing the news he was about to break. 'The DAS are going to arrest you, Hernán, and hand you right over to agents from the US Federal Bureau of Investigation. And the Feds, they're going to be taking you on a nice, all-expenses-paid journey to the Golden State of opportunity – and capital death. And do you know how they can do that? They can do it because, like my friend here just told you, when you ordered the hit on the woman who was producing the movie, you crossed American borders, Hernán, like you crossed the street and walked right into a Federal jail. Boy, they're going to be happy punks the day you get out of here, because they can kill you legally, Hernán. That's right, legally, because that's what happens to scum like you in the United States of America.'

Galeano wasn't fazed. 'Gómez, you don't know shit,' he told him mildly.

Gómez continued to smile.

Galeano moved his eyes to Chambers. For a while he merely looked him over, then taking another sip of water he said, 'I owe you, Tom Chambers. I owe you big time for what you did to me and my people. All that bullshit evidence you spread over the papers; all the lies the cheating, double-crossing sons of bitches you got into bed with gave you. You came after me, Chambers, and let me tell you, boy, I been lying awake here at night dreaming about how I'm going to come after you. I've got a thousand different ways of making you pay, and my boys, they all know every one of them.'

'You hit the jackpot the day you killed Rachel,' Chambers told him.

Galeano's eyebrows rose. 'You think that was me?' he said.

'I know it was you.'

Galeano nodded. 'They sure made it look like it was me,' he said. 'And how difficult was that? I was the guy you were focusing on, so it made sense I'd want you to back off. So Molina took your girl and let you think he was acting under my instructions.'

Chambers merely stared at him.

'He had some issues with her, right?' Galeano continued. 'She wrote about him, told the world what a corrupt, perverted little toerag he is. She hurt his package-tour business real bad with that report, so I'm told. You know, the packages he runs from Europe, setting up all those shitfuck paedophiles with as many kids as they can bang in a fortnight. So he wanted to get even, and he reckoned putting you and me in the frame together was a clever way of doing it. Thought he'd get away with it, and he might've if I hadn't paid someone to go find out the truth.'

Chambers looked at Gómez.

Gómez looked at Chambers.

'And that's what you've managed to come up with, after four years behind bars?' Chambers sneered. 'You reckon you can slither your way out of this by dumping it all on the creep *you* paid to kidnap, torture and kill the woman he already had issue with? You're a piece of shit, Galeano. A stinking, lying, useless piece of shit. Your nephews were there when she was killed. They were the ones who raped her along with Molina. They tied her up and did things to her that no decent man would even know how to do. They're like you, Galeano. They're not fit to tread the same earth as normal human beings.'

Galeano's gruesome teeth were showing in a smile. 'You're not helping yourself here, son,' he warned. 'You're not helping yourself one bit.'

'The way I see it, you're the one needs help,' Chambers told him. ''Cos you're the one who's top of the Feds' dance card.'

Galeano found that amusing. 'You just don't get who I am, do you?' he said. 'And that's surprising when you got yourself more information on me than my own mother – God rest her soul – ever had. You did a good job with your investigation, I'll hand you that, but despite what you learned about me back then you still don't seem to be connecting with who I really am. But that's OK, because you will. You're going to find out just how much your FBI boys scare me.' He looked at the men around him and they all started to laugh. 'You Americans have got no power here, my friend. I know you like to think you have, but you're oh, so wrong about that.'

Chambers's lips were twisting into a sneer. 'So tell me, just why do you think you're in prison here, Galeano?' he challenged. 'Four years it's taken you to buy your way out, so just who do you think your friends out there were trying to appease by putting you in here at all, if not the Americans? And I don't know about you, but I'd call four years a pretty long gesture for a man who likes to think he's got as much power as you do.'

'Chambers, you don't know the half of it,' Galeano responded. 'And I'm sure as hell not going to take the time to explain. But I will tell you this. If you think the general here is your safe ticket around this city then you're running straight up a blind alley, because he's got no more power to help you than your dead girlfriend's got power to come back and fuck you.'

Chambers's face hardened, showing that the barb had struck home.

Gómez stepped in. 'All right, let's cut to the chase, Galeano,' he said. 'You got us here to talk about a deal, so let's hear something before we get on our way.'

Galeano handed his water to a flunky, then massaged his heavy chin. 'The woman who went on the Larry King show and told the world my nephews killed your girlfriend,' he said, 'she did a lot of damage. It could be she's put us in a position where there's no longer any deal to be cut.'

'Get on with it,' Gómez snapped.

Galeano shot him a look. 'But like with most things,' he said, dragging his eyes back to Chambers, 'there's always a way round it. So the deal is this: you lay off my nephews and I'll give you Molina. That means you're going to have to go public and tell the world the woman on Larry King got it wrong. You do that, and Molina's all yours. Tell you what, we'll even give you evidence to get him shipped to the States to stand trial. Unless you decide to do with him what he did with your girlfriend.' He shrugged. 'It's your call.'

Chambers looked at Gómez.

Gómez nodded and they turned to walk out of the room. At the door Chambers turned back. 'What about the kids?' he said.

Galeano waved a hand. 'Gutter scum,' he snarled.

'I want your word that you'll lay off them as of now,' Chambers said.

Galeano's piercing eyes narrowed. 'You got it,' he said.

Gómez opened the door.

'So do we have a deal?' Galeano demanded.

Gómez looked back over his shoulder, then started to grin.

Galeano's face twitched. 'Deal or no deal you're a dead man, Gómez,' he growled. 'And you, Chambers. What they did to your girlfriend is going to be nothing to what they're going to do to you, you motherfucking son of a bitch.'

Chambers turned back. He too was grinning.

'Don't underestimate me, Chambers,' Galeano warned. 'One word from me and you won't even get as far as your next step out of here.'

'Give the word,' Gómez challenged. 'Give the word and watch your whole fucking empire go up like Apollo 13.'

'Shove it up your ass, Gómez,' Galeano snarled. 'You don't scare me.'

'And you don't scare me,' Gómez responded. 'But I'll tell you what does,' he added, glancing at his watch, 'is all the shit those nephews of yours are going to give up now that my men have got them in jail.'

Galeano visibly blanched, but made a quick recovery. 'You're bluffing,' he growled.

'And do you know why it scares me?' Gómez continued, taking a knife from his pocket and going back into the room where he began cutting all the cables that connected Galeano's impressive technology. 'It scares me because of all the hits you're going to order the minute you get word I'm telling the truth. I wonder how long we can keep your nephews alive,' he mused, 'before you pay one of my men enough to get your *sicarios* through?'

'You can bet your ass,' Galeano seethed, 'that if you're not bullshitting me here, then it'll be you they come for first, Gómez. You and that shitfuck journalist there who I should have had killed four years ago along with his cock-sucking whore of a girlfriend.'

Chambers and Gómez looked at each other. Gómez's eyes were gleaming. '*Adios*, Galeano,' he said, pocketing his knife. 'We won't be meeting again, 'cos not even all those lawyers you're aiming on getting lined up to keep your extradition dragging on for years can save you from what's coming your way.' And with a final salute to the chef, Gómez led the way out.

Minutes later Chambers and Gómez were back in the fresh air, where one of Gómez's bodyguards helped him detach the recorder he had strapped inside his shirt. When they were finished Gómez pocketed the tape, and slipping in behind the wheel of his car he waited for Chambers to get in beside him.

'I think we got all we needed,' he said, as they drove out of the complex. 'A confession to ordering the hits on the kids, and on Rachel. It'll be up to the Feds to get a confession out of their arrests in LA–' He looked at Chambers. 'I did tell you they'd made arrests, did I?' he said.

'No,' Chambers answered.

'A couple of days ago. So it'll be up to them to get a confession from the punks they reeled in that they were getting their orders from Galeano. Anyway, he'll have figured out by now that one of us was wired, so once he's got his command station active again there's going to be a price on our heads that'll make this nation's GNP look like a poor man's power bill. And having his nephews in custody isn't going to cut us any slack either.'

Chambers looked at him in amazement. 'You mean you weren't bluffing about the nephews?' he said.

He shrugged. 'The raid on the Tolima estate is scheduled for midnight tonight,' he said. 'Our intelligence informs us that's where the nephews are holed up, and as they've been reneging on some deals with the guerillas in recent months, they're not going to be able to rely on their paid protection the way they once could. In fact, I've got good reason to believe the guerillas are going to start shooting any of the bastards that look like escaping.' He glanced at Chambers. 'And if you're thinking you want to be a part of that raid then you just start thinking again. As of now you're going underground and if need be I'll put you in chains to keep you there.' He grunted. 'Though why I should care about your miserable ass when I got my own to look out for sure beats the hell out of me.'

Chambers turned to stare out of the window.

'I know what you're thinking,' Gómez told him. 'You're thinking all this should have happened four years ago, right after Rachel was killed. And you're right, it should have. But I couldn't even get close to Galeano back then. His friends in the Government had him all padded out with their own protection – that is, the ones you didn't manage to send down with him. It's taken time, a lot of time and a lot of manpower, to get us to the point we're at now. Even getting into the prison with a wire on and a knife in my pocket, the way we just did, would have been impossible as recently as a month ago. You just got to wait for grudges to come up, disaffection to come down and allegiances to break apart. That's the way things work around here, and well you know it. But if you think you'll ever get Galeano back to the States to stand trial you're falling into a fool's haven, because it's never going to happen. Yeah, I know I told him it would, but he's got enough cash and enough lawyers to keep that case stalling until long after the world's lost interest. What he doesn't have, though, is the crystal ball that's telling me he's going to be in La Picota for the rest of his worthless existence.'

Chambers looked at him, waiting for an elaboration, but Gómez only chuckled and pressed his foot down harder on the gas.

'The next few days are going to be critical for you and me,' he said finally. 'That's how long it's going to take for all this to wrap up the way we need it to, that's presuming it does. Until then, you could spend your time making up your epitaph, 'cos you're likely going to need it. Or,' he added, glancing over with a grin, 'you could start working out what you're going to do with Molina, because, in my opinion, you deserve a shot at that bastard before his arrest becomes official.'

'You mean you've got him?' Chambers said, feeling a twist in his gut.

'Not yet,' Gómez answered. 'But have faith, my boy, have faith.'

An hour later Chambers was inside a run-down *finca* on the road to Medellín, with a dozen armed guards in the surrounding tangle of shadows and trees. The moon was just a pale ghost of itself as it rose in the twilight; and the eerie sense that he was never going to see Gómez again, as the Mercedes disappeared in the distance, was something he was struggling to put down to nothing more than an understandable paranoia.

Alone in her room Sandy kept a near twenty-four hour vigil on the news, not daring to pick up the phone to anyone for fear the call might be traced back to where she was. So far she had learned nothing about Tom, but comforted herself with an assurance that if anything had happened it couldn't fail to make many more bulletins than one. Ellen was still unconscious, and according to the news an hour ago, it was now feared she was slipping into a coma.

Sandy's heart went out to Michael. She knew that Ellen had been breathing unassisted for a while, so Michael's hopes must have been soaring, until some kind of complication had set in and the life-support machines were reconnected. And this on the day that the FBI had announced they were charging the two men they had arrested in connection with the murder of Kris Santiago, and the shooting of Ellen Shelby McCann. It was looking much more likely now that the charge would turn into one of double murder.

Sandy looked down at the cluttered desk in front of her. If Ellen died, and with Rachel already dead, she couldn't help but be aware that she, the woman neither Michael nor Tom wanted, would be the one still left in their lives. It was a horrible, painful reality to face, that she might occupy a place in the world that others wanted for somebody else. But she wasn't in control of the way things turned out; there was nothing she could do to bring Rachel back, nor could she perform a miracle to save Ellen.

It wasn't likely that Galeano's men would find out where she was, but if they did, she had already written a will. The thought of dying terrified her, though perhaps it was the kind of death she would suffer, should they manage to track her down, that terrified her the most. So she stayed locked in her room, reading, watching TV and checking that nothing was overlooked in her will.

Her remaining shares in World Wide she had left to Tom – or to Michael if Tom didn't make it. Right now it didn't seem that the movie would ever start shooting again, but if it did she knew how vital it was to remove all of Ted Forgon's power. Apart from allocating her shares, she had taken further steps to ensure that Forgon never again made a single decision regarding the film that meant so much to Tom. What was more she had made certain that Forgon would know she was behind the ignominy and defeat he so badly deserved.

Her apartment and jewellery she had left to Nesta, and everything else she owned she had bequeathed to the people who were looking after her now. Even if no-one else understood that, Tom would, presuming, of course, that he made it through whatever hell he was enduring now, and that he didn't fall into the trap of taking the revenge he had promised himself on Salvador Molina.

Michael sat at Ellen's bedside, his head resting on one of the blue padded bed rails, his hand barely touching hers. He was almost asleep, so exhausted now by his vigil that the whole of his life had lost shape and meaning. He didn't understand what had happened, why her lung had suddenly collapsed again and she had started slipping away when she had been doing so well. With all his heart he had believed that it was only a matter of hours before she would open her eyes and look at him; before they could ask her to cough to help them remove the tube that was still in her lungs. Instead, they had been forced to reconnect the tube, which was once again pumping and sucking air in and out of her body, along with all the other life-preserving elements that were keeping her there.

434

By contrast the baby was coming along so well that he was now breathing alone, and one of the IVs in his scalp had just been removed. His skin was no longer red and shiny; it was turning pink and healthy, and his hair was coming through quite thick and black. Not long now, the doctor said, before Michael would be holding him and feeding him. Each time Michael looked at him he could feel the tears sliding down his face. This was Ellen's son, the child she wanted so badly, that he loved not only because it was theirs, but because it was hers. It didn't matter whose loss would be the greater, his or his son's, all that mattered was that they remained together, the way Ellen would want.

Her parents had gone back to the house now, leaving him alone with her, the way he preferred. It wasn't that he wanted to keep them away, but their fear, their terrible anguish and confusion made his own worse. He guessed that his gaunt, unshaven face held the same hardship for them, though they all, in their own ways, tried to comfort each other. He wondered how they would all be managing without his mother, who was going quietly on with the everyday chores, and driving back and forth to the hospital bringing food and the kind of solace only a mother could provide.

Selfish though it was, he wished desperately that Robbie were there, as he couldn't bear the thought that Robbie might never see Ellen again. The house felt silent and empty without him – Spot's pining was hard to watch without wanting to hold the scruffy little dog and weep into his fur. He wondered how it would be, just him, Robbie, the baby and Spot. It felt all wrong without Ellen, in fact without her he knew nothing would ever be right again.

He tried to tell her some of this, leaning on her bed rail and whispering over the monotonous hiss and puff of the ventilator. But in the end he was so tired that he fell asleep where he was, moving into a dream that was so deep and impenetrable that he didn't feel her hand stir beneath his, nor did he see her eyes flicker open before, very gently, they flickered closed again.

Chapter 24

The TV was on, the sound turned down low, as Chambers, now wearing the combat clothes he'd been allocated, dozed in a badly sprung chair behind the boarded-up windows of the *finca* where Gómez had left him. The room was spare and dusty, plaster flaking from the walls, damp creeping across the ceiling, and the boards underfoot creaked with every move.

There was no satellite or cable, so he had no idea what was happening in LA, but an earlier local bulletin had informed him of the successful police raid on the Galeano estate in the department of Tolima late last night. It was reported that General Javier Garcia Gómez and his élite force of British SAS-trained men, in a fleet of Huey choppers fully equipped with electric Gatling guns, multiple grenade launchers, bazookas and M60 machine-guns, laid siege to the fifty-acre estate around midnight, and by morning had secured more than twenty arrests, as well as the seizure of four private jets, a small arsenal of Russian, US and Israeli manufactured weapons, a fully equipped laboratory and some eighteen tonnes of cocaine. The arrests, the newscaster had reported, were rumoured to have included Gustavo and Julio Zapata, the nephews of Hernán Galeano, who had recently been named in connection with the killing of the American journalist, Rachel Carmedi, four years ago.

There had been no mention of guerilla assistance in the raid, nor, as yet, had there been any update on the whereabouts of General Gómez and three of his men. Gómez's second-in-command had reported last seeing the general and the missing officers running towards a building only seconds before it exploded, but so far no bodies had been recovered.

For Chambers, next to Ellen's death, this was the news he least wanted to hear. He'd sat up all night waiting for word from the general, knowing it wasn't likely to come until much later in the day, but unable to sleep anyway. Then the news had reported his disappearance, and by mid-afternoon he'd already begun to detect a nervousness in the officers around him. They were clearly unsettled by the general's failure to make contact, and the lack of any instruction on how to proceed with the protection of the general's friend.

It was dusk now, though somewhere nearby a cockerel crowed incessantly, and a dog let up an occasional yowl. As he drifted in and out of sleep Chambers could hear the officers outside, the low mutter of their voices, and the flare of a match as they lit their *barillos*.

He wasn't exactly sure when he began picking up on the increased level of their tension, or what it was about their change in mood that was now alerting him to how vulnerable they were – in the heart of a small valley, remote from the world, with only a few Berettas, M16s and MGLs to protect them. In any other country that would be way above requirements – in Colombia it wasn't going to do it.

He went outside to get a better sense of the air. It was dark now, and the dozen officers guarding the *finca* were all squatting in shadows, rounds of ammunition laced through their guns, combat knives and grenades bulging from their belts. Seeing him one of them loped over, drawing him down against the wall of the house, and edging him to the cover of a mushrooming shrub.

'Any news?' Chambers asked.

'No,' the young man answered. His darkly handsome features were smeared in mud, the whites of his eyes gleamed like moons. 'It is not usual for the general to go so long without contact,' he said.

Chambers glanced at him, then dropped his eyes to the dirt. 'Do you think he's still alive?' he said softly.

'They have found no bodies,' the man answered.

Chambers took heart from that, mainly because he needed to, rather than because he termed it conclusive. He looked up at the looming hillsides around them where the darkness hung in thick, impassive shadows, and the air was as warm as his breath. His ears were tuned for the slightest sound beyond the grate and screech of night creatures; in the distance an owl hooted, while hidden in the impenetrable forest the stealthy prowl of jaguars, ocelot, deer or armadillos made a soft crush on the scrub.

'Who are you in contact with?' Chambers asked.

'Major Rodriguez,' the man answered.

'What are his orders?'

'For us to sit tight. If there are any signs of an attack, we are to make it our priority to get you out of here.'

Chambers gave an ironic smile. 'Cut and run,' he murmured, knowing that would go down hard with these fighting men.

'I have some whisky,' the man offered, and digging into his belt he handed Chambers a flask.

Chambers sucked in a mouthful, and passed the flask back.

They sat quietly together, watching and feeling the night and listening to each other's breath. From time to time Chambers saw a shadow move and tensed, though he knew it was another of the men shifting position. His heartbeat felt abnormally dense, and as the hours passed his skin began to prickle with the prescience of danger.

439

It was an hour before dawn when they first heard the distant sound of an engine. All over the garden the thumbing-down of safeties and readying of machine guns made a short, muted resonance through the drooping trees and brush. The man with Chambers disappeared for a moment, and returned with another officer. They took position either side of him, then signalled for him to follow.

As he moved Chambers could feel the stiffness in his limbs, and the dewy dampness that had seeped into his clothes. In one hand he carried the Beretta, in the other he held the grenade he had been given during the night. This wasn't the first time he'd been in a situation like this, it had happened many times before in El Salvador, Nicaragua, Sarajevo, the Lebanon, but the fear never got any easier to handle. If anything, it got worse, for there was only so much luck a man could count on before it finally ran out.

The rumbling of approaching vehicles was getting louder by the second. It was impossible to tell how many there were, though he heard someone guess six. By now he and his escorts were at the side of the house, edging backwards into one of the barns. More men were in front of them, retreating too as they swept the garden with eyes and guns.

They drew into the barn, the rank, stale smell of old molasses and camphor clogging on their chests. The first officer pointed Chambers to the armoured Jeep, nodding for him to get in. Chambers did as he was told. The barn door remained open. The roar of advancing engines trailed through the valley as the front line of his guard moved forward towards the rusted chain-link fence and thorny scrub.

His two escorts got into the Jeep with him, one in the back, the other in the driver's seat. Their faces were taut and pale. Each was acutely aware that an attack was unlikely to come by road like this, alerting them well in advance with the blatant noise of engines. But six vehicles could hold twenty-four men and up – at least twice as many as at the *finca*. And with the constant betrayal, switching of allegiances and easy bribes in this nation, there was a very good chance that the detail of the *finca*'s set-up had been reported to Galeano's men within minutes of being established.

From where they were sitting they could see the swell of a nearby hill, visible now in the greyish light before dawn. Their eyes were trained on the road that looped round it. The vehicles suddenly burst into view, one, two, three, four of them, headlights beaming, speeding around the bend like evenly-timed missiles. Then they were gone, descending fast down the track that led to the *finca*.

Chambers glanced at the man beside him. He was still clutching his gun, eyes rooted on the tangled sprawl of garden and open land beyond. They listened as the vehicles screeched to a halt, expecting gunfire, hearing none. There was the sound of men shouting, then running. The driver leapt out of the car and moved swiftly to the barn door. There was more shouting as someone called out, 'Don't shoot! Italo, César! Put down your guns!' Two camouflaged figures appeared in the doorway. Behind them came half a dozen more.

Chambers dived for cover, then spun round, ready to shoot, as the door beside him was suddenly yanked open.

'Señor Tom! Please, come with me.'

'What is it? What's happening?' Chambers asked, jumping down from the car.

'We have orders,' the man told him. 'Valerio has come from the general. He is here. He will tell you.'

Valerio, the man who had been one of his escorts for the past five days, was standing in the midst of the group, looking dishevelled and seriously hyped up.

'Señor Tom,' he grinned when he saw Chambers

441

coming towards him. 'The general will be relieved to know you are safe. But you must come with me now.' He was already walking away.

'Where are we going?' Chambers asked, as they all started across the garden. 'Where's the general?'

'He is safe,' Valerio answered. 'Please, get in the car, I will explain on the way.'

The four vehicles turned out to be more armoured cars, this time three Chevy Blazers and a Ford Explorer. All were black or dark grey. Valerio pulled open one of the front passenger doors and gestured for Chambers to get in. As he did so two armed men climbed in the back, and Valerio got behind the wheel.

Minutes later all four vehicles were speeding back towards the mountain road. The sun was half over the horizon by now, and a steamy mist was beginning to rise from the ground. For a while no-one spoke, and the further they got from the *finca* the more unnerved Chambers became. Twenty-four hours ago he'd been in no doubt that Valerio was the general's man; now he remembered that it was only a fool who didn't doubt.

'It said on the news that the general was missing,' he ventured.

Valerio glanced at him, then leaned over as he took a sharp bend fast. 'They say many things on the news,' he answered. 'They know nothing.'

'But the raid. It did happen?'

Valerio grinned. 'Sure, it happened,' he confirmed. 'We took the Zapata boys. They are in custody now. By tonight we will have their confession that they killed your girlfriend.'

If he was telling the truth about the arrests, then Chambers had no problem believing him about the confession. He knew more than he wanted to about their methods of extraction. 'And Molina?' he asked.

Again Valerio grinned, and this time threw him a look. 'I am taking you there now,' he responded.

'He's in custody?'

Valerio shook his head. 'No, but we know where he is.'

Chambers waited and Valerio started to laugh.

'At ten o'clock this morning,' he said, 'our friend Molina has an appointment with a man who makes bulletproof jackets. The man, he is a good man, has a fine reputation, and he doesn't like to provide jackets for guerillas or *traficantes* or lowlife scum like Molina. So when he gets someone like that approach him, he always tells them no, then he informs us so that we can protect him from the offences these men take. In Molina's case, because the general has asked him, Señor Gavira has agreed to make an appointment. But he won't be there. It will be just us. Already we have our people in place, at the sewing-machines and in the offices, looking like Señor Gavira's staff. When you arrive Salvador Molina will be all yours.'

Chambers turned to look out the window. The Beretta was back in his belt, and he could feel his palm itching to hold it. Just thinking of Molina incited the urge to kill. But not only to kill, to hurt and mutilate, terrorize and humiliate too. Four years had done nothing to deaden the need for revenge, nor to lessen the loss that between them Galeano and Molina had inflicted. How many nights had he lain awake longing for the woman they had taken; torturing himself with images of the way things might have been, of the way things were when they had loved and laughed, shared dreams and passions, known anger and outrage and such a depth to their love that few ever got to experience. She was the only woman he had ever loved, was probably the only woman he ever would love. He wanted no closeness with others; he wanted only her and the life she had been so brutally deprived of.

But that could never be, and because of it he knew what he wanted to do to Molina – had known since the day he'd discovered that it was Molina who had sent him the photographs of her rape and torture, that it was Molina who had killed her. The only emotion that surpassed his hatred for this man was the love he still felt for Rachel. He was so torn apart by the force of both that he sometimes despaired of ever knowing peace again. In his heart he knew she wouldn't want him to take this revenge, that she would fear the damage it would ultimately cause him, but this knowledge couldn't prevail, for she wasn't having to live with the daily guilt of the fact that he had taken a gamble with her life and lost. For more than three years he had lived with the blame for her death, truly believing that had he done as he was told she would have been allowed to live. But then he had learned the truth, that Molina was the one who had abducted her, so no matter what he had done, what ransom he'd offered, or deal he'd struck, Molina would have taken it all and killed her anyway. So he owed Molina, he owed him not only for the trickery, the deceit, the rape, the murder – but for the dreams of a future that could now never, ever come true.

It was a quarter to ten when the three escorting vehicles broke from the convoy and left them to continue on alone to the jacket-maker's on Carrera twenty-six. By now they were well inside the city limits of Bogotá, driving through an area Chambers didn't know, but one like so many others on the outskirts of town, crumbling, uncleansed and as dangerous as hell. Every window and doorway was barred, every store had a spyhole to vet clients before allowing them in. Few walked the streets, several lay hunched up against walls, flattened cardboard boxes acting as blankets. It was as run-down as any place Chambers had seen anywhere in the world, so much poverty, tragedy, abuse and addiction that it seemed to be eating the streets like a cancer.

Soon they passed on to a neighbourhood that had

more people on foot, fewer in doorways, some freshly painted storefronts and garbage dumped in piles rather than strewn about the sidewalks. Still there were bars on everything. They came to a stop behind a dark blue Toyota that was parked outside a tall, purple-fronted building with green-painted bars that protected a bulletproof door.

Valerio got out first and went to ring the bell. Chambers watched him speak through the intercom, then turn to gesture them out of the car.

'He is here,' he said, grinning as Chambers reached him.

Chambers felt the knots tighten inside him. Despite the many fraught and dangerous situations he had been in in his life he had never yet killed a man, and was now beginning to wonder if when it came to it, he could actually go through with it.

The few neighbours hanging about watched with small interest as four men in combat fatigues and carrying M60 machine-guns crossed the pavement and disappeared inside Gavira's purple shop.

The door clanged shut behind them, leaving them facing a steep concrete staircase. They mounted swiftly and quietly, stopping at the third floor where a middle-aged, suited man opened a door and stood back for them to enter.

The room beyond was a medium-sized rectangle, with a half-dozen or more hanging rails stuffed full of vests and jackets of all sizes, colours and descriptions, pushed down one end. There were a couple of desks where a receptionist and secretary were seated, and beyond them through an open door were the machinists and cutters, apparently intent on their work.

Valerio looked at the middle-aged man who nodded towards a closed door in the opposite wall. 'He is with a sales representative,' the man said.

Valerio turned to Chambers. Chambers looked at him,

his grey eyes glowing in his unshaven face, which was showing cruel signs of the stress he was under. He knew these men would think him a coward if he started to back off, but goddammit, now he was here he just didn't know that he had what it took to kill. The shame he felt at this sudden weakness was as bitter as the anger, but right now he was finding it impossible to move.

Then the door opposite opened and a man, a stranger, came out. He took no notice of either Chambers or the armed officers, but went to a hanging rail and took down a smart brass-buttoned blazer. Then he re-entered the office, leaving the door wide open. There were two men inside, both seated, one with his back to the door, the other with his feet up on the desk. This man must have been able to see them, but that he showed no sign of it indicated he was one of the general's men. He and his companion appeared relaxed and confident, enjoying their coffee and the importance they obviously felt at their need for bulletproof clothing.

'This is one of our newer designs,' the salesman was saying, as he took the blazer from its hanger. 'It is a little expensive, but it is of excellent quality and with this Kevlar padding it will stop .357 magnum, .45 calibre or 9mm sub-machine bullets.' He opened the jacket to reveal the inside. 'These pouches here are for the steel plates which, should you choose to insert them, will protect your vital organs even against 7.62 NATO rounds. Perhaps you would like to try it?'

Molina put down his coffee and got to his feet. The other man walked behind him, helped him off with the full-length leather coat he was wearing, then took the blazer from the salesman. As Molina slipped it on, Valerio walked into the office.

'Salvador Molina,' he said.

Molina's head snapped up. 'What the–?' He stopped, almost physically shrinking at the sight of the combat gear and heavy artillery.

'We have someone here to see you,' Valerio told him.

Molina swung round. His tall, muscular frame was dwarfed by the blazer, his wide-set eyes were slits of terror and confusion.

'You remember me,' Chambers said. 'I'm the man you sent photographs. The man whose girlfriend you raped and murdered.'

Molina started backing off, eyes darting from side to side as he tried to assimilate this sudden change in his surroundings and work out who everyone was. His large face was yellowing with fear; his shaking legs stumbled into a chair. He was trapped and he knew it, but still wasn't quite accepting it. He began reaching inside his jacket, then squealed and flung his arm against the wall as Valerio fired at his wrist.

'What the *hell*?' he cried. 'Who are you? I don't know who you are.'

'He just told you who we are,' Valerio reminded him.

'I don't know him. I've never seen him before in my life.'

A man behind Chambers fired a handgun into the wall next to Molina. Molina jumped. His face was starting to twitch.

'You've got the wrong man,' he cried. 'Jesus Christ, look what you did to my hand.' Blood was dripping from the wound and running into the sleeve. 'What are you doing? Who the hell are you?' he demanded, as Valerio delved inside the leather coat and pulled out Molina's ID.

'Just wanted to remind you who you are,' he said, thrusting it at Molina. 'We didn't have any doubt. But you said you were the wrong man. Seems not. So, why don't you start by getting down on your fucking knees and begging Señor Chambers here for your life, the way you made his girlfriend beg for hers, *cochino*!'

Molina's eyes were flat with horror. The nightmares he'd had that the bitch's boyfriend would one day find

447

him were suddenly right here in this room. He knew already that he was going to die, and if he was then he had nothing to lose.

'Beg nicely,' Valerio advised him, 'because all the decisions around here belong to Señor Chambers, and he doesn't have a lot of reason to like you.'

Molina's eyes darted back to Chambers. 'Are you out of your mind?' he sneered. 'I don't beg no scumbag *gringo*. Let him beg me. Let him ask me what she did those three days we had her. Let him get off on how we all fucked her and how she begged us for more and more.' He put on a female voice. '"Oh Salvador, Salvador, please come and fuck me, Salvador. Oh, Gustavo, I love your cock. Give it to me Gustavo." The bitch just couldn't get enough,' he snarled. 'This asshole here wasn't man enough for a *moza* like her, so we gave her what she wanted, up her cunt, in her ass, down her throat . . .'

He flew back hard against the wall as the first bullet hit him with all the might of a boxer's fist. Seconds later, the echo of the gunshot still ringing fiercely in his ears, he looked at Chambers and grinned. 'You want to hear how many of us fucked her?' he jeered.

Chambers fired again. And again, and again.

Molina danced and jerked, grunted and twisted and attempted to keep on laughing. He was like a punchbag inside the blazer, the bullets hitting him with punishing force, but none could reach him. 'Asshole! Lily-livered *gringo* cunt!' he spat.

Chambers suddenly grabbed his throat, glared into his eyes, then head-butted him in the face, breaking his nose. The man screamed. Blood poured from his nostrils. Chambers stepped back and aimed his gun at Molina's groin.

Immediately Molina's hands dropped from his face, the terror of Chambers's intention registering hard in his eyes.

448

'You'll never rape another woman in your god-damned life,' Chambers growled. His heart was thumping fast, his loathing was tightening the trigger. 'I don't know how many women or children you've beaten, abused, or got working on the streets for you even now, but this is going to be for them. Every single one of the poor bastards you've corrupted, victimized, tormented, and killed. And when I'm through, when your cock is on the floor and your balls are all full of bullets, you're going to pick your cock up and you're going to fucking eat it, do you hear me? You're going to shove it down your own fucking throat, the way you did to Rachel.'

Molina's eyes were glassy with panic. He was shooting glances at the others, seeing if there was any help to be had. 'He's crazy!' he yelled. 'He's a fucking madman. You can't let him do this. She was just a whore. A no-good fucking whore, who couldn't mind her own fucking . . .'

Chambers fired.

Screams tore out of Molina as he slammed back into the wall. Blood and urine burst from his groin. He clutched it frantically, his face twisting in shock and agony, his skin rapidly turning grey as he slid, whimpering, down to his heels. 'Aaaay, no, *hijoeputa*! *Mis huevos*! No. No.'

'I think my friend here means what he says,' Valerio remarked mildly.

Shaking uncontrollably, Molina looked up at him. His breath was fast and shallow, shredding his voice as he struggled to speak. For the moment it was only possible to groan as he rocked forward in pain, jerkily fumbling with the end of his tie as though to bandage his wound. 'You've got to stop him, *dios mio*. Please, stop him,' he choked. 'I am a man. He cannot do this to me.'

Valerio looked at Chambers, whose face was ashen and strained as he stared down at the man in loathing.

449

'What did you do when Rachel begged?' he demanded. 'Did you give her any mercy, or did you just find ways of shutting her up?'

Molina was crying with his mouth open. Blood, mucus and saliva ran down his face. 'You've ruined me, man,' he wept. 'You've ruined my fucking cock.'

Chambers watched him in disgust. His hands were shaking. His head was spinning. He couldn't hold on to the gun. He hated what he'd done, but knew he'd do it all over again. 'You're going to jail, Molina,' he snarled. 'You're going to jail for the rest of your fucking life where every pimp and pervert that ever crosses your path is going to do everything to you that you did to Rachel and more.'

Molina looked at him, his wild black eyes starting to dim as his body continued to shake and jerk in shock and pain. For a moment he didn't understand what was happening. Was the *gringo* backing off? He wasn't going to kill him? No eating his own cock? Holy Mother of God, yes, the *gringo* was backing off.

Chambers was walking out the door, vomit rising in his throat.

Valerio and the others were watching him.

Molina was slipping a bloodied hand to his waistband. Then, before anyone could move, he whipped out his gun and fired twice with a .44 magnum. Both bullets hit Chambers full in the back and mushroomed on impact.

Chambers flew forward, crashing into a desk and taking it over with him. Then the entire place erupted in gunfire, as every armed officer in range shot Salvador Molina with ammunition that no bulletproof blazer could stop.

It was only when the mayhem was over and the final echo of gunfire drifted into silence that Chambers allowed himself to move. Valerio came to stand over

450

him, offered him a hand and pulled him to his feet. He was winded, cut and bruised and shaken to the depths of his being.

'I think Señor Gavira's vests are to be recommended,' Valerio stated.

Chambers could barely hear him through the deafening aftermath of gunfire. He slipped off his vest and held it up to look at where the bullets had entered. The bitter stench of gunsmoke mingled with the meaty smell of torn flesh and blood. For a moment he blacked out, was revived with water, then dropping the vest he looked over at Molina. There wasn't much more to see than a pile of bloodied clothes and the splash of brains on the wall. Again he felt his stomach rise, and turning aside he threw up on the floor.

General Gómez stepped out of his Mercedes as the dark grey Explorer came to a halt beside it. The wind was blowing a gale across the huge flat plains of the airport, driving bracken and brush to this far, empty corner.

Valerio got out of the Blazer and saluted the general. 'Everything is in order, sir,' he reported.

The general turned to watch the take-off of an American Airlines 757. He stayed with it as it soared overhead, and rose on higher and higher into the clouds. Then looking back at Valerio he said, 'Did you tell him?'

'That Hernán Galeano is dead? Yes, sir.'

The general nodded.

'He said,' Valerio continued, eyes straight ahead, '"Seems you just can't get the chefs these days."'

The general allowed himself a grin, then got back into the Mercedes and drove away.

Chapter 25

Michael was standing in the doorway trying to see past all the white coats that were gathered round the bed. Ellen was watching him, her eyes shining with forced humour and tears. She had regained full consciousness a few hours ago, after drifting in and out for the past day, coming around just long enough to murmur and hold his hand before slipping away again. In all that time he hadn't moved from her bedside, except to visit the bathroom and make way for the doctors.

Now she had been breathing unassisted for long enough to start becoming agitated by the need to speak. To enable that the ventilator tube had to be removed from her lungs, which was what the respiratory therapist was now doing.

'OK,' the therapist said, 'are you ready to cough?'

Ellen looked up at him and nodded. Her face was still frighteningly pale, but to see her eyes open and to watch her respond felt like such a miracle to Michael that he could barely contain his emotion.

'Off you go then,' the therapist instructed.

Ellen took a breath, then coughed. The therapist eased gently on the tube. There were murmurs of well done, and squeezes of her hands. She coughed again, and after two or three more tries the tube came free.

More congratulations. More coughing. Her lips were dabbed, the inside of her mouth was washed, then after checking the rest of her IVs the room finally started to empty.

Michael walked forward. She looked up at him, her eyes so anxious and full of love that he felt tears come to his own.

'Hi,' he said.

She smiled, then tried to speak, but nothing came out.

He leaned forward and kissed her softly on the mouth. There was still a tube in her nose, and all kinds of other attachments he had to be careful of, but to feel her lips beneath his, and the touch of her hand seeking his, was all that mattered.

'I like the beard,' she managed to croak.

He smiled and kissed her palm as she touched his chin.

'You look terrible,' she said. Her voice was so faint he could barely hear, but he laughed at that.

'You look wonderful,' he told her.

'Can I see the baby?'

'They said in a couple of hours.'

She looked disappointed. 'Tell me some more about him,' she said, rallying.

Michael grimaced. 'Well,' he said, 'he looks a lot better than he did a week ago. A week ago he was a bit scary. He looks more human now.'

She smiled and laughed as a tear trickled down onto the pillow.

'He's off the respirator and his lungs are good,' Michael went on. 'So's his heart. You know, he looks a bit of a backchatter to me, and he's not keen on the ICU so they're moving him to the intermediate ward.'

She swallowed hard. 'He's doing that well?' she said.

He nodded.

'Does he have a name?'

'Not yet. I was waiting for you. But I told him this morning that if he didn't stop acting up I'd call him Jasper.'

Ellen laughed.

'He doesn't like me,' he stated, 'because I'm not very good at feeding him. Well, that's not true, I can do it, but he doesn't like the frock and mask I have to wear while I'm doing it.'

Ellen bit her lip as more tears welled in her eyes. 'I want to see him so bad,' she whispered. 'I want to see you feeding him in your frock and mask.'

'Don't worry, you will,' he assured her.

He turned round as her parents came into the room, then stood back to make way for her father.

'Hello Dad,' she rasped, as he took hold of her hand.

The big, brusque Nebraska farmer tried to speak, but for the moment was too overcome to get any words past the emotion in his throat.

Michael looked at his mother-in-law, who smiled and squeezed his arm before stepping forward. 'Hi honey,' she said, her tired face showing so much relief it seemed to lighten her by years. 'How're you feeling?'

'OK,' Ellen answered. 'A bit of pain, but not much. I just want to see the baby.'

Nina smiled. 'You've got a fine son,' she said. 'Dad and I are real proud.'

Michael put a hand on his father-in-law's shoulder as the old man began quietly to sob.

Ellen tightened her hold on his hand and cried too. 'I love you, Dad,' she whispered.

He nodded, then nodded again. They all knew how precious she was to her father, his only child, the daughter he loved so much he had been too terrified to allow her out into the world for fear of something like this.

'Come on, we don't want to tire her now,' Nina said.

Frank got to his feet, but Ellen held on to him. 'Don't go home yet,' she whispered. 'Please stay in LA for a while.'

'We're not going anywhere until you're out of here

and at home with your baby,' her father assured her.

Ellen turned to look up at Michael. He came forward and took the hand that Frank released.

When her parents had gone she continued to cry, tears running from her eyes as she clung to Michael's hand and tried to speak.

'It's OK, darling,' he whispered. 'Take it easy now. Just take a breath. It's going to be all right.'

'Oh Michael, I'm sorry,' she choked. 'I'm so sorry.'

'Hey,' he laughed. 'There's nothing to be sorry for.'

'I should have told you,' she said. 'I should have told you as soon as I knew the baby was yours. You deserved to know. You're his father, and I didn't tell you right away. Oh Michael, I'm sorry.'

'Sweetheart, it doesn't matter now,' he said. 'All that matters is that you're here and so's the baby and you're both going to be just fine.'

'I should have told you about the phone call too,' she said. 'Someone threatened me. I don't know who it was, but he told me to back off the movie. I didn't tell you, because I didn't want to worry you. You had so much going on with everything else, and you were going to lose everything . . . Oh God, I made such a mess of things and I love you so much.'

'I love you too, and you're a fool not to have told me. You should have known that you'd matter more to me than anything. But it's in the past now. We can't change it, so let's just look forward.'

Her eyes gazed up into his and stayed there for a long, long time, looking at him, loving him and wanting so much to hold him. In the end she drifted into sleep, her hand still holding on to his.

He stayed with her until a nurse came and told him gently to go. He needed some rest too, and, though she didn't say it, probably a shower and definitely a shave.

*

Chambers took a cab in from LA airport, not sure this time how long he'd be staying. Presuming his hotel bill would no longer be picked up by World Wide, he checked into a room at the Four Seasons rather than a suite and ordered the belongings he'd left in storage to be brought up by a porter.

It was early evening. He was tired, hungry and in desperate need of a drink and some company. But he knew he wouldn't go in search of any, for he was still too bruised and shaken by the events of the past week to want to venture far from this room. Besides, the only person he really felt like talking to was Michael, but with so many issues between them right now, that call would have to wait. At least Ellen was pulling through, or so it had said on the news, but the first few months of doubt over the baby, and the collapse of the movie, were matters that he and Michael would have to sit down with sooner or later.

He toyed with the idea of trying Sandy's London apartment again, but didn't imagine Nesta would welcome being woken up at three in the morning. He'd tried earlier, during the stopover in Miami, but neither Nesta, nor any of Sandy's colleagues at the agency, knew where she was. They hadn't heard from her in over a week, but Nesta had been hopeful that once Sandy heard that the Colombian threat had now been dealt with, she would surface from wherever she was hiding.

Tom certainly hoped so, for he was anxious to let her know that he was no longer mad at her for disclosing his plans – if anything, as Gómez had pointed out, he wanted to thank her for saving his life. He wanted to see her, too, for, in a surprising kind of a way, he was missing her.

But any catching-up they had to do would have to wait until she decided to come out from wherever she was, and in the meantime he would take a solitary dinner in his room, sleep for at least twelve hours and then try to start piecing together some kind of plan for the future. That wasn't going to be easy, for what had just occurred in Colombia was bringing back Rachel's loss as though it had only just happened. He knew there was a good chance it would pass a lot quicker than before, but for now the memories, the pain and the longing were welcome, for it was all there was to hold them together until such time as he was ready to let go. And he'd do that soon, he was sure of it; and he prayed to God that when he did he would be able to find some kind of peace at last, and maybe even a life that felt worth living.

It seemed everyone was smiling at Michael as he made his way along the sixth-floor corridor to where Ellen had now been moved into a private ward. He smiled back, and was so euphoric that he might have shaken everyone by the hand, and even embraced them, had he not been so overloaded and in a hurry to get to Ellen.

She was holding down solids now, could manage the bathroom unaided, and the small infection that had concerned them a couple of days ago was all cleared up. In fact, there was a very good chance she'd be home by the weekend, which was going to be an event it would be hard not to celebrate with fireworks, brass bands and magnums of champagne. But since she wouldn't be up to that, both their mothers were planning a small family dinner which had already turned the kitchen into a no-go zone, unless you had the courage of a madman. And since neither Michael nor Frank quite qualified there, they were left either to starve, or eat out.

Spotting Michael coming towards her, one of the nurses got instantly up from her work station and went to open Ellen's door.

Ellen was sitting up in bed, the baby cuddled in her arms as she fed him his formula and gazed adoringly into his cute little face. There were no IVs or monitors cluttered around her now, just a TV set perched high on a bracket, a nightstand full of flowers and a pretty good view of the Santa Monica mountains from the window. And of course her son, who had been discharged from the hospital the day before and had been left here earlier by Michael while he went off to get her a surprise.

Hearing the door open she turned to see who it was, then immediately started to laugh as she saw Michael struggling with a pot plant that was on the fast track to becoming a tree.

'It's not from me,' he told her, manoeuvring it in through the door.

Ellen frowned curiously, and was about to ask when Michael put a finger over his lips for her to stop.

'OK. Surprise!' he called.

Ellen looked at the door, then gave a sudden gasp of joy as Robbie's little face peered anxiously round the corner. 'Oh my darling,' she cried, holding out an arm for him to come to her. 'What are you doing here? When did you arrive? Oh, let me see you. I've missed you so much.'

More certain now of his welcome, Robbie looked at his dad, then went sheepishly over to the bed. 'They wouldn't let me bring Spot,' he said, looking sideways at the baby.

'Oh, never mind,' Ellen laughed. 'I'll see him soon. Do you want to jump up here, next to me? You can see the baby better then. He's your brother, you know.'

He nodded, then lifted his blue eyes to Ellen. He looked so solemn and worried that she glanced at Michael to see if he could explain it.

'I've got to go talk to the doctor about the insurance,' Michael said. 'I'll be right back.'

Surprised by his abrupt departure, Ellen turned back to Robbie. 'You going to climb up?' she offered.

He nodded, and tugging on the blanket he hoisted himself up next to her.

'Can I give you a kiss?' she asked, as he gazed down at the baby.

Again he nodded, and hugging him close she kissed him hard on the head. 'I'm so happy you're here,' she told him. 'It's the best surprise ever.'

Robbie kept his head lowered, apparently entranced by his new brother.

'Do you like him?' Ellen said softly.

Robbie shrugged. 'Yeah, he's OK,' he said.

She smiled and hugged him again. 'So when did you get here?' she asked. 'I'm so glad you kept it as a surprise, and my plant is wonderful, by the way. Definitely the best one I've had. We can probably put it in the garden when we get home.'

'Dad said that,' he responded. Then he turned his head to look at her. 'I'm sorry I was nasty to you,' he suddenly blurted. 'I didn't want you and Dad to be unhappy, and for you to go and leave Dad on his own and I know it was my fault, but Dad says it's all right now and that you're not angry with me . . .'

'Oh Robbie,' she cried, pulling him to her. 'It wasn't your fault, honey. None of it was your fault, and you mustn't think it was. And you weren't nasty to me, you were just confused – you wanted your mom, which is understandable, because she loves you very much and I know you love her too.'

His eyes continued to search hers, as though he were taking a while to digest what she was saying. Then he nodded and said, 'I love Mummy.'

'I know you do.'

'And I love you.'

'Oh, I love you too,' she said and kissed him again. 'You're my big boy, my best boy. And this is my little boy, and my other best boy.'

He turned back to the baby. 'Can he sleep in my room?' he said.

'When he gets a bit bigger, sure he can. And when you

459

get fed up with him we'll put him in the room Gran's using now, shall we, because he might get in the way when your friends come over.'

'Yes, he might,' he agreed. 'I think Spot will like him.'

'Oh, I hope so,' Ellen said.

'So how are you doing in here?' Michael said, coming back and sitting on the edge of the bed. 'Did you say what you wanted to say?' he asked Robbie.

Robbie nodded, and snuggled in closer to Ellen as Michael ruffled his hair. 'So what do you think of the baby?' Michael said.

'He's good,' Robbie answered. 'What's his name?'

Michael and Ellen looked at each other. Then Ellen turned back to Robbie.

'I know, why don't you choose one?' she suggested.

'Steady on, remember the dog,' Michael muttered under his breath.

'Oh God,' Ellen mumbled.

'Shut up, Dad,' Robbie said. 'I'm not going to call him Spot.'

'Oh, well there's a relief,' Michael commented. 'So what do you want to call him?'

'Ummm, I know, what about Mervin?'

'*Mervin!*' Michael cried in disgust. 'I'm not calling him Mervin.'

Robbie turned to Ellen, who wrinkled her nose and gave a quick shake of her head.

'I know,' Robbie cried excitedly. 'Why don't we call him Derrick after the . . .'

'I'm not calling him Derrick either,' Michael declared.

Ellen leaned forward and whispered in Robbie's ear.

'Oh, yes, yes,' Robbie responded, clapping his hands together. 'Let's call him . . . what?' he said, twisting back round to Ellen.

Michael glared at Ellen. 'This is cheating,' he accused.

Ellen was laughing as she whispered again.

'Galen?' Robbie repeated in a whisper.

She nodded.

'I never heard of that name,' Robbie said.

'Precisely. Whoever heard of such a ludicrous name,' Michael agreed.

'It's Irish,' Ellen said.

'So's Connor and that's a much better name. Don't you think?' he said to Robbie.

Robbie looked at the baby, then up at Ellen.

'Connor McCann,' Michael said, pushing it home. 'It's got a great ring, don't you think? Not like Galen McCann. That doesn't work at all. They'll call him Gay. Or Len.'

The baby farted.

Robbie burst out laughing.

'See, even he agrees with me,' Michael insisted.

Ellen was laughing too. 'What do you think?' she said to Robbie. 'Galen or Connor?'

'He's going to say Galen to keep you happy,' Michael protested. 'Tell her you prefer Connor. It's a good name.'

'Do you prefer Connor?' Ellen asked him quietly.

Robbie looked up at her. 'I think so,' he said.

She smiled. 'Then Connor it is,' she declared, and they all burst out laughing again as the baby let go a loud, healthy burp, as though to endorse his brother's decision.

A little later in the day Michael's and Ellen's mothers came to collect their two grandsons, while Michael, though he desperately didn't want to, returned to the office.

Since the shooting he'd barely seen anything of Ted Forgon, wasn't sure if the man had sent Ellen any flowers, or even remembered that there was a baby involved. He couldn't see Forgon concerning himself with such minutiae, but that was fine by Michael, as Ted Forgon was the last person he wanted getting into his family life. The question now, however, was how the hell to get him out of his professional life.

The share aspect of World Wide aside, he needed to look into the new contracts Forgon had drawn up for his personal SWAT team to go in and screw up the movie after he'd fired Vic Warren. Warren's was just one of many lawsuits now pending following Forgon's interference, though Michael believed he could persuade Vic to withdraw his suit, except it would probably be under the proviso that he managed to get Ted Forgon out of the picture.

With the Colombian threat now taken care of there was nothing standing in the way of the film's completion, though Michael had been worried for a while that Ellen might not want to carry on after what she had been through. However, from the brief discussions they'd already had, there seemed no doubt in her mind that they must continue. It wasn't only that they both still totally believed in the movie, it was also the only way of saving their entire assets, not to mention reputations. Though getting it all up and running again, when actors, co-producers, assistant directors and even the directors might already be committed elsewhere, wasn't going to be easy.

However, Michael was at least going to try for the same team; they knew the original script and most were already way down the line in pre-planning and spending. Hopefully most of that could be brought back on track without too much trouble, or extra expense, though he needed to find out how the financial picture was now looking, since Forgon's band of cowboys had appropriated the budget during those insane few days before they'd been forced to stop.

But even more important than all the re-hiring and firing that needed to be done was where Tom Chambers now wanted to go with the movie. He still owned the rights to the story, though the script, naturally, belonged to World Wide. There was no question that it worked as it stood, but because of all the recent publicity, Tom's latest experiences in Colombia needed to be incorporated into the final scenes. And without his permission – and co-operation – there was no way that could happen.

Ten days ago Michael wouldn't have had any doubt about Chambers's readiness to give all for the movie, but now he wasn't so sure. With Galeano and Molina both dead, and the Zapata boys in custody on charges that included the rape and murder of Rachel Carmedi, Chambers had the vindication he'd been seeking, so what need did he now have of Hollywood and a movie? If anything, he was probably much keener to get away from the place, to move on with his life and finally put Rachel's memory to rest. And Michael couldn't blame him for that, since the pain he'd been carrying these past four years had to come to an end some time, and there was no getting away from the fact that now certainly seemed like that time.

After spending three hours with his lawyers and managing yet again to avoid Ted Forgon, Michael went back to his car, and on a sudden impulse drove over to the Four Seasons. He'd heard on the grapevine that Chambers was back, had even been hoping he'd call, though wasn't too surprised that he hadn't. He was probably just planning on staying long enough to wrap things up here before moving on out to the next war zone or corrupt regime that needed exposing. Despite all that had happened, Michael didn't feel good about him leaving, especially not with the way things stood between them now, nor when he knew how badly Chambers must be feeling after the events of the past week.

After getting the receptionist to announce him, he rode up in the elevator and took a right turn down the corridor to the room he'd been told. When he got there he hesitated a moment, still not sure how he was going to play this.

'Hey,' Chambers said, when he opened the door. 'How are you? It's good to see you.'

'Good to see you too,' Michael responded, taking his hand. He was immediately struck by the dark circles around Chambers's eyes, and the apparent weight loss that made him look both younger and older. Apart from that, however, he seemed in pretty good shape for a man who had just undergone the kind of ordeal he had.

He stood back for Michael to come in. 'Can I fix you a drink?' he offered. 'There're most things here. How about a Scotch, to wet the baby's head, or did you already do that?'

'No, not yet,' Michael responded, certain there was no bitterness in Chambers's tone, though he wouldn't have blamed him if there were.

Chambers took a couple of miniatures from the mini-bar, then turning to face Michael he put the bottles down and fixed him with dark, earnest eyes. 'You know, I want to get this out of the way,' he said, pushing a hand through his untidy hair. 'I mean, I'm not too good at this sort of thing, but I want you to know that if there'd been anything I could do, anything at all to change what Ellen went through . . . To have prevented it, even . . .'

Michael held up a hand. 'Let's not get into it,' he said. 'We both know you weren't to blame, for any of it, so how about we just work on putting it behind us and cut right to the celebration – not only for the baby, but for the fact you managed to get yourself back in one piece.'

Chambers's grin was slow in coming. 'Now there's a sentiment I never expected you to have,' he remarked, and Michael could hear the relief in his laugh. 'In fact,' he continued, 'when I boarded the plane in Bogotá I got the feeling I could be letting you down big time by not getting myself bumped on to the Great Hereafter.'

Michael was laughing. 'Well, I won't deny there were moments there when I wouldn't have minded if we'd never met,' he confessed.

'Believe me, I felt so bad I wouldn't have minded myself,' Chambers responded. 'So how is Ellen? Is she doing OK?'

'She's doing great,' Michael answered. 'She should be home on Saturday. The baby came home yesterday.'

Chambers smiled and turned for the drinks. 'A boy?' he said.

'Yes,' Michael answered and watched him pour. God only knew what he was feeling now, whether he was disappointed, relieved, or even bitter that the baby wasn't his but if it were anywhere near as bad as Michael suspected, Michael could only admire how well he was handling it.

'We're having a family dinner on Saturday night, if Ellen does come home,' he said. 'Would you join us?'

Chambers looked at him in surprise, and felt himself start to colour. 'Are you sure?' he asked.

Michael shrugged. 'Sure I'm sure. You kind of feel like family, so it would be right for you to be there.'

Chambers touched his glass to Michael's. 'Then I'd love to come,' he said.

Michael hesitated a moment, then decided to go ahead with what had just occurred to him. 'Ellen's got something to ask you,' he told him, hoping she was going to agree to what he had in mind more readily than she had agreed to a name for their son.

'Are you kidding?' she laughed, when Michael told her, just before they were leaving their bedroom to go and join the rest of the family on Saturday night. 'I can't think of a better idea. You're a genius, my darling, and I love you for coming up with it.'

Michael laughed and pulled her gently into his arms.

'You know what I thought you were going to say?' she murmured, as he kissed her. 'I thought you were going to get me to ask him if he'd carry on with the movie.'

'Ah, well, *he's* got something to ask *you* about that,'

Michael responded, stroking her hair back from her face and looking far into her eyes.

'Oh?' she said. 'So you two have already discussed it and didn't tell me?'

'Kind of,' he said. 'Does this hurt?'

'No, you can hold me even tighter if you like,' she told him.

Wrapping her more closely to him, he pressed his mouth to hers and kissed her for a long, long time.

'Come on,' she said, finally, 'or we'll never get out there.'

'Are we taking him?' Michael said, nodding towards the cradle.

Ellen laughed. 'Oh God, I almost forgot,' she confessed. 'I guess I'm just not used to him being around yet.'

'You wait until three in the morning,' he warned her. 'You'll know you've got him then.'

'Oh and to be sure he was the one who got up,' Clodagh said, coming in through the open door. 'We're all waiting for you now, so come along with you. I'll bring little Connor. Such a good idea to let Ellen and Robbie choose the name, I dread to think what you'd have come up with, Michael.'

Michael looked at Ellen and Ellen grinned.

An hour or so later they were all gathered around a table next to the pool, candles flickering in the early evening breeze, dish upon dish being transported back and forth by Nina and Clodagh. Matty was at the foot of the table, sitting with her Uncle Frank on one side of her and Robbie the other, while Ellen, at the head of the table, was between Michael and Tom. And for the brief moments they allowed themselves to sit down Clodagh and Nina were in the middle, Clodagh between her son and grandson whom she regularly and happily scolded.

'You know, I can't tell you what a relief it is to see you here,' Ellen said to Tom. 'None of us wanted you to go to

Colombia the way you did, and to be frank, we weren't at all sure we were going to see you again.'

Chambers's eyebrows went up. 'Would have made a great end for Forgon's movie,' he said.

Ellen grimaced and looked at Michael. 'We've got to do something about that man,' she said.

'I'll make a note of it,' he responded.

Cutting him a look she turned back to Tom. 'I'm sorry if I'm being dense here, but I'm not sure I understand how Galeano died,' she said.

'Food poisoning,' Chambers answered. 'I know Gómez would never admit it, but the minute we walked into Galeano's cell and Gómez laid eyes on that chef, he knew exactly who he was and what was going to happen.'

'Do you think Gómez planted him there?' Matty asked.

Chambers shook his head. 'No, that wouldn't be Gómez's style. The guy was very probably from a rival drug cartel, put there by one of Galeano's enemies to stop him ever coming out.'

'And Gómez turned a blind eye?' Ellen said.

'I guess it's what you call Colombian justice,' Chambers responded.

'Which'll probably be the South American version of Clodagh's justice,' Michael responded, affecting an Irish accent as he hugged his mother. 'So maybe we should get you working in Forgon's kitchen, Ma? What do you say?'

'I say you're a cheeky little blighter,' she replied. 'My cooking never did away with anyone yet. But for certain folk,' she added with a menacing glare at her son, 'it can always be arranged. Now, what's been happening to the wine? Did we run out?'

'No, Ma, you drank it all,' Michael told her.

'Michael!' Ellen laughed. 'Don't tease her and go get some more.'

'. . . and then,' Robbie was saying to Ellen's dad, 'we changed my bedroom all around, so that Connor's bed can fit in there too, and afterwards Grandma couldn't find any of my clothes. So then Grandma Nina came in and they started playing on my computer and wouldn't let me have a go.'

Frank was chuckling at Robbie's indignation. 'That's women for you, son,' he told him. 'Get themselves all in a confusion and go off doing something else while we men sort it all out.'

'Did you hear that, Mom?' Ellen enquired.

'Oh, I heard all right,' Nina replied. 'And I'll lay money Clodagh's got a good answer.'

Everyone looked at Clodagh. 'Well, we've got to remember who won the war,' she said.

They all burst out laughing at the ludicrous non sequitur, and raised their glasses to Clodagh. Then Ellen tapped her plate with a fork and called for everyone's attention. 'I have something to ask Tom,' she announced when everyone was quiet. She looked at Tom and smiled, then turning to Michael she took hold of his hand. 'Actually, we both have something to ask Tom,' she corrected. 'Tom,' she said formally, 'Michael and I would be honoured if you'd agree to stand as Connor's godfather when it comes time for his christening. But a quick warning,' she hastily added, 'if you accept, you really will become family. And just look at them.'

Tom looked around the table. 'I can't think of a family I'd rather belong to,' he confessed, 'or of a little boy I'd rather have as a godson.'

'What about me?' Robbie wailed.

'It goes without saying you're his godson,' Michael jumped in, certain he could square this with Michelle. 'Didn't you know that?'

'No,' Robbie answered. 'You don't tell me anything, Dad.'

'Wait for the facts of life,' Matty advised. 'He'll be

468

happy to share those with you.'

'What are *they*?' Robbie said.

'They're something that fit rather snugly into godfatherly duties,' Michael answered with a grin in Tom's direction.

'Well it definitely won't be his grandfather,' Nina sniggered, then pulled a face at the scowl she received from her famously puritanical husband.

'OK, OK,' Tom said, tapping his glass for attention. 'My turn to ask something of Ellen now.'

'Do we all get a go at this?' Matty wanted to know.

'If we do, then I've got something to ask Michael,' Clodagh responded.

'Do we want to know about this?' Ellen enquired.

'No, we certainly don't,' Michael responded. 'Over to you, Tom.'

'Ellen,' Tom said, turning to face her, 'I want to ask you if you'll write the end of the movie, according to the facts I give you, and if you can do it without me, so that I can get on with a life that's been on hold for too long.'

'Oh my God!' Ellen cried, fumbling her glass back to the table. 'Are you serious? Sure I'll do it. But it's your movie, Tom. You should be here making sure we get it right.'

He was shaking his head. 'I know you'll get it right,' he answered. 'And if you come across any problems and need to speak to me, the world's small enough now for you just to pick up a phone and call.' He smiled at her and lifted his glass. 'I don't know when you're going to be strong enough to get back to work, but hopefully this is something you can do at home for a while, while taking care of my godsons here.'

Ellen leaned forward and taking his hands in hers she kissed them hard. 'I'll do you proud,' she promised. 'I swear, I'll do you proud.'

'Oh my, I think I'm going to cry,' Clodagh threatened,

reaching for a napkin.

Michael took it from her and dabbed his eyes. 'You know, I hate to be a killjoy,' he said, as Ellen slapped him, 'but there's just one problem. Ted Forgon. He's still got a thirty per cent holding of World Wide and ever since he got his hands on the controls of this movie . . . Well, I've got to tell you, from the talks I've been having with the lawyers, we're going to have a pretty difficult time getting him to back off.'

'If Chris Ruskin keeps voting in our favour, then we've got nothing to worry about,' Ellen reminded him.

'I'd feel happier if I knew which way Sandy was going to go,' Michael confessed. 'Do you know where she is?' he asked Chambers. 'Has anyone heard from her yet?'

Chambers was shaking his head. 'I was going to ask you the same question,' he said. 'I found an e-mail from her that she sent just after she did the Larry King show, but it didn't give any clue where she might be.'

'But surely, wherever she is, she's got to know by now that the crisis is over,' Matty said.

Tom nodded thoughtfully. 'You're probably right,' he said. 'Maybe she's just not ready to come back yet.'

Ellen looked at him curiously. 'You make that sound as though you've got an inkling where she might be,' she said.

'Mmm, I think I do,' he answered. 'I could be wrong, but . . . Well, we'll see.'

Ellen smiled and turned back to Michael. It had come over her very suddenly, the dizziness, and she didn't want to make a fuss, but she had to leave now and she didn't think she could do it without him.

One look at her face was enough to tell him what she wanted, and getting behind her he helped her up from her chair and joined in with her as she told the others not to fuss.

A few minutes later they were lying together on their bed, gazing down at their newly born son who was

470

sleeping between them.

'It's going to be all right,' she whispered, trying to fight back the fear. 'I know it is. I just . . .'

'Ssssh,' he soothed. 'It's still early days.'

'We'll get through this,' she said.

'Of course we will.'

'Do you promise?'

He smiled and reached over to touch her face. 'I know I've come pretty close a couple of times,' he said, 'but have I ever let you down yet?'

'No,' she said, swallowing hard. 'I just hope to God that I don't let you down.'

'If you'd called this boy Galen I might have been worried,' he said, and she laughed.

Then, leaning over, he brought her mouth to his and kissed her with such tenderness that tears came to her eyes. Sure the next couple of months were going to be tough, getting through an ordeal like this could never be easy. But all that really mattered was that she was alive, and that their love, despite everything, just seemed to get stronger all the time.

Chapter 26

Night wouldn't be long now in settling over the wide, sweeping landscape that glittered with every shade of green, and basked under a sky of a hundred different blues. All around hills rose from smooth, lush pastures and plunged to the depths of rocky gorges, where streams and rivers bubbled and gushed a journey to the distant sea.

The afternoon had been warm, but as evening approached and the sun began to fade, the temperature was dropping fast and the wind was starting to bite. Soon they would hear the whistle of ghostly gusts that tore through the mountains at night, and the ageing creak of trees bending to the force of the gale. Sandy's guide, Colin, could identify almost every bird that called in the night, and every one of those that sang by day, along with all the living creatures that scuttled over the hills and dales and the endless variety of shrub, plant and tree that called this glorious place home.

Right at that moment though, as they strolled unhurriedly over that small stretch of highlands back to the house, Colin was in the midst of telling a joke, while Sandy, used to his humour by now, was already bubbling up with laughter.

'So,' he said, the earflaps on his hat bobbing as he walked, and his eyes glowing like coals in the warm hearth of their sockets, 'the architect's dog goes up to the pile of bones, arranges them neatly, in a kind of Eiffel Tower, then comes back to his master for praise. Fantastic, say the others. Then the mathematician's dog goes up to the bones, arranges them in a straight line, counts them, then goes back to his master for praise. Amazing, say the others. Then the Hollywood producer's dog goes up to the bones, crushes them to powder, sniffs them up his nostrils, screws the other two dogs, then asks for commission.'

Sandy burst out laughing, and carried on laughing as he treated her to one of his drier expressions.

'Sounds like you know that dog,' he remarked.

Still laughing she said, 'I'll bet I know its owner. So exactly how long were you in Hollywood?'

'Twenty-six years,' he answered. 'I was an agent, then a producer, then I worked for the studios – then I got a life.'

Sandy laughed again. 'How come you never mentioned it before?'

'Because boasting about being a Hollywood producer would be a bit like boasting you got ebola.' He grimaced. 'OK, I'm being harsh, but there's not a lot of reason to tell anyone who I was, or what I did in my earlier life. Besides, it was different back then, more about talent and loyalty, not like today. Today it's all about deals; who's making the biggest and fastest buck. There was no way I could beat 'em, so I joined 'em for a while, made myself a bundle, then came here to repair the abuse to my soul.'

Sandy smiled. 'So did you know Ted Forgon?' she asked, taking a set of earmuffs from her pocket and hooking them on.

'I certainly knew of him,' Colin answered. 'He was one of the big players even then, but I don't recall any dealings with him personally.'

'You were lucky,' she remarked.

His irony made a return, for during their many long

and lively conversations these past two weeks he'd got to hear quite a bit about Ted Forgon.

They walked on quietly for a while then, descending the hill towards the small grey stone castle where orange lights glowed a welcome at the windows and a Scottish flag flapped from the turrets. By the time they reached the door Sandy was laughing again, her cheeks red from the cold, her eyes tearing up from the wind and mirth.

'Och, Sandy, your timing is scary,' Olivia said, as they brought a cloud of cold air into the large, flagstoned hall, which was home to a discreet reception area, several French antiques and an enormous log fire that was currently crackling and roaring in the magnificent hearth. Olivia, Colin's rotundly pretty wife, was holding on to the phone while trying to bat away the cat that was making a languorous inspection of the desk. 'There's a call for you, dear,' she told Sandy.

Sandy's heart immediately jumped.

'Will I put it through to your room, or would you like to take it here?' Olivia offered.

Sandy was nonplussed. Though no-one knew she was here, she was well aware that the only person who was likely to guess would be Tom. She wondered if, subconsciously, she'd been waiting for him to find her, but that was absurd, she was ready to go back now, had even told Olivia and Colin that she'd be leaving at the end of the week.

'Are you going to take it?' Olivia asked, leaning over the desk for her husband's dutiful kiss as he passed.

'Who is it?' Sandy asked.

Olivia smiled and Sandy's heart turned over.

So it was Tom.

Taking the receiver, she held it in both hands and watched Olivia follow Colin through to the kitchens.

As the door closed behind them her heart tightened again. This was a call she'd been dreading, as well as longing for, ever since she'd arrived. It seemed suddenly

474

strange that it was upon her, and though she'd rehearsed what she might say a hundred times, she knew even before she spoke that all her preparations had been in vain.

'Hello,' she said.

'Well hi,' he responded. 'I was beginning to think you weren't talking to me.'

She smiled. 'I've been looking forward to talking to you,' she told him.

'Now that's good to hear. Are you OK?'

'Yes. How are you?'

He paused. 'In need of a friend.'

Sandy's smile wavered, as she sucked in her lips.

'Will you see me? If I come?' he asked.

Her eyes closed as warm emotions swept through her. 'Where are you?' she said.

'At Heathrow. I can fly up there tomorrow.'

'Then I'll tell Colin and Olivia to expect you,' she said.

It was just before lunch when Sandy finally spotted his rental car coming along the narrow winding lane towards the Retreat. Beneath her carefully cultivated calm she was a thousand times more nervous than she'd care to admit, but she was keeping it under control by insisting vigorously to herself that she really was ready for this. It wasn't going to be easy, she knew that, but few things were.

Colin was behind the reception desk, sorting out paperwork, when she ran down the wide oak staircase into the hall.

'He's here,' she said.

Colin looked up and smiled. Then, coming round the desk, he gave her a giant hug. 'You're going to be just fine,' he promised.

She nodded, swallowed hard and put on her bravest smile. He was right, of course, but keeping her courage forward was going to be tough. Easier now, though, than it would have been before she came here, and because of the subtle and tremendous changes it had wrought in her, she understood why Tom had taken refuge at the Retreat so many times himself.

He knew Colin and Olivia well. They had helped him through some of his bleakest, most despairing moments during the turbulent months after Rachel's death, buoying him with their quiet strength and infinite kindness. They would never call themselves counsellors, nor did they welcome any such labels as spiritualists or healers, they simply liked to think of themselves as friends. But they were much more than that, for the way they shared their view on the world, and on life, was so enriching to the soul and inspiring to the mind that it was impossible to go away from here unchanged for the better.

They saw everything life delivered, whether good or bad, as a means of measuring courage or appreciation; or perhaps as a reassurance of existence, or an exercise in endurance; almost always it would involve a strengthening of character, and an often necessary levelling of ego. They never preached or advised, nor did they lay claim to any special affinity with God; they simply welcomed their friends, and friends of friends, with warm, open hearts, and a wry irreverence that was as rewarding to be a part of as the tranquillity and seclusion of this wild terrain.

Perhaps two weeks wasn't long enough to effect all the changes she'd have liked, or felt she needed, but she was sure some of the more important ones were taking place – those that were going to help her to experience and explore her life much more fully and less fearfully than she had before. She was now beginning to understand the reasons behind her desperate attachment to Michael, her piteous search for love and acceptance, that had come from her feelings of inferiority and lack of self-esteem. It was as though she had needed Michael, then Tom, to validate her existence, to give her a place in the world she didn't feel worthy of alone. Until now she'd had no appreciation of herself, nor of her success, hadn't understood at all who she was, or why she should matter. All she'd known was the anger and bitterness that was locked up inside her, the self-pity and resentment that had driven her to inflict injury and malice on those who refused to recognize and accept her. She'd been all twisted up in knots of jealousy over Ellen, whom everyone seemed to love, and who made her feel so inadequate and unattractive. She realized now that it was her own mind that had created these problems, that she had allowed her ego to set up defences and hostilities that had no need to be there, for only she saw herself as undeserving and meaningless, so only she could do something to change that.

In fact, it was Tom who had first tackled her warped and damaging view of herself and set it on the right track. He had done so in many subtle as well as obvious ways, like taking the kind of interest in her that no-one had much bothered with before; getting her to feel good and right about herself after all the disastrous flirtation, thinly veiled prostitution, and heavy-duty desperation. She realized now that one of the reasons he had never slept with her was because he didn't want her to use her body to befriend him – he wanted her to understand that she was worth knowing as a woman first, a woman of many more qualities and much greater depth than just those of a lover.

Of course, the other reason he had resisted her was because he didn't love her, but though it hurt to know that, she was up to dealing with it now. At least, she certainly hoped she was, because his car was drawing up outside, and though she'd worked hard trying to persuade herself these past two weeks that she only *thought* she was in love with him, underneath it all she was still a long way down the road to believing it was the truth. After all, he was an extraordinary man, with

477

such complexity of character and so many great qualities that even Olivia agreed it would be very hard not to love him.

Giving Colin a last quick hug, she took a glance in the mirror at the simple jeans and big sweater she had chosen, then went to open the door. A blast of icy wind barged past her and rearranged Colin's desk on its way to the hearth. Hurriedly she pulled the door closed, then seeing Tom walking round the car, she broke into a smile and ran across the forecourt to greet him.

'Hey, look at you!' he cried, catching her up in his arms and spinning her round. 'You look great. The cold weather obviously suits you.'

'Oh, it's so wonderful to see you,' she told him, hugging him hard and looking up into his laughing face. 'I can hardly believe you're here.'

He grinned. 'It's a great place to get me to come find you,' he responded. 'Are you planning on staying for good?'

'I'm leaving at the end of the week,' she answered, slipping an arm round his waist as they walked back to the house. 'I've thought about you such a lot – I was so scared for you, terrified that you might never come back and if you did that you might never forgive me. But now you're here, and I'm going to tell you right out that I don't have a single regret about what I did.'

He was laughing. 'Well, I'm sure glad to hear that,' he told her, 'because there's not much doubt it saved my life and I wouldn't want you to be regretting that.'

Her eyes were sparkling as she looked up at him, then, giving in to the urge, she hugged him again. 'Are you hungry?' she said. 'Olivia's got some soup on the go, and guess who baked bread this morning?'

'No!' he said incredulously.

'Well, I had to do something, I was so nervous about seeing you,' and letting go of his hand she skipped on ahead to open the door.

'They're looking forward to seeing you,' she said, turning back. 'Colin's threatening to bring out one of his best wines for dinner tonight – if you're staying.'

His eyes were dancing, but before he could reply the door opened and Olivia came out. 'Tom Chambers!' she cried, pulling him into her plump embrace. 'It's been far too long, and what have you been up to in Colombia, we want to know. Oh, look at you, you gorgeous thing, if Colin knew what you did to my heart he'd never let you over the threshold.'

'There's no fool like an old fool, is there?' Colin remarked, standing his wife aside so that he could shake Tom's hand. 'Welcome, my friend,' he said, looking warmly into Tom's eyes. 'It's good to see you.'

Tom was laughing. 'I've got to tell you, it's good to see you too, but after the Colombian and Californian sunshine I'm freezing my whatsits off here.'

'It's you, Colin, blocking the way,' Olivia scolded, shoving him aside so that Sandy and Tom could go through.

'Do you have any luggage?' Colin asked.

'Nothing to speak of,' Tom answered.

Though Sandy's smile remained, her spirits sank. He obviously wasn't planning to stay.

'I hope you're hungry,' Olivia said. 'We've all been preparing for your arrival. And if you can bear to tell us what happened in Colombia, Colin might be persuaded to dig out one of his better vintages right away to help us along. On the other hand, you two might not want any company,' she added, looking at Sandy.

Tom looked at Sandy too.

'Oh no,' she said, colouring, 'let's all eat together. Then maybe you and I can go for a walk later,' she said to Tom.

'Sounds good to me,' he said, putting an arm around her. 'So where's this soup? I'm starving.'

*

Though the sun was bright it was still bitterly cold as they climbed over the huge grey boulders that cluttered the path, high above the loudly gushing river, and way below the soaring mountain peaks. Sandy, complete with earmuffs and woollen gloves, was zipped snugly inside a down-filled jacket, while Tom considered himself pretty cool in Colin's snazzy old deerstalker and fur-lined duffel. Since he'd tied the earflaps under his chin and buttoned the coat right to his neck, Sandy couldn't look at him without laughing. Nor could she properly hear him as he shouted directions above the roar of the water. But it didn't matter, she knew the way to the cave, she'd walked there many times with Colin or Olivia.

When at last they reached it, it provided a welcome relief from the biting wind and partially muted the deafening rush of the river. The view from the cave's entrance was stupendous, for it looked right down over the fir-studded valley which rose again in the distance to yet more snow-capped mountains and a stunningly azure sky. There was nothing, in all those wondrous miles, that showed a single touch of human creation, and as they gazed at the beauty Sandy couldn't help being aware of its timelessness, and felt a quiet exhilaration moving through her – an exhilaration that was gently weighted with awe.

'You know,' Tom said, slipping an arm round her shoulders, 'this is one of my favourite places in the world.'

'Mmm,' she responded, resting her head on his shoulder. 'I can understand why.' She paused, then spoke again. 'Standing here like this makes you realize how small and irrelevant we are, don't you think? Or how briefly we're here, while these mountains, this landscape go on for ever, seeing everything there is to see and enduring everything there is to endure.'

He smiled and hugged her. 'Do you want to sit down?' he said after a while. He was already taking a blanket from his backpack, and the flask of coffee Olivia had made.

'Here, I'll pour,' Sandy said, taking the flask.

They were soon huddled cosily up against a rock, steaming mugs of coffee cupped in their hands, the walls of the cave curving round them like a huge protective shell. Outside the elements were battering the world, while inside the air was dank and earthy and soothingly still.

'You know, I don't want anyone else in the world to be here,' she said, watching the birds soar and dive on the speeding currents of air, 'but I wish there were some kind of magical camera that would swoop down now to take a picture of us like this.' She turned to look at him, and started to laugh. 'We, at least *you*, look so ridiculous.'

He grinned widely and drank some more coffee.

She did the same and settled back against the rock. 'So tell me about Ellen,' she said, after a while. 'I know she's home from the hospital, but how is she, you know, in herself?'

'Good question,' he answered, his eyes losing focus as he thought. 'I didn't realize how touch and go it was there for a while, until Michael told me, but she seems to be pulling through. At least physically she is, but I think they've still got some way to go on other fronts. Michael told me just before I left that she's started getting bad dreams, you know, about the car going over, and losing the baby and Kris being dead. Apparently she's not too keen on going out of the house either, at least not without Michael. Her parents are still there, but they're leaving next week.'

'What about Clodagh?'

'She's staying. She's moving into the apartment attached to the house. I think the plan is, six months in England with her daughter and grandkids there, then six months in LA with Michael and Ellen – and my two godsons.'

Sandy turned to look at him.

He waggled his eyebrows and sipped his coffee.

'Congratulations,' she said. 'I take it the other one is Robbie?'

He nodded. 'Though I don't think Michelle's been consulted yet.'

'Well, I can't see her having a problem with it,' Sandy remarked. 'What did they call the baby, by the way?'

'Connor. He's a cute little thing. Doesn't do much except cry and sleep, but he can produce a pretty mean fart when he's up to it, much to Robbie's delight.'

Sandy laughed. 'I'm sorry to hear that Ellen's having some problems,' she sighed after a pause. 'I suppose it was only to be expected though. I mean, it was a terrible thing to happen.'

He turned to look at her. 'Michael tells me you saw it.'

She nodded. 'Most of it.' Her head went down. 'It was horrible. I've never been so afraid in my life, so I can't even begin to imagine what it was like for her. Just thank God she came out of it alive. And the baby, of course.' Putting her cup down, she hugged her knees to her chest and gazed out at the hills. 'I was wondering,' she said. 'How did you feel when you found out the baby wasn't yours? Were you upset? I mean, did you want it to be?'

He laughed drily, and sucked in his lips. 'The truth is, a part of me did, yes,' he answered. 'But I'm glad for Michael and Ellen that it wasn't.' He sighed. 'I kind of figured that if I'm ever going to have one, then it might be better if it weren't with another man's wife.'

Sandy smiled, and moved her thoughts away from the dangerous ground they were approaching.

'So what's next for you?' he asked, reaching for more coffee.

'Me?' she said, surprised. 'Well, I'm going back to London on Friday, where I imagine there's a mountain of work waiting for me, and where I need to be to get all my new plans in motion.'

482

'Oh?' he said, intrigued.

'Tell me,' she said, turning to him and resting a cheek on her knees, 'have you and Michael made any decisions about the movie yet?'

'Sure,' he nodded. 'He's going to carry on.' He laughed as she made an exaggerated collapse of relief.

'I'm sorry,' she said, 'I know you don't want it to be about money, but all the people who gave us so much . . .'

'It's OK,' he said. 'And it's me who should be apologizing. I should have been more understanding.'

She smiled, then lowered her eyes.

'Of course, there are a few minor complications that have to be sorted,' he said, 'like licking Ted Forgon into shape, and dealing with the stack of lawsuits the company's facing. But Michael's optimistic he can get it back on line.' He paused, and waited for her eyes to come back to his. 'I know what you did with the shares,' he said softly. 'How you gave them to Ellen so she could vote with Michael, so you could help save the kids and maybe still salvage something of your career. So I've got to tell you, I'm real sorry about the way I got mad at you for not coming right out with the commitment I wanted. I guess I just wasn't being rational.'

Sandy's lips flattened as she looked away. 'And I wasn't being so honourable,' she confessed. She looked at him again. 'I don't expect Ellen told you about the condition attached to those shares?'

He frowned and shook his head.

'The deal was that she told Michael the baby was his. In other words . . .' She stopped, and dropped her eyes again. 'Well, you know what I'm saying,' she said.

Putting a finger under her chin, he lifted her head up. 'Don't be too hard on yourself,' he said softly.

Feeling her heart turn over, she smiled and looked to one side. Then, wanting to get past her shame, she reached for her cup and held it out for more coffee.

'So, did you find it helpful being here with Colin and

Olivia?' he asked after he'd poured.

'Helpful?' she laughed. 'I'm only feeling like a completely different person, and one I could even get to quite like. Though how long I'm going to be able to keep up all these good feelings and generosity of spirit once I get back to the cut and thrust of London, God only knows. I can see myself ending up coming back here for monthly, if not weekly fixes. I wonder if they do phone-ins?'

He was laughing. 'Believe me, a little bit of Colin and Olivia goes a very long way, so you'll probably do a lot better than you think.'

She didn't look convinced, but grinned when he poked her. She rested a cheek on her knees again and looked into his eyes as she wondered whether to broach the subject his comment had brought to her mind, that of Salvador Molina and the revenge Tom had sworn he would take. It seemed that not even Colin and Olivia had been able to dissuade him from that, and with Molina now dead and so many mixed reports coming out of the killing, she was curious to know what really had happened, and how troubled, or not, he might be.

He was quiet for a long time after she finally asked him, a wry, though thoughtful expression on his face as he assimilated the truth of his answer. 'You know,' he said, after a while, 'I keep thinking I should feel bad about what I did, but I just can't say I do. I shot the man's balls off, I stood there and watched him bleed and twitch, and scream in agony, and I didn't feel a single moment of remorse. And if I had it all to do over again?' He shrugged. 'I'd do exactly the same. Next time, I might even kill him.'

'I'm glad you left that to somebody else,' she said quietly. 'I could be wrong, but I don't think you'd find that so easy to live with.'

'Maybe not,' he agreed.

She wanted to ask him about Rachel, and if Molina's

484

and Galeano's deaths had changed anything in the way he was dealing with that now, but guessing it was probably still too early for him to know, she decided to leave it. 'So what's next for you?' she said. 'You're carrying on with the movie.'

He shook his head. 'Not me,' he answered. 'I've left Ellen with all my notes so she can rewrite the end, which works for her, since it means she can be at home with the boys, and Michael's bringing in another exec. producer to cover.'

'So what are you going to do?' she said, forcing the words past the dread of his answer.

'Me? I guess you could say I'm shipping on out.'

Though her heart twisted, her eyes managed to show nothing but interest. 'To where, and to do what?' she asked, teasingly.

He inhaled deeply. 'Well, I'm booked on a flight to Karachi tomorrow night,' he answered. 'Michelle and Cavan are still in the Afghan refugee camps in the north of the country, so I'm going to catch up with them there. Then I thought I'd give war and turmoil a rest for a while, and visit some exotic lands and curious cultures. The Indonesian or South Sea islands, maybe. I don't know, I guess I'll firm up a decision once I'm over that way.'

Though Sandy was still smiling, she didn't, for the moment, trust herself to speak – she was too afraid that her voice might falter on the terrible loss that was already building inside her. But this was no more than she had expected, was precisely what she had feared, so she must just make herself accept it and move on.

'So what are these plans you've got for when you return to London?' he asked.

'Ah, those,' she said, allowing her eyes to shine. 'I'll need to talk to Michael first, but I've got to tell you, no matter how wonderful and considerate and forgiving being here has made me feel inside, I'm still not anywhere near a place where I can stomach Ted Forgon.'

He laughed. 'So?' he prompted.

'So, I've been thinking about it and I reckon Michael and I can go one of two ways. We can either bounce the old sod around a bit, keep voting him down and kicking out all his suggestions, which, I've got to tell you, I favour, because it'll provide me with the ongoing pleasure of watching him froth at the mouth and run round in circles of rage and frustration: or we can work on a way of throwing him out of World Wide altogether. For that, we'll almost certainly need the support of the movie's investors, but I don't see too much of a problem there. We'll have to speak to the company lawyers, obviously, but I've got the makings of something devastating worked out, I just need them to make it legal.'

He gave a shout of laughter. 'You're not a woman to be messed with, Sandy Paull,' he told her.

'And don't you forget it,' she warned darkly.

Her eyes went down then, as the prospect of his impending departure, and a future that was already moving them in different directions, stole over her in a horrible, swamping wave. She leaned back against the rock so that he could no longer see her face and tried to tell herself that this wasn't as bad as it felt, but the ache in her heart wouldn't be moved.

In the end she was the first to break the silence, though it took several attempts to push the words past the pain, and make them strong enough to be heard. And even then the emotion was catching so hard on her heart, it was as though it was trying to pull the words back. 'I know . . . I know you don't love me,' she finally managed, 'but I hope we can always be friends.'

She waited, keeping her eyes fixed to the ground and hardly daring to breathe as the seconds ticked by. Then she felt him reaching for her hand, and turning her to face him he looked far into her eyes. 'Me too,' he whispered.

He continued his gaze, and as she returned it she felt an ocean of tears rise from her heart. Then she found herself laughing at how silly he looked in that hat, and the tears overflowed. Oh God, he really was such a very, very special man and this was so very much harder than she'd expected.

He smiled and waited for her to look at him again, then leaning forward he put his mouth gently over hers. Her lips trembled, then a sob suddenly escaped from all the emotion that was caught in her chest. But it was OK. Everything was all right. She accepted that he didn't love her, she truly did – she just hoped that one day someone might.

ALSO AVAILABLE IN ARROW

Summer Madness

Susan Lewis

After finishing work on their sensationally successful TV series, Louisa, Danny and Sarah take a much-needed holiday on the French Riviera. All they want to do is party, soak up the sun and have a good time.

Danny, the actress, with her sensual beauty and impossible temper, soon has the eligible men of the Riviera chasing her. Louisa, the scriptwriter on the rebound from a broken love affair, finds herself more and more drawn to the mysterious Jake Mallory. While Sarah, the producer, just wants to hang out and have fun.

But they quickly discover that the sparkle of Riviera life conceals a dark presence that pulls them into a game no one can win. And when mayhem and madness begin to stalk them, they find there is only one way out . . .

'An irresistible blend of intrigue and passion' *Woman*

'Spellbinding!' *Daily Mail*

arrow books